The Storm Knight IV:
Green Horizon

by Zachary Watson

For more information, address: z.watson.author@gmail.com.

Website: https://zachwatsonauthor.com/

Edited by Dana Morck, John Watson, Jordan Perona, Catherine Hariton, & Samantha Watson

Cover Art by Ed Bourelle

ISBN 979-8-9860285-9-0 (Kindle ebook)
ISBN 979-8-9896510-0-9 (Paperback)

For my family, friends, and everyone who told me I could do this.

Semper Victoria

Other Stories by Zach Watson

The Knights of the Compact

The Lost Knight
Awakening
Fealty
Ronin
Huntsman
Vengeance
Einherjar

The Storm Knight
Dark Skies
Falling Mist
Howling Winds
Green Horizon

Warblades of Saerda Novellas
The Amethyst Blade

Other Stories in the Knights of the Compact Universe

Welcome to Nowhere by Keven Karaki

Glossary of Terms

Caranat; Literally meaning 'The Language', Caranat is the primary spoken word of the Trahcon people and the Empire in particular.

Humanity; The newest addition to the Empire after Earth was conquered roughly a century in the past. Not particularly well regarded by most other species, they are increasingly being forced off of Earth and scattered across various colonial regions. An Imperial Human's term of conscription begins at the age of 15 Imperial (roughly 17 Terran), and lasts until they're 27 (roughly 30 Terran).

Hyperspace; A nebulous, dangerous sub-dimension that allows for faster-than-light travel. Filled with rolling storms of plasma capable of destroying ships in an instant, vessels are often forced 'shallow', moving relatively slowly in exchange for safety, and only 'descend' to pick up speed along safe currents that avoid the worst storms.

Imperial Intelligence; While its official main purpose is espionage and counter-espionage against foreign powers, the sheer size of the Empire ensures that most of its agents are dedicated to internal security and investigations.

Index; The record of an Imperial Citizen's life, used to determine both military promotions as well as to evaluate their progress through the technocratic civilian government.

Naule; A four armed, simian species counted among the five Humanoid races. Universally covered by long strands of hair, their small interstellar nations were overwhelmed and conquered by the Empire several centuries ago.

Sorcery; A range of telekinetic and pyrokinetic abilities focused on manipulating the same sub-reality that allows for FTL travel. Organized as 'spells', the difficulties in learning the more complicated spells ensures few Trahcon learn more than basics in the modern era.

Trahcon; The founding species of the Empire, and the only Humanoid species naturally capable of manipulating energy without cybernetic enhancement. On average shorter than Humans, they have uniformly gray skin but extremely bright eyes. Unique in possessing a nearly three to one gender imbalance between females to males, and for having a five century long lifespan.

Glossary of Nations

Ascendancy; After the destruction of the United Clans by the Empire, the Thondian-dominated Ascendancy became the premier power in the Near Reaches. This state of affairs lasted for several centuries, until political and cultural fault lines caused the nation to fragment into a civil war that has been raging for several years.

Ark Fleet: An unified collection of Kelthi and Humans descended from refugees after the loss of their homeworlds. Usually operating in isolated flotillas across the Near Reaches, the Ark Fleet relies on a mixture of temporary colonies, the strip mining of dead worlds, and piracy in order to sustain itself.

Crescent of Cathia: Formed from the ashes of Cathia's Fourth Republic by the remnants of the Republic's Army. Ruled by Iriahn'kolkris, it is a rare monarchy ruled by Trahcon. Extremely militaristic, they have inherited Cathi's millennia long feud with the Mikiran people.

Empire of the Homeworld: The most populous of the original Compact states, formed by the Trahcon people who dominate it. Located on the Spinward side of the Core Regions, it has made significant incursions into the Near Reaches over the past few centuries, conquering both the Naulian and Human homeworlds.

The Kingdom of the Lost: A scattered state of loosely aligned worlds on the fringes of known space, the Lost was created by refugees and exiles who simply wished to be left alone. While technically a Compact signatory, the Lost are stringently isolationist, and generally ignore events in the wider galaxy.

Scarlet Tears: Officially a dual-kingdom ruled by a Mikiran and a Naulian dynasty, in reality it is more of a loose alliance of warlords, mercenary units, and piratical groups. How united or disunited they are is largely determined by how dominant their current Kings are, and how strong the vein of Mikiran-Naulian nationalism is within their society.

Xenthan-Empire: Once the Xenthan-Imperial Alliance, its blatant corruption led to a a military coup saw the ruling dynasty overthrown and replaced by Empress Yan'Ravt. Her reforms have led to a massive rise in the nation's military and economic strength, culminating in it making enormous gains during the recent wars.

Prologue
Rerth'riah

Date: Day 5, Month 1, 2165 Imperial
Location: *Shrouded in Onyx*, Orbit Above Altair, Empire of the Homeworld

---

Chemical Interrogation was such a cowardly way of saying 'torture by drugs'.

It had been more than a week and I was still recovering from my own 'session' in the chair. I still felt the ache in my tarah, even if the doctors insisted that I shouldn't be feeling anything anymore. That the pain was entirely in my head.

They were probably right about that, but that didn't change the ache that just would not go away.

Not that going through the experience myself made me feel any degree of empathy for those I'd subjected to the process in the past. None of them had been innocent children, undeserving of what happened to them. They'd been criminals, murderers, and worse. Only a few hadn't broken and given me information that I'd badly needed to protect the Empire, to save Imperial lives.

It just made me decide that, in the future, I'd forgo the official phrasing. Both in person and in my reports. If we were going to do it, we might as well be fully open with what was going on.

"I've been saying that for decades." Holde chided me when I said such thoughts aloud, my bond walking beside me down the Void-Ship's corridors. "Probably because I'm the one that went through a level one demonstration during training."

I huffed, tarah quivering. "Because you volunteered as part of the resistance course. Doing the non-chemical training was tiring enough."

"Because you were taking five classes at once that year." He reminded me.

"How else was I supposed to make sure I graduated before you?"

My bond snorted, though his humor and his smile both faded as we drew nearer to the pair of guards waiting outside of the briefing room ahead.

It was a sign of how bad things were that even here, in the heart of a Void Fleet's flagship, we had to have our rank badges scanned, then go through a facial recognition scan, and *then* be scanned for weapons.

I was half convinced they were going to force nullification bars onto our tarah before they finally waved us in.

Chashti'tahze Sever'amiar'delarah, the Eighth Void Lord, current heir to the position of Torlah, was lounging inside. And I do mean *lounging*. She had her boots kicked up on the wooden table, her cheek resting in one hand while she watched a slow stream of information flowing above a projector.

The Void Lord shut down the feed with a gesture, rising with a languid motion to better look at us as we entered her sanctum.

Now that I could really take her in, now that I wasn't half-out of my mind on a cocktail of drugs, I realized that images and videos didn't do her justice.

She was... almost perfectly androgynous. Incredibly tall, but as lean as a long-ship beneath her black and star-field uniform. A feminine jaw was matched by tarah so long that any man would kill to have them, while her green eyes were so bright they practically glowed. And though her high-collar mostly hid it, I could see the beginning of a tattoo covering her neck, and intricate patterns of ink trailed out of her sleeves to cover the backs of her hands.

"I see you're finally sailing about once more." Her Icar accent made her sound more like a newscaster than a decorated soldier, more soothing than commanding. "Sit."

"Yes sir." I quickly obeyed, Holde taking the seat on my right as the Void Lord returned to her seat on the far side.

Delarah regarded us in silence for several minutes, taking our measure as we remained quiet, waiting for her as we should.

"I sent my initial report to the Torlah." She said finally. "I am to proceed into the Near Reaches at once, to Trinity, where I will relieve Void Lord Obdel'rilem and place the entire system on lock down. You are to assist me in cleansing the Intelligence Regional Headquarters there, and determining how much of their staff is compromised by our new enemies."

I swallowed, "Yes sir."

She looked amused at my response, "This is a Void Fleet, Agent Riah. We don't act like conscripts here."

I felt the smallest smile come and go, "Yes sir. Then I may ask questions?"

"That is what I implied, yes." Delarah chuckled.

"What of the Altair branch?" I asked. "And the other sectors in the Empire?"

"The other Void Lords are being pulled off of their other duties to investigate, interrogate, and if necessary, shut them down." She replied. "All except for Grine. The Torlah wants to hear exactly how he allowed Trinity to be so compromised in person, and I doubt she'll let him contribute even if she accepts his reasons. He'll probably be sent to the Twins to make sure the Federation doesn't get any ideas while we sweep our rivers clean of the filth."

Holde stirred on my left, "That is good to hear, sir, but what of our missing packmate?"

Delarah rolled a shoulder. "You will be free to examine all of the data we recover from Trinity. Surely there must be something there to hint as to where she was taken, and I will allow you to sit in or watch the recordings of all interrogations."

"Thank you, sir." I said, Holde echoing me a heartbeat later.

"Do not thank me yet." Her voice hardened slightly, those brilliant eyes narrowing. "Your old packmate gave me a great deal of information when she reached the Watch. Enough to convince me that something was rotten in our Empire, but I want to hear it from the first pack to discover these... Faithful."

I bobbed my head, "Yes sir. What do you want to know?"

"Your packmate, the missing one who directly encountered them. Tell me just what she experienced."

And so we told her everything that Ashe had gone through on Oshflara, then on Trinity's surface. That lead us to Nueva Genova, and its extremely strange circumstances. A one-time Ark Fleet colony somehow living in fear of a Faithful outpost that preyed on its alien citizens.

We told her of how Ashe had been tortured by the Burned Hand. How, on Trinity, she'd been batted around as a Blue-Shark might amuse itself by torturing its prey before feasting. How luck had been the only thing to save her from a horrible death both times.

How that dismissive torture matched too many cold cases across the Empire, and then again on Nueva Genova.

The Void Lord listened, interjecting occasionally with sharp requests for clarification. When we finished she changed the subject to the Group of Five, asking for our own words as to what had happened there.

"This was all in the reports." I said once we'd described our operations on those worlds. How Void Lord Grine'obdel'rilem had ruined our long-term insertion plans with his invasion and raids. "Why ask about it?"

A tarah lifted in amusement, "Our enemy can apparently manipulate our very systems, corrupt our reports. I wanted to hear it from you, hear it in your voices."

Holde blinked. "We *are* Intelligence assets, sir. We could be lying."

Gray lips twitched away from her teeth. "Yes, but you'll find that I am very difficult to lie to. For now, put Grine out of your mind. He is the Torlah's problem, and she will deal with him as she sees fit."

We both nodded without hesitation.

"As for the rest." A finger tapped a few times on the rich wood of her table. "Your clandestine group within Intelligence is being gathered together to form a new investigative task force. I am promoting you to Operative, and placing you in command of the initial work."

I stared at her for a long moment, "You... can't promote us, sir. That's-"

She reached under her desk, pulled out two small metal objects, and tossed them across the table.

Glancing down as they tumbled to a stop let me see a silver bar holding three bronzed mountains in place, each with a silver starburst atop their peaks. The rank badges of Void Fleet officers.

"You've been transferred." She said. "You'll find the appropriate uniforms in your assigned quarters. I expect you to be in them the next time you provide a briefing for me."

"Sir-"

Delarah interrupted me, as was her prerogative. "From how furious the Torlah is, I believe it extremely likely that Imperial Intelligence is going to be disbanded. Something will obviously have to be created in its place, to maintain our security in the DataNet at a minimum, but Intelligence has seen a complete systemic failure."

I thought of the massive shortages of Agents and Assets we'd found in several regions, even as other sectors had so many that they were sitting becalmed, or else playing local security out of lack of work. Of our reports on Oshflara being manipulated, changed, within months of being filed.

"Worse," She went on, voice lowering in anger. "This was not a rapid failure caused by one of our traditional rivals. Such things have happened before, and can be excused in their own ways. This... this was infiltration on *our* timescales. Failures at every level, failures that an entire generation of Intelligence leadership was either blind to, or sailing along beside."

I hadn't even wanted to consider that the Oasis Commanders had been involved in the Faithful, but now that Delarah had said it aloud... it was a very real concern. One that would likely stay in my mind for years, swimming about and gnawing at me.

"Do you disagree?" She asked.

"...no sir." I admitted quietly, reaching out to take the badge in front of me. "We'll be merged into the Void Fleets then?"

"It will depend on the Torlah, and I suppose on the Imperial Circle." Delarah waved an arm, "We shall be breaking orbit as soon as the remainder of your new staff arrives."

I swallowed before speaking, "There are already Operatives among our group, sir. I don't have a strong enough Index to supersede them."

That amusement seemed to return. "An honest spy?"

"One that respects her fellow spies, sir."

Delarah huffed, tarah once more twitching to show that she wasn't offended. "The other Operatives will be analyzing the data coming in from other sectors until my fellow Void Lords begin to form their own Intelligence units. Once that occurs, I will revisit the command hierarchy as I see fit."

Meaning whichever Operative impressed her the most over that time would be moved into a command position over the others.

"Yes sir." I said.

"If that is all," She nodded toward the exit, "Finish your recovery, Operative Rerth'riah. These will be the last quiet days you'll have for many years, unless I miss my guess."

Holde and I rose, saluting together. Delarah gave us a lazy one in return, motioning for us to go.

We were just at the door when she spoke one last time. "Riah."

"Sir?" We both turned.

Her eyes had half closed, tarah elevated fully. "We will be a poor Empire indeed if we stop a pack from finding out what happened to one of their own. If we stop them from avenging her, if she proves to have been killed. If you find any hint of Ashe'lori, you have my word that I will allow you to chase that lead."

I swallowed, drawing myself up to my full height, fist coming before my throat in a second salute. "We are yours, Void Lord."

"Good." She said. "Go. Get into proper uniforms. You will join my morning councils to provide briefings once we depart from Altair. Until then, you are off duty to rest and recover."

"Sir."

We left our new commanding officer then, my arm sliding around Holde's shoulder as his own wrapped around my waist. As we leaned on one another, the relief washing deep through the currents of my soul.

Intelligence would be purged. Would be rebuilt into something else. Something better, Aspects willing. The Torlah and her Chashti'tahze would allow nothing less, now that they knew of the corruption that had taken root.

And more importantly, if Ashe was still out there... we would find her.

And if she wasn't, we would have the authority to kill everyone responsible for her death.

I
Ashe'lori

Date: Day 5, Month 1, 2165 Imperial
Location: Unexplored Space

"It's beautiful in a deadly way, isn't it?" I murmured, cheek resting on a fist, the rest of me slouching in the co-pilot's chair of our stolen yacht.

No one else was around to hear me talking to myself. Well, not unless there was something out there in hyper-space that could. It was theoretically possible, I supposed. There were a few fringe cults that believed the Aspects actually lived in this reality. That faster-than-light was heretical because we were plowing through the souls of the dead.

"Hope they're wrong... this is hardly Aysh's embrace." I sighed, watching as something like lightning phased in slow motion between green and turquoise clouds. As arcs of plasma the size of stars appeared and vanished far ahead, far below.

Any one of them would have melted our little yacht, killed those few of us who'd escaped the Faithful in an instant. There would be no warning, no chance to prepare for our fate. We would simply be dead. We'd have wasted the lives of the people who'd died so that we could escape.

It was why we'd gone shallow, skimming along hyper-space's rough 'surface'. Accepting a far slower speed in exchange for the safety of calmer waters.

It was necessary, yes, but the slow speed meant that we were burning fuel that we didn't have. It was limiting our options of where we could go before our reactor simply cut out.

Which would also kill us. Just a little more slowly, since we'd have to wait to either freeze to death, or asphyxiate when the oxygen ran out.

"I really need to stop thinking about it." My head fell back against the rest, the luxurious cushion easily supporting it. "Been thinking about it too much."

Not that I didn't have a reason to. Watching someone immolate themselves in front of you, blowing herself up with a sacrificial sorcery, would do that to a person. Especially when the old Director had done it just so that the rest of us could escape. Could have the chance to live. A chance to get home, to tell every nation of the Compact what had been done.

So that those pathetic few of us who'd lived could avenge everyone who hadn't.

It had been five weeks since that day. Since our escape. There hadn't been a single day that had gone by where I hadn't found myself here, alone. Acting more Human than I should have, lost in my own thoughts, cut off from the others.

My eyes were half closed when I heard the heavy thumps of footsteps approaching. The decadent wooden deck groaning at the weight of the alien as he made his way into the yacht's tiny bridge.

"Imperial..." Irkan's rumble paused, then he corrected himself. "Ashe. She should not be lingering alone yet again."

"Couldn't sleep." I replied, turning my chair so I could look over my shoulder at our pilot, and one of three survivors of Last Stop. "You're not supposed to be up for another three hours either."

Mikira were a high-gravity species, and it showed in his thickly built, short frame. They were incredibly strong, well protected thanks to the heavy shell that wrapped around his chest and back, and exceptionally dangerous with a razor-sharp horn protruding from the end of his narrow snout.

Oh, and his blood was toxic to nearly all other species, something his bright green and blue shell, horn, and chin-quills warned you about.

"True." His mouth fell open, showing off sharp teeth in what passed for a lazy grin for him. A hand idly tugged at the roughly sewed cloth wrapped around his waist and legs, a replacement for the bright green prison wear he'd sported as long as I'd known him. "But this sailor... *I* had hoped to check our course, to see if any additional speed could be gained."

Mikira also had a thing about people's names. Escaping Last Stop had convinced Irkan we'd all earned ours, but it was proving to be an adjustment for him.

"You won't hear me complain about going a bit faster. Are we still on track to survive, even with how things are?" I asked.

"We are, though we shall have fewer options than we hoped." His wide feet made the deck groan some more, until he squatted down where the pilot's chair had once been.

We'd had to rip it out, since it hadn't been designed to hold anything like a Mikira. Not that he'd really seemed to mind.

"I ran the calculations while you slept. Cashihto remains within reach, we should land in a week's time." Irkan went on, poking at the controls for a moment before looking out at hyper-space as well. "The navigation system claims it to be an agricultural world of little value, but one that has a respectable population. We may be able to trade labor for fuel there."

I heard myself sigh again. "Let's hope so. If we can't, all we've got to trade are the fancy clothes we've found in the cabins back there, a couple of guns, and one small case of Imperial credits that won't get us very far."

He waved a short arm dismissively, "Fuel and food shall both be found, one way or another. Then we shall move to the capital so that all may send messages home to warn our peoples."

Which was the entirety of our plan at the moment, mostly because the three of us couldn't really agree on where to go from there.

I wanted to go to Cathia. Its ruling dynasty definitely hated the Empire that I was a citizen of, that I was a conscripted soldier of, but it had been the Director's last advice to me. A promise that, as crazy as the Kolkris could be, they were enemies of the Faithful. That telling them what happened would see them protect us until my pack could come for me.

Irkan wanted to go to Cathia's enemy... *his* nation's capital of Lushrivers. I didn't know much about the Dual Kingdom of the Scarlet Tears, beyond the fact that they were a mixed nation of Mikira and Naulian exiles. People currently at war with half of the Far Reaches in an attempt to take back what they saw as 'their' region of the known galaxy.

He also had the greatest advantage in our debates; Lushrivers was far closer than Cathia to where we were. And, given that a war was raging, the route there was far less likely to see us attacked than if we tried for the Crescent's territory.

It was also infinitely closer than the nearest Ark Fleet outpost, which was where our final member, Johanna, wanted us to go. That we'd have to refuel two more times to get that far, once in the middle of the war's heartlands, was a problem even she'd admitted. Not that it stopped her from simply wanting to go home regardless of the distance.

I didn't, couldn't, blame her for trying to convince us despite those facts.

If Altair had been even a remotely plausible destination, I'd have tried to argue for it too. Even if I would have known, just like she did, that it really wasn't a choice.

"...we're going to end up going to Lushrivers, aren't we?" I asked.

"Only once the stubborn savannas agree." He rumbled, amusement clearly audible in his low, slow voice. "It is the only practical option given our location."

I huffed, putting my hands on the armrests. Pushing myself up to my feet came with a quiet groan, and a twist at my waist to try and loosen up stiff muscles. "All right. I'll start trying to convince Johanna if you can get us a few light-years per day faster."

"This sailor shall try." He paused, then corrected himself yet again. "*I* shall try, and I shall do my best not to see our lives ended pointlessly in the void."

"Thanks." I patted his leathery arm as I slipped past, stretching my own out above my head. "Is she up too?"

A huff. "Yes. In the engines."

Of course she was.

Groaning and rolling my eyes at her behavior, I padded on bare feet down the hall, the novelty of being surrounded by the yacht's splendor and wealth long faded. The faux-lantern lights that left it dimly lit, everything covered in rich wood, every closet filled with luxurious outfits. The kind of yacht that only the top level members of Delne'lir should have been able to afford.

Gorgeous, but knowing who'd owned it had helped kill the sense of luxury pretty quickly.

Honestly the most important thing we'd found had been the clothes. We'd all been sick of wearing a mix of disintegrating prison uniforms and cloaks made of hide.

I tugged my warm bathrobe around me a little tighter against the chill in the air, allowing myself to enjoy the comfort of it. In having real clothes. In being able to shower with real soap for the first time in... Ashahn's Blood, a bit more than a year now.

Hands rose to run through fur that was still far too long, hanging well below my shoulders, down my back, but which was finally free of oil and grime. Letting the strands play over my fingers for a few moments, I started tying it near my neck just as I made it to where my old cellmate was lurking.

Muscles made her paler skin shift as she hauled back a grate, her still-recovering body visibly straining with the effort.

"Johanna!" I groaned, racing in to help grab the other side. "Not again!"

Between us we got it set aside, leaving her to slump back, brushing her own dark fur out of her green eyes.

We were a study in contrasts for Humans. I was tall, taller than most Trahcon women. My skin was a tanned brown, with fur only a few shades darker, and sharp scarring on my face from where the Burned Hand had lived up to her alias by pressing fingers wreathed in sorcererous flame against my skin.

Johanna was short enough that I could comfortably rest my chin upon her head. Her skin was a light, pale tan, making her black fur stand out in contrast. My cellmate's features were sharper, narrower, and had only just begun to fill out from how gaunt they'd once been.

"Ashe." She panted, leaning back against the bulkhead, absently tightening the robes she'd chosen for herself. "Sorry. Thought I could get it up on my own."

Shaking my head, I walked around the now open-access to the ship's innards, reaching out to take her right arm.

There was a frustrated little sigh, but she didn't resist as I pulled it closer, rolling her sleeve up enough to check the thin lines in her skin. The legacy of where her arm had been broken in our desperate escape.

"Does it hurt?" I asked, carefully running my fingers along it to make sure nothing felt out of place.

"No." She insisted. "Ashe, the regenerator says my bone is put back together. I'm fine, just... not strong enough yet."

I huffed, letting her go. "You would be if you worked out with me in the mornings."

"I have been!"

"Every other morning at best." I countered, crossing my arms. "The rest of the time you're in here, poking at systems you don't understand."

Her features pulled into a scowl. "I'm not stupid, Ashe. I'm sure of what practically everything in here does."

"You know what I mean. You still can't read Caranat, which means you can't be *sure* since you have no idea what any of the labels say." I said. "And you've been refusing to let me teach you that too."

"Have not been. I know some of the letters now." She claimed.

I gave her a flat look, saying nothing.

"...dammit." Her chest heaved in a sigh. "No, I don't know what any of the letters are."

"Thank you for admitting it. Could you *please* let me teach you?" I asked. "Ashahn's blood, Johanna. I'm not asking you to move to Altair, be conscripted, and join me in the Empire. Just trying to help you learn how to read a language you already let me teach you how to speak."

It was her turn to cross her arms, eyes dropping to the floor. "I know. And yes, I know it's important. Not like anyone out here is going to write in Deutsch, or Englisch. I'll... start today."

"Promise?"

"I promise." She nodded down. "Just let me work on this for a bit on my own. I need to check the port side, make sure there isn't anything hidden in the access tunnel."

I took a deep breath, letting it out. "All right. Just keep the wrist-comp on you, all right? Don't get stuck somewhere we can't get you."

Johanna huffed, a small wave of confidence making her straighten. "Ashe. I've been crawling through ships since I was born. I'll be fine, just like I was fine every other time I've done this."

"All right," I said, holding my hands up in surrender. "I'll make breakfast in a few hours. Think you'll be done and showered by then?"

She nodded, squatting down next to the open space. Within a few breaths she'd swung her legs inside, giving me a small smile when she looked up. "I'll be back in a bit."

Then she was gone, vanishing under the floor, the sound of her movement vanishing against the deep hum of the yacht's reactor.

Leaving me with nothing to do besides trundle back to the cabin she and I were staying in. To crawl into a bed sized for a Half-Sword, a bed that felt depressingly empty with just me in it.

Well, it felt empty even when it was Johanna and I together, but it felt especially empty without her.

"...should exercise." I told myself. "Maybe finish cataloging everything we can pry off the walls to sell."

The former was tiring, and dull when it was done by myself. The latter was nearly complete as it was, and we had another week to finish it regardless.

What I really needed to do was spontaneously learn how to hack encrypted systems. Figure out how to pull information from the ship's secured files, from the three locked wrist-comps we'd found in cabin drawers.

Any one of those could have critical information on the Faithful, on the Burned Hand, on their mysterious 'Process'. Information I needed. Partly to give to the Empire, to Rerth, once I got back home, to my pack.

Partly that... but mostly because I *needed* to know just why they'd done what they had. Why they'd tortured us. Why our memories of how long we'd been on the prison barge didn't line up with this ship's calendar. Why they'd horribly mutilated Naule, Kelthi, and Xenthans. Why they turned people with souls into little more than rabid attack beasts.

Attack beasts with cybernetic enhancements and overrides. Overrides that had let them be controlled, talked through.

Why? Why do that to someone? What possible reason could there be?

"They're definitely petty enough for it." I slid an arm over my eyes, feeling my body sinking into the bed. "But just because they're cruel Trahcon supremacists doesn't explain it. It's too much effort for just... casual cruelty like that."

That fact kept striking me as significant. As the key to figuring out just what seas I'd been dragged into.

The Faithful were obviously wealthy; this yacht proved that. They were well connected within the Empire. Had to be, to have abducted me right off of Trinity like they had. To have inserted at least one agent deep into Imperial Intelligence, even if he'd committed suicide rather than be interrogated when found.

But why? Why murder random alien citizens of the Empire? Why create Last Stop so far beyond the borders of known space, absolutely nowhere near that same Empire? Nowhere near *anyone's* borders, for that matter.

"Why?"

I had no idea. I couldn't figure it out, couldn't think of any logical reason that could explain it. Bits and pieces, maybe, but put together? Entire convoys of barges bringing tortured prisoners beyond the edges of the map didn't line up with casual, dismissive murder.

Inserting Trahcon agents into Imperial institutions didn't seem to have anything to do with using cybernetics to convert people into animals. Into puppets.

"Why?" I growled, turning my hand over to rub at my face. "The answer is probably in the damned computers that I can't unlock. That I won't be able to look at until we get this ship to the Empire. To Jet."

My most annoying packmate would be able to get through the protections. He'd have already unlocked it all, read it, and summarized it if he'd been here.

...but he wasn't, and I had no skill or training in hacking.

"...fix that." I mumbled, forcing myself to calm down. "When I get home. Lessons on that, first thing.'

It still took me a little while to relax. To let my arms drop to my sides, my eyes closing against the dim light.

"Soon. We'll be there soon. Just have to keep sailing a bit longer... and then I'll be home."

II

Johanna and I sat down at the small dining table, Irkan comfortably squatting in place of a chair. All three of us had cups of cool water at hand, and I had a factory-new tablet stolen from one of the empty cabins ready to take notes on.

"All right." I tapped away, opening up my note file. "We're one day out from Cashihto, and you promised to tell us everything you knew about the Lost."

Irkan jerked his long head in an angular nod, "Yes. The Lost are... only somewhat like those others who call this region home. They are those who seek freedom in isolation. Those who lack the desire to become involved in the great struggles of the age."

I nodded, tapping out my first note even if it was just a reminder of what I'd been taught as a child. "I know that much. I just didn't know they had colonies this far out."

"There are far more of them than most know." He replied. "And they are far stronger than most who do not live in these Reaches know. There is a reason the Kings never seek battle with them, nor did arrogant Cathia even when it sought to rule all of what is now called the Far Reaches."

Johanna huffed, the two of us exchanging an amused look and shake of our heads at Irkan's usual anti-Cathia bias. While I rolled my eyes, she spoke up. "We don't really need to know how many ships they've got, Irkan. We need to know if we're trading one prison for another."

"We are not." He assured her, "The Lost are fiercely private, and respect the privacy of others. While this ship will certainly draw interest, few questions will be asked so long as we do not ask questions in return."

Her eyes narrowed, my cellmate beating me to asking the question by a single heartbeat. "Is someone going to try and take our ship when we land?""

Irkan blinked, as if surprised that the question had been asked. "Of course they will. It is a luxurious vessel, worth a great deal in these Reaches.

It is this sailor's belief that we should sell this yacht before we must battle for it. It is the most efficient means of funding our voyage."

"No." I said, not hesitating for a moment. Selling this ship was out of the question, no matter how much we'd get for it. How much easier that would make our journey. "We need it. We need what's on the servers Johanna found buried under our feet. Under no circumstances can we give up this ship."

He let out a heavy breath. "The wrist-comps and tablets secured must surely be enough proof for what the Faithful have done to us, to others. It will be enough to prove our claims of where we have been."

I was shaking my head before he finished, "They might be, but they might *not* be. There could be terabytes of information that we can't access in the computers. You've admitted you can't touch most of the navigation system beyond the basics. At a minimum that's got to have the location of other bases, other facilities."

Next to me, Johanna shifted, leaning an elbow on the table before resting her chin on that palm. "Ashe has a point. That's the kind of thing we'll need if we're going to convince anyone of what happened out here. At a minimum, the navigation system will have what we need to make sure people actually listen to us. Believe where we came from."

"Exactly." I said, "What happens if we sell the ship, make it to Lushrivers, and then it turns out there's nothing on the wrist-comps after all? If the tablets are just full of what we already know? What if the Faithful get away with what they did because we can't *find* them again?"

Irkan closed his eyes, his chest letting out a deep rumble of frustration.

"They'll have abandoned Last Stop by now." I went on, increasingly sure of my point. "That's the first thing you do when a secret operation is compromised. Even if we memorize those coordinates, anyone who goes out there isn't going to find anything but an empty base."

Johanna grimaced, "Assuming they don't find a way to take the entire base apart or something. They'll know it's going to be a long time before we get home, before anyone could get that far out to even check the place."

"Right." I agreed. "Point is, Irkan, we need this yacht as evidence. We can't sell it, or worse, let anyone take it."

"...the savannas have made their point." He allowed. "But that shall complicate matters. Selling this yacht for a more conventional ship, for fuel and food, was the best plan that this... that *I* had. Without credits of some form this voyage shall be incredibly difficult. And likely longer than we desire."

Johanna shrugged. "We knew that even before we left, and if our old plan is shot then we'll come up with a new one."

Irkan and I both eyed her, though I found my voice first ."You're not usually this confident."

"I'm finally on a ship, where I belong." She countered, lips curling on one side. "I know what I'm doing on a ship. What we'll need and not need to survive. Couldn't say that when we were in tiny cells, or stuck in a swamp, or running through pitch black tunnels while *things* chased us."

I smiled back at her. "And everyone's glad that you're feeling better."

Her grin widened for a moment, then she turned back to Irkan. "Point is that we'll just have to do something else for cash. Didn't you say we'd be doing manual labor or something to pay for fuel?"

Irkan shook his head, quills swaying under his chin. "Yes, but it was not a serious consideration for me. I was... reassuring you both, while truly hoping that we would simply sell the vessel instead."

"Of course you did." She rolled her eyes. "Well, back to our old ideas then. What do we do? Work on a farm? I don't think any of us knows anything about that kind of thing."

It was my turn to shrug, "Machine repair, maybe. Offering to drive goods around, or fix up the trucks and aircars that handle that kind of traffic. I've got plenty of experience on that, and I'm sure you can figure out the differences between a ship and a truck when it comes to maintenance."

"...maybe." She paused, then asked, "Could we steal what we need instead?"

My tongue ran over my lips. "...not sure I'm comfortable adding to our list of enemies, Johanna."

"Fair," Johanna allowed, "But what if it's the only way to get moving quickly? I don't like the idea of spending another year working on a farm just to get enough fuel to make it to the next planet."

While I didn't think it would take *that* long, I had to admit it was a valid concern.

"Besides," She went on, looking uncomfortable, "I don't think we've got many other options that don't involve prostituting ourselves to aliens who might want to have a fling with a Human girl."

The last word drew a grimace, a memory of Tasir caustically asking me if that was my plan to make money once we'd escaped. It had been during one of our arguments, and it had left me just as uncomfortable then as the idea did now.

"...let's not go there." I said, recovering after a moment. "And we're drifting away from the main topic. We'll decide how legal we're going to be about getting the fuel once we're there, and know who and what we're dealing with. Speaking of, Irkan, what are the Lost actually like? What can we expect when we land?"

A clawed hand rose in a negligent little wave, "They are people of the Reaches, like any other. Merely ones who do not involve themselves in its wider affairs, as I said."

"Species?" I asked, typing a few thoughts down about what we'd already said.

"We can expect peoples of many species united in their devotion to being left alone. Perhaps..." He let out a bird-like chirp, then twitched his hand once again. "...most shall be those of the Near and Far Reaches. Mikira, Naule, Thondian. Trahcon, of course, as their kind are everywhere, along with some Kelthi."

I nodded absently, noting that done. "Kelthi-Kelthi, or Xenthan-Kelthi?"

"The former. Most exiles from the Ark Fleet seek to make their way to the Lost in order to survive, given that they are so rarely welcomed on their home-world."

Johanna grimaced. "That's not exactly encouraging, Irkan. Anyone exiled from the Ark Fleet is someone who either made a whole lot of enemies, or did something pretty disgusting. There's a reason even the blood-thirsty Xenthans turn a lot of them away."

Our Mikiran companion grunted. "Yes, and they shall likely not be pleased at the sight of two savannas. Nor shall the others be pleased that newcomers have arrived unasked for."

"Especially not this far out." I guessed.

His long head moved in another of his strange nods. "Especially this far out, yes. With hope our desire to simply move on will soothe them. See them tolerate us, work with us to arrange a means we might depart most swiftly."

I leaned in a little. "You mean there's a chance they might just give us the fuel, to get us off their planet as quick as they can?"

"Not a high chance, but a chance." He said. "Or, perhaps, the cost will be something low enough that we can easily pay."

Teeth worked at my bottom lip for a moment. "...a chance is better than nothing. What are the odds we'll find an FTL buoy that we can use? I know you said there wasn't one, but is there any hope at all?""

Irkan let out a deep rumble. "Such odds are non-existent."

Johanna frowned. "You're sure?"

"Yes. The Lost do not communicate with the wider galaxy. Do not connect to the DataNet." A clawed hand fell to the table, fingers tapping away slowly. "Only their capital and a few select military systems have such access as far as I know. All other communication is done by courier vessel."

Her frown stayed. "How far away is that capital?"

"Aonu is perhaps five weeks further travel from Cashihto, if the void between stars remains calm." He paused, then admitted, "We are well and truly beyond the borders of known space, and there no safe currents listed in the navigation system."

I put a hand on Johanna's before she could say anything hot in response to his statement of the obvious.

"And what," I asked, "Could we expect when we reach Aonu? The Lost are a Compact signatory. Will they help us, if we report what we found to their government?"

Irkan's broad shoulders twitched as much as they could. "This sailor does not know. The nature of the Faithful complicates their position in the Compact, as the Imperial savanna well knows."

It did, as much as I'd been doing my best not to think about that. Yes, what the Faithful had been doing violated a whole lot of the Compact's laws... but *only* if you considered the Faithful as a nation-state of their own. As a rogue group operating outside the boundaries of any existing nation.

Which we all did, but what were we?

An Imperial Conscript, a civilian citizen of the Ark Fleet, and a middle-ranked sailor from the Scarlet Tears.

We weren't exactly the people that the Torlah, or Scarlet Kings, or politicians of any kind would listen to. Doubly so when our only real proof was our testimony, or else locked away beyond passwords and firewalls. Assuming that my prayers were answered, and the ship's servers did have critical information locked away within them.

And I really wasn't sure I trusted anyone out here to hack through those.

Strike that. I definitely didn't trust anyone besides Jet to hack into those devices.

"Especially," He went on, "As those Faithful are made up entirely of the river-sharks. This sailor can well imagine other nations simply claiming them as an Imperial problem, so that they might attack that Empire both politically and physically."

"...I could imagine that too." I admitted, chewing on my lip some more, typing out a few more thoughts. "What are our honest odds of getting an audience at all, on Aonu? At being heard out, even if they don't believe us?"

He mused on that for a minute, scratching at both the table and his chin before replying, "We come from a strange direction, in a type of ship that should not be here. That, and the tale we tell, could be enough for some.... but this sailor-"

"I." Johanna interrupted. "You're back to the third person."

"Ah. Thank you." He cleared his throat, "*I* believe that it shall depend on if their current ruler is present. He is a Trahcon himself, and may be more inclined to react to a group of his own species acting in such a fashion."

"And if he's not there?" I pressed.

Another of his micro-shrugs. "Perhaps one chance in four. Greater if we can convince a Lost from Cashihto to give us a marker, indicating we truly visited the world. That we truly came from beyond known space."

Johanna and I both grimaced, my expression tightening further when she added another worry to the pool. "Assuming that the Faithful aren't all over the place inside of the Lost too. I mean, they'd have had to go through their territory to make it as far out as Last Stop."

"...yeah." I admitted, eyes dropping to the table. "They would have. That was one of the many things I've been trying not to think about."

"It is unlikely." Irkan countered, "The Lost pride themselves on accepting all who desire to move on. All species are welcomed by them. Such an obvious group would be quickly dealt with."

I heard myself let out a little huff. "All species are welcomed by the Empire too, officially. Doesn't mean we really are. All the Faithful would have to do is pick a group or species no one else on a colony likes, and they'd get to have their sick fun. And with no DataNet access out here, it would be a lot easier for them to cover up what they're doing."

He grunted as if I'd just poked him with a stick. "The Ashe makes a fair point. I correct my statement; it is unlikely that the Faithful will be operating openly there. If they are present at all, it shall be in the shadows, just as elsewhere."

"Let's hope so." I told them. "We're straining the yacht just to make Cashihto, and it's one of what, two Lost colonies are that in our range at all?"

"Three." Irkan corrected.

I waved a hand, accepting the correction just as he'd accepted mine.

"So three colonies that this ship could get to Last Stop from, meaning there's every chance that it's been to one of them to refuel before."

"Or," He offered, "There are coordinates for other Lost facilities in the locked systems of this yacht. Locations in unexplored space where they take on provisions during their long voyages. Last Stop proves that they are no stranger to enormous expense and effort in their outposts."

"...maybe, but I think we have to assume that the Faithful will be around. Somewhere." I said firmly. "We have to assume they're going to come after us. For all we know there's a tracking device on this ship that we can't find."

He let out a grumbling noise, reminding me, "There are no FTL buoys for such a signal to route through."

"I know, I know, but what happens when we get to Aonu?" I asked.

That seemed to make him pause, then admit, "You have another point. We likely will not be able to linger there for long."

Johanna blew out a frustrated breath, "We're just talking in circles here. We can deal with what happens on Aonu when we get there, and our plan isn't to stay long on Cashihto to begin with, right?"

When we both nodded, she sailed on. "So we get to this colony, we try to be polite and beg for fuel, trade a week or two worth of work if we have to, or else figure out how to steal what we need. Then we do the same thing once we make it to the Lost's Capital, sell what we can from the ship to pay for messages home telling everyone what happened, and then we sail for Lushrivers however we can."

I glanced to Irkan, then back to her. "Yeah."

"Agreed." He rumbled.

"So how about we just go with that." She suggested. "And figure out the rest as we go. Not like we can make a better plan until we get there, and see just how they react to us dropping in on them."

I made a low sound in my throat. "Didn't you complain once about Tasir's plans not having enough details for you?"

She colored a little, "That was different."

"Uh huh. Because it wasn't you coming up with the plan?' I teased.

"I think the fancy Imperial spy should be embarrassed a nineteen year old girl from the Ark Fleet just came up with a better plan than she did."

"Hey!" I glowered at her, "I came up with most of that plan!"

Irkan chuckled as the two of us bickered, our little group enjoying what peace we could before we made landfall once again.

III

Cashihto didn't look like much from orbit. Large stretches of brownish red, with only the occasional bits of green. What little blue I could make out seemed to be confined to inland seas, rather than existing in proper oceans. Here and there white clouds covered up what little else there was to see, and there really wasn't much to see.

No major cities lit up the night side, no great sweeping agricultural projects were taming the wilderness. There wasn't even a primary orbital station. It was just us, and what our sensors claimed to be an old cargo scow that had been laboring its way onto an FTL exit from the system before we'd arrived.

It was... incredibly bland, and incredibly welcoming for that fact.

Against Cashito's lack of features, the radio challenge we received when we entered orbit was far more interesting. Doubly so considering that it came in the mix of chirping and snarls of the Mikira's dominant language.

Johanna and I sat in the remaining chairs on the right side, wearing pants and shirts that mostly fit us, nervously waiting as Irkan handled the initial negotiations.

"The scow just hit FTL." Johanna reported, "Or it blew up. One or the other."

I gave her a look, "You'd be able to tell if you'd taken my reading lessons seriously."

"I *am*." She hissed back, "I'm doing better than you are with *Deutsch*."

"Because your penmanship is terrible." I countered.

That got me a huff in response, "Not like yours is any better. You just get to cheat by typing things for me to read."

I was ready to continue our distracting argument when Irkan tapped a button, ending his call. We both shut up at once glancing over at him as he got his hands back on the primary flight controls.

"We are allowed to land." He told us, not dragging things out in the slightest. "We must negotiate for fuel once we are on the ground, but they promise that they will give us food if we are truly escaped prisoners. At a minimum we shall not starve."

"You told them?" I frowned. "How much of the story?"

"The broadest tale only. They were hesitant to believe, but also greatly confused as to how else a small yacht may have reached the farthest known colony of the Lost."

Johanna cleared her throat, "Did they sound like they're actually going to talk to us, or like they're pretending so that they can kill us and take our ship?"

"The former." Irkan replied, though he promptly ruined that reassurance by adding. "Though I cannot be sure. My people prefer to discuss such matters face to face. To do so over mere radio is... unseemly. We shall learn more once we land, unless the savannas wish to try another colony? Should we do so, we will be on the last dregs of our fuel tanks."

We mere Humans exchanged another look, this one both more worried and more skeptical.

Then it was my turn to speak again, "I don't like the idea of being trapped, and if we land here we can still leave and make a run if really need to... so I think we risk this harbor. Johanna?"

She gnawed on her bottom lip for a moment, then nodded. "I guess we risk it."

"All right." I exhaled, nodding. "Let's sail down down. Irkan? If they're mostly Mikira, you can handle the negotiations and I'll cover you with one of the guns. Johanna?"

"I'll be ready to seal the ship, and watch for anyone trying to sneak around." She said.

Irkan settled into position, nudging our small vessel onto a new course. "Agreed. Shields?"

I tapped the appropriate buttons, "Coming up... now."

And with that, we began our descent. The first waves of heat began to lick over the barriers shielding the fragile hull, the glass polarizing in response to the rising temperatures.

Irkan began to ease up on the speed relatively quickly. The air cleared to reveal Cashihto's largely barren surface, proving that it wasn't any prettier up close than it had been from orbit.

I fought the urge to grimace at the sight of so much sand and heat-baked clay, but didn't hide my relief when we began to follow a massive river.

The green laying on either side was far more promising to my eyes. Especially when we slowed further, letting us see isolated farmsteads. What looked like miniature canals stretched out to their little plots of land, with neat rows of crops sprawling out on either side of the water.

Our pilot checked his course once or twice, but otherwise seemed content to follow that broad river until we caught our first side of proper civilization; a small village clustered on one side of the river.

"Not many prefabs. Local materials, looks like." I noted as we swung over it, "Ten thousand people maybe?'

"I would trust the savanna's eyes." Irkan replied. "She is the trained observer."

Johanna glanced at me, seemingly ready to make a smart comment. A second look outside seemed to leave it becalmed, her attention quickly turning back to the screens she could only sort-of read.

Not that I had time to reassure her, or myself. Irkan was already slowing us to a crawl, more hovering than flying. We swung out over the outer edges of the community, my hands hitting the appropriate buttons to extend the landing gear when he called for me to do so.

And then we were touching down on a hill perhaps five hundred yards from the village's outermost buildings. A narrow trail ran from the outskirts to our position, betraying that this was a commonly used landing zone rather than anything special.

"Company." Johanna was already pointing even before Irkan had finished putting the reactor into low-power mode. "All Mikira, looks like."

I narrowed my eyes, peering at the group tromping our way along the path between tall reeds. "Six of them... shells are red and green, if that means anything."

A huff from our own Mikira. "Only that they have no royalty in their blood. Come. They will not appreciate tardiness, not when there are matters of import to discuss."

I nodded, quickly unbuckling myself. Irkan was already lumbering down the hall by the time I was up, but my longer legs made it trivial to catch up to his slow strides.

He waited at the hatch just long enough for me to grab the rifle we'd left near it, and for the display to inform us that the air quality was sufficient for our survival.

Not that I was prepared for the blast of heat that struck me the moment the hatch was opened. I heard myself gasping, almost swaying against the shock of it. My vision actually darkened for a moment before I managed to steady myself.

It was a struggle to follow Irkan partway down the ramp, to crouch in place with the rifle to cover him in case the locals tried anything.

For his part, he trundled a dozen yards away before settling into a lazy stance. Our hosts slowed their trek up the small hill, heads and horns bobbing as they spoke among themselves. A couple pointed me out, which drew another round of conversation before one was apparently chosen to sail over to us.

He strode forward confidently until he was within reach of Irkan. The two aliens seemed to take a long measure of one another before reaching out at the same time, clasping clawed hands. They seemed to tense for a moment in some silent contest of strength, then let go by equally silent accord.

I could only shake my head as they fell into comfortable crouches, their conversation largely muted by the reeds rustling in the wind. Shifting the weapon around a little, I got as comfortable as I could without compromising my readiness to shoot.

And then I waited.

An hour later, I mused on the fact that being a conscript had prepared me well for this kind of trial. I'd soaked my shirt and pants with sweat, and was thoroughly uncomfortable, but I refused to let it stop me from covering my companion.

"Ashe?" Johanna called from just behind me.

"Still talking." I said, just as I had twenty minutes ago. Johanna had more than proven herself in our stay on the ship, but her old nerves were apparently coming back now that we were on the ground. "Stay out of sight."

"I know." Johanna grumbled, "How much longer can it take to ask for fuel and food?"

My shoulder twitched. "Who knows? I'm just glad there hasn't been any fighting, or any more of them trying to encircle us. Speaking of..."

There was a long groan, "I know, I know. I'm heading back to watch the sensors. I'll bring you more water in a half hour if they haven't finished up by then."

Huffing quietly, I smothered a grin in favor of watching the five Mikira waiting just as patiently as I was for the conversation to be over.

In the end it would be another hour and a quarter before they finished, clasping hands once more before separating. Irkan walked back, placing one foot on the ramp without coming the rest of the way up.

"They are cautious." He reported, returning to Caranat. "But well believe that we are no lost travelers. Not in a luxury yacht from a far-off Empire. Two of us are to accompany them back to speak with their leader about our tale. That conversation shall decide our future here."

I frowned at him, "What about fuel, and food?"

"The latter shall be delivered, enough to keep us alive. They are willing to give us enough of the former to reach the nearest world, but not enough to reach Aonu. Not without payment, and they have no interest in what baubles we can strip from the vessel."

Dammit. Not what I'd wanted to hear, but at least he'd hidden that we already had enough fuel to make it that far. That could give us a few more worlds as options.

"Labor?" I asked.

"Perhaps. We shall have to negotiate." He jerked his head back, "Who shall go?"

...that was a hard question. One that had me biting my lip.

The smart call was for it to be me and Johanna, if only because we couldn't risk Irkan more than we already had. He was the only one of us who could fly the ship. The only one of us who might be able to make it back to civilization if something happened to either Johanna or I.

But I really wasn't sure Johanna would be up for this kind of negotiations either. Not when she clearly more comfortable in space than she was on the ground.

Not that I was really feeling up for negotiations with a local planetary leader either... but if I was being totally honest, now that we were off of Last Stop, I was the most expendable member of our strange little pack.

Irkan could fly the ship, and Johanna could at least try to repair it. I didn't have any skills beyond translating labels for the latter, and Irkan could manage that just as well as I could.

"...Ashahn's blood." I sighed, straightening with a quiet groan. "Get inside and lock the ship up. I'll... I'll handle this on my own."

He stilled, turning his head in what I thought was his way of conveying a worried frown. "Is the Imperial savanna sure?"

"She isn't." Swallowing, I started to walk down toward him, "But she doesn't see a choice. Does the sailor?"

"...no." Irkan admitted, "Be polite, young one. Be humble.... and be cautious."

I bobbed my head, swinging my rifle around, getting its sling over a shoulder. "Lock the ship down until I'm back, or until I call."

"We shall."

I slowed my pace as we moved past each other, took a final breath, and said, "If they try to take me hostage or something.... just leave. Get to another colony, steal what fuel you can, and go home. If I call you, um... right. If I call you, and I tell you I want to go to Alum, it means I'm a hostage and that you need to leave without me."

Irkan paused... and then nodded. "You do your kin proud, Ashe'lori. We shall await your word."

Swallowing, I gave him a final nod and got going. It was a struggle not to look back when I heard the ramp rising, the hatchway closing. Leaving me stuck out here with people I knew very little about, our very fate possibly in my hands.

"Aspects watch over us." I murmured before plastering what I hoped was a polite expression on my face.

The Mikira who'd been speaking with Irkan tilted his head at my approach, saying nothing even when I walked right up to him and stopped.

"I'm the negotiator, I guess." I told him, hoping he understood Caranat. "Just me. The others are staying on the ship."

Yellow eyes blinked slowly, then he let out an amused little chirp. He tapped an old wrist-comp, its tiny speakers offering a translation when he began speaking in his own tongue again.

"The savanna is more wise than she appears." He paused there, waiting for the synthesized voice to finish before he went on. "Does she not wish to retrieve armor first?"

"No." I said, avoiding mentioning the fact that we didn't have any aboard. Not any that would fit me, anyway. "I'm ready."

He seemed to shrug, turning slowly in place, motioning for me to follow him.

I did, walking in stride until we reached his waiting companions. The six of them formed up around me in an unmistakable escort...

...leaving me surrounded as they led me away.

IV

The village's buildings were a lot like the Mikira themselves; squat, durable, and painted in extremely bright colors. I appreciated that last part. The gaudy and mismatched coloration made it feel a bit homey as we walked down the dirt covered street. That feeling was the only thing that was helping me stay calm as people began to take notice of us.

Taking notice of me in particular.

They weren't subtle about it either.

I felt my heart speeding up a bit as the staring got worse the deeper into town we sailed, the moment reminding of those few times I'd turned down the wrong streets on leave back home. When I'd sailed into neighborhoods where Humans were very much not welcome.

Nearly all of the locals were Mikira, and the vast majority of them were making sure I saw them staring at me as I was led past. What few aliens I saw weren't any better. Most of those were Trahcon wearing masks, probably humidifiers, but their quivering tarah betrayed their distaste even with half of their faces covered up.

"I don't think we're very welcome here." I murmured, fingers tightening around my rifle's strap.

The only one of my escorts who'd spoken glanced at me, twitching his head in a nod before speaking through his translation software once again. "The savanna is not. This world is the farthest Colony of the Lost, settled by those who desire to leave all else behind. That she is here at all is an unpleasant mystery."

I grimaced. "We guessed that might be the case, but we didn't have many options."

"So she and the sailor claimed." He replied, turning ahead once again. "It is a strange tale, one that others must hear."

"Can you think of another reason for us to be out this far?" I asked, practicing the argument I'd need to make once we got wherever they were leading me. "And it isn't as though we're asking to settle, or the vanguard for an invasion. All we're asking for is the bare minimum we need in order to leave as soon as possible."

There was a rumble in his broad chest, a bird-like chuckle following it. "This speaker admits he cannot think of another reason, and her desire to leave is a welcome one. It may earn her honor and aid, if she remains both wise and polite."

"Will it earn us fuel?" I asked.

"It is possible." He replied. "We approach."

The government building, I assumed that's what it was, proved to be a decent size square with two layers of domes rising from the top. It seemed to be one of the few structures left without paint, leaving the sand colored stone it was built from exposed to the elements. If nothing else it helped it stand out, I supposed.

My escort guided me up the stairwell leading inside, marching me through the front door.

I tried not to groan in relief at the far cooler temperature in the shade. As relieving as it was, I had to observe what was going on around me. Our survival could depend on it.

A very strange lack of guards was my first observation. No one challenged us at the door. I hadn't seen any sentries outside either, and there wasn't a checkpoint inside. Ashahn's blood, there wasn't even a receptionist's desk. Just open stone hallways, largely empty.

My second observation came with the next wave; the building felt... unfinished. I hadn't been in many government structures back home. Not civilian ones at least, but what few I'd had to go inside of had all followed a pretty similar decorating pattern. Pictures of respected locals, pictures of the current Torlah, of past Torlah, paintings of famous moments in the colonial or Imperial history... that kind of thing.

The walls here were barren. By the Aspects, some of the rooms didn't even have *doors* on them, letting me see that the vast majority of them held nothing but dust and sand. A couple had what looked like storage crates inside, but none looked to be in use as anything but idle storage.

Once we got upstairs, things changed a little on that second floor. For starters there were actually people up there, working, talking, and bustling about in that self-important way that bureaucrats seemed to affect regardless of species.

There still weren't very many of them, but this part of the building was clearly in use, unlike the floor below.

Our path eventually reached a desk, behind which another Mikira sat. A female, I thought, from the stubbier horn, and the fact that her quills were on her cheeks rather than her chin.

She and one of my escort had a short conversation, then I was pointed to the door behind her. A glance at the others saw them simply staring at me, waiting... and so I gathered up my courage and walked on as instructed.

I strode through the door to find myself face to face with yet another of their species, this one's coloration red and blue around his leathery skin. He seemed older, from the cracks in his skin, and the almost dull colors on his shell, but I couldn't be sure.

"Savanna." He spoke Caranat in the slow, measured way Mikira always did, a clawed hand held out to me.

"Sir." I replied politely, grasping his wrist like I'd seen Irkan do to the first messenger outside of the ship.

He started squeezing my own at once, and I squeezed back, mostly to try and bear with the pain. It felt like he was about to break my wrist, but some instinct told me not to show how I felt.

I couldn't stop myself from trembling, but I could keep my jaw clenched. Could stop myself from letting out any noise.

He kept up that tight grip for most of a minute before grunting in what sounded like approval, releasing me. "Interesting. Sit, savanna."

The chair was more of an elevated bowl, better suited to his people than my lanky body. It did prove strangely comfortable once I figured out how to settle into it with my legs crossed. For his part, my host shifted around his desk, easing his way into his own seat.

"In your tongue, I am called Chakin, ruler of Cashihto." He

41

introduced himself. "What do you claim to be called?"

"My name is Ashe'lori." I licked my lips, then went on, "The Mikira named Irkan who is our pilot said I earned my name during our escape from Last Stop."

There was another of those avian chirps, "I would hear this tale, to judge its worth for myself."

I bit my lip, hesitating. Not sure if I should tell him or not, not until I had a better idea of what he already knew. If anything.

"...have you heard of a group called the Faithful?" I asked.

"I have not." He replied.

"Do you swear it?" I asked. "There aren't ships coming through your system, refueling, and then going on into deep space toward the core? Imperial made barges doing the same?"

His reptilian eyes blinked slowly. "You are wary."

I couldn't exactly deny it. "Yes, with good reason."

Chakin stared me down for several silent heartbeats before saying, "I swear by my name, by those who dwell beyond, that I have not heard of such a group. You are the first foreign visitors to Cashihto in many decades."

It was still probably foolish to tell him. Rerth wouldn't have. She'd have come up with a smooth, elegant lie. Holde would have already had everyone convinced he was their best friend.

Jet... well. He'd have probably flailed about just as badly as I was.

Neither one of us was as good of a liar as our packmates. I certainly wasn't. Not yet.

Worse, I hadn't been practicing like I should have. Hadn't thought of something in advance like I should have. And besides, Irkan had already told them the broad details. That meant I was stuck with that much truth.

Left with little choice, I told him the surface level of what had happened. That my companions and I had been three of many people stolen away from our homes. Abducted. Tortured. I described the trip on the barge, of waking up to find the cell beside us empty save for the blood of those slaughtered within.

I didn't say much of our broader group on Last Stop. Only that we'd had a plan, that we'd been found or betrayed, and that everyone else had died. That we'd determined to risk our escape anyway.

Chakin listened intently as we told him of finding the ancient mines, built by his people's long dead kingdom. Of the things we'd killed in those tunnels. Finding our way into the Faithful's base, Tasir's final sacrifice leading to our escape.

"...concerning." He rumbled when I had finished. "To my knowledge, there are no lost colonies five weeks travel coreward from here. This was not a direction the kingdoms of the past ever explored or settled."

I could only roll a shoulder. "The computers there were definitely Mikiran made, and Irkan was certain it was from the kingdom before your homeworld's Judgment."

"And I must believe you." Chakin scratched at his quills, looking contemplative. "It is a wild tale. An unbelievable tale. Yet I struggle to discover just why you would say so outlandish a story if it were truly false. A claim to have escaped from pirates, to be fleeing the war now raging, was what I expected."

"Getting to that war is kind of our goal right now." I told him. "Well, getting to Lushrivers is, but that means going through that war. We have to call the Compact."

He huffed. "Three lost souls, seeking a Judgment? You do not lack for boldness, Ashe'lori. Such a thing has not been called since the invasion of your kind's homeworld, when the most foolish of your nation-states were exterminated for violating the Compact's laws governing war."

"I know." I said.

"And you would presume that these... Faithful would be considered a state onto their own, not merely rebels to distant Empire."

I grimaced as he voiced my very real worries, repeating myself. "I know it's not likely."

"Yet you would still try?" He asked.

"Yes." I cleared my throat, "We have to try. After what they did, what they're still doing... they're scattered across the Near Reaches, have infiltrated the Empire. We need an agreement of the Compact nations to hunt them all down. To end them."

His eyes seemed to gleam, and there was a low, almost dark chuckle. "There it is. The cry for vengeance within the soul of Ashe'lori. I can see it in your dull eyes, smell it in your scent. You shall never be calm again, not until they lay slain."

I swallowed. "I... they have to pay for what they did. What they're still doing."

"Yes." He said. "That emotion is what leads me to believe you."

I nearly sagged in pure relief, only barely keeping my back straight. "...you'll help us?"

Chakin chuckled. "I did not say that. Not yet. Do not be impatient, savanna. This is matter is important, and must be treated with the respect it deserves."

Nodding, I forced myself to lean back in my seat. Force myself to relax, to breath evenly, to be less of an impatient Human.

"Of course." I said. "I apologize. I'm merely concerned that the Faithful will come for us, sooner rather than later."

"A valid concern." He replied, folding his arms across his armored chest. "A people who act as they do... no. They would not react well to the chaos that you caused, to the insult of your escape. Not well at all. Their blood surely hungers for your pain and death, just as yours does for theirs."

I wasn't really sure how to reply to that, so I went with my old standby of saying absolutely nothing at all.

Chakin regarded me across the metal and wood of his desk, apparently fine with my silence. He let it linger for a time before he spoke again, his slow voice contemplative. "Decisions shall have to be made. Those who dwell here have no desire for visitors, especially not ones who may inspire more to come. You say that your destination is Lushrivers?"

My own arms crossed, just to stop them from twitching. "Eventually. We plan to go to Aonu next, to call the Lost to the Compact if we can, or else just bargain for what we need to make it back to the Far Reaches."

"Wise." His claws scraped at his tough skin, head tilting one way, then the other. "You would ask us for fuel for such a voyage to the capital, and for sustenance?"

"Yes. And a message from you to your leader, verifying that we really did stop here." I said. "Otherwise they'll probably just think we're refugees or pirates who stole the yacht from Cathia or something."

He showed me his teeth, "Wise indeed. I already find your company far less taxing than any other savanna I have met. That you intend to depart only makes it more pleasant."

I bowed my head, licking my lips once. "Thank you."

"You are welcome, but what does Ashe'lori offer for my compliments? For my resources?" He asked. "Her warning of these Faithful shall mitigate the price, as does the logic of sending her to speak at Aonu... but a price must still be paid."

"Um, we don't have much to trade in exchange for your generosity." I replied.

"I will believe that." Chakin replied. "Yet such a trade must be made. I honor you with my belief of your tale, and shall except an unworthy exchange for the fuel and food you require."

"Did... you have something in specific you wanted?" I asked. "We have luxurious clothes, fit for Trahcon, but I can't imagine you'd want those."

"You imagine correctly. I have more practical desires." His narrow eyes turned to the weapon still hanging from a shoulder. "That is a rifle from the Empire of the Homeworld, is it not?"

"...yes." I admitted, "We found a few in arms lockers aboard the ship."

"I desire them." He said.

Another bite of my lip. We had the three rifles we'd grabbed from the armory, a few pistols, and then two more carbines we'd found in the ship's cabins... and that was it as far as weapons went. Unless you counted the cutlery we'd found in the yacht's galley, which I really didn't. Or the one sword that none of us knew the first thing about using.

"I can give you three, and two pistols that are just as new." I said after a long moment.

"Is that all of them?"

I lifted my chin, and tried not to shake when I repeated myself. "I can give you three rifles, and two pistols. They're the newest models, reserved for Imperial Wind Formations. You won't find any like them this side of Alum. Those have to be worth a lot on their own. They're probably worth more than the actual cost of fuel."

Chakin rapped his skin with his claws once more. Ignoring the remark about the value of the weapons against the value of the fuel.

There wasn't much room to argue with him about it. He had what we needed, and he knew it.

"Three such rifles, two such pistols, and the coordinates of the prison world you claim to have been upon."

"Agreed." I certainly wasn't going to get a better offer.

"Agreed." He rumbled. "You shall return to your vessel to inform the others. We shall bring the fuel and supplies to you tomorrow, along with a coded message from myself for the government."

I could only nod again, even if the notion of having to wait until tomorrow left me nervous.

"We will make the exchange in even allotments, you will provide part of the payment, we shall provide our resources. That will continue until all of it is done." Chakin went on. "After that, you shall depart from Cashihto as soon as the process is complete with no further delay."

"Agreed." I repeated. "We'll stay on board the ship, and won't bother you further."

His long mouth dropped open in a pleased smile, "How good that we are both reasonable beings. Go, savanna who has earned the name Ashe'lori. Tomorrow you shall leave this world, and I shall question the River-Sharks who live among us."

I swallowed, "You think some of them may be Faithful?"

"I think only that it is foolish to assume loyalty." He replied, slowly shifting his weight. I mimicked him, standing as he did, "And wiser to be cautious. Go, Ashe'lori. We shall not meet again in this realm."

My head bowed, "May your river be calm, elder."

There was a final wave, and then I was led back to the yacht to tell the others of the arrangement. Without once being threatened, or taken hostage, which meant it had gone far better than I'd honestly dared hope.

...considering my usual luck, that was a minor miracle.

Considering that same luck... I made sure the yacht was fully locked for the evening, one of us awake at all times to watch the sensors, and that we kept guns near at hand at all times.

Johanna and Irkan didn't complain. They were equally ready for something to go wrong...

...and we would be prepared when it did.

V

Two trucks pulled up an hour after dawn. One had the look of a vehicle that carried fuel, parking closer, while the other was open-topped with its bed occupied by three enormous crates.

A group of Mikira had already begun to offload the food by the time that we got the hatch open, my legs carrying me down the ramp while Johanna covered me with a rifle. That she wasn't a very good shot, that she hadn't had more than a few hours training in the middle of our escape, would hopefully go untested.

"Khash, bless me rather than curse me." I whispered the prayer before plastering a smile on my face for our hosts.

"Savanna." One of them rumbled, not offering me further greetings than that. "Payment."

In response I pulled out a pocket-drive, holding it out for him. "The coordinates that Chakin wanted."

His eyes narrowed, and he didn't make any effort to take it. "The weapons."

"I arranged the order with Chakin last night." I countered. "Coordinates now, then you load the food. Then you get one rifle, we get Chakin's message, and you start fueling. You get one more rifle halfway through that, and the last gun when it's finished."

Thick lips pulled back from sharp teeth... but he grabbed the drive. "Very well. Where is the cargo access?"

"Port side."

A sharp nod came along with deep barks in his own tongue, his feet carrying him back to the others. Between them they got all of the crates up in short order. I bit my lip, watching as two of them casually carried the food we'd need to make it farther into the Lost's scattered kingdom.

Bringing my wrist up to my lips, I whispered into my comp, "Irkan, they're coming around. Drop the cargo lift."

His reply was in doing just that. The sight of the small platform lowering from the yacht's belly made one of the locals turn, clearly irritated that they'd have to load the crates one at a time.

"We're not letting you aboard the ship. You can load it onto the lift." I said, hearing the defensiveness in my tone.

The man glowered a bit longer, then jerked his head back around to help put the first of the containers in place. Another whisper had Irkan bring it up, the process repeating two more times.

Asking them to wait, I went back up the ramp, patting Johanna on the shoulder as I went past. She was sweating just as badly as I was in the morning heat. At least I hoped it was from the heat, and not from the stress of having to stand guard like this.

Or maybe it was from wearing some of the armor we'd found. It mostly fit, though lacking a helmet gave her a rather obvious weak point. Still, it was more than I had.

"Halfway." I murmured, grabbing the first of the guns from where we'd set it in the hall. "You all right?"

"No." She whispered back, weight shifting. "I'd really rather be back in space."

"Soon." I promised.

All six of the Mikira were waiting as I came back down with the first rifle, holding it out for the man I'd originally spoken with. "Khadel Eighty-Two, Ix model. Two clips of ammunition. As agreed."

Clawed hands took the long rifle, turning it over slowly. He peered at it, inspecting the rich wood worked into the bronzed metal, the elegant way the electronics had been hidden within.

"...how much is such a weapon truly worth, savanna?" He asked.

"The Empire doesn't sell them." I replied. "Fuel?"

There was a chirping grunt, "Yes. Begin."

I half expected 'begin' to mean 'tear her apart so we can get more of these', but to my relief, the phrase saw three of them stride off to start the long process of refueling the ship.

I got a second surprise when the man gave me a final nod, pulling out a drive of his own from his belt. "Chakin's message for the True Lost."

"Thank you." I said, taking it, sliding it into a pocket.

He grunted. "Give the remaining weapons to the others. This speaker returns to Chakin."

"Uh, okay?"

They were already turning away, one clambering into the cargo truck. By the time the others had the fuel lines hooked up, and Irkan reported it was flowing, they'd pulled out and were on their way back to the city.

Pursing my lips, I forced myself to focus on the ones managing our fuel intake. They were close enough to the truck, and ship, that I couldn't really think of them doing anything untoward. Not with what amounted to an enormous bomb right next to them.

...unless they were Processed by the Faithful, and willing to die to take us out with them.

The thought made me shudder. "...by the Aspects, I'm going to be paranoid about that for the rest of my life, aren't I?"

None of them heard me muttering to myself, which was probably for the best. They seemed fine ignoring me completely until a soft chime sounded, one of them hauling back on a lever before turning to me.

"Half." He announced. "Weapon now."

My comp came back up to my lips. "Irkan? They really halfway?"

"*Yes.*" Irkan replied at once.

I nodded to the others, trudging back up the ramp to grab the next rifle. That time, though, I had something besides reassurances to give to Johanna.

"Go up front. Help Irkan get the ship ready to take off as soon as possible." I told her.

She glanced at me, "You sure? I can stay, keep covering you."

"Not sure at all, but... I don't know. I just want to be ready to leave." I exhaled, picking up the second gun. "As soon as possible. I'm probably just paranoid, but..."

"Tiny cells?"

"Tiny cells." I sighed. "Thanks."

It was her turn to pat my shoulder, then she was darting down the hall, already calling for Irkan to start bringing the reactor up to full power. Leaving them to it, I headed back down the ramp with the next part of the payment.

The one who took the gun was even less polite than the first had been. He simply yanked it out of my hands, chirping and growling excitedly as he waved it around. I couldn't help but flinch when he pointed it at me for a moment, despite the fact that it wasn't loaded.

Not that it remained that way for long.

I caught him sliding a magazine into place as I returned to stand on the ramp, the others trying to hide his preparations by bustling around to get the fuel pumping once more. They failed miserably, but were clearly making the effort to not let me see what they were up to.

"I'm starting to hate being right." Swallowing, I forced myself to look bored and tired, rather than ready to bolt the rest of the way back up the ramp.

By my rough guess, we were about halfway through the next portion when the situation changed... but not in the way I honestly expected.

The harsh crack made me flinch, my brain slow to realize it had been a distant explosion rather than a nearby gunshot. Closer in, the Mikira had a similar reaction; all of them half-ducked, then jerked upright.

My head snapped around along with theirs to stare at the plume of smoke rising in the distance. It was rising quickly, somewhere on the far side of the village. For a few long breaths there was silence... and then I heard the distant thunder of gunfire.

A few shots at first, then a rising deluge along with a second, sharper boom from a second blast that set a three story building to toppling amid another huge plume of smoke and dust.

"Ashahn's blood." I gasped, already backing my way up the ramp. We had more than half of the fuel, we had Chakin's message, and we had food. That was hopefully enough to both make it to Aonu and help us once we got there.

No reason to stand in the open, or reason to stay if things were exploding. My arm rose, letting me shout into my wrist-comp. "Irkan! Are we ready to leave?"

"*Nearly!*"

The shouting drew the attention of the remaining three Mikira, who only then seemed to realize that I was making a run for it. The nearest of them let out a furious noise of his own, though the effect was ruined by the sound of a third explosion going off somewhere.

"Savanna!" He boomed. "Halt!"

"We have a deal!" I called back, making one last attempt to get the fueling process finished. "I'll throw out the third gun once you're done! I swear by Ashahn!"

He took a threatening step forward, "Savanna caused this? Answer!"

"I-"

The one closest to the fuel lines turned slightly, letting me see the one with the rifle already bringing it up to aim at me. My steps turned into a frantic lunge for safety, though I knew I wouldn't make it before he could pull the trigger.

I could tell when he did, because he started screeching in rage when nothing happened. I couldn't understand his language, but I knew the tone of a man swearing up a storm well enough.

Which was about how I'd figured they would realize we'd disabled the rifles before we'd handed them over.

His chorus went on until I slammed my palm on the door controls inside, making the hatch drop down with an enormous clang before the others could try to race after me. A second, slightly less frantic tap of a command saw it lock and seal in preparation for departure.

"They tried to shoot!" I called down the hall, "Time to raise anchor!"

Johanna's head stuck out from the cockpit, fur framing her nervous features, "I'm shutting the fuel intake! Irkan's bringing up the core to full power now!"

Nodding, I stayed just long enough to bring the ramp back in, glancing at the security feed next to the controls to see one of the Mikira scrambling off of it when it began to retract.

"...blood of the Aspects." I raised my voice again when I saw the boxy object he'd had in his hands. Something that must have been hidden on the fueling truck. "Irkan! They have some kind of charges!"

His reply was in the deep thrum of the yacht's engines throttling up far more quickly than they probably should have been. I had to grab onto one of the fancy light fixtures when the entire ship tilted around me, its mass leaving the ground without any further warning.

There was the briefest pause before the fuel lines were disconnected; fortunately by a fail-safe and not by them tearing apart.

I stayed long enough to check that, just to be sure, then staggered my way down the lurching hallway. Irkan steadied us out at the same time as I made it to the cockpit, falling into my usual seat just as he began a lazy circle of the village.

"Fighting all along the river." I muttered, already bringing the shields up. Just in case. "Look there. Sorcery."

"I see it." Johanna winced at the blue-black flames that were clearly starting far more natural orange-red ones in quite a few of the local buildings. "Trahcon are torching everything they can get to on that side of town."

Irkan grunted, "It would seem that the Faithful were present here after all."

"...maybe." I admitted.

"You do not sound convinced." He rumbled.

I could only roll a shoulder in a shrug. "No theories without evidence. Could just as easily be the locals just not having gotten along to begin with, and we're just the excuse for a miniature civil war."

There was a huff from my right, Johanna leaning back in her seat. "I guess it doesn't matter, does it? What's important is knowing if we have the fuel to make Aonu."

Irkan tapped at the controls before him, gauging them for a long moment before replying. "Yes."

"Comfortably, with fuel to spare?" I asked. "If we have to go shallow again?"

"No." He said flatly.

My cellmate grimaced as she spoke, "Well, let's get moving in that direction. We're just burning fuel up here, and I don't think I want to know what's going on down there. Not enough to stay."

"Agreed." He rumbled, already adjusting our course. Pointing our bow to the sky, our altitude beginning to rise at once. "Speaking of our hosts, they wish to talk."

Hesitating for a moment, I bit my lip before reaching out to accept the transmission. "Yes?"

"*Ashe'lori.*" His use of my name let me realize it was Chakin speaking, even if I honestly wouldn't have been sure otherwise. "*You were assuredly telling the truth in your warnings it would seem.*"

"I was." I said. "Your men refueling our ship tried to attack us, by the way."

His shrug was audible. "*Did you expect anything less?*"

"Well, no." I admitted, "Was it on your orders?"

"*Had it been, you would all be dead or prisoners already.*" Chakin replied. "*You certainly would not have been allowed to leave my palace as you did.*"

...that was fair, even if I didn't think the word palace worked for the building I'd been in. "I hope you forgive the question. They had satchel charges of some kind, so I was more than a little concerned."

There was a low rumble, "*If that is true, then I am most curious as to where mere attendants acquired such devices. When you arrive at Aonu, add a recording of this conversation to your proof. I trust you have adequate video of the events in my city?'*

"We will."

"*Good. Be gone from this system, Ashe'lori. Do not return.*"

He cut the channel there, leaving me frowning while Johanna let out a huff.

"Well," She muttered, "Planet one and we're already being told to leave and never come back. Suddenly I'm a whole lot less certain about us even making it to Lushrivers."

I wanted to argue with her... but it was rather hard to. "At least we got away without any problems."

Johanna gave me a tired look. "Can we check the food for poison before we say that? Do we even have a way to tell without eating it and hoping we don't die?"

That was another good question, fortunately it was one I actually had an answer to. "The medical suite has a food scanner, thank the Aspects. I'm still sure this was the Burned Hand's personal ship. It would definitely explain both the luxury, and the fact that it has a scanner for poison sitting around and ready to be used."

She gave me her up and down style of shrug. "So long as the scanner works."

Taking the hint, I took one last look at my console before pushing myself upright once again. "I'll go get started on that, unless you need me for anything, Irkan?"

His long head jerked in a negative motion. "Not so long as no other ship arrives. I shall call should that happen, otherwise we should be on our next long march soon enough."

Patting his shell, then Johanna's shoulder, I lingered until the final bits of blue sky had turned to black stars. Then I made my way back down the port side hallway, stopping just long enough to grab one of our remaining guns. With pistol in hand, I opened up the small cargo space tucked in on this side.

No one had contrived to get aboard, which made my paranoid clutching of the Strike pistol a little silly. I still kept it ready until I'd circled all three of the crates, cracking each one open to double-check that there wasn't anyone hiding inside either.

Only once I was absolutely sure did I put the weapon aside and start poking around at the food we'd been given.

Interlude
Rerth'riah

The shuttle's roaring engines sent crops flying in every direction, completely ruining half a field's worth of harvest. Several men and women scattered back at the sudden landing, scurrying to take shelter in nearby treeline.

Only one of them stood their ground, an arm thrown up to shield their eyes.

I waited for the shuttle's landing struts to sink into the soil before stepping off. Armored boots trampled shredded leaves and half-grown fruits, carrying me toward the woman in her bright green penal clothing.

"Mok." I greeted the murderer.

"Riah." The former security officer looked ready to lay into me for ruining their food, but must have seen the Void soldiers stepping off the shuttle behind me.

She visibly swallowed a hot reply, instead asking, "...what are you doing with Voiders, and what in Ashahn's bloody name are you doing here this time?"

"I was transferred, and I'm doing something I strongly advised against." I said, voice flat, pulling something out of a pouch on my belt. "Here. Catch."

A hand snapped up, catching what I'd just thrown at her. Eyeing me suspiciously, she glanced down at it... and her tarah splayed outwards in shock. "Riah. What in the Aspect's names is this?"

My arms crossed my chest, new armor creaking a little with the motion. "Your new rank badge, *Agent* Tia'mok. Your sentence has been commuted by the order of Chashti'tahze Delarah, who also signed an order drafting you and your pack into the Eighth Void Fleet."

For the first time since I'd met the smug bitch, she seemed at a complete loss for words. Her mouth opened and closed several times until she managed to croak out. "...why?"

"We found out who the Burned Hand works for." I said.

She jerked her attention back up to me. "Oh. Are they as bad as I suspected?"

"Worse." I told her. "Imperial Intelligence is compromised. All vetted Agents are being reassigned to Void Fleets. Any and all possible Assets who can assist in locating the persons responsible are being drafted, regardless of past convictions, dishonor, or dismissals."

"...and if we don't want to work for a Void Lord?" She asked.

I rolled a shoulder, "I just told you that you were drafted. Refusal to serve is desertion, and I can shoot you here and now."

Mok huffed, glancing down at the badge in her hand once again. She took a shuddering breath, fingers closing around the badge. "What's our task?"

"Aggressive investigation and interrogation." Pausing, I exhaled before making myself walk the rest of the way over to her. She watched me approach, saying nothing until I settled in just a foot or two away.

"We don't have enough security or intelligence trained assets." I admitted, "That's why the Void Lord is pardoning you, and several others. People we're certain aren't involved in this new group, or their infiltration of the Empire."

She met my stare. "And you're certain I'm not one of them?"

"You swear by the Aspects."

A small frown. "Yes? So?"

I let out a tired breath, "The Faithful, that's what they seem to call themselves, react violently to any mention of them. As in they attempt to rip apart their bindings to kill you for speaking their names."

Mok blinked rapidly. "You can't be serious."

"I am. I didn't get through the third common prayer before they were all screaming for my blood through their gags."

The woman in front of me was a lot of things, but slow on the uptake wasn't one of them.

"Blessed is Ashahn, bringer of inspiration. Wrathful is Ashahn, the stormbringer." She recited in an instant. "How many more would you like?"

I huffed, shaking my head. "You'll get to read the entire book, out loud, once we're on board. You will not be allowed off of the ship without escort. Everything you do will be supervised until we're certain of your loyalty to the Empire."

"...I see." She glanced aside, seemed to take a breath, then nodded slowly. "This is a full pardon? We're not going to be thrown onto a new one of these primitive holes once the crisis is passed?"

"You really think Delarah would do that?" I asked. "You know her reputation, and how she treats those in her fleet."

Her head tilted a little, right tarah flicking out, then in. "Point. Am I under your command then? I do see the markings for an Operative on that shiny new armor."

"Yes." I said.

Mok seemed to mull that over before accepting it. "...all right, and where are we going?"

My left hand rose, motioning around us. "Get your packmates into the shuttle. I don't want to repeat myself when I give the details."

There was a deep breath, and Mok nodded once before bringing her own hands up. A moment later her new rank badge was affixed to her penal uniform, looking horribly out of place, but I didn't fault her for wanting to wear it.

After twenty years on a low-tech colony like this, I'd have been thrilled to have a rank insignia as well.

Leaving her to gather the others, I strode back to the shuttle, nodding to the two soldiers standing guard in the hatch. Holde was lounging within, his eyes closed. They didn't open when I sat down beside him.

Not that it stopped him from speaking. "You can admit we need the help even if you don't like Delarah's plans."

"I never denied that we needed aid." I countered. "Releasing Mok isn't a bad plan either."

His tarah quivered. "It's that the others releasing three packs we've put on penal colonies that has you in a mood."

I'd have elbowed the irritating man, but his armor would have made it a pointless exercise. "Obviously. And if you try to get me to calm down about it again, I'm going to punch you."

"Do you mistake me for Jet, love?"

I couldn't help but snort. "No."

"Good, I would pray I have not become so ugly in your eyes." He grinned, eyes still closed. "We just got a message in from Fyvn and Jet. They'll meet us at Trinity on schedule, and she confirmed that the others were picked up by the Second Void Fleet without problems."

My own eyes closed as well, exhaling. "Good. The sooner they get their projects done the better. Any word from the capital?"

A tiny shake to his head. "The Imperial Circle is still debating the matter, and the Torlah is still on the Homeworld."

I fought the urge to clench my fists, to summon up my sorcery to better display my anger and annoyance.

The Torlah and the Circle had been on poor terms ever since her ascension. That wasn't exactly news, nor had it seriously inhabited the Empire's safety or security. Until now, I supposed.

We needed quick action to deal with this crisis if we were going to get it under control before the other nations of the Compact recognized our weakness. How long would it be before the Federation or the Concordat acted? How long until their hackers were tearing their way through the DataNet and finding our own security assets were now insufficient?

Not long. Not long at all.

And that was just one of the many battle fronts. Pulling the Fifth Void Fleet out of the Contested Region to deal with the Icar Intelligence Branch was probably necessary, but that would leave the Imperial Navy without its most flexible force.

If the Chezzek decided to push us out there, hard, I didn't know what the Torlah would do.

"...focus on the project." I muttered, shaking my head against the unwelcome thoughts swimming around in my mental seas. All of that was well above my level.

I had to focus on my project, and only on my project.

Mok helped by arriving shortly after, her four packmates all eagerly following her inside. I watched them get settled, though only Mok sat anywhere near us. The guards fell back inside as well, sealing the hatch once everyone was seated, and shouted for the pilot that it was time to lift off.

"What are our orders, Operative?" Mok asked, leaning forward. Her normal reserve gone beneath a Huntress's excitement to be moving. To have duties. To be leaving her prison behind.

Taking a deep breath, I let it out with my words. "We sail for Trinity, to dismantle the Imperial Intelligence Headquarters there. By the time we arrive it's expected that any compromised personnel will have fled. You will pick three of your packmates to investigate every project they ever touched."

"And the remainder?" She asked. "Interrogations?"

I nodded. "Yes. My packmate Jet will work with yours on the digital investigation. Holde here will command the group handling the live sessions. And yes, you will have full authority for chemical torture if it's required."

"All right." Mok shifted in her seat, tugging the restraints a little tighter. She didn't look surprised or taken aback by what I'd just told her. "What will you be doing?"

"Working with combat assets." I let my own head lean back against the rest, eyes closing. "You don't need to know more than that. Not yet. Relax as best you can, it's going to be a long verification process once we make orbit."

Mok's chuckle was swallowed by the rising sound of the engines. "They can take as long as they like, so long as we don't get put back on that damned planet. Serving the Empire is all I've ever wanted to do."

I supposed that was true.

I could only hope that she kept the collateral damage to a minimum this time.

VI
Ashe'lori

My arms burned as I labored through my last pull up. It was a real struggle to get my chin level to the bar, my hands opening the moment I hit that goal. Feet hit the floor, arms thrown out to keep my balance as I took a few gasping breaths, trying to settle myself in the back of the cargo hold.

"...ow." I groaned, turning so that I could lean against the bulkhead. The back of my head struck the wood, my eyes closing ."Ow."

There was a matching groan from the floor, Johanna speaking slowly. "Told you... it was too much..."

"...you did." I'd definitely tried to jump into my old pattern too quickly, after too few sessions working my way up to the more strenuous activity. And Johanna had been right to say I should have stopped after our first session.

I focused on my breathing, letting my heartbeat slow before I heard my friend getting to her feet. Cracking an eye open let me see her shuffle past the nearest food container to grab the water bottle that we'd brought with. She guzzled half of it, throwing her mess of fur over her shoulder with her free hand.

She lowered the bottle with another groan, offering it to me. I took it with a tired nod of thanks, finishing off what was left.

"Sure we have enough water for this?" She asked.

I nodded, turning the empty bottle over in my hands. "Yeah. Would have been nice to refill them, but the humidifier tanks alone have enough water to get us wherever we want to go. So long as we don't flood the living spaces or something."

Johanna shuffled over, leaning against the crate. "Right, right. Sorry. I'm more used to being paranoid about water than food. And we've been showering almost daily. That's... luxurious for the Ark Fleet."

"You're also used to being on overcrowded ships." I said. "And eating food that's kept as powder."

She huffed, "I wasn't *that* poor on the Fleet. Eating military rations didn't start until we got sent to that mining colony. I'd figure you'd be more used to rations than me, Miss Conscript."

I snorted. "We only had to eat those things when we were out on training maneuvers. The Empire definitely has its problems, but feeding its soldiers real food isn't one of them."

The mention of problems seemed to make her perk up a little, "Oh? Finally admitting the Empire isn't perfect?"

"I always admitted that." Reaching up, I wrapped my hands around the bar above my head again. I didn't start doing more pull ups, I'd scream if I did, but I did use it to start stretching out my sore limbs. "That doesn't mean I don't think it's better than any alternative I've heard of."

"You've never tried any of the alternatives." She shot back.

"And you," I countered, "Have never really lived in the Empire either."

She rolled her eyes, turning to lean her back on the nearest crate. "I've heard enough, thank you. How many times have you been assaulted by sorcery, framed for something you didn't do, or nearly raped again?"

I paused my stretching to glower at her. "Plenty. How was life on an Ark Fleet penal colony again? How many of your childhood packmates left you when you started calling a Kelthi *onkel*? I've got as many bad stories from you about the Ark Fleet as I gave you about the Empire."

Johanna's jaw clenched a little at the retaliation. "It was awful, and most of them left, but I would have still been free to choose my own way when I turned eighteen."

"And I'll be free to do the same once I'm twenty-seven." I said.

There were a few deep breaths, then she shook her head and closed her eyes. The words a mumble. "Tiny cells."

"Tiny cells." I echoed.

We both went silent after that. Johanna relaxing, myself stretching. Both of us coming down from our mutual refusal to go with the other one to their homes, even if I was... all right. Yes, I wanted her to come back with me. She and Irkan had become the closest things I had to packmates out here. People I liked having around.

People I'd like to keep close if I could.

She apparently felt the same. At a minimum she liked me enough to want me to go back to the Ark Fleet with her. Telling me I needed to *see* what an alternative to the Empire was really like in person. My rebuttal that she could do with seeing what the Empire was actually like had seen our first argument on the subject.

This had been the... Ashahn's blood. I didn't know. Fourth or fifth debate, abortive as it had been. It probably would be the last either.

Our mutual silence lasted until I finished my post-exercise routine, tapping her on the shoulder when I was done.

She cracked an eye open, nodded once, and walked along with me to the yacht's bridge. Irkan was asleep, at least I hoped he was actually sleeping, so we took a few moments to check over the sensors. Making sure our trip through hyper-space was proceeding smoothly, that no storms were creeping into our path, that kind of thing.

No alarms were screaming, and we were still alive, so I took that as good enough.

A second short walk down the hallway on the vessel's other side led us to the galley, where we got started on our evening meal. It wasn't much. Most of what we'd gotten from Cashihto had proven to be the ingredients needed to make bread, plus a variety of vegetables, and some dried meats.

Not exactly the kind of food fit for a feast, but it was hopefully the kind of food that would keep us alive until we made it to Aonu. We'd spent most of the day working our way through the process of actually baking some of it, and testing it for poison far too many times along the way.

By mutual agreement, we took our first bites of the freshly baked loaf at the same time. Neither of us choked and died in the opening moments, which I accepted as a victory, but the flavor was...

"...bland." I announced when I'd finished chewing. "Incredibly bland."

She hummed, swallowing hers down as well. "Can't argue with you. It needs butter, or... I don't know. Something."

"We don't have anything." I sighed. "We ate all of that on the way to Cashihto. No sauce, no butter... this is what we have for the next month."

Her lips turned down even as her fingers slowly tore off another piece. "...it's not a gross rodent that we had to skin first. That's something. No fur to pick out of our teeth either."

The snort came out of me before I could stop it, my head dipping in agreement. "Yeah. Ashahn's blood, I'll be very glad to never eat one of those things again. Or trap one. The squeaking was horrifying."

She made a noise of agreement, the two of us slowly working our way through our little meal. Between us we ate two thirds of the bread, leaving the rest for Irkan once he woke up, though we went through our full allotment of the vegetables.

He couldn't eat most of them, just like we wouldn't be able to eat most of the meat, so it evened out.

After that it was a short walk back to the cabin we were sharing, Johanna glancing at me when I started poking through the closet I'd filled with things that mostly fit me.

"I'm guessing," Johanna asked quietly, "that talking about what we'll do when we get home isn't on tonight's agenda?"

"I don't feel like arguing about staying together and going to your Fleet or my Empire, so no." I said, pulling out a new robe to wear tonight. I set it on the bed for now, I'd put it on later, once I was clean. "You can shower first. Maybe... I don't know. Trim our fur after?"

She looked doubtful, "It's going to take forever. All we have are those tiny scissors for working on clothes."

"We've got knives too." I pointed out.

Her voice dropped. "You're *not* cutting my hair with a knife."

I rolled my eyes, making an impatient gesture. "Go shower, then I'll shower, then you can cut *my* fur with a knife."

"You'll look terrible." Johanna shook her head, muttering some more about lunatics raised by aliens as she stomped over to the small bathroom attached to the cabin.

That left me free to sit down on the edge of the bed, closing my eyes, letting my arms go limp. I heard the sound of the shower starting up, listening to the water as I let myself sink down into the meditative depths.

Sadly I didn't get to enjoy that calm for long. Johanna took pathetically short showers, and was out within a few minutes. That left it free for me to slip into the tiny space, discarding sweaty clothes to enjoy the steam she'd left behind.

As much as I wanted to take my time, and despite my earlier assurances, I didn't want to waste too much water just washing off a light sweat. So instead of enjoying myself, I rushed through scrubbing my skin, and got out nearly as quickly as she had.

Then I sat down on the floor beside the bed, Johanna seated on its edge, her fingers gently running through my mess of fur.

"I'm not shaving it down to your scalp."

I pouted, not that she could see it. "It's so much easier not to have any on your head."

She scoffed, still trying to arrange it to her satisfaction. "Yet you let the rest of it grow out without a care."

"Because my clothes cover it up, and it's too annoying to deal with cutting it every day." I countered. "Just shorten it? Please?"

"*Mein gott...* fine, fine." There was a heavy sigh. "I've never actually done this before, so it's going to look awful."

I crossed my arms, getting settled in. "It already looks awful. I doubt you'll make it worse."

The bed shifted behind me, then I finally heard the tiny pair of scissors start cutting. Felt the freeing sensation of fur falling away from my scalp. She hummed quietly after the first few sections, sighed again, and then started on another.

I sat patiently, feeling and listening to her work.

"...this is going to take a long time." She said after ten minutes or so. "It's very ragged. You really never had this done before?"

I nearly shook my head, stopped myself, and instead simply replied. "Nope. I had a mechanical razor I used to keep it all shaved down from when I was... fourteen or so. Well, my childhood pack stole one that I used. I bought a proper one with my first pay as a conscript."

"And you liked being bald?" She asked.

"I don't have to wash it, or dry it, or have it get caught in things." I listed off. "And I'd let it grow out a little bit. Didn't shave it down more than once a week or so. You never tried?"

"No, it's... a cultural thing, I guess." Johanna's hands paused, then she resumed, carefully trimming around my ears. "In the Ark Fleet you keep your hair short, makes it easier to deal with zero-gravity events, but women still keep it longer than men do. It's considered a sign of femininity."

I hummed. "Weird. Why?"

The bed creaked again as she slid off it, coming to kneel on my right to work more on that side. "I don't really know to be honest. Just the way things are. Like how you said Imperials get tattoos for everything. Oh, speaking of, are you going to get one for our adventures?"

"Definitely. Going to have to be on my back, or maybe my chest." I said. "I'm out of space on my arm and shoulder. Not sure how to symbolize what happened though."

She leaned in, very carefully pulling the fur just above my eyes down, measuring it with her fingers before bringing the small scissors up to start cutting. "Does it have to be nautically themed, like the storms and broken ships you've already got?"

I considered that for a moment. Those broken ships represented each of the packs that I'd been on, and been forced to leave, over the course of my career. The story of my life written on my body.

"I think it would look strange if I went with anything else. Especially for our trip on the barge."

Johanna's breath hitched for a moment at the reminder, then the cutting resumed. "What about... fog and a galley? On Earth those were rowed by slaves, if I remember my history classes right. Symbolism fits."

"Hmm... could work. A mist trailing down, with a blood soaked galley coming out of it."

"Stop nodding."

"Sorry." I froze again, letting her work her way around to the other side of my face, still thinking through the idea. "Maybe... more mist on the other side of the galley, trailing into shadows in a forest."

It was her turn to hum. "Not a mountain?"

My right hand rose, finger trailing as I tried to imagine the scene. "Maybe somewhere. The ship would be from my left shoulder to my right... put a river trailing down from the forest, curling around a cracked mountain. Have that river turn into a sea, with a small sailboat fleeing from fire."

She paused again, giving me an almost startled look. "That... sounds kind of cool actually. You just came up with that now?"

I let myself sound a little smug. "I'm a daughter of the Empire. We're an artistic bunch you know."

Johanna scoffed, but her lips curled a little. "Uh huh. I saw an Imperial movie once. It was three hours long and it didn't have an actual ending. It just cut to black right when the climax was supposed to happen."

"That's because you're supposed to figure out the ending on your own. It keeps it in your mind, keeps you thinking about it."

"And you think the Ark Fleet is weird. Our movie makers aren't lazy like yours." She said.

I scoffed, "They do release the endings later you know. That way everyone who was right can properly brag about it."

"So. Weird."

We bickered and bantered as she kept cutting away, until she thought she was done. I got up, feeling wonderfully light above the neck. Brushing loose fur off of me, I quickly head to check my appearance in the bathroom mirror.

I looked... good. I actually looked *good*. The cut was uneven, asymmetrical. It would certainly attract attention, especially since a bit of it hung down near my right eye. It left it contrasting very nicely with the scars on the other side of my face.

"Wow." I leaned back out of the bathroom, "If you need a job in the Empire, I think a lot of Humans there would pay you to cut their fur like this."

Johanna gaped at me. "You're a mess! It's not even!"

"Asymmetry is big right now." I told her seriously. "Do you want me to do yours? You'll look great!"

"Nein!"

I kept trying to convince her as we cleaned up the dark fur all over the floor, up until we laid down in bed to sleep another night away.

VII

Aonu was nothing like Cashihto. According to Irkan, it had a population of around four billion or so. By Imperial standards that was middling; prosperous without being anywhere close to the regional hubs like Altair or Icar.

By the standards of the Lost, it was incredibly cosmopolitan, and it had the orbital traffic to suit a proper harbor.

I gazed out of the view screen as Irkan followed the traffic controller's instructions, sweeping over an endless field of green toward the sprawling city awaiting us. It seemed to have been built between and around a trio of enormous lakes, and there wasn't much of a proper skyline.

There *were* plenty of skycars in the air though, forcing Irkan to stay close to the flight path we'd been given.

"There," he rumbled, nodding, "That port is our destination."

Johanna leaned forward, following his gaze just as I was.

"We're in the outskirts, I think." She said.

I shrugged, tapping the commands to start dropping the landing gear. "We're lucky the cash we have is enough to pay for a proper hangar at all. I thought we'd have to land out on a farm or something."

She grimaced. "I thought we'd have to dock with one of those cruisers in orbit. Be questioned or have the yacht seized or something."

Another shrug of my shoulders. "That's why we didn't say anything about where we're from, or what happened on Cashihto. We're playing this one slowly and quietly."

"I know, I know." Johanna leaned back in her seat, looking at me while Irkan brought us into a low hover above the open-topped hangar. Well, less of a hangar and more of a stone box lacking a roof, if I was being honest.

"I remember the plan," She went on, "I just still expected things to go wrong already, I guess."

"...me too." I admitted. "We'll see what happens when we try to contact the government. For now let's get the hangar paid for, and get all of the fancy clothing sold off so we can afford to send our messages home."

"You mean while you two do that, while I say here and make sure no one steals the yacht."

Irkan let out a low chuckle, the yacht rocking gently as it settled onto the ground. "Would you rather take my place in exploring this world?"

"...not really." She admitted. "Just try not to get killed, please."

"Do our best." I replied.

We spent a few minutes putting the ship back into low power mode, preserving what little fuel we had left. By the time we finished the hangar's owner had walked in; a Mikira with a red and yellow pattern to their shell. They gave us a wave, then moved to wait for us to drop the ramp.

By our plan, Irkan handled that while I retrieved our small case of hard currency, and Johanna grabbed one of our remaining rifles to be ready.

Our host was still speaking to our pilot in their native tongue, leaving me to wait for them to finish. Fortunately it didn't take them that long to complete the negotiations. Less fortunately, I ended up having to turn over half of our credits to pay for two weeks of harbor space and a refill of our water tanks.

The other man left without doing more than glance at me after that, leaving a trio of automations to handle the rest of it. They were wheeled rather than bipedal, and they looked well cared for even if I couldn't begin to guess how old that particular model had to be.

While they hooked up hoses, pumping clean water into the ship, Johanna and I got one of the crates from Cashihto offloaded. The food it had once held replaced with all of the spare clothing, jewelry, and trinkets we'd found in the various cabins.

Plus the sword and all of the armor that didn't fit anyone. Those would probably get us more money than the rest of it put together.

Irkan worked away at a small console in the hangar wall while we were occupied, trying to find us both directions and transportation.

"There is a nearby rental facility." He confirmed upon his return. "The prices are reasonable."

"Good." I accepted one of the Strike pistols from Johanna, inspecting it, and then getting it settled onto the belt I was wearing. I'd have preferred one of the carbines, but carrying one would be a little awkward on a calm, civilized world.

She gave another pistol to Irkan, his clawed hands carefully checking the safety, power levels, and clip just as I had before attaching it to his own waist.

Then I gave her a quick hug, and we split up to start getting things done.

Irkan and I waited outside until she'd closed and sealed the ramp, only then heading for the personnel exit. It opened right out onto the street, a few battered ground-trucks rolling by in either direction. None of the drivers did more than glance at us, and we were the only ones walking when we set off for the rental facility.

It wasn't the longest walk. Just a short sail past three hangars identical to the one that we'd landed in. There we found a small lot with a two dozen vehicles, evenly split between ground and air models, all surrounding a small building.

Inside the structure, the man behind the counter was a miserable looking Trahcon man in an olive uniform. He perked up a little when we entered, then straightened even more when I drew closer.

A Hunter, and one whose tarah were angling out to let me see just how elegant and long they were.

I couldn't stop from smiling back, feeling just a little bit smug when his eyes kept going up to my ragged fur. Swallowing the urge to lick my lips, or flex my arms, I forced myself to think like a spy.

To think like Holde. It would be my first time trying *that* kind of interaction with a target, but... this seemed like a perfect opportunity to try.

Irkan clearly noticed the young man's excitement on seeing me, one of his low chuckles coming out. "I shall remain at the door, and leave this to you."

Snorting, I patted his shell before he wandered off, leaving me to go forward alone. The Hunter's grin widened when I approached without my companion, his slender tarah twitching a few more times in excitement.

I read his name tag, voice cheerful. "Good morning, Garu'lok."

He shifted his posture a little, making very sure I could see just how long his tarah were. When he spoke his accent was a rolling, lilting thing that made him sound more adorable than suave. "Good morning. May I say that you have wonderful scars?"

"You may." Turning as well, I leaned a hip on his counter, "Your tarah are wonderfully elegant, Hunter."

Said tarah quivered in excitement, "Your fur is... very striking, Huntress. Oh, are you a huntress?"

"I am." I said. "One who needs a vehicle on a budget. Preferably a truck so that we can move some light cargo. I don't suppose you'd be able to help with that?"

He was all too happy to slide around his counter, beaming as he waved me toward the door. "We're not the largest rental facility, but I'm sure we'll have something for you."

Irkan was chuckling again as he followed us outside, even if he again stayed near the door, leaving me to walk with the young man around the lot. His quick listing of the usual prices had me remove the aerial vehicles at once; they'd cost us most of what we had left.

That left him helping me go over the two ground-trucks that looked as if they'd work... and since one of them was configured for a Naulian driver, that really meant there was only one option.

I flirted with him through the discussions. And not just because he was cute, which he very much was. Or because I was enjoying someone actually finding me attractive for the first time since I'd been with Pack Vet, which I also very much was.

It was an easy way of mimicking how Holde gathered information. True, I was nowhere near as ridiculously handsome as he was, but I was apparently good enough for a young Hunter with a thing for Humans. That meant I had an easy way of sounding him out.

Well, a less obvious one than praying to the Aspects to see if that set him off like it had the tortured Xenthan in the mines. I couldn't imagine a member of the Faithful being a xenophile, and the more I made him stammer the more I was sure he really was smitten.

Which meant we had a chance to avoid putting our names down in any kind of database, which I desperately wanted.

Flirting with a cute boy to get a discount on a rental truck was easy.

Coming up with a false name, then remembering to answer to it? That was a lot harder. In fact it was an exercise I'd failed miserably at in the past, and this wasn't really the best time to try that in the field.

"I'd really rather avoid that much paperwork." I told him once we were back inside, approaching his counter in step with one another. "We're in hanger number fifteen. Surely that's good enough. We're in a yacht, not going to fly off with your company's truck."

He hesitated, "I mean, the hanger number and payment up front is all we *really* need, but we're still supposed to get your names and identification just in case something happens."

Huffing, I put a hand on his shoulder to get him to stop. When he did, turning, I quickly ducked down and grabbed him around the waist. He let out a quiet gasp when I picked him up, turning to sit him down on the counter in a casual feat of strength.

"Please?" I asked, keeping my hands on his waist as if he was a packmate I was extremely close to. "I'd appreciate it."

The young Hunter's tarah gave away his feelings, and his answer, even before I went a bit farther, leaning in to kiss the base of one of them.

Five minutes later I was driving the truck back into our hangar, Irkan riding comfortably in the back as his shell stopped him from fitting into the cab with me.

"Amusing." He laughed when we got back, waving to where Johanna was watching us from the cockpit. "I did not think Ashe'lori capable of such."

A bit of heat rose to my face, "That was another of my packmate's usual jobs. I just tried to act like he would."

He grinned, the pair of us heading over to the waiting crate. "She certainly succeeded. That river-shark would have eagerly let her take him into a back room, perhaps unclothe him right in the open."

More heat came with a clearing of my throat. While it had been a bit fun in the moment, in the aftermath I felt... incredibly awkward, and a little uncomfortable.

"I know, but I don't go that far outside of my packs. He'll have to be content with a little kiss and getting to ruffle my fur a bit."

"For now. He will likely hope for far more when you return the vehicle." He noted.

That...was probably true, and not something I'd considered before I'd gone ahead with my plan. Ashahn's blood, I really needed to get better at thinking through my spontaneous ideas.

Pushing those thoughts back into the deeps for now, I got my hands settled on the crate just as Irkan did the same on the other side.

A quick nod saw each of us lift it up, our conversation pausing as we worked to get it balanced. Wrestling it into the back of the truck didn't take all that long, and soon enough he was clambering up there with it while I got back into the driver's seat.

Waving to Johanna once again, I pulled us onto onto the street, parking again so that Irkan could hop off and close the vehicle-sized door behind us. While he did that I opened the back windows so that we'd be able to converse while I drove.

I also fiddled with the navigation system, doing a quick search for the kind of shop that would buy what we had to sell. There were apparently several nearby, but only one of them had a decent trust rating on the local net. Picking that one, I was ready to go when he returned.

"Ten minute drive." I called back, getting us rolling once again.

"Heading for the Driftwood Exchange."

He ducked his head down, hanging on to the back of the cab as I picked up some speed. "With such a name, it is surely a business owned by a river-shark."

"Yeah." Following the navigation's instructions, I took the right turn after the rental facility, joining a steadier flow of local traffic. "I'm hoping that means they'll be interested in the latest Imperial fashions, and willing to pay enough for us to be able to afford more fuel."

"And food."

I nodded, keeping a good distance between myself and the car ahead. "And food. If we can get enough for what we've got, I think we should change the order. Pick up food, better fitting clothes first, and then go pay for fuel at the hangar."

"Agreed." He said. "Ideally, I would prefer if we could do as much of that today as we can. Our experience on Cashihto leads me to believe we should be prepared to depart as quickly as possible."

"We're in the same river." I told him. "We need to be paranoid, and assume the worst until we're out of this Kingdom."

I saw him nod in the rear-display. "Yes. Armor for you and I would also not be amiss."

"Would love some, but I don't think we'll be able to afford any." I shook my head, easing onto the breaks as we hit an intersection. "Let me guess. You agree with Johanna, and think we should just steal some?"

"Ideally we would simply pay, but if we have no currency to do so... then yes." He replied firmly. "We are in dire need of proper battle equipment, and even Johanna's does not quite fit. On Cashihto we escaped only because you felt that things were off in time for us to bring the engines online."

I rolled a shoulder, "We were all in agreement about disabling the guns before we turned them over. That was just as important."

A clawed hand rose, scratching at his narrow chin. "True, but the point remains. Paranoia and preparations cannot guide us in these Reaches forever. Sooner or later we shall be brought to battle, and we are not prepared for that."

It was a pretty good point, and a convincing argument. I still didn't really want to try and break into the kind of store that sold battle armor. If the local shops were anything like the ones I'd seen on Nueva Genova, or in the Group of Five, they'd have plenty of security features.

But... we might have to make the attempt. Like Irkan was all but saying, our lives could depend on it.

"All right." I said when the traffic finally began to move again. "If we can't afford it, I'll find a shop that we can scope out. But don't expect miracles. I don't have my packmate's hacking skills, or their experience."

"Ashe'lori had skills enough to keep her alive upon Last Stop." Irkan said, voice sanguine. "We shall find the path."

I wasn't nearly that confident, but then Irkan had a very different way of looking at the galaxy around him.

Falling quiet once again, I focused on the road and the map. Following the route led us to a small part of the city clearly inhabited by Trahcon from the wildly varying styles of paint and art covering every building in the area.

The Driftwood Exchange was a surprisingly sizable building, and one with its own signs directing those bringing in goods to sell to a lane around the side.

We pulled in beside a door, and a young Trahcon Huntress strolled out to greet us...

...and her tarah rose, quivering in excitement when she saw the burn scars on my face.

I smiled once again, getting out of the car, and set about seeing just how many credits we could get for our cargo.

VIII

"So you had the first one eating out of your hands." Johanna said, "But then her boss came out and had a fit about you being Human?"

I sighed, leaning against the side of the truck, both of us watching as the hangar's automations worked around the yacht once again. This time pumping fuel rather than water, and going about their task with a silent diligence that I appreciated.

Despite the fact that we'd been able to buy some clothing that would actually fit both of us, were still in our ill-fitting silks. In her case because she hadn't had the time to change yet. In mine, because the clothing would hopefully help to convince others of our story later in the evening.

"Pretty much." My head came to rest on the window, eyes flicking to where she was standing with her arms crossed. "Good news is that we still have enough local money for what we need, but only barely. Between the food and fuel that we bought, we're back down to about as much as we started today with."

Johanna knew what I meant. "Not enough to afford armor?"

"I suppose we could buy you a helmet, but it would cost everything we had." I paused, then admitted, "For Irkan and I... we might have enough for shield belts. Cheap ones. "

Her lips pressed together for a long moment. "I'm not really a combat expert, but don't those only last for one or two shots?"

I nodded, "The kind we can afford? Pretty much, yeah. Meant for civilians who want enough time to run if a fight breaks out nearby. There are nice ones, full harnesses that can hold up in a real fight, but I don't think we'd be able to afford more than one of those."

"So we're stealing some then." She said.

"Eventually." I replied. "I think that should be the last thing we do while we're here."

My companion frowned. "What if something happens when we send the message? Or when we talk to the government?"

"I'm going to do both tonight, one wave hitting the shore right after the other." I told her. "And if the Lost's soldiers come after us, I don't think having armor would really help. Especially since they could just blow us up when we leave."

"...great, now I'm going to be worried about that until we depart." It was her turn to sigh, "When are you going to go send our letters home?"

I waved toward the automations. "As soon as they're done. I'll try and contact the local government right after."

She shook her head, "I still don't like you going off and doing that alone, Ashe."

I felt my mouth curl into a little smile. "And I appreciate that worry, Johanna, but Irkan's still the only one who can fly the ship, and if anything breaks you've got the ability to help him fix it. I'm expendable right now."

"No." She countered. "You're the paranoid spy who'd stop us from walking into an ambush, or get us out of one like you did on Cashitho. None of us are expendable."

That brought out a wider smile, and I pushed off the truck so that I could wrap her up in a hug. I felt her take a deep breath, returning the embrace even as she muttered, "You're still going alone, aren't you?"

"You think leaving the yacht without anyone in it is a good idea?" I murmured back.

"In a cheap hangar like this?" Her huff blew warm air over my ear, the two of us separating by mutual consent. "No, of course not. I know you're probably right, but that doesn't make me like it."

"And I appreciate that too."

Her skin pinked slightly around her cheeks. "Ashe. You're doing it again. That staring thing."

It was my turn to cross my arms and huff, "I was not."

She muttered something in Deutsch that I couldn't make out, spinning on a heel so that she could stalk back to the ramp. "Yes you were. If you're going to practice lying again, you need to do it about things that aren't obvious."

Snorting, I called after her, "Check the fuel tanks, and make sure Irkan didn't think of another person to send his message to!"

Johanna gave me a tired wave without turning, striding back up into the ship. I watched her go before turning around, pulling the rental's door open so that I could drop into the driver's seat.

Refueling was done around the same time I got the route to the nearest DataCenter set on the screen. A ping on my wrist-comp from Irkan confirmed that he hadn't thought of any other addresses to route his letter to, and neither had Johanna.

Tapping out a quick reply that I'd be back as soon as I could, I followed that up with a reminder that 'Alum' still meant I was a hostage, and 'Tasir' meant I'd run into Faithful. After a moment I added a second reminder to take off if they hadn't heard from me by midnight.

That done, I pulled back out onto the road, gently getting the truck up to speed.

It was more than an hour's drive to the center, which left me with little to do besides think. I did my best to avoid musing on the ongoing project for too long. Not because there weren't far too many things to worry about, there were, but because I'd already had a little more than two months of doing nothing else aboard the yacht.

Well, two months aboard the yacht, too many months on Last Stop, and too many months on the prison barge before that. Plus the time spent chasing them down in the Near Reaches with Rerth, and Holde, and Jet. I'd spent a *lot* of time focusing on them, and all I had were a few vague theories with minimal evidence.

"Which means." I covered a yawn, putting on more speed as I got onto one of the cross-city highways. "There's no point drowning in that whirlpool. I don't have more evidence, so I'm not going to suddenly figure it out now."

Trying to think about anything else made me think of the two people

I'd tried to flirt with today. The brief enjoyment I'd gotten in the moment, followed by the uncomfortable aftermath. Well, uncomfortable at the first stop.

The hissing insults I'd gotten from the Elder at the Driftwood Exchange had left me with my usual mix of hurt, upset, and frustrated.

Sighing, I put on a bit more speed to keep up with traffic, my thoughts turning to the last person I'd actually been with.

Fyth would have hated this truck. Loathed it. It was big, it was ugly, and it was slow. She'd have been complaining endlessly about the handling, or how it liked to pull to the right if you didn't keep a gentle hand on the controls at all times.

...but I still found myself wishing that she was here to complain.

"Irony." I muttered. "I keep getting stuck being the one driving around, to the point where I'm actually starting to enjoy it. And it's too late for us to share that hobby together."

I... Ashahn's blood. I was going to message her, when I got back to the Empire. Maybe it was just me being a stupid, short-lived, impatient Human, but I *missed her.* I missed everyone in Pack Vet, nearly as much as I missed Rerth, Holde, or Huvu.

More than I missed Jet, for sure. As much as I admired his competence, and wished I had his skills, I still couldn't bring myself to actually want him as a packmate. I missed the Vet far more than the Thun as well. They'd been fun, but it had only ever been casual flirting with them. Friends, but not packmates.

I shook my head, shoving those thoughts back into the depths as well. I could dwell on how much I missed everyone in the Empire once the three of us were safe on Lushrivers.

Reaching out with a hand, I started playing with the radio, eventually finding a station covering a local Strike-Wave game. Neither team's names meant anything, nor did the players, but I let myself get swept away by the commentator's enthusiasm, by his excitement over what proved to be an extremely close game.

It was exciting enough that I had to force myself to turn the truck off when I finally reached the DataCenter, not listening to the last minutes of the game in favor of getting out.

I paused after doing so, adjusting my belt a little as I took in the building. It was framed nicely by the setting sun, the light highlighting a stepped pyramid, five stories tall from what I could see. Perhaps more importantly there were a large number of cars in the lot, several more coming and going even as I looked around.

A pair of Naulians were exiting just as I approached the doors. They didn't hold them open for me, but they didn't sneer or glare either.

Walking in revealed a line up to a counter, and I quietly took my place behind a Naulian elder wearing an old suit, his red fur peppered with gray and white. Ahead of him the Lost were apparently determined to show me that they really did accept everyone; I could see three Trahcon, a Mikira, another Naule, and a pale skinned Human.

I tried to stay relaxed as the line shuffled along. Fortunately there were enough receptionists that it didn't take very long before I was walking up to an open counter.

Said receptionist proved to be a Mikira with similar colors as Irkan, his bulk more adorable than intimidating when it was forced into the little cubicle.

"Good evening." I told him, very careful not to not giggle at his awkward position. "Uh, I need a DataNet connection to send messages."

He gave me a polite nod, "DataNet is on the second floor. Fifty kozn charge for general access."

Reaching into a pocket, I pulled out the appropriate amount of the local currency. He took it, counted it, then used one hand to slide it into a slit on top of the desk while his other tapped a few controls on his console.

A similar slit on my side hummed, then began printing out a small card.

"Access token. Use it to activate the lift and consoles upstairs." He instructed, "Is that all?"

I nodded, taking the little card. "Thank you."

He made a noncommittal noise, and I took the hint to move on without any additional conversation.

Forgoing the lift, I followed the maps for the stairs instead. Those didn't have any locks on them, and gave me more of a chance to run in case something unfortunate happened.

Two flights later and I was on the appropriate floor, walking between a field of small privacy units. A surprising number were occupied, until a bit of logic reached my mental shores.

Aonu was one of the few Lost worlds with Datanet access at all. There was probably a lot of people who visited the Capital solely to send messages back to the galaxy at large, or who were sent to download news. Especially now that there was one, maybe two wars raging in the Reaches. Depending on if the Ascendancy's civil war was over or not.

Sadly the one in the back most corner was occupied by someone else as paranoid as I. Or maybe by someone antisocial enough to want to be that far in the back.

I found an alternate three units down, along that same back wall, and closed and locked the door behind me. Then, to make sure I acted like a proper spy, I spent a few minutes checking over every inch of the unit to see if I could find any listening devices or cameras.

Nothing, but that didn't mean they were there.

It especially didn't mean that what I did with this console wouldn't be recorded.

"No choice." I muttered, taking my seat and plugging my card into the labeled slot.

The machine booted up at once, a cheerful greeting in what looked like ten different languages flashing. It stayed there until I realized it was actually a prompt, and selected the one in Caranat.

A quiet chime sounded, and then...

...and then I had access to the DataNet.

Blowing out a breath, I pulled my wrist comp up, linking it to the device. One quick transfer later and I had the three letters, one written by each of us, along with a text file containing the addresses to send them to.

Licking my lips, I opened the mail program, exhaling in relief when it politely informed me that it was operating in Guest Mode. That I was free to mail anyone I wished, but that I would not be able to receive a reply without logging in.

Good enough considering that we weren't staying.

I sent the letters in order; Irkan's being the first. His people were closest, his home the one we hoped to reach. Copies went to his old commanding officer, another on what he said was an inbox for emergency communications, and then a third to an address used by his blood-pack.

After that I briefly considered changing which terminal I was using for each message, then decided it really wouldn't matter. Anyone good enough to track me would be good enough to track me no matter which one I was using in here.

Johanna's was next, again for the simple reason that the Ark Fleet was closer than the Empire. There was more of a chance her people would be able to respond, to send someone to Lushrivers. Hers went to her Onkel and to Captain of the ship she'd been born on.

Then it was my turn. Swallowing, I typed in identification numbers; each of my packmates got a copy, I sent another to my own inbox, another to Huvu, and after a long hesitation, I sent one to Fyth as well.

"...Ashahn's blood." I tensed when the system pinged, informing me that the messages were on their way to the system's FTL buoy. I stayed that way until yet another chime sounded... and it confirmed that they'd hit the buoy and were on their way through hyper-space.

We'd done it. We'd...

My hand came up covering my mouth as I struggled to breathe.

We'd done it. Everyone back home would know that we were alive. Would have the shortest version of what happened to us, would have the coordinates for Last Stop. Would know that we were on Aonu, hoping to make it to Lushrivers.

They would all know.

My pack would know.

Rerth would know.

I don't know how long it took me to calm down, to get control of myself. Too long, probably, but I felt that I'd earned that small collapse. After everything that had happened on Last Stop, on the real fear that we wouldn't even make it this far...

Closing my eyes, I took in a final few breaths, calming my mental seas.

"...messages sent." I whispered, opening them to bring my wrist-comp up. A few quick taps sent a more local communication back to the others, telling them I'd done it.

That I was now on to stage two.

Shaking my head, I focused on the screen in front of me. Fingers began tapping on the keyboard, navigating through the system. "Now it's time to see if the Lost believe what happened to us, and if they know about the Faithful."

IX

Of all of the things I considered would happen when I tried to report a Compact violation, ending up in front of a very bored clerk was...

Well, all right. I'd figured that it would be what would happen, but I'd been praying that Khash would bless us with a bit more luck today. That he'd let me get to talk to someone higher up in rank, have a chance to make our case quickly and cleanly.

Instead the only woman working this late, a tired looking Guide, pushed a tablet across her desk. Her tones the bored ones of someone who didn't believe me in the slightest, and expected this to be a complete waste of her time.

"Fill out which pirate organization you are accusing on line one," she recited, eyes fixed over my shoulder rather than on me, "personal information on lines two through ten, then the specific Compact Violation you are alleging occurred in field eleven. It'll be processed with all of the other claims, expect a follow up in the next year or two."

I tried to keep my tones diplomatic when I said, *again,* "I'm not accusing a pirate organization. This is something completely different."

Her left tarah flicked outwards in a dismissive little motion. "I heard you, just like I heard the same thing from every other refugee we've let in since the war started. Just fill out the form, it'll go on the list. Investigators will get around to it. Eventually."

My fingers twitched. "What pirate group operates six weeks coreward and spinward of Cashihto?"

"Cashihto?" The name finally got a small reaction from her, blue eyes narrowing and finally meeting mine. "Isn't that one of the far outposts?"

"Yes." I said. "It took us another five weeks just to get here. I have a message from its current ruler confirming that we were actually there to pick up enough fuel to make it this far."

The clerk took a deep breath, as if I was massively inconveniencing her by refusing to just fill out the form.

"Fine." She said. "Give it to me, I'll make a copy and file it as evidence of your claim. Should bump you closer to the dock, shave a few months off the response time."

I pulled out the small drive containing the original message, I'd made several copies that were on the yacht, and handed it over. She took it, plugging it into her console, her attention turning to the device as it processed the files.

Her annoyed expression turned into a puzzled frown as she read the short letter. "Iriahn's.... what? You're claiming that you're from the Empire of the Homeworld?"

"Yes." I said.

Tarah flicked, eyes narrowing further as she read on. "This can't be right. You have an Imperial luxury yacht you used to escape from a world in unknown space, that you claim also had evidence of Mikiran civilization?"

"Yes." I repeated.

"Impossible." She muttered, scrolling further. "The old kingdoms never made it that far. They didn't even make it *this* far. I know the history, all of their explorations went rimward thanks to the storms of that era."

I crossed my arms, reminding myself that it really was a fantastical story. "One of our number is a Scarlet Tears officer. If he said that it was a Mikiran ruin, I believe him."

A finger starting tapping on her desk, her attention returning to me. After a long stare, she finally took the form back, setting it aside, and booted up something new on her console.

"All right. Give me your version of events then."

I did, in the shortest possible version. Skipping everything that happened before my abduction on Trinity, instead simply laying out our journey on the barge, our arrival on Last Stop, and our desperate attempts to escape.

Finding our way into the tunnels through the mountain, through the old mines, and into the Faithful's facility. Being hunted by tortured souls, releasing more in a mass riot, and then Tasir's sacrifice that had let the rest of us have enough time to escape.

The clerk started typing away as soon as I started, occasionally asking me to stop and clarify a point so that she could get the proper words into the system.

"...and then we made it here." I said finally, "Hoping to warn your government about the Faithful, and get them to prepare for a Judgment if we can get home to warn everyone else."

"Quite the hope." She muttered, still typing. "And quite the story. You know it's impossible, right? I mean, the alternative is that you found a way to loop all the way out to Cashihto in a *yacht*, so that's impossible too, but I can't imagine anyone actually believing this."

Huffing, I reached up and pointed to my face. "I assure you that the woman who gave me these scars was very real."

She glanced at my face, started to turn away, then jerked her attention back as she took a closer look. "...Iriahn's bloody dick, I thought those were cuts from an animal. Burns?"

I nodded, "She wreathed her hand in it, and grabbed my head while she was interrogating me. Not because she cared about my answers, but because she felt like it."

The clerk winced, finally looking sympathetic. "By the Aspect's, that's... unpleasant."

"So you believe me then?" I asked.

Her head titled one way, then the other. "...it's still impossible, but I don't see anything on the surface for why you'd make it up either. Still, it's not my place to make that kind of decision, thank the Aspects."

Swallowing, I waved toward her console. "How long until someone important reads that?"

"I'm flagging it for priority review, but there's plenty of refugees making claims about pirate groups. Or agents of the Warlords trying to make claims about one another to get the Lost involved in their latest spat."

I sighed, "So a while."

"Sorry, savanna." She said, voice quieter and more earnest than before. "Having the record from Cashihto will bump it up since you have *some* evidence, even if it it's only confirmation you were on that colony. Looking at the list... a month, maybe? It's better than the years that it would take anything else to be looked at, if it ever actually is."

A month. I didn't really want to stay here for a month, but I supposed that we could. We had enough food, and we had enough currency to buy more if we needed to. The ship wouldn't really use up any fuel just keeping the lights on and plumbing working.

I just wasn't sure if that was the best call or not. Would staying on Aonu and getting the Lost to investigate be better than going to Lushrivers, then getting the Scarlet Tears to do so?

The Lost were far more likely to actually find something. They were closer to Last Stop, and not involved in a war. They'd have plenty of ships to send out there, *maybe* in time to find the Faithful before they abandoned the place.

But... we also knew very little about the Lost's government, and had no contacts here. On Lushrivers we'd be assuredly be safer, and free to stay with Irkan's blood-pack even if the Tears own government officials proved to be just as skeptical. Even if they refused to pause their war just on what three escaped prisoners were saying.

Most importantly though, Lushrivers was closer to home. It *was* home for one of us. Even if they didn't believe us, Johanna and I would have a far better chance to make it back to the Empire and the Ark Fleet from there, than we would from here.

"Thank you for listening." I said finally. "And sort-of believing me. Here's my wrist-comp ID, for whenever a follow-up actually happens."

She entered that as well, along with the name Ghai'vet. It was a pretty poor one, as far as an alias went, but I was still too wary of putting my actual one into official systems if I could help it. Plus it wasn't like I'd have someone running me down, shouting the name.

It would work for conversations over a wrist-comp, or in letters.

"Report compiled." She said finally. "It's in the stack. I or another clerk will contact you once it's been reviewed. Do not leave Aonu until such a time or the report will probably be flagged as a false claim."

Thanking her again, I rose, took the drive with Chakin's original message on it, and then left her little office. It was one of many in the little government building, but thankfully it was the one nearest to an exit.

I didn't waste a single breath in getting outside, inhaling the cool night air once I was outdoors again.

A short walk through the lot, weaving around a few aircars, and I was back inside of the rental truck. Getting the motor running, I synced my wrist-comp to the small console, starting a call.

"*Ashe'lori.*" Irkan answered. "*Do you wish to travel to Altair?*"

"Not yet." I confirmed I wasn't a hostage, putting the truck into reverse to pull out. "I don't see Tasir either."

"*Good. Situation?*" He asked.

"I just finished filling our a report with the only clerk working this late into the day." I said.

"*Did they believe you?*"

I blew out a breath, getting the truck back into forward drive so that I could start to crawl through the lot. "Not at first, but she was starting to come around by the end. Between the letter and my story I got her to flag it for actual review... but that's going to be a month from now in the best case. Probably farther out than that."

His answering chirp betrayed his annoyance.

"I know, I know." I said, "But apparently we're not the only ones complaining about Compact Violations. She made it sound like everyone fleeing from the war in the Reaches is pointing fingers at one another about their enemies."

"*I am not surprised, though I remain irritated.*" He replied. "*Do you wish to remain on Aonu, until such an investigation is complete?*"

I bit my lip, considering it for the few seconds it took me to pull out of the lot and onto the street. "If we leave, I don't think the Lost will believe the report. The clerk outright said as much."

"That is a complication." Irkan said.

"Yeah, but that doesn't mean I think staying here is all that smart either. Who knows how many more government masts we'll have to climb? On Lushrivers you'd help us bypass some of those."

Irkan was silent for a time as well, then replied. *"I must agree with Ashe'lori, and not merely because I wish to return home. We would have more options there, and the Lost would be compelled to aid us regardless if we should convince the Dual-Kings of our tale."*

"Agreed." I swallowed, easing to a stop at an intersection. "I'm going to return the truck, then get back to the yacht. Let's get out of here as soon as I return."

"I will wake Johanna and begin the preparations." He assured me.

"Thanks. It's going to be a long drive, I'll be back in an hour and a half, maybe longer depending on how returning the truck goes." Where I hoped someone besides the young Hunter would be working this late into the evening.

"Understood."

He cut the line there, leaving me with nothing to do but focus on driving once again. There was far less traffic with the sun long set, which made it much easier to make my way back to the main through-way.

Sadly there wasn't a late-night Strike-Wave game on, and I only caught the very aft end of a talk show on the local league. That left me with nothing to listen to besides music.

Getting the truck up to the local limit, I locked that speed in place, and did my best to get comfortable for the long drive while some kind of local orchestra played. They weren't bad at all, the upbeat music helping to keep me awake and mostly focused.

I spent the first half hour just watching the road, noting that most of the traffic seemed to be cargo trucks with logos that made me think they were hauling food into and out of the city. There were far fewer personal vehicles out than there had been earlier, but considering the time that wasn't all that surprising.

Once I saw a pair of cars race past the opposite direction, clearly racing, and saw a security air-car come roaring down after them, yellow lights flashing.

I watched them all whip past, glancing at my rear display to see if they were going to stop or not... and found another truck coming right up behind me. They kept coming until they were right up on my stern, refusing to simply pass on the right.

Pursing my lips in annoyance, I glanced to my right before shifting lanes, giving them the chance to simply accelerate past as they clearly wanted to.

"Honestly." I muttered, glancing left as they began to pick up speed. "There's no one on this side of the road for a half mile. Even Fyth wouldn't get up behind someone like that."

It made me miss driving a shuttle crawler on Nueva Genova. No one dared getting that close to one of those. Not when it could easily smash their own vehicles under its treads.

...and now I was annoyed about how someone else was driving on a planet I'd never been on. Ashahn's blood, I really was turning into Fyth.

Huffing, I shook my head, and let myself glare at the truck as its cab drew even with mine.

The Trahcon riding in the passenger seat had slid their window down, one arm coming out, palm pointed right at me.

Paranoid instinct had me slam on the brakes before the torrent of blue fire vomited forth, scorching the hood of the truck. Fingers clenched hard on the controls, turning the vehicle, foot shifting to shove down on the accelerator again, pulling up behind them.

My heart was hammering in my chest, a shaking hand slapping at the console.

It had just begun calling Irkan when the passenger shoved their torso through the window, one hand holding them in place as they sat with half their body in the wind.

A second slam on the brakes had them shoot ahead before they could throw another spell at me, even if it nearly had me rear-ended by a heavy freight hauler that only barely swerved into the other lane. I had a brief glimpse of a Naulian driver, his horn blaring furiously as he fought to keep the massive vehicle upright.

He managed it, and gave me a bit of cover as I got back into that lane, desperately trying to remember if there'd been a sign for an exit.

"Ashe'lori?" Irkan finally answered, *" What-"*

"Tasir!" I shouted, cutting him off, finding the breath to explain beyond the code word. "Faithful attacking me on the road!"

There was a startled noise that I barely heard when an off-ramp appeared around the side of the freight hauler ahead of me. It was my turn to fight to keep the truck upright when I abruptly swerved onto it, desperately trying to ease off on the speed before I slammed into another hauler waiting for the turn signal at the intersection ahead.

I managed it with a few feet to spare, gasping, frantically checking my rear view for anyone else following me.

"Ashe'lori? Ashe!"

Shaking my head, I found my voice. "I'm going to try and take an alternate route back. Forget about returning the truck, I'm heading right for the hangar. Keep the doors locked until I call again, and be ready to leave."

"We could pick you up at a clear location!" He replied.

"I..." I swallowed, "I don't know how they found me. They could be listening to this call. If someone tries to breach, lift off and try to pick me up."

He didn't sound pleased, but he still said, *"Understood, we shall listen for your arrival."*

"Thanks. Cutting the line."

A finger stabbed down at the same time as the signals finally changed, letting me get moving again.

I'd just started the turn when I saw a low-slung ground car come roaring at unsafe speeds down the ramp behind me... and I jammed my foot down once again.

X

I owed that Hunter at the rental facility a proper kiss; the truck he'd given us was proving to have a monstrous engine.

Blowing through the frontage road's stop signal, I shot back up another ramp, getting back onto a different through-way, keeping my foot all the way down as the car behind me kept up its pursuit.

"Come on, come on." I heard myself whispering, fingers cramping thanks to how tightly I was clutching the controls. There wasn't much other traffic on this one either, which was good because there wasn't nearly as much of a risk of me running into someone else.

It was also bad, because it made it very easy for the Faithful to keep close to me.

At least I was assuming it was the Faithful. I couldn't imagine anyone else randomly trying to murder me, but I didn't exactly have proof either. Not yet, .

The car behind began to slowly close the distance, its more efficient design giving it the advantage it needed to begin catching up. I tried to push my foot down harder, but the truck was already giving me every bit of speed it had.

I frantically ran through what I knew about ground-driving. Everything I'd been taught in training, everything Fyth had referenced, everything I'd picked up during Del-cycles or in my fake job on Nueva Genova.

I wasn't going to lose them. Worse, this road was taking me east rather than south, though I thought there was connection point somewhere ahead that would let me turn in the right direction.

But even if there was, this kind of elevated street lacked the turns, buildings, and corners I could have tried to use to lose the car behind me.

Frantically licking my lips, I kept my eyes snapping back and forth as my pursuit drew closer. Far ahead I could see the rear lights of a few other vehicles, and began trying to figure out if I could make it to them before the Faithful fully caught up.

The answer turned out to be yes, but only barely. I had just pulled ahead of some kind of van when the first Strike spell made the entire truck rock, nearly sending me careening into the bystanders front half. Swearing, I kept my speed up, swerving just ahead of the van the first heartbeat I could.

Said van began hammering their horn when I nearly clipped them, then again when I eased off the accelerator, a shaky plan coming together.

The pursuit car came screaming in, their own engine still going all out, and proved to have passengers ready in both the front and the back. Both were locked on to me, one with a hand raised, the other not bothering, but I knew they were ready to hit me with two Strikes to try to roll the truck.

Which was why I yanked the controls over, and rammed them before they could cast at me.

The impact slammed me against the restraints, and it was a struggle to keep my grip on the controls. I did better than the Faithful's driver; they kept their course straight and tried to pull ahead rather than slowing or trying to shove me back.

What that meant was our cars grinding on one another, my arms still holding the truck in a turn into them, until they pulled ahead enough that I was ramming my bow into their aft-side rather than their middle section.

I saw the lever action Fyth had mentioned work in real life as their driver lost control, their car beginning to spin in place against the pressure.

They tried to get it back, but they went side-on before they could...

...and then they spun out, past me, leaving me to frantically swerve back in before I tumbled into opposing traffic. I glanced back just in time to see the same van we'd just passes ram into their car, unable to stop in time.

One body went flying out of an open door, and I quickly looked away before I could see more than that.

Shaking fingers tightened again, my speed picking up as I wasted no time in trying to get back to the others.

My eyes were constantly moving as I got to the southern turn, looking for any vehicle that seemed to be following me. Any sign of a Security air-car starting its own pursuit for what I'd just done.

I didn't see anything when I got back on course.

I didn't see anything over the next hour, when I reached the off-ramp to approach the small collection of hangars.

That very first signal light flashed for a stop as I pulled onto the road leading there, something I ignored in my paranoid need to *leave.*

And for the second time in the night, that bit of paranoia saved my life.

My quick check for crossing vehicles as I approached the intersection let me see the idling truck to my right, two figures standing upright in the back.

Yet another shove of my foot got me hurtling forward just as they cut loose with sorcerers flamethrowers. Blue-black fire roared over my windows, my voice rising into a scream as I pushed through that horror before it could do more than scorch the paint and blacken the glass on the right side.

I felt myself starting hyperventilate, the old terror of those flames welling up.

"Control. Control. Get out of here." I slapped at the console, getting the line to my companions open again. "Irkan! I'm almost there, being pursued!"

Johanna replied, sounding nearly as panicked as I felt. "*I think we've got someone trying to get inside!*"

"Ashahn's ass!" The blaspheming swear escaped my lips, "I see them!"

Another car like the one I'd rammed was sitting in front of our hangar, three figures working at the door. They all heard me coming, heads locking onto my roaring vehicle when my lights highlighted the group of Trahcon in casual clothing.

Ashahn's blood. I didn't let myself hesitate when I began to swerve right at them.

"Unlock the hangar!" It was the last word I managed before the Faithful realized what I was doing.

Two of them managed to scramble out of the way, but the third didn't.

I'd just begun to slam on the brakes when I hit him, then hit the car right behind him, his body crushed between us. The sudden stop sent air-cushions exploding out of every panel, my restraints digging tightly into my chest.

Shaking hands yanked the restraints off, shoved the cushion away and my door open. I fell out, lunging for the opening door.

A spell hit me before I could make it, but the attacker's angle was off. The agonizing blow to my back drove me through it rather than away from it, my body rolling as I hit the ground just inside.

"It's inside!" A man barked, "Go! Go! Go!"

I couldn't run. You couldn't outrun sorcery. Grabbing at my belt got my pistol out just as the first man tried to come through the door, his eyes widening when I started shooting.

He must have had a different spell in mind, something offensive, because he didn't get a Barrier or a Wall up before I put three panicked rounds into his chest.

His body toppled, a women shouting out for Barriers while I scrambled up to my feet. I shot again at the first figure that tried to look through the opening, forcing them to duck while I ran for the waiting ramp.

"No!" That same woman rushed through, the swirling lights of a barrier protecting her as she sprinted after me. "You will answer for this, beast!"

I ran harder, firing wildly, inaccurately behind me, praying it kept her spells defensive rather than offensive.

I looked back in time to see her realize I was going to make it. To see her barrier fade, tarah lifting as she prepared a different spell.

Wild gunfire snapped over my head, tracer rounds skipping off the ground all around her, two hitting her legs. She went down with a scream of pain, a third and fourth Faithful only surging into the hangar as I reached the ramp.

Johanna, her eyes wild, kept shooting at full automatic from the top of the ramp until I was nearly in her line of fire. Only then she did she jerk back, clearing space for me to dive inside.

"Irkan!" She screamed, dropping the gun to get the door shut. I nearly had another heart-attack when the rifle bounced, but it didn't go off even if the barrel was pointed far too close to me.

She didn't even seem to notice, slamming the button to retract the ramp before grabbing at my arms, babbling in Deutsch. "Come on! Come on!"

I got my legs under me with her help, stopping just long enough to safety her gun, then mine, and then I let her haul me up towards the cockpit.

The yacht was swaying long before we got there, Irkan bringing us up and off the ground before the Faithful could try to do anything with their sorcery to damage our hull, our landing gear, or the engines.

"Shields." He growled, focusing on what was in front of him, "I already requested an orbital path, and it was granted."

"Good thinking." I gasped, dropping into my usual seat, getting our protection online. "I'd really rather not have fighters after us."

He chirped, pushing us onward and upward, not taking the time to circle like we had on Cashihto. "What happened?"

I sagged back into my chair, trying to catch my breath, to stop the shaking in my hands. Johanna hadn't bothered to sit, and instead moved to stand behind me. Her fingers found my shoulders, a gentle massage doing more than anything else to lull me back into calmer waters.

"...they came up behind on me on the road." I told them. "Tried to hit me with fire right there in the open. I avoided them, but there was a second car that followed me onto the side roads. I... I managed to turn them, roll them."

Irkan glanced at me for a brief moment, "You slew them?"

I swallowed, "Maybe one of them, maybe all of them. I don't know, I didn't stop to look. I just kept driving. Nothing else came after me until I was nearly here, and then that first truck was waiting in an ambush on the local street. Avoided them, then hit a third group trying to break into the hangar like you saw.."

Johanna's fingers paused for a moment, then resumed. "Um... how did they find you in the middle of the night on a planet we've been on for less than a day? Are they tracking our wrist-comps?"

"Don't see how. We pulled them out of the packaging. And if they're tracking the yacht they'd have attacked you two first, not me on the road."

She took a deep breath, "What about the clerk you talked to? Maybe they warned them, or had a hack in their system. You could have been followed from there."

I was shaking my head before she finished, watching as the stars began to become visible with our increasing altitude. "They'd have already had to be close to move that fast, and I'm pretty sure I wasn't followed like that. I think..."

When I trailed off, she prodded me, "What?"

I took one more deep breath, then let it out. "I think I know who the traitor was, on Last Stop. The one who gave away our group's position when we were making for the Faithful's base. We must still have transmitters inside us, broadcasting our locations, and the Faithful must have an outpost here. Picked up on them."

Johanna wasn't a spy, but she wasn't stupid either. She figured it out from there, "God. Marzin. He's the one that scanned us."

"Yeah." I chuckled bitterly, "Aspects... I liked him too."

Irkan's growl was a low, furious thing. "As did this sailor. All liked him. An act to lure out those who escaped, to corral them as herd beasts for future slaughter."

That sounded exactly like the kind of language that the Faithful would have used.

"Should have figured it out earlier." I muttered, closing my eyes. "The cybernetics they forced into those poor people in the mines, in their prison cells in the base. Marzin was filled with cybernetics. Faithful could have been puppeting him from the very start."

Johanna managed to stay more focused on the here and now. "Do we have scanners we could use on board?"

"No. Well..." I exhaled, thinking about it. "Just the one attached to the regenerator, but it'd be really awkward to use that to scan every part of our bodies. And even if we find it..."

She finished the thought. "...we don't have the training to do that kind of surgery, especially since it's not close to the skin like the ones Marzin helped us get rid of."

"Yeah." I cracked an eye open, glancing at Irkan. "Do we have the fuel to get to Lushrivers?"

A single angular nod of his head. "Yes."

"Then I think we go straight there." I said. "And pray that they can help us."

"Agreed." He rumbled. "Johanna?"

"Agreed." She said at once. "Let's get to the Far Reaches."

Irkan reached out, and pressed the throttle down a bit farther, taking us away from Aonu as quickly as possible.

Interlude
Rerth'riah

An Intelligence Headquarters for an entire Sector was not a small operation. Even Trinity, whose Near Reach Sector was officially the second leanest organization, had thousands of men and women working directly in the Trinity system itself.

Then were were the hundreds of Agents currently in the Reaches themselves, operating either openly or quietly, on long term projects or short term hunts.

And *then* there were the packmates of everyone actually of rank within the organization, nearly all of whom were working as support staff of some kind, or else had qualified for low-level clearance to keep a pack from having to keep secrets within itself.

And to clear all of those people, we had just a few dozen qualified Intelligence assets, a hundred or so repurposed Security Officers, and then about forty private investigators that Lord Delarah had yanked from the sea.

We'd been in the Trinity system for just over a week, and we were still flailing in our efforts to determine out just how large the problem actually was.

I strode in to yet another briefing room, finding my 'team' already present; Holde, Jet, Tia'mok, and Huvu'ithi. The latter pair were representing their own packs, who were still hard at work while we suffered through yet another meeting.

"How's the Void Lord?" Jet asked, not looking up from the tablet he was reading. "Impatient as always?"

Huvu snorted, "Of course she is. Impatience is a requirement to be a Voider."

I gave the scarred woman a flat look, sitting down at the head of the table, a gesture activating the built-in console. "That joke was old a century ago. Find a new one, especially since *we* are in the Void Fleets now."

The soldier rolled her eyes, ruined tarah giving the slightest quiver.

When she kept her mouth shut after that, I turned to Jet. "Jet, report on the data analysis teams?"

"We've hardly begun." He replied, finally setting his tablet down. Looking my way let me see the increasing wrinkles underneath of his eyes, and the way his lower arms crossed his chest betrayed how stiff they were.

None of us had been sleeping well, but Jet had been sleeping even less than the rest of us.

"We cleared one of the DataNet Security Administrators, they're creating the keys we'll need to go through both the modern data and the backups." He said.

"How many other Admins were there?" I asked.

"Three, not including the Director." He replied.

I tapped out a short note to myself, nodding once. "Their status?"

"Two are still going through interrogation and clearance. The last was on a religious pilgrimage to the home-world." A hand waved tiredly. "Still waiting on a response to see if she's actually there or not."

Another few keystrokes added that. "What about DataNet Security as a combined group?"

There was frustrated noise before his words, "As of this morning, the count is twenty four missing Agents, and we're up to five missing Operatives."

My tarah rose in anger, harder taps of the keys updating those numbers. "Mok?"

"Thirty nine field Agents unaccounted for." She replied at once. "That's up three but minus one since yesterday. We found what was left of their corpse in an abandoned shack in the valley. Preliminary evidence is that they were tied down and executed."

I exhaled, "Their pack?"

"Missing." Her head shook slightly, "We didn't find any missing persons reports filed by them about their absent packmate, which tells me they probably didn't survive much longer than them. Assuming that they weren't vanished first."

"Confirm that, but treat it as a lower priority." I ordered. "We don't have enough people to waste time on corpses."

Mok's head bobbed, "It's on the list for once we're farther along with vetting local assets. Until then it'll wait."

Good. Mok was proving to be just as good at her job as her old index would have indicated. She and her packmates needed very little direction, and their decision making hadn't left me with any complaints so far.

I'd still grabbed the first Agent who'd been cleared and vetted to watch her wake, but so far that precaution was proving less necessary than I'd feared.

"All right." My eyes moved to Huvu. "Any updates today?"

The soldier shook her head, resting a broad arm on the table. "No attempted break ins, no suicides among the prisoners, and the local army officers are maintaining their alert. I have another meeting with-"

A loud chime on her wrist comp made the big woman jump slightly, my tarah rising in amusement even as her ruined ones tried to lower in embarrassment.

"Really, Huvu?" Holde chuckled, reaching out to pat her arm. "Don't tell us you're an Elder now, forgetting to silence your comp."

Mok and Jet chuckled, drawing grumbling even as she tapped the device, glancing down at it. "Unknown contact? What is..."

"Huvu'ithi." I pursed my lips, lifting my tarah a little as well. "Not the time."

"You can wait." She muttered, peering down to read the subject line. I was already looking at her, which made it easy to see her eyes widen, ruined tarah shaking as wildly as her muscles would allow.

"What-" I began.

"Shut up!" Her finger was already stabbing down, bringing the full message up. For a long heartbeat she seemed to freeze, then her hand come up to cover her mouth. "Most sacred Aspects, I never.... it's from her!"

I needed the time between two waves to realize just what, *who*, she meant. Then I was on my feet, hands planted on the table. "Where is she!?"

"Someplace named Aonu." Huvu shook her head, reading quickly. "You're all listed as contacts, you should have it as well."

A swift glance at my own forearm betrayed nothing, which made me turn to Jet. He was already pulling his own up, frowning. That continued as he shifted through a few menus, "Damn. It's an unauthorized account from... I don't even recognize the path she used. My routines quarantined it."

"Unlock it." I demanded.

"I am, I am."

The moment my wrist-comp vibrated with a new message I was opening it, reading just as frantically as the others, feeling my hearts beginning to race wildly with each word.

Everyone,

I'm currently on Aonu, capital world of the Kingdom of the Lost. Was taken to penal colony named Last Stop by group called the Faithful along with Ark Fleet prisoners, coordinates to follow.

Faithful appear to prey on all non-Trahcon species; Mikira, Kelthi-Xenthan, Human, Naule, Thondian, Regnon, and Chezzek all confirmed targets.

Faithful conducting experiments on prisoners: confirmed focus on a form of mental adjustment and extreme cybernetics, including remote puppeting. Purpose still unknown.

Myself and two other escaped prisoners only survivors of escape effort. We are attempting to reach Lushrivers to secure the protection and reaction of a Compact Signatory. Will attempt to make my way home from there, or else wait for further contact.

Encountered Director Ashul'tasir of Alum Intelligence Branch. Killed in action during our escape, indicated she was betrayed by her own subordinates. Intelligence May Be Compromised.

Burned Hand confirmed present on Last Stop. Was badly wounded, survival unknown, but considering Khash's opinions I suspect she lives. Have additional evidence, but cannot currently access it.

Will send second message once we reach Lushrivers.

Ashe'lori, Rifle-Experienced, AL-875-678DEL-2708

I focused on my breathing, forcing it to be steady. Forcing myself to focus on the possibilities. This could be from Ashe, but it could just as easily have been the Faithful attempting to lure us into some kind of ambush.

It was far more likely to be such an ambush, if I was admitting the full truth. Ashe had been gone for nearly a year and a half. Someone who was not her packmate would suspect she was long dead.

I *was* her packmate, but I was also a paranoid Guide who'd spent nearly seven decades as an Imperial Agent. I'd already noticed several things wrong with that letter. Things that could simply be a young Huntress trying to squeeze in as much information as she could without giving away too much if it was intercepted...

...or it could be markers that it was too good to be true.

"Jet... can you confirm this letter?" I asked, keeping my voice under control.

"Apart from her index key at the end, and her reference to her luck? No, and we both know that someone could have tortured that much out of her." He shook his head, "I just ran a trace on the send path. It's definitely reading as coming from the Far Reaches at a minimum, but that part of the DataNet is such a mess I can't say if it actually came from Aonu right now."

Holde glanced at him, "What would it take to confirm that it came from the Lost, and not from somewhere else in the Far Reaches?"

"Data." He said. "I'll need other communications from there to be sure, but I don't know if Trinity will have any. Any intelligence reports from that region would have been routed through Alum, and probably to Shaidan from there. And I can't imagine finding any personal or official messages either."

Neither could I. The Lost didn't have a reputation for communicating with the wider galaxy to begin with, and certainly not with the Empire. They were an isolated little island of civilization in the farthest seas of known space, which was exactly how they liked it.

I gave him a tired wave, eyes returning to the message hovering above my arm. "Check anyway, and compare the language to her prior reports and correspondence... dammit. She included one of her old packs on the distribution. Holde? Contact the Void Lord's flagship at once. That Half-Sword might still be on Oshflara, but we need them recovered before they start talking to the wrong officers about strange messages."

He was already pushing himself to his feet, reaching over to give my arm a firm squeeze before he made for the door.

"Mok, Huvu." I turned to them. "I need everything you can get me on Aonu and Lushrivers. Everything on the war going on between the warlords, and any viable way we could get a team to Lushrivers to pick her up."

Huvu'ithi was already scowling, glancing at Holde as he vanished into the hallway, "We should send someone *now*, so that they're there when she arrives."

I throttled the urge to release my sorcery, "Even if this message isn't a lure of some kind, Lushrivers is nearly as far away as the Home-world, and we'd have to traverse a region filled with pirates and warlords trying to kill one another, nearly all of whom hate us."

Mok stirred, "What about Alum? It's much closer, and there's an Imperial facility there. And apparently an Intelligence branch in dire need of a cleansing."

"That... is an option." I admitted, "But first I need to confirm that, which is what Jet will be doing while you two get me the information I already ordered you to retrieve."

Mok nodded. Huvu still didn't look pleased, but she nodded after a longer heartbeat.

"Jet? You heard me. Fyvn is the one working the Far Reaches right now. Contact her, get everything you can find on Tasir. Tell her we have new evidence, but don't trust sending anything."

His head bobbed, glancing rapidly between his tablet and his wrist-comp. "Full precautions in effect, got it boss. I'll get you a full report ready to go in the next day. Priority?"

I flicked my right tarah. "She's our packmate. She is our priority unless Delarah orders otherwise, and her office is where I'm going next. I'm going to press for Fyvn to rotate back here to take command of this search, and for us to go to Alum in her stead."

There was a slow, quiet breath from Huvu. "Good. It's time to get her back."

It was past time to get her back. I was ready to say as much when Mok hummed, clearly reading from Jet's device as he worked.

"More evidence." She mused. "That she can't access. Database? You think they stole a ship? I didn't think she was that capable."

Huvu growled at her, "She was plenty capable."

"In her own way." I agreed with her, before having to agree with Mok. "That being said, she had no training in piloting or ship engineering. And having only two others with? Three people, one of whom knows nothing of sailing, aren't about to steal a barge or a corvette."

"So they stole a shuttle." She countered.

In response, I tapped the table's console until I had a map of known space up. A glance at my copy of the message let me enter the coordinates that had been provided...

...and the auto-zoom feature had to pull very far out to show the blinking red dot.

"A shuttle, from there?" I was already feeling my excitement ebbing. "Look at the distance to Aonu. That's two, maybe three months travel unless there is a hyper-space current that the Empire doesn't know of."

Her eyes met mine, her gaze colder than ice. "I know Ashe. This letter is from her. She's alive."

My left tarah flexed very slightly. "I want to agree, and we will proceed as if it that's true. But we have to be ready in case that it's *not* Ashe. That this is the first attempt by the Faithful to eliminate one of the teams trying to clear out their rot from our port."

Mok perked up a little, her own tarah lifting. "Which we could turn against them, so long as we're ready for it."

"Exactly." I said, my own voice hardening just as Huvu's had. "And if they knew Ashe's index key, of her relationship with Khash... then they will know what happened to her."

Both women nodded once more, Jet mimicking the motion a beat late, still distracted as he brought up yet more reports to read with one hand, and seemed to be composing a message to Fyvn with another.

I took a final breath, let it out, and pushed away from the desk. "Get to it, both of you. I want a full report on the situation in the Far Reaches within the week. Jet? Remember to sleep."

He gave me an absent wave as I walked past, mind already turning to just how I would convince Delarah of what needed to happen.

Of what I would need to find the truth.

Of that fragile crest of hope, the first I'd felt since I'd let her be taken.

Since I'd failed her, as I always did.

XI
Ashe'lori

A shrieking alarm had me kicking my way out of the blankets, submerged reflexes having me try to dive for the nearest locker. I was halfway through trying to yank it open when I fully woke up and realized that it wasn't a snap-inspection of my Half-Sword.

I was on a yacht in hyper-space, yanking at a decorative light, and that I wasn't in a barracks about to be put through a midnight drill.

Reaching up, I gave myself a light smack across the face, shaking my head against the cacophony coming from overhead.

I'd just begun to turn for the door when the low noise of the faster-than-light drive cut out, and the heavier rumble of the standard engines kicked on.

"Irkan!"

Either he somehow heard my scream over the alarms, or else he just had good timing. The screeching cut off a heartbeat later, his voice coming across the speakers instead, *"Blockader!"*

"Ashahn's bloody ass!" Being out here was ruining my language. That was the probably the tamest curse to escape my lips on my run to the cockpit, getting there just ahead of Johanna bursting through on the other side. She must have been messing around under the deck again from how ruffled her clothing was.

"Whose blockader!?" Johanna demanded, both of us scrambling to get into our seats. "Where are we!?"

"Shields!" Irkan barked, clawed fingers flying across the controls, adjusting our course. "There is a battle ahead!"

Getting my own hands working, I quickly scaled our shields up to full power while Johanna proved she'd finally mastered written Caranat by getting the sensor display overlay projected onto the glass window. Seeing that reminded me to hit a second control, dropping armored shutters, though I doubted they'd help much.

If a warship took notice of our little yacht we'd live only as long as our shields lasted. Anything that got through them would kill us, regardless of whether or not we blocked off the glass holding the vacuum of space at bay.

Johanna read the display while I fiddled with the controls, and while Irkan focused on piloting.

"Pirates... I think." She shook her head, "They're all reading as non-national, so that has to mean pirates right?"

"The Faithful would know the Warlord's identification keys." I agreed, trying to make sense of the three dimensional battle occurring in the middle of interstellar space. "Irkan? What are we looking at?"

He grunted, made a final adjustment, then gave the display a longer look.

"The Blockader lurked in ambush near the mouth of a stable hyperspace current. This is the only such current in this region, which is why I planned to take it as near Lushrivers as possible." Irkan replied, pointing to one group of ships. "There. That is the Blockader, see how that group of ships is attempting to pressure it. Force it to shift power to its shields rather than its nullification field."

I started to see the pattern after a few more moments.

The ship that had made us slam back into reality was in the center of a rough sphere of escorts, with a pair of heavy but unidentified ships staying closer to it. Their entire formation moving in pursuit of another group of ships that read as a trio of 2nd Rate Liners to the yacht's sensors. In between the two fleets were several dozen much smaller vessels, who seemed to be skirmishing.

I couldn't really tell what they were doing, but I trusted Irkan's view of the battle. If he said it was an attempt to pressure the Blockader, I believed him.

A longer look let me see that we weren't the only poor fish caught in the net. Two freighters were trying to get clear of the Blockader's field as well, along with three smaller ships that may be have been other yachts or personal transports.

...and a fast moving icon had broken off from the main battle, accelerating our way.

"Um, Irkan?" I asked. "Is that ship running away, or is it coming to kill us?"

His own eyes fixated on the same marker. "That, Ashe'lori, is an excellent question."

Johanna swallowed in the silence that followed. "Can we get out of here in time?"

Our pilot was already adjusting our course once again, the pitch of the engines changing as he put more power into them.

"We shall try." He replied. "Adjust the negation's field on the display, I must see it properly to chart our path through the void."

It took her a few moments of fiddling, but soon enough the hazy gray sphere changed to a sharp blue color. The broad circle was centered on the Blockader as it moved, clearly working to keep its main enemies within its radius.

Which was a problem for us, because that movement was bringing us progressively deeper into the field, rather than letting us have an easy route out.

A few taps on Irkan's side brought up a golden line that I presumed was our course, revealing that he'd hoped to cut across the 'bottom' of the sphere as the battle moved well above us. Johanna took that as a cue, fiddled with her own controls a bit more, and then a red line appeared to show the incoming pirate's path.

They were going to cut through the middle of the fleeing bystanders. We'd be the farthest from them, but I didn't know how much that would matter when it came to naval weaponry.

"Will we be in their range?" I asked.

"Yes." Irkan replied. "We likely already are."

I licked my lips, fighting the urge to clench my fingers as well. "Why aren't they shooting at anyone then?"

Johanna answered, "We could avoid it at this range, and they're pirates. They want to get close, give us the option of surrendering. If we give up, they get an intact ship to loot. If we don't, they want to be close enough to try and shoot out our engines without completely destroying the ship."

That made sense.

"So what do we do?" I asked.

Irkan made a final adjustment, the golden line bending into a curve that would take us out of the negation field by plunging us away from the Blockader's course.

"We see if they care enough." He replied, deep voice grim. "They should not. We are a mere yacht, where there are two fat merchants struggling to make speed. If these pirates are reasonable, they will not waste their time and effort on us."

I nodded, "And if they're not reasonable?"

"They fire a missile at us, and gamble that it merely disables us to be dealt with later." He said. "If we survive, they shall board us, implant us with slave rigs, and use or sell us as they see fit."

Johanna promptly made the sky even darker when she added, "That or they fire a few missile at us just for the fun of blowing someone up. Some pirates in the Near Reaches... they're so sadistic that they make the Faithful look normal."

Swallowing, I forced my attention back to my control console, flicking through the menus. I was very sure that there wasn't some kind of hidden anti-missile system, Irkan or I would have found such a thing a long time ago, but it didn't hurt to check.

When that search revealed nothing... I found myself left with nothing to do but sit there and wait.

Irkan glanced my way when my chair creaked, his sharp teeth showing in a small grin. "The wait is always the worst part of a naval battle. When there is nothing one can do but watch small marks move on a screen, and wonder when the violence shall begin."

"It already did." I said, nodding to the two fleets. "What do you think that is? Rival pirate bands?"

"Likely pirates nominally loyal to my Kings, warring against those nominally loyal to Cathia." He shrugged. "One group waiting to ambush the other at a common entrance to the local currents. Neither bears markings that I know. A shame we did not stay on Aonu long enough to gather proper news on the war."

I grimaced. "I'm sorry. I know you were hoping to hear about how that's going."

He shook his head, quills rippling under his chin. "Do not apologize for the actions of enemies, Ashe'lori. None of us anticipated that the Faithful would so quickly realize we were present, or else we would have acted with far greater haste."

Johanna snorted, though her nibbling at her bottom lip betrayed her nerves. "I thought we were running around pretty quick as it was. I mean, we didn't exactly sit around before we got to work getting money, fuel, food. And we sent our messages out first thing."

"Yes." Irkan acknowledged, "But you could have pulled news while you waited, rather than merely checking over the engines."

"...true, I guess."

She didn't say anything else, neither did Irkan, leaving us in yet another tense silence.

It wasn't broken until our communications suite lit up with an incoming hail. The others both turned to me, leaving me to take a deep breath before pressing down to accept it.

A man spoke before I had a chance to think of a greeting.

"*Unnan vassal.*" Whoever was speaking was doing it in Caranat, but I didn't want to know how much they were twisting their mouths to pronounce it. "*You surrandar! Kill power or ba dastrayed!*"

It took me a moment to recover from the assault on my native language.

"This is Ghai'vet," I remembered to give my alias instead of my real name. "I'm afraid to tell you that we're just a yacht out of Aonu."

There was an almost baffled pause, then the man said, *"Not care! Surrandar or die!"*

Tapping the mute button, I asked, "There's not point in talking, is there?"

Johanna cleared her throat, "No, there is. Buy us time. Demand to talk to the Captain. No pirate group in the Reaches would have a captain who speaks Caranat that badly."

She was hardly an expert on Caranat, but I supposed the Ark Fleet would make sure its citizens understood how pirate groups operated.

Rolling a shoulder, I unmuted the system and made the demand. "I want to speak with your Captain."

"No! You choose dath!"

"No!" I half-shouted, "By Ashahn, put your Captain on the line!"

For a brief moment I thought they'd ended the transmission, then a woman began speaking in the cutting accent I'd heard from the Cathian Trahcon on Last Stop.

"Presumptuous little thing, aren't you, Vet?" She began. *"Let me guess, you're going to say that your little yacht has nothing of value, and so I should simply let you go."*

I swallowed, flailed about for a moment, then tried to improvise with a joke. "Well, I was thinking about it, but you kind of drowned me right at the pier."

A chuckle, the cold tones warming up in amusement. *"Heh. A realist maybe? Power down your engines and I won't fire a brace of missiles at your little toy ship."*

"What will-"

"You're stalling to reach the edge of the Negation Field." She

interrupted me. *"Yes or no, Vet. Right now."*

Irkan shook his head on my left, and Johanna made a cutting motion at her throat on my right.

I cut the channel without replying. "A smart pirate?"

"An experienced one." Irkan huffed, "Adjust our shields, all power aft... yes. There are the missiles."

My fingers shook a little, but I managed to adjust our protection as he'd ordered. Only then did I look up to the sensor display once again, promptly finding the small icons racing out from the warship.

Another alarm blared a second later, red circles appearing around the missile's icons while yellow lines snapped into place connecting the weapons to our little ship.

Irkan growled, another heavy shake of his head. "Experienced indeed. They fired them in sequence rather than a single volley. One missile to breach our shields, the next to follow through and destroy our engines. Or our hull."

"Can our shields hold both off?" I asked.

"I do not know. There was no need or ability to truly test their power." He admitted, voice quieting. "If they remain intact, we shall survive to escape. They will not have time to fire further weapons before we reach the edge of the field."

"Good." Johanna whispered, "Um, do you have the hyper-space path ready?"

"Yes." A hand shifted, patting that control. "Seal the rear doors, Johanna. Then allow me to speak to my ancestors while the savannas pray to their own spirits."

I didn't watch as Johanna got up, heading back to seal the doors. I just kept staring at the two dots, at the ever shortening tethers between them and us. I couldn't look away, even if I wanted to.

All I could do was bring out the chair's restraints for the first time, locking myself against it. A worried glance at a crouching Irkan, his eyes closed, evidently content though he lacked anything keeping him in place.

And then... all I could do was whisper to the Aspects.

"Khash... please, bless us with your luck today. Let us escape. Let Ashahn spend her fury on the others, not upon us."

Closer.

"Yurah, guide me back to my packmates. Tzus remind them of my love for them."

Closer.

"Bodelbe, guide me home."

Closer.

"And if not... Aysh accept our souls."

My fingers tightened around the armrests when the first icon reached us.

The entire yacht shuddered, the alarms reaching a fever pitch of screaming. My display lit up from the damage to our shields, too many colors shifting as it tried to show me just how much our protection had been compromised.

I didn't have time to try and understand it.

The second missile hit a few seconds later.

XII

The second impact was far worse than the first. The ship seemed to buck around us, Irkan's chest slamming into the control panel, Johanna and I bouncing off of our restraints. Somehow he managed to avoid falling, hands seizing his console when the artificial gravity abruptly cut out.

More alarms were screaming, the sensor display vanishing as an automatic damage-control pop-up appeared. I felt my heart hammering, waiting for the air to explode outwards, for fire to roar through the cabin.

None of that happened, though my racing heart didn't begin to slow.

"Primary engines are out." Johanna recovered enough to speak, reading off what she was seeing while I grabbed Irkan's arm with a shaking hand, making sure he was all right. He seemed to be, but he was coughing with a crack on the shell covering his chest. That he was floating ever upwards probably wasn't helping either.

Johanna went on while I tried to make sure he didn't drift away from us, or from the controls. "Shields are trying to cycle, gravity's down... power plant is still online though. We must have military grade shields on this boat."

That didn't surprise me, and I quietly thanks the Aspects for the Faithful's militant paranoia. For once it had worked in our favor; ensuring our survival against something that really ought to have killed us.

Johanna seemed to feel the same, going quiet for another moment before finding her voice again. "Uh, I don't see any damage to the FTL system. No breaches to the forward hull.... *scheise*. I think we're losing fuel."

That drew my eyes back to her and the readout of the damage. "All of it? Please tell me we're not losing all of it."

"I, uh...." Her attention lowered to the console in front of her seat, a hand sending it scrolling as she checked something. "No, *dank Gott*. There was a cut off that sealed the starboard tanks. We're just losing what's in the the port side tanks."

That still wasn't good, but it was better than the alternative. "Half our fuel. I guess it could be worse. A lot worse."

Her nod was quick, "Agreed. Uh. Irkan? Are we going to drift out of the blockader's range before the next missiles can get to us?"

Our pilot managed to clear his throat, shaking himself as best he could considering he was parallel to the floor, only staying in place thanks to his firm grip on the pilot's console and my grip on his scaled arm.

"If our engines are no longer firing, they will presume we are disabled." He said, sounding as if he knew what he was talking about as usual. "They will not shoot again so long as we do not fire them and keep the shields down."

I glanced at him, finding him nodding to my hand. Taking the cue, I carefully let go, asking a single question for both his words and his actions. "You're sure?"

"Yes." He replied, "If they wished us dead, they would have fired three missiles, not two."

"Point." I said, using my freed hands to turn the shields off when they began attempting to recharge. My thundering heart was finally beginning to return to normal with the hope that we truly had survived.

That we would survive, thank the Aspects. I'd have to pray to Khash more often.

"What do you need us to do? Gravity or engines first?" I asked, not sure on the priority.

There was another hacking cough before he replied. "Gravity. The standard engines can wait until we are safe in hyper-space once again. Until then it is best to drift as though we are disabled."

Nodding, I turned the other way. "Johanna? Do you need help with that?"

She was already unbuckling herself, a shake of her head sending her wild fur all over the place, "I'll let you know when I get back there, but hopefully not."

Acting as if zero gravity was a completely normal thing to endure, my old cellmate pushed herself out of her chair. Floating up to the ceiling, she twisted around in place, kicked off from the armor protecting the view-port, and flew straight to the door.

She opened it and vanished down the hall almost before I could blink, leaving me to assist Irkan as best I could.

After a bit of checking the displays, we realized there wasn't much more for us to do besides be ready to make the transition to hyper-space as soon as we could. The FTL drive was still charged and ready to open the way, and our path into the local current was still set.

Further, the pirates weren't trying to communicate with us, likely certain we were helpless, and the yacht was still going in the right direction to make our escape.

All we really had to do was not die for the next three minutes, and then Irkan could push the button to hurl us back into hyper-space.

I wanted to check the crack on his chest, but my medical skills were middling even with gravity. Without it I was more likely to make him start leaking toxic blood than I was likely to actually help him. That would have to wait until Johanna got the system back online.

Speaking of, I tapped the internal comms, "Johanna? How bad is it back there?"

It didn't take her more than a few seconds to reply, "*Not as bad as it could have been. I think the gravity turned off automatically when the shields got hit, some kind of power saving program... trying to reset that right now.*"

"Thanks." I glanced at Irkan, "Once you get that generator working again, bring a medical kit up. Like he said, we'll fix the thrusters later if we even can fix them from inside."

"*Got it.*"

Irkan let out a sound of approval at my priorities, adding his own. "Open up the navigation suite. We will need a new destination with our fuel drained."

...right. Dammit. A few keystrokes got the screens reset, getting rid of the damage control display to show us the local battle once again. I took a minute to look it over, just to make sure that Irkan's guess about the pirates was correct.

It seemed to be. The ship that had fired at us must have also shot at the two bulk freighters. Our yacht's sensors had begun reporting that both of the larger vessels were displaying 'unusual readings – possible damage' next to their icons.

The pirates looked like they were in the process of running one of them down, the acceleration taking them even farther away from us.

Swallowing, I started getting the navigation system on the main projector, asking another question while I worked on pulling it up. "Could the pirates have actually caught us if we really were disabled? I mean, we're drifting at speed in the opposite direction."

"If they are good enough for such a precise FTL motion? Yes, easily." He let out a little grunt, swinging his stubby legs back down, arms straining a little to get him settled in preparation for gravity's return. "If they lacked such precise navigational systems, they would simply make the transition far enough ahead of us to easily match our velocity. They could then intercept us, or force us to approach them on their terms."

"That's a lot of work for a yacht." I said.

"Yes." Irkan agreed. "Our survival would have depended on the quality of the loot to be found aboard. Otherwise they would demonstrate their displeasure at the waste of time and resources."

I grimaced, "Loot like the kind we just sold on Aonu to pay for the fuel leaking out into space?"

His mouth opened in what passed for a grimace. "Yes. Given our current lack of cargo or items of worth... this sailor believes it likely we would have all been shot at once. If your shard of luck was benevolent, slave-rigs would have been used to torture instead."

I wouldn't have called that lucky, but then I supposed we'd have been alive. Tortured, abused, and raped, most certainly, but alive.

Pushing those thoughts back into the depths, I nodded to the updated screen, "Where can we get with our fuel?"

He was about to reply when Johanna came across the speakers again, cutting him off. *"Gravity in five seconds! Four, three, two, one, now!"*

I was promptly jerked downwards into my chair, Irkan letting out a deeper grunt when his feet were yanked onto the floor. We both took a moment to shake ourselves, then I was working at loosening my restraints while he got a proper hold of the primary controls.

"Negation field will be away within moments." A quick check of the sensors had him settled a hand on the button. "Johanna. Does the FTL system read operational in engineering as well as at my seat?"

"Checking." We waited for less than a minute before she replied, *"Yeah, it's fine, thank God. Get us out of here."*

A push was all it took for the low hum to slowly build up, the yacht giving a single micro-shudder that had me tense up before everything stilled again. Irkan gave me an amused look before checking his instruments.

"We are away and approaching the current." He reported, sinking back into a relaxed crouch with a relieved chirp. "Now there is only the question of where we are away to."

Still an excellent question.

"No chance of Lushrivers?" I asked.

His head was jerking in the negative before I finished the last word. "No. We could not even get close to it, nor even make this current's end near Terminus. Our engines drew from each fuel tank, not one over the other, and we'd expended nearly half of our total volume."

I got the math. "So we're actually down to a quarter of what we left Aonu with."

"Yes." Irkan confirmed. "Somewhat less, if these systems are truthful. Fuel was likely lost before the safety cut off sealed the remaining tank. I shall bring up our options."

While he surveyed out possible destinations on the main display, I did a few more checks on the yacht. Bringing the damage control screen up on my own console helped me get a better understanding of how battered we actually were.

Soft footfalls heralded Johanna's return, her head appearing over my shoulder as she took in what I was looking at.

The missiles had clearly been tracking our engines, hitting us on the port aft side. Flashing red and orange panels made me think that entire back section had simply been blown out into space. Those cracks ran down and up to the fuel tank, which tracked with us losing the precious liquid required by our reactor.

Of the five thruster nozzles that let us actually accelerate, one was a solid red, while another was a less certain orange. Considering that I wasn't really sure I wanted to start up a damaged engine, who knew it would explode or not, we were down to the central mount, and then the two on our starboard side.

Enough to fly well enough, I hoped, but we'd be awfully slow to pull away if we got caught by another Blockader out here.

"...that's a lot of damage... ugh. We lost a water tank as well." I muttered, "Less of it than we lost fuel, but it's just as gone."

Johanna hummed, "We have enough?"

"More than enough. We'd have to ration if we were still trying to make Lushrivers, but since we're not... I think we'll be okay. I'll do the math later, but at worst I think we'll just have to cut down on the showers." I glanced at the medical kit in her hands, "You going to help Irkan?"

She colored a little. "Right, sorry."

Irkan chuckled without looking away from his own work. "I am fine. I shall treat it later."

"You sure?" She asked.

"Yes. It is not bleeding, it merely aches." A hand patted his chest, "My natural armor served its purpose. Let us instead consider the worlds we may reach."

We both looked up to see that he'd cut it down to three options.

"The first is the safest once we arrive." Irkan adjusted the view, highlighting the name in the center; Karrorkash. "It is the nearest outpost of the Scarlet Tears, and should still be under their control."

I pursed my lips. "But you can't guarantee it's still under their control with the war on."

A low chirp. "No. I cannot. Further, it is at the very edge of our theoretical range. Even a single disturbance in hyperspace, a day or two when we are forced shallow, and we would not make it."

Damn. "I think we have to eliminate that one, then. What's closer?"

"Jahrth'flara." He supplied. "It is the only real hub in the region between the Lost and coreward most colonies of the Scarlet Tears, or of the Riush's territory. To compare it to a world you may know, Johanna, it is said to be much like Neues Hamburg."

Johanna hissed, "Neues Hamburg is a den of slavers and pirates!"

A clawed hand waved dismissively. "As is Jarath'flara, but that also means it is a world where few ask questions. A world where there are countless ships coming and going at all times."

I understood where he was sailing with that. "A world where we could easily find someone to repair our ship, or a place where we could hide until you could call for help from home."

Irkan nodded. "Yes."

Another huff from the woman standing behind me. "I don't like that any better than risking running out of fuel. And if it's such a hub, isn't it more likely that there'd be Faithful agents there? We could end up just repeating what happened on Aonu, except we won't have the money for a quick refuel and exit this time."

That drew a frown. "Yeah, she's got a point. What's your third option for us?"

A claw tapped the controls, making the other two vanish and leaving only one world's name and location in place.

"Kagarraht." I read before guessing. "Is it another pirate den?"

"Yes, but a far smaller one." Irkan replied. "A population of only a few million, nothing like Jarath'flara. It is also well within our remaining range, so we would have a few lingering options on our arrival."

I hummed, reading the quick description he'd pulled up.

Apparently it once been a Scarlet Tears base, which had been taken over by the Riush when they'd seized Terminus a few centuries ago, and then simply been abandoned by them as a world not worth the cost of holding onto.

Now it served whatever smaller pirate groups couldn't afford to operate out of a larger world.

"Not ideal." Johanna voiced her opinion. "There's really no quiet planets in range? There's got to be plenty out here."

"There are, but who does Johanna believe these pirates prey upon?" Irkan asked.

She let out a little huff. "Yeah, but that's a *chance* that a pirate will attack while we're there. Not a guarantee we'll be surrounded by them."

His voice deepened slightly. "That is not this sailor's meaning. Our ship is damaged, possibly beyond our ability to repair. A world harassed by pirates is not one that will wish to give charity to unknown visitors."

"But a pirate world," I let out a heavy sigh, "Will have repair facilities if we can find a way to pay for them, or they'll have people interested in buying a damaged ship if we can't."

"Yes." He said. "I know that you wished to keep this vessel, Ashe'lori, as evidence of our trials and victories. I agree with your logic, but we may have no choice. Further, if we are on Kagarraht or Jarath'flara, we shall have more choices to sell or buy a new vessel than we would on a simple farming or mining world."

I took another deep breath, and forced myself to nod. "And if we go to Kagarraht and don't like what we see, we'd still have enough fuel to try for one of those independent colonies, right?"

His reply was grudging. "Yes."

"Then I vote for Kagarraht." I said. "Johanna?"

126

A frustrated little groan came out, "Ugh. Fine, if I have to pick one of the three, I guess I'll pick Kagarraht, but I'm sure we'll be leaving there the moment we land and someone tries to kill us for the yacht."

I turned back to Irkan in time to see him shrug, already reaching out to adjust our course. "We shall arrive in six days. We shall have that long to see what repairs we can make to the engines from the interior, and work out a means to approach the world as confidently as possible."

Biting my lip, I stared at the display as our course updated, watching the blue line shift away from Lushrivers, and to a world in contested space.

A poke at my shoulder finally made me look away, Johanna jerking her head toward the back. "Come on. I need an extra pair of hands, and Irkan needs to stay here to monitor the systems while we work on them."

And so we headed aft, to see just what we could do to fix our stolen vessel.

XIII

I got to sit on the ramp, rifle in hand while Johanna and Irkan tromped through the light rain and heavier mud to check the yacht's damage. While they tried to see just how bad it really was, I surveyed the collection of other ships we'd landed among.

All of the real hangars in the largest city were reserved for the pirates who owned them, leaving everyone else parking in what clear spaces they could find just outside of it. We'd found a spot in a small field among several other vessels roughly the same size as ours.

There were two other yachts, not nearly as luxurious as our own, what looked like a small gunship of some kind, a few light transports, and one extremely battered looking personal cargo hauler. Several had their own crews out and about, working on various maintenance tasks despite the fairly miserable weather.

It didn't take a real Agent to notice the way many of them were looking over our vessel. The fancy exterior was drawing attention in ways I'd really rather it hadn't.

I kept a wary eye on our surroundings until my friends returned, both of them already coated in muck nearly up to their knees.

"Well?" I asked when Irkan made the ramp, Johanna tromping along behind him. "How bad is it?"

His entire body shook, the quills on his chin swaying with the motion. "It was wise not to start thruster number four, and we discovered the reason for the central mount's fluttering."

Johanna's dark expression gave me the answer even before I asked the question. "I'm guessing it's not good?"

"No." He said flatly, cautiously moving around me as best his bulk allowed, though he stayed in the hatchway rather than heading fully inside. "The damage is severe, and the strain of atmosphere likely made it worse. I would not risk activating it again as it currently is."

Grimacing, I glanced from him to Johanna to see her scowling. "We can't fix it, can we?"

"Not without a *lot* of money." Johanna replied. "The problem's not that specific thruster. We can see the damage to it, and I think Irkan and I could patch it if we could find the equipment. We could get it safe enough to use. The problem is that we can't physically get in there to make those repairs without pulling thrusters four and five out of the way."

I tried to imagine the equipment required to pull those massive sections out of the yacht... and I gave up on those thoughts almost at once.

"Dammit." I forced myself to press on, toward the other repairs. "What about the fuel tank? Could we patch that, refuel it, and work with the two engines we still have?"

Another shake of Irkan's head. "Two side engines are not powerful enough for us to break orbit properly. We need either the central engine, or three of the side thrusters."

"And," Johanna muttered, "Even if we gamble with turning the central engine back on as it is, the fuel tank on the port side is cracked wide open. That's not going to be a quick and cheap patch job, even if it would be a little cheaper than pulling the engines."

I blew out a breath, watching as it turned to foggy mist in the air. "All right. What about repairing engine four, and patching the fuel tank?"

Irkan twitched in a little shrug, "Possible, I suppose, but we would still need heavier equipment than we have, and likely need to remove engine five to have full access to four. Assuming we do not need to pull four to repair it."

It was a fight to keep my hands on the rifle, to not run them over my face in frustration.

"...we're stuck here, then." I mumbled. "Until we come up with something."

Johanna's expression darkened even further, muddy feet carrying her past me. "Pretty much. I'm going to go shower and scream at the walls for a bit. Let me know when we have a plan."

I tried to talk to her, "Johanna-"

She was already stepping around Irkan, vanishing back into the ship without looking back.

I sighed at her reaction, then my lips pressed into a line when I heard Irkan let out a low, amused chuckle.

"It's not funny." I said.

"Perhaps not." He replied, still chuckling, "Yet her petulant anger remains quaint to me. She brings to mind younger blood-kin, still learning respect and patience."

Blowing out a frustrated breath of my own, I waved for him to move back. "She'll calm down, she always does. Come on. Let's seal the ship up and talk about our options so we can vote on them when she's ready."

He did, backing up so that I could follow him inside. Closing and sealing the hatch behind me, I followed him up to the yacht's prow so that we could keep an eye on the various camera displays while we discussed just what we were going to do now.

I elected to remain standing, leaning against the back of my chair while Irkan began a slow pace of the room, scratching at his chin, at the slowly repairing crack on his chest.

"You think we need to sell the yacht, don't you?" I led with what seemed to be the most obvious question. "I mean, you already did, but now that it's this badly damaged you think we really need to."

He glanced at me with one eye, grunting softly. "Yes. It is the most logical choice in this one's opinion."

I took a deep breath, willing my mental seas to remain calm and flat. Losing control of my emotions wouldn't make this situation any better, or easier to deal with.

"What are our other options, logical or not?" I asked.

"I am considering." He replied. "Does Ashe'lori have any for consideration?"

Crossing my arms and leaning my head back gave me a little bit of time to try and think.

Our central problem remained the same as it had been since we'd first tried landing on Cashihto: money. We needed far more of it than we had, and we lacked any real way to make more of it. I supposed we could try stripping out even more of the yacht's interior than we already had, sell it, but I doubted we'd get all that much for the fancy light fixtures or wooden panels.

Maybe enough for more fuel and food, if we combined it with the leftover money from Aonu. Enough to survive off of for a little while. Enough to have made Lushrivers if the yacht had been intact.

But since it wasn't... no. There was no way we'd get enough to pay for repairs. Not on the levels that Irkan and Johanna clearly thought were necessary to make this ship functional once again.

"FTL buoy?" I asked.

"There is one." He allowed, "But my ping on our arrival indicated that it is locked down. I do not know by whom."

So we couldn't call for help, not right now. Maybe we could investigate that, if we really were here long term.

"If we can't contact anyone, then only other option is labor." I said finally. "Getting some kind of local jobs until we can afford repairs, or until we can figure out who owns that buoy and how to send a call for help. The Tears aren't far from here, are they?"

"They are not." He agreed, "If I could craft a request, it is likely they would dispatch a small vessel to retrieve one thought dead."

So that was an option. "All right. What about working locally in the meantime? How long would it take us to get enough local credits to pay for the repairs?"

He slowed his pacing, turning to face me as he considered the question.

"It would depend upon the employment, but many months to years is likely. It is more likely that Ashe'lori would discover a means to message my kingdoms, or her Empire, long before we earned enough."

That's what I'd been afraid he'd say. "You're sure? Keeping the lights on in here doesn't take much power, so we wouldn't really be paying for a place to live."

"This is true." He allowed, "However, retaining this yacht would demand we be ready to defend it at all times. That would limit our opportunities for employment, and extremely limit your own investigations. It is likely that that those watching us would notice a pattern, and seek to exploit it if we routinely depart the ship."

Meaning one of us would have to remain here at all times, and any of us heading out alone would be at serious risk of being attacked. Maybe captured as leverage against the others, or else simply killed to make taking the yacht easier.

And since Johanna was the only one of us with partial armor that fit, I didn't really think we had much of a chance of fighting off a dedicated attack. I mean, I supposed I could resize some of her equipment to fit me, but even then it would still be just one of us. And I'd still lack a helmet.

I groaned as the notion of being attacked brought up the other thing we needed money for. "And we need to find a doctor we could trust enough to scan us for transmitters, and then remove them."

Irkan let out a quiet huff, apparently having forgotten that as well in light of our many other problems. "This is true. If the Faithful are present, that shall be a complication."

"That's an understatement." I said, chewing on my lip for a few heartbeats. "On Aonu, we had about twelve hours before they attacked me on the road, and when they also came for the ship. I propose we stay in the yacht, on alert, for one day. If they don't come for us by then, I think we can assume that they either don't have a team here, or that they aren't scanning for escapees like Aonu's group was."

There was a low hum in his throat, then a quick nod. "Sensible, agreed. If they do come, we can relocate to another of this world's cities. The engines will be sufficient for that purpose. Then perhaps we sell this yacht, and then find any way we can to depart."

"What are our options if we do have to make that kind of panicked sail?" I asked.

"Pirates always need more crew, especially those who actually understand how to repair and maintain a starship." He waved a hand slightly. "It would be dangerous, but it could remove us from this world quickly."

My weight shifted uncomfortably. "...not sure I like the idea of having to do that. Could we just steal another ship instead?"

"Of course, but such a thing would be risky. Especially on a pirate world."

I clicked my tongue, "Meaning everyone else is going to be just as paranoid as we are about their ship getting stolen."

"Yes." Irkan shrugged. "Joining a crew, and then departing their company as soon as possible, would be safer."

Safer, maybe, but I didn't want to imagine how I'd explain that to Rerth or the Imperial authorities once I got back home. I was pretty sure they'd forgive a lot, and overlook things like burglary and self-defense... but if we couldn't leave the pirates right away, we might have to actually do some piracy to stay alive.

Raiding an independent colony on behalf of pirates... I could well imagine being made to kill a civilian to 'prove' myself as a fresh pirate recruit. It was the kind of thing I'd seen in movies. True, little else in those films had much to do with reality, but it was easy to guess that such a proof of loyalty might be demanded.

That could be the kind of thing that saw me welcomed home, debriefed, and then immediately thrown onto a brand new penal colony. Assuming I didn't have a mental collapse from having to kill someone who did not deserve such a death.

"Let's save that for emergencies." I said finally. "The kind of emergency where we will die or be captured by the Faithful within an hour if we don't turn pirate."

Irkan's eyes started to narrow, then he gave one of his quiet chirps. "Ah. Yes. Your Imperial masters do not tolerate such activities."

"No, they don't." I drummed my fingers on my arms. "But I'd rather spend my life on an Imperial penal colony than be taken by the Faithful again, so we'll treat that as our we're-about-to-die plan like I said."

"Agreed." He dipped his head. "Then we have such a plan in place, and shall remain in this vessel for a time to determine if the Faithful are present. The question remains what we shall do after the first day passes, beyond accrue currency and seek to access the DataNet."

I'd been avoiding that question, if only because I still didn't have a real answer for it.

Selling the yacht in the hopes of buying a more practical ship, or passage on a non-pirate vessel, was likely our best option left to us. Even if we couldn't find passage immediately, then it would give us enough money to find a doctor, lodging, and investigate the FTL buoy's ownership.

Living in a cheap hotel or apartment would probably be far safer than living in a gilded yacht. True, we'd lose the protection of the shields, easily sealed hatchways, and the mobility of being able to move to another region of the planet... but we'd also draw less greedy attention.

And as I'd just seen outside, there was already plenty of that greedy attention even with our battle damage. It would only get worse as other people heard about our ship.

Every logical wave was striking the beach, telling me it was wisest to sell the yacht as soon as possible to the highest bidder. To simply find passage on another ship to the Tears' Kingdoms, to reach some degree of safety as soon as possible.

Every wave save one.

There remained the servers below our feet. The locked portions of the navigation systems. Things that we couldn't take with us if we sold the ship. Couldn't preserve as evidence for when we made it to Lushrivers, or when I made it home.

"I can't." I muttered, shaking my head. "I can't say that we should sell the yacht, Irkan. I have to know why they were doing what they did on Last Stop. I *have* to know, and those might be the only things with records on them."

Irkan's rigid expression did not change. "I know Ashe'lori feels that way, but I believe it is our only true path to our next destination."

I let out a ragged breath and pushed away from the chair. "Johanna gets to cast the tie breaking vote then. If she sides with you... I'll... respect the pack's voice."

A low rumble emerged from his chest. "I do not believe that we are a pack as the river-sharks create. We are also not blood kin."

"Well we're not just companions either." I told him. "Or you'd have proposed that we split up and each try to make our way home from here. Or you'd just go off and join the first pirate crew heading towards the Tears' territory and leave us behind."

His heavy mass shifted in what looked like discomfort, his voice lowering. "Ashe'lori... perhaps has a valid point. I would prefer not to leave her company, nor that of Johanna, until we reach my home. The savannas are... comfortable to have as companions."

The awkwardness made me smile a little, "It's comfortable to have you around too, Irkan. I'll let you watch the cameras while I go talk to Johanna about our options."

He seemed relieved, even when I patted him on the shoulder as I walked by. I looked back to see him settling in to his usual place, already double-checking the various external cameras.

Leaving him to it, I made the short walk to our cabin, brushing the door open to find a robed Johanna toweling water out of her fur. The look she sent me when I closed the door behind me betrayed her lingering disapproval over the situation.

"Well?" She demanded in Deutsch.

I sighed, replying in her native language. "We're going to stay in the yacht for the next day. See if any Faithful show up and attack us or not. If they do, we'll relocate to another city. Maybe put our emergency plan into motion."

"Which is?"

"Join a pirate crew." I quickly held a hand up, "No, I'm *really* not happy about it even as an emergency plan, but it might be the only way for us to sail out, and sail out quickly if we really have to."

Her lips twisted, fingers clenching in her towel... then she visibly forced herself to relax.

"I guess I can see it." She said. "Not happy about that either, but I can see it being a way to run away as quickly as we can."

"Yeah."

Her chest moved with a deep breath, then she slowly resumed drying. "What's our plan if the Faithful don't attack us?"

Swallowing, I forced the words out. "Irkan and I are split, which means it's your decision."

She froze once again. "...options?"

"I want to live in the yacht, find local jobs here or in another city. Earn money for repairs, buy ourselves time to figure out who has the local DataNet locked down." I explained. "Then we either call for the Scarlet Tears to come get us, or we pay for repairs. Whichever one comes first."

Johanna nodded slightly, "And Irkan? Wait, let me guess. Same thing, but he wants to sell the yacht so we've got money to actually spend. Give us the option of just buying passage to Lushrivers."

"More or less." I said.

"...and it's up to me?" She asked.

"He and I aren't changing our minds." I told her. "So... yes, it'll be up to you to decide if the Faithful don't attack."

Teeth appeared, working at her bottom lip in that display of nerves we shared. They kept pressing down until a long groan came out of her mouth, and the pale skin of her cheeks took on a pinkish hue.

"Ashe." She did her best to growl my name. "Stop. Staring. I don't like you like that."

I rolled my eyes, turning around, "I don't like you like that either, Johanna."

"Well you act like it sometimes." She muttered.

"That's just me being a good packmate." I countered, staring at the door. "Which is still the only reference I really have for what we are to each other at this point."

"Did you tell Irkan that?" She asked.

"I did, actually. He was adorably awkward about it. Can I turn around now?"

"No, and I don't know what we are either, but it's still weird to have you staring at me like that."

I shook my head. "I try not to."

"I know, which is why I'm not really that mad. About that, at least." There was a heavier sigh. "I *am* a bit mad about being the one put on the spot like this. I'm... Ashe, I'm nineteen. You're the spy's apprentice, and Irkan is a military officer. You two should be the ones making the big plans."

"We have been." I noted, shaking my head once again. "But... we don't agree this time. You've heard us both, you've survived the same things we have, Johanna. I think you have every right to have your own opinion of what we're doing, which is why I'm not upset that you're upset about being here."

"I..." She trailed off for a long moment, then she said more quietly. "Fine. I'll think about it. Go away, I want to get dressed, then see if there's anything else I can do in engineering."

"All right." An arm waved, waving at her, "I'm going to wander the ship, do inventory on anything we might be able to sell to local brokers."

"All right." She echoed.

I left her, murmuring a quiet prayer to the Aspects that she'd side with me as she often did.

Because I didn't know what I would do if she didn't.

XIV

The damage to the yacht drove the price down considerably, though the amount we received was still fairly substantial. I supposed it could have been a lot worse. The Naulian Clan who Irkan found to buy it were polite, professional, and didn't try to murder us to get their money back.

Not that I was in any mood to appreciate that, since they'd also refused my request to get us copies of any electronic data found on board. They'd made it clear they were simply going to force all of the systems through a hard reset, wiping all of the data to make space for their own information.

The Elder had even lectured me. Saying that out here, in the Reaches, you didn't want to know what lay in systems like that. That it only led to problems.

It was safer to not know. To clear the systems and move on.

I'd forced myself not to create a storm. He'd meant well, was paying us well. He didn't know how badly I had needed that information.

Information now gone, obliterated.

All I had were the wrist-comps we'd found on board, and a copy of the navigation system's encrypted data. All of it shoved into a bag I refused to let go of for the rest of the day.

I sailed listlessly along behind the others as that first day without our ship continued. Irkan picked out a bank he judged to be reputable, putting our new credits into an account there, and then we paid for a hotel to last us until we could locate an apartment to stay in. We'd stay there until we could buy a new ship, or find safe passage.

We ate a frugal dinner consisting of the last bread we'd baked aboard the yacht, and then tried to settle in to the small room.

I managed about a half hour of trying to participate in their inspection of apartments on the local Net before my Human weakness had me pushing myself off the bed I'd been laying on.

"You two can decide on the apartment." I said, "I'm going to start investigating the DataNet connection."

Johanna looked up from her wrist-comp, blinking several times. "Alone? I thought none of us were going to go anywhere alone."

"I'm not leaving the building." I told her, "And I'll have a panic alert on my wrist-comp."

She frowned, watching as I grabbed the pistol we'd left on a dresser. "You're going to the bar downstairs, aren't you?"

"Bars are good for gathering information. People talk freely when they have alcohol in them." I said defensively.

Her frown deepened, "And you haven't had alcohol in more than a year, Ashe. I don't think it's a good idea. One of us should go with you."

I got the weapon settled onto my belt, turning to face them properly. Johanna sitting at the little desk, Irkan far more awkwardly seated on a bed not at all designed for a Mikiran body.

"I'll be fine." I crossed my arms, trying to sound calm and confident instead of exhausted. "And I'm not actually going to drink. I know my tolerance is probably gone, so I'm just going to sip a cheap beer and listen to the people around me. It will be easier to do that alone."

Irkan tilted his head in consideration, then chirped softly. "Ashe'lori has a point. A Mikira and a savanna would draw more attention than a single savanna, or a pair of them when one has no training in such things."

That didn't make Johanna look any happier, glancing between us. "I suppose, but are you actually doing that, or are you just going to go get drunk since we sold the yacht?"

My own expression turned into an irritated scowl, "I'm depressed, Johanna. Not stupid. I just want to get started on figuring out the DataNet so that we can get home as soon as possible."

The snap in my voice had her blink rapidly, awkwardly lifting a hand in surrender. "All right, all right... just, um, be safe."

"I will."

I swept out of the room, knowing she hadn't actually deserved the snap. She'd made the decision she thought gave us the best chance to survive, as had Irkan. They'd had every right to make that decision, to outvote me in our strange little pack.

I... Ashahn's blood. I couldn't even seriously argue against it. The yacht had been a loss as soon as that second missile had hit us. Realistically there hadn't been any real chance we could repair it on our own, and our single day inside of it had betrayed just how many people would be willing to kill us to have it.

The Faithful might not have attacked us, but we'd had two local groups who'd tried to make offers or threats during the night. Neither had taken our refusals well, and only the fact that they'd started arguing between them had saved us from serious problems.

A third group had arrived around dawn, demanding we open up or see our hatches blown off. Irkan had lifted us off before they could, moving us to the far side of the city, but that had been enough to make up Johanna's mind.

She'd agreed with Irkan; the yacht was simply too rich a prize for us to simply use as a make-shift apartment. There was no way any of us could see that a mere three people could defend it, work local jobs, and handle local investigations. One or more of us would have been dead within a week or two, and we'd have lost the yacht anyway.

I knew that, in my rational mind.

But that didn't stop me from being miserable about losing a possible ocean's worth of information on the Faithful. Hating the fact that we might have just given away everything we might have needed to destroy those evil creatures once and for all.

To survive another few days, we may have traded away our chance at justice.

"Grow up." I muttered to myself, a shoulder shoving open the door to the stairwell. "You're acting like a petulant child. You knew this was going to happen. Get over it, focus on what you have to do to make it home."

My ill-fitting boots struck each step, carrying me down to the first floor, then into the lobby.

The hotel was a respectably average little place. Neither gaudy nor run down, and busy enough to make its popularity clear. Several Naule in olive and blue uniforms were in line to get rooms from the Thondian receptionist, while a Mikiran security guard stood vigilant near the doors.

No one looked twice at me as I sailed past, walking into the dimly lit restaurant attached to the hotel.

Another Mikira was acting as the host, but waved me past when I muttered that I was heading for the bar. Like the lobby, the restaurant proved to be doing a fairly brisk business, with most of the tables and booths occupied.

The bar was just as full, but fortunately there was a seat in the back corner near the wall. I took it, feeling dwarfed by the Thondian woman who was sipping something electric blue on my right. Like many others she was wearing a faux-uniform, though hers was a pale green with white highlights. I couldn't tell if she was armed, though I didn't doubt that she was.

Dark lips pulled back to show me her sharp canines, head tilting to the right sharply enough to make the numerous gemstones hanging from her long ears sway with the motion.

I met her stare, the black scelera of her eyes making old nerves tremble under the surface.

She growled something in that Human language that sounded vaguely like Deutsch, but wasn't.

"Imperial, not Ark Fleet." I told her.

A slower blink came, her neck straightening slightly. When she spoke again it was in the same tongue. "A strange claim, short-fur."

The slur made my fingers twitch a little, but before I could reply the Naulian bartender came ambling over. The tan furred man tossed a coaster down with one hand, giving me a toothy smile as he did.

"Your order?" He asked.

"Whatever your best dark ale is." I replied. "Bottled."

He bobbed his head, quickly moving to a cooler and pulling out something.

...and then he turned his back to me, all four arms vanishing behind his torso for nearly thirty seconds before he turned around again. If that wasn't clue enough, I saw one of the Thondians who could see what he was doing smirk without quite looking at me.

I took a deep breath as the bartender came back over, all smiles as he set the bottle down in front of me.

"Hakka's Dark Ale." He said, stepping back. "Did you need anything else? Food perhaps?"

"I could use something, yes." Taking a second breath, I channeled Rerth and theatrically rolled my eyes. Grabbing the ale, I picked it up, rose onto my feet so that I could lean well over the bar...

...so that I could drop the full bottle at his feet. It didn't shatter dramatically like I hoped, but enough of it splashed over his shoes that he yelped, scrambling back and drawing plenty of attention all the same.

"How about an ale without whatever drugs you just put in that one?" I asked loudly, half of the bar turning in interest at the noise. "If you're going to try something like that, be less obvious about it."

The bartender gaped at me, mouth opening and closing.

I nearly hesitated when he didn't give me the angry denial I'd expected, but quickly forced myself to turn to one of the Trahcon sitting at the bar near the cooler.

"Do you mind sending me one?" I asked, pointing at her.

The woman grinned, rising up enough to reach down and grab one. She tossed it up, her tarah flexing as she called on her sorcery to fling it in a gentle arc.

I got both hands up in time to catch it, "Thanks."

She gave me a cheerful wave before returning to speak to the Human male beside her, leaving me to twist off the top. The bartender recovered enough to scowl at me, stalking over to grab the fallen bottle.

"You." He growled. "Are paying for both."

"No." I said "I'm not."

Two hands slammed on his side of the counter, pushing him up, "You *will-"*

The Thondian woman beside me casually reached out before he could finish, grabbing half the man's face in a single massive hand. Then she gave a single yank, slamming his chin into the bar hard enough to bounce his head up.

Her follow up shove was just as casual, sending his stunned frame crashing to the ground.

"You have keen eyes, for a savanna." She said, turning in that full-body way Thondians did instead of simply turning her head. Acting like absolutely nothing of note had just occurred. "An Imperial, you say? Conscript?"

"Rifle-Experienced." I said, taking an experimental sip of my ale. It was rich and heavy, the flavor honestly far better than I'd expected. "Ashe'lori."

"Yerra ul Gothin." She supplied.

"Pirate?" I asked around a second drink, making sure to leave a finger over the top when I wasn't looking at it. The last thing I needed was to get overconfident at spotting one attempt to drug me.

Those sharp, ivory teeth appeared again, this time in a clear grin. "I prefer to call myself an independent mercenary, currently self-employed due to the state of the war."

I couldn't stop a snort, even if my eyes warily returned to the groggy bartender as he got himself upright. He seemed to have learned his lesson; he staggered back, away from our little corner rather than trying to confront us again.

"Thank you, by the way." I said. "I thought I'd have to pull my gun on him."

A low chuckle came out, the towering woman bringing her own drink to her lips. She took a long sip, setting it back down before saying, "You are welcome, little savanna. I would demand an answer to a question in exchange for the debt you owe me."

I tipped my head, "I suppose I do owe you, so go ahead and ask."

"When you say Imperial, you do not mean Xentha, do you?" When I shook my head, she sailed on. "I thought as much. Then I would know what you claim to be doing here."

Ah. She thought I was lying about where I was from. Given how far of a distance it was to even the most remote Imperial outpost from here, I supposed I couldn't blame her.

I considered my answer, debating using the old cover as a deserter, then decided we were simply too far out for that to really be plausible. The truth, or an extremely shallow version of it, would have to do.

Besides, it might get me some kind of reaction.

"Abducted by a group called the Faithful." I told her. "Hardcore Trahcon supremacists. Heard of them?"

Her blink was slow, body language turning to something I couldn't read. "I have not. A mercenary group?"

"Terrorists." I corrected. "They enjoy torturing everyone who isn't a Trahcon. They're the ones who gave me the scars."

Gothin's eyes flicked to the burned skin on my face, head tipping ever so briefly left. "Unpleasant."

I shook my head, glancing down at my ale. "They're a lot farther out to sea than unpleasant. When we tried to escape they sent Kelthi that they'd put so much cyber into that their bodies were almost falling apart. Full remote control rigs, claws for hands... disgusting.... and you don't believe me."

There was the tiniest twitch of her shoulder. "Not especially. It is a unique cover, do not get me wrong, but a bit too outlandish. Still, it is not the most extreme tale I have heard from one of your kind, and I have heard many in my years out here."

144

Biting my lip for a long moment, I hazarded a guess, "You think I'm from one of your rival pirate groups."

I still couldn't read her well, at all, but something in her deep voice made me think she was either impressed, amused, or both. "Assuming you are not from the Ark Fleet's band of ship thieves, I think it most likely. It seems clear you are no slave, and after that, piracy is your species most common occupation in this galaxy."

That was true enough to depress me further, another swig of ale letting me find my voice again.

"Well, I'm not here to steal your ship." I assured her, bringing up a hand to motion to our height difference. Even with both of us sitting down I barely came up to her shoulder, and I wasn't exactly short. "I'd like to think I'd have gone after someone smaller."

Her laugh was more of a bark, but that time it was easy to tell it was genuine.

"Yes." She managed, posture losing a bit of stiffness. "I suppose you are wise enough for that, little savanna. You amuse me, and so I shall allow you to continue to sit beside me."

"Thanks." I did my best to sound like I meant it, if only because I'd definitely have backed down if she'd told me to go away. I wasn't sure if she really was a pirate or not, but that didn't change the fact that she could probably snap my neck before I could draw my gun.

Assuming she didn't just pull out whatever weapon was hidden in her uniform.

"If I may ask a question of my own?" When she gave me a permissive flick of a wrist, I asked, "I'm a bit behind on the war. What's the latest news on it?"

The next two hours passed in a blur of polite conversation, with the pirate regaling me with every major advance, retreat, and counter-attack that had taken place over the past two years. I didn't quite get as much of the full horizon as I hoped; Gothin had an understandable tendency to focus on her own raids and exploits.

I still got the basics; the Xenthan Empire and Crescent had crushed the Tears' on the rimward side of the Far Reaches, but the Tears were similarly overrunning Riush's territory on this side.

Supposedly the Tears were about to launch a major offensive of some kind, with the odds-makers sure that Terminus was the target.

"It is leaving this region wide open for operations." Gothin had told me. "Though I do not think any will risk traveling through the current nexus near Terminus for some time."

Eventually I managed to turn that discussion into asking about the local DataNet, making it sound as though I merely wanted access to keep track of the war so I could place a few wagers of my own.

Access was apparently controlled by monthly subscriptions... which were so hilariously expensive that only the wealthiest of pirate bands operating from the system could actually afford them. Which was exactly how the 'Big Four' who apparently ruled the system liked it.

I'd sighed, thanked her, and left enough cash to pay for both my drink and hers before I rose to leave.

"You are a respectable little thing, Ashe'lori." Gothin said, one of her hands catching my shoulder before I could depart. "We shall speak again."

Her tone made it an order, rather than a polite farewell.

And so my streak of making contacts in bars continued... though I had a sinking feeling that this one would prove to be more complicated to handle than the others.

XV

Bringing the cheap cup to my lips, I sipped the hot tea within. The herbal liquid helped ward off the chill in the air, and allowed me to focus on watching Kagarraht's largest spaceport.

It was our third day away from the yacht, and I was doing my best to learn everything I could about our temporary home.

At that moment, the 15th Flotilla was lifting off as a full force; the pirate bands' vessels were rising across the city. Barges for holding loot, gunships to escort them, light corvettes, and too many shuttles to count carrying crew up to the larger warships waiting in orbit.

"Heading spinward?" I asked the man who'd just sold me the tea.

A wrinkled Human elder nodded, his blue eyes following mine. "That's the rumor. Plenty of worlds without enough defenses since the Riush pulled back to protect Terminus."

I hummed around another small sip. "What kind of loot are they getting though? I wouldn't have thought colonies out here would have much of value."

The old man chuckled, "You are preaching to the choir, young lady. They'll come back with century old toys, and art that's been out of style for longer."

"And say it's the latest from Cathia." I finished with a smile, pushing the odd Human phrase to the back of my mind in case I needed to try blending in with my own kind.

"That they will." He smiled, showing teeth as weathered as his skin. "Did you need anything to eat?"

"Not today, thank you." My cup rose in salute. "Have a good evening, sir.'

"You as well, miss."

Leaving his little cart behind, I casually started walking out of the lot and back toward the street. Other food and drink vendors were beginning to pack up for the evening.

I'd honestly been a little surprised. They'd gotten excellent business from the pirate crews heading back to their ships, and from the pack members coming along to wish them good hunting.

I supposed I shouldn't have really been *that* surprised that pirates would have packs, would have blood-kin. From how Irkan described it, piracy and raiding was practically a legitimate career in the Far Reaches. Those who treated it as an honeset profession would naturally have packs, and would seek to leave them in the relative safety of worlds like Kagarraht.

A world just large enough, teeming with enough pirates, that no one else was going to raid it.

Sure, by my standards it was practically lawless. No one from the hotel had come pounding on our door to evict us for what I'd done in the bar; casual attempts at drugging and enslaving people was apparently common, and reacting with violence was considered totally normal.

Apparently Kagarraht was still floating somewhere near the surface compared to many of the worlds around it, which made very sure I never wanted to visit those other planets in these Reaches. As it was, everyone I'd met easily assumed I was a fellow pirate just from my species, something I didn't bother correcting them on.

I sipped more of my tea, humming to myself as I left the parking lot that the food vendors had anchored themselves within. The setting sun had the streets in this part of the city slowing down already; something else that suited me just fine.

My strides lengthened, eyes up and alert as I moved.

For once the paranoia didn't end up paying off. No one jumped me on the way back, or threw spells at me from an alley. A couple of Naule seemed to consider me from the far side of the street, but either my height or the wary tension in my body made them think twice about approaching.

A block from the hotel I found my next destination; a place Johanna had called a 'hole in the wall restaurant'. I didn't really get what she meant by that, but it was a pretty small little building squeezed in between another hotel and a grocer.

There wasn't much space; a single long counter and a pair of tiny tables, but nearly every seat was taken by Trahcon.

My entrance caused a chime to sound, and the woman behind the counter got up on a step to see over her customers.

"Ah!" She beamed, tarah rising. "The scarred and handsome savanna did return after all!"

"Told you I would!" I had to raise my own voice over the general rumble of conversation. "Is the order ready?"

A gray hand waved toward the register at the far end. "Come on."

I had to turn sideways to fit between the chairs and the wall, even with a few of the patrons trying to scoot in a bit to give me more space. A few others didn't, but that seemed less because of my species and more because they were simply too occupied in their meals or their conversations.

"You need a bigger building." I said once I finally made it to her.

The cashier grinned, already bringing my order up on the small screen. "We're having one built, but it's not ready yet. Let's see... two orders of Hoallen Bowls, and then one Redburn Loaf. Did you want to add anything else while you're here?"

I shook my head, "No thanks."

"You sure?" She added a bit of a purr to the last word, "We have plenty of alcohol."

"I'm sure." I said with a smile. "Maybe next time."

"I'll hold you to that." She reached out, taking the hard currency that I pulled out of my pocket. A bit of counting later and I had change back, along with a heavy bag of hot food.

Squeezing back out was just as difficult as getting in had been, but it wasn't a long walk back to the hotel. A brisk walk got me inside within a few minutes, striding into the lobby just as the sun finally finished setting.

For the first time since we'd arrived, that lobby was actually pretty quiet, and the evening's security guard was lounging near the restaurant's door. The Mikira didn't even seem to watch me walk past, more occupied buffing the stubby claws on one hand.

Taking the stairs as always, I used my elbow to get the door open on our floor, and I would admit to being relieved when I didn't see anyone else in the hall.

It was probably stupid, but I didn't think I'd ever be comfortable in hotel hallways again. Not after what had happened on Trinity.

With my hands occupied holding my tea and the food, I settled for kicking our room's door to announce my return. Irkan opened it after the fifth boot, chuckling in amusement when he realized what I'd been doing.

"That would explain the odd note to the knock." He rumbled, stepping back to let me in. "Perhaps you should have had one of us accompany you after all."

"One human draws less attention." I told him, finally relaxing when he shut the door behind me. "Can you take the food?"

He could and did, setting it on the little dresser while I walked over to the bed Johanna was lounging on.

"Here, and yes, it's filled with too much sugar." I said, offering her the tea.

She beamed, eagerly taking it... until she felt the weight. "I said you could have a *sip*, Ashe! This is half empty!"

"And it was good." I grinned, sitting down to work on getting my boots off. "Plus it would have been weird if I'd bought it and not drank any."

Johanna pouted around a few quick sips of her own.

Fortunately Irkan had the bag open by then, and tromped over with our bowls full of blue noodles and bits of fish. Taking mine, I waited for him to head back to get his own meal before getting up again, walking over the desk in the corner.

Hopping up onto it, I settled the bowl in my lap and pulled the disposable utensils off the sides.

We all dug in quickly, relishing food that we hadn't had to make. Food that wasn't bread, or dried meats, or the kinds of things we'd been forced to eat on Last Stop. That lasted until the heavy spices started to get to me, forcing me to grab a bottle of water, and give one to Johanna.

After that, I slurped down one more mouthful of noodles, then finally gave my report.

"So," I coughed a little against the heat filling my mouth and making my eyes water, "Uh. Yeah. I talked to a few of the people watching the departure, and they confirmed what Ul Gothin's said. DataNet access is strictly controlled. Have to be one of the Big Four pirate bands, or else arrange a deal."

Johanna bobbed her head, a long noodle vanishing between her lips. "Wow this is hot. Um, could we hire a hacker?"

I shook my head. "I tried to imply that, but the dockworker said that's the kind thing that gets you and the hacker shot. And all of the hackers make better money working for the pirates unlocking things they steal. I said I got it, and changed the subject."

"So no chance unless we decide to work for pirates." She said.

Irkan huffed, swallowing the bit of whatever he'd been chewing on. A 'Redburn Loaf' was apparently... I had no idea what it was, to be honest. A cross between burnt meat and bread was the closest thing I could compare it to.

It didn't look appetizing at all to me, but he was attacking it with every sign of real enjoyment.

"Doubtful even if we were so employed." He spoke around another sharp bite. "We would be those of the lowest rank, hardly those who would be given access."

"Yeah." I agreed, nodding to him. "Not without proving ourselves, or working for them for a set period of time or something. I'm going to ease up on that for a while, don't want to draw too much attention, but I'll see if there's any kind of deal we could make."

Johanna pointed a fork at me. "What about your new pirate girlfriend? Could she help?"

I snorted at the term. "Pretty sure I'm more of an amusing pet. Something to entertain her during shore leave, and to be forgotten once they leave port. And I'm pretty sure she's still convinced I'm some kind of spy from a rival group, one she's keeping close for now.

"Sounds like a Thondian." She muttered, "Still, what about her? Does she have access?"

I gave her a flat look at her usual anti-Thondian attitude, but I didn't feel like arguing with her about it. She knew my opinions, just like I knew that the bad blood between the Ark Fleet and the Thondians went back for more of a century.

Not that long by Imperial standards, but plenty long by most other people's. I wasn't going to change her mind anytime soon.

"She doesn't." I provided. "She does data pulls from other systems, and only comes here to sell loot and get her ship worked on. Right now she's loosely affiliated with the Star-Runners, but she gave me the impression that's a temporary thing."

Which it might or might not. From what I understood, a *lot* of Thondian culture involved posturing. Making yourself seem like the biggest shark in the river at all times. So... maybe she was a temporary contractor, or maybe she was drowning in a debt owed to that pirate band.

I'd need to do more research to know either way.

Before I could say as much, Irkan's attention returned to me. "If she has her own ship or ships, that may present options. Would she be interested in providing us passage?"

I hesitated, then admitted. "I haven't asked, and I don't know if I'd trust her. Or her crew, since I don't know any of them. Can't say I know her either. Not after just a few nights of chatting. Give me some time to ask other people about her, see if the local Net has anything."

Irkan's head bobbed. "I believe Ashe'lori should do so. If nothing else, such a search might result in discovering other pirates who might be enticed to accept an easy charter."

My shoulder rolled, "Working on it, but if you want me to be sure that we won't just get tossed out of an airlock while they keep our money, it's going to take a while. And I won't be able to guarantee anything even then."

"I know, I know." He waved his food to show he understood. "This sailor merely seeks to expand our options."

I twisted my fork around, getting more noodles onto it while I spoke. "Agreed. What about your search? Any FTL shuttles we could buy and fuel up as soon as possible?"

Irkan gave Johanna a look, betraying that he'd passed that part of the search onto her while I'd spent the day exploring and talking with whoever would talk to me. She grimaced around another mouthful of noodles, quickly swallowing so that she could speak.

"Good... woah." A hand grabbed her water, bringing the bottle to her lips. She guzzled a bit, swirling it around to try and help. It still took a few long breaths before she managed to resume, "Uh. The good news is that there's a few for sale on public auctions, and it seems like that's a pretty routine event. But the bad news is... um, that they're public auctions."

"Auctions?" I blinked, "As in actual bidding? We can't just buy them?"

"Yeah, bids only, no direct sales. Some kind of agreement between the pirates to make sure all of them have a chance to buy stuff." She shrugged, glancing down. "I checked the last few sales, and... they were kind of far out of our price range."

My fingers tightened a bit around my utensil. Shoving the spicy food between my lips gave me something else to focus on, until I swallowed.

"Ashahn's...." I exhaled, feeling the burning on my tongue as I did. "...blood. How far out of our price range?"

"A little less than double." Johanna said.

That wasn't as bad as I'd feared, if I was being honest... even if it made me turn to glower at Irkan. "I think we got cheated on how much we got for the yacht if a stolen shuttle is going for double."

A grumpy little noise was his initial response, though he followed it up with actual words. "It wasn't capable of leaving atmosphere, Ashe'lori. Nor is it a vessel whose parts are easily located in this region of the galaxy. We were lucky to get what we did."

I wasn't entirely sure that was true, but it was too late to do anything about it. So instead of complaining further, I ate the last of my noodles, setting my empty bowl aside when I finished.

That left me free to put everything before us. "All right. So, here's how I'm seeing the horizon. We've got a few advantages. We have actual credits, and the Faithful either don't have agents here, or haven't found us yet."

Johanna slurped down the last of her noodles, coughing as I had before speaking, "Guessing not here. Just from how fast they found us on Aonu, I mean."

I pointed a finger at her, "I'm pretty sure about that too. They probably only keep long-term agents of their own on hub worlds like Aonu, or on colonies close to their operations like Cashihto."

"Relatively close." Irkan corrected.

My finger swung to him. "Either way, I think we finally have some time to tread water, to recover. The problem is that's really all the wind we have in our sails. We've got no way to call for help, and we need double our current money if we expect to afford a new ship capable of FTL travel. Maybe we can get lucky, not need as much cash, but we might also get unlucky and need more."

Irkan let out an affirming chirp, Johanna nodding in agreement.

"I think..." I hesitated, then said. "I think we have to accept that we've got trackers in us right now. I'll try and search out a doctor, but if we pick the wrong clinic we might wake up on a different kind of slave barge."

A long, low growl from Irkan. "Agreed. A risk not worth taking yet."

Johanna made her own noise of agreement. "That leaves us with focusing on money?"

"Earning more of it in specific." I said, crossing my arms. "That means that we need jobs, and means that we need a more affordable place to stay than this hotel. Irkan? Any progress on that?"

"Jobs?" His long head flicked in a negative. "Nothing I am certain of yet. Apartments are more promising. There are three that shall make our stay comfortable, and minimize the amount of currency spent. I hope to inspect them and their surroundings tomorrow."

Johanna flicked her eyes between us, "Do we all go?"

That was an easy decision. "Yeah. Let's make sure we all agree since we'll be here for a few months unless we get lucky. How affordable are they?"

Irkan provided a number, making me blink a few times. "That low?"

"My searches lead me to believe that few choose to live here long term." He said. "There are many open homes, and not enough tenants."

I hummed at that. I'd seen plenty of families out and about today, but this was a pretty big city. Maybe too big for the amount of people now living in it. Something else to add to my list of things to check.

Johanna rubbed her chin, speaking up before I could, "Buyer's market. That's something, . If we can get decent paying jobs, keep our rent low, might have a chance to start attending ship auctions in a month or two, instead of five or six."

"Agreed." It was my turn to nod. "We stay focused on the project. Aim to get off planet as quickly as we can."

There wasn't any disagreement.

Interlude
Rerth'riah

I managed three steps on the roof of the Imperial Embassy on Alum before the resident Ambassador came storming forward, her bronze tinted robes thrown back from the shuttle's exhaust.

Her expression was somewhere between annoyed and furious, a sentiment backed up by the crackling of imminent sorcery in the air.

"Ambassador." I greeted her, offering a salute even if it wasn't technically required. "Did you-"

"What in Irihan's fucking name is this?" She spat, cutting me off. "They finally, *finally* send help after years of silence, and it's a single Aspects' damned Operative!?"

Blinking rapidly, I tried to soothe the waters. "I have plenty of support, Ambassador, and the backing of Void Lord Delarah. We're-"

"Delarah?" She demanded, eyes narrowing as she interrupted me once again. "She was in exile in the Wastes. What is she doing commanding Intelligence assets?"

"Intelligence is being disbanded." I said, voice sharpening with my own annoyance. "All vetted assets are being transferred to Void Fleets until the Torlah and the Imperial Circle authorize a replacement organization."

Her tarah flicked outwards once, then twice, her jaw finally clenching shut.

I kept speaking before she could get over it and interrupt me for a third time.

"We are here to investigate what happened to Director Ashul'tasir, arrest and interrogate any remaining members of her staff, and conduct investigations on the Void Lord's orders." Bringing a hand up, I motioned for the soldiers waiting in the shuttle to get moving. "Included in that is a hold order for you and your entire staff until your loyalty is confirmed."

Those tarah rose even further as Huvu'ithi and her troops began storming out.

To my surprise she didn't resist when the officer came for her directly, a nullification bar in her hands. It was locked into place on her tarah within moments, quickly followed by standard handcuffs locking her hands behind her back.

Another wave of my hand sent Holde to guide the restrained Ambassador inside, making sure to keep her calm, Jet joining me in striding along in their wake.

More shuttles were coming down all over the lovely grounds surrounding the building, disgorging men and women in the black armor of the Void Fleets. I paused at the edge of the stairs leading down into the building, making sure that the cordon was perfect.

"Ithi does good work." I said finally. "The Voiders seem to respect her as well."

Jet chuckled, "Don't sound so surprised, boss. She might have been invited to join them if she hadn't gotten blown up on her first combat mission against the Concordat."

"If she hadn't lost her entire pack and developed Lost Hunter, you mean." I corrected him, turning away from the view. "Go. I want this building cut off from the DataNet and any local access."

He bobbed his head, using his extra arms to propel himself along at speeds I couldn't hit without running. My packmate vanished down the stairs while I followed at a far more sedate pace.

The stairs leading down from the shuttle pads lead to one of the more ostentatious rooms that I'd ever seen. Three artificial waterfalls were hard at work keeping the air moist, while little canals carried their water to gardens filled with miniaturized trees from the Homeworld itself.

Paintings of past Torlah and great Void Lords were strategically placed so that one was always in sight. Enormous floor to ceiling windows were done up with plenty of bronze and golden decoration, letting everyone see the equally overdone gardens waiting just outside.

It was about as subtle as a hurricane.

Ithi was waiting for me on the ground floor, her rifle slung once again, though she'd kept her helmet on.

"All staff accounted for." She reported, "No resistance besides confusion."

"No attempts at escape?" I asked.

A quick shake of her helm. "Nothing. If anything, I'd say a lot of them are... relieved."

Relieved. I hadn't expected that, but if I combined that with both the Ambassador's attitude, and Director Tasir's final desperate attempts to contact home...

...it was easy to see the masts on that particular horizon.

"Ensure double guards on the staff." I ordered. "Unless I'm wrong, the Faithful have still been interdicting communication between this embassy and home."

"Yes, Operative." She started to turn, paused, then reported, "We've got an incoming group of aircraft. One aircar escorted by three gunships.'

My eyes narrowed at once. "Identification?"

"Crescent." Came the reply.

That was faster than I'd expected. I'd hoped to have a few hours to work in peace before the latest Cathian warlord tried to swim about in Imperial business.

"Contact the Admiral, get the second wave released." I said, "Bring everyone inside until reinforcements arrive."

She moved off, helmet only slightly muffling her bellows for defensive positions. I shifted as well, taking partial cover behind one of the ornate waterfalls, focusing my attention on the broad windows.

It didn't take long before I saw the four aircraft coming in from the direction of Alum's capital city.

That the Crescent was sending someone to confront us over our actions didn't surprise me. Alum was governed by complicated treaties, and was *technically* an independent world governed by an Executive Board. In truth, however, the Crescent of Cathia ruled the system, and everyone, including the Empire, knew it.

It was why I'd fought down the urge to descend by stealth, why I hadn't given in to the temptation to send out teams to capture every off duty worker, every packmate, and every Imperial citizen I could find.

I focused on keeping my breathing even, watching as the distant aircar landed just outside of the grounds... and a single tall figure emerged, already striding in our direction.

"Gunships?" I called, trying to locate them through the low sun.

One of the soldiers called back, "Circling the compound."

My eyes returned to the solitary figure, observing as they walked right to the embassy's gate before stopping.

Shaking my head, I took a deep breath and let it out. "Posturing. Everyone maintain positions and orders. I will go and speak with them."

Holde's voice came across the comm-piece covering my left tarah. *"You sure?"*

"Yes. Keep the prisoners secured and under watch. Jet? I want your first results when I get back, and send a signal to open the gate. Ithi?"

"Covering you." She replied.

Nodding a silent thanks, I took a few heartbeats to straighten my uniform, make sure my pistol was secure on my left hip. Then I started walking, moving around the armored soldiers taking cover wherever they could.

They stood, knelt, and crouched as silent, immovable sentinels. A sign of professionalism and control that was more reassuring than any words when I stepped outside.

My boots struck the stone path leading from the building to the slowly lowering gate, hands folding behind my back as I approached the woman waiting for me.

She wasn't as tall as I'd first thought. My height, perfectly average, as was her build. Her features wouldn't have been anything of note either, except for her eyes. They were a striking turquoise, somehow bright yet deep in a way that made it difficult to look away. White tattoos drew even more attention to them, curling down her cheeks, chin, and neck before vanishing under the silver robes she wore.

Those ornate robes, and the silken belt holding a sword to her side, betrayed her occupation.

I stopped my march a few feet away, giving her a polite incline of my head. "Honored Priestess."

She regarded me without any particular emotion, speaking with the obnoxiously sharp accent of the local Trahcon. "Operative. What are you doing here?"

"Dealing with internal Imperial problems." I replied, keeping my voice even. "Which we will resolve as swiftly as possible."

One tarah flexed in a lazy little motion. "I will repeat the question. What are you doing on Alum, daughter of Empire?"

My own lowered, a bit of my power trembling through them. "Dealing with internal Imperial problems, priestess."

A deep breath came as she felt my sorcery shifting... and then she responded in kind, drawing in power...

...and I felt my mouth dry as she *kept* drawing in power, until it felt like the air itself was going to combust.

"I," She said, only the slightest shaking of her tarah betraying the fact that she was holding onto enough energy to incinerate me and everything within a dozen yards of me. More power than I'd ever felt a living soul hold onto in my life.

"I," she repeated, voice hardening, "am Uko'kolkris'irkah, daughter of Iriahn'kolkris, Queen of the Crescent. I speak with her voice in her absence."

I needed another deep breath to straighten my spine. To remind myself that I was a battle-hardened Guide, not a scared child.

"I," I said, mimicking her tones. "am Rerth'riah, Operative of the Eighth Void Fleet, commissioned by Chashti'tahze Sever'ahmiar'delarah herself. It is by her order that I am here, and by her orders that I will proceed."

If this Kolkris was impressed by my response, she didn't show it. "To what waters do your orders lead, Operative? Your Empire has not cared about events in these Reaches in centuries. Not even when your own spies were being slaughtered or else made to vanish."

My fingers clenched at the blatant attack. "We were blinded, but are blind no longer."

"I doubt that." She murmured, one of her own hands casually coming to rest on the hilt of her sword. "Your kind are always blind."

"As yours are always consumed by greed." I replied. "Do you want to trade further barbs about our cultures, or may we focus?"

The comment didn't quite draw the reaction I expected. I assumed she would react with anger, but instead she actually smirked, visibly relaxing.

"Not as bland and stoic as the others. Well, perhaps this won't be boring then." Fingers drummed her weapon's hilt. "You are here to hunt the Matriarch then?"

Matriarch? The name or title was a new one.

"Our business is our own."

"And you are right back to being both foolish and boring." She exhaled, shaking her head. "Imperial, you may speak with me now, or with my mother once she returns from her campaign against the Scarlet Tears. I assure you that I am far less likely to make you scream and beg for mercy."

My eyes narrowed, "The Empire will work with the Crescent regarding our investigations, but only when we have completed our initial work within the Embassy."

Kolkris'irkah huffed, "Stubborn bitch. You are aware that Tasir was working with our Whisperers on the Matriarch problem, are you not?"

"I am aware that Director Tasir was coordinating with your people." I replied. "I am also aware that she was betrayed and abducted."

That got me another tarah flick. "You are the most irritating combination of amusing and annoying. Very well, do step aside so that I might observe you at work."

I kept up my glare, "The embassy is closed."

Her lips curled on one side, a single lazy step bringing her across the gate. A second brought her closer, and only me shifting my arms, holding a hand up to block her stopped the priestess from moving right into my personal space.

It didn't stop her from leaning in, the power still constrained around her making my tarah begin to shake regardless of my self control. "You have one Void-Ship and one Long-Ship in orbit, with a few dozen soldiers on the ground. I have two dreadnoughts and their attendant battle-groups, dozens of GTS batteries, an entire army, and fighters ready to intercept those reinforcements you tried to call in."

My teeth ground as she leaned in even further, smirking as she dropped her voice to a whisper.

"Now," she went on quietly, "Either you have Delarah lurking outside this system, ready to storm in to back your play... in which case I will have to accept your refusal. Or you don't, and you will get out of my way before I lose my temper."

I worked my jaw for several long heartbeats, a vicious oath finally escaping my lips. "Ashahn's fucking blood. They told me your blood-pack was obnoxious, but you're even more arrogant than I thought possible."

She smiled as if I'd just paid her a compliment. "You yield?"

I had no idea if they'd actually attack or not, but if they did...

...if they did, they would win, and they would win quickly. Likely quickly enough that none of us would survive, neither ship able to escape. And with the Crescent in full control of the local DataNet, they could probably cover it up well enough.

Not forever, Delarah wouldn't accept her people dying like that, but that wouldn't save us.

That wouldn't save Ashe.

"This Matriarch." I said, still not moving. "Is she affiliated with a group known as the Faithful?"

Her head tilted, balance shifting even if she didn't retreat. "I have not heard the term before. Are they Trahcon supremacists with a penchant for mental manipulation and control, who prefer explosive suicide to capture?"

"That's a yes then." I exhaled, and finally turned, motioning with an arm. "The Imperial Embassy is open to the Crescent. I believe we have a mutual enemy to discuss."

"It would seem that we do."

XVI
Ashe'lori

I was comfortably lurking in the back of the shipyard's main conference hall when a man finally returned to the stage after a long delay. The broad Thondian elder moved with a bit of a stoop, but his voice was strong even without the speakers that carried it to every corner.

"Our last auction for the day." He said without any preamble. "A Conquest Model Forty Five personal freighter. In full working condition, and I am assured that the prior owners were hosed off of the walls appropriately."

Dark laughter ran through the crowd. I didn't join them; three months on Kagarraht hadn't made me any more comfortable with pirate humor. I doubted that three decades would.

Their sense of humor wasn't why I was here, surrounded by people I was increasingly sure I wanted nothing to do with. No. I was here to try and gauge the price for the kind of ship that we were looking to buy as soon as possible.

The man running today's events went on once the seas had calmed. "We shall begin the bidding."

I listened intently when the first offer from a Naulian clan was half of our current fortune. They were promptly countered by a Thondian house who raised the bid by several thousand local credits. No one else seemed interested in a ship as small as a personal freighter, leaving the two of them to rapidly go back and forth.

"Sold to House Collaxix. Pick it up in Lot Twenty-Two by nightfall or it will be resold during our following session." Two wrinkled hands clapped together. "That concludes this month's sales. The next regular auction will be in thirty days."

My feet were already carrying me to the door, getting me out of there before the crowd could really begin to get moving.

Loosening my light coat, I made sure I could reach for the pistol in its shoulder holster if I had to. Not that I really expected to need the weapon inside the city's main spaceport, but the paranoia was becoming a habit. Three attempted muggings while simply doing your day job would do that on its own, even without all of my other reasons to be constantly on alert.

It was a short walk to the nearest exit, where the warming air of a late spring was waiting.

Unzipping the jacket the rest of the way, I took a moment to tap my wrist-comp online. It connected to the speaker settled in my left ear, a quiet chime repeating itself as the system made the call.

Three went past before Irkan answered, *"Ashe. How close?"*

"Depends on the model." I reported, "Only two ships were sold in the size range you gave me, but we're very close for both. A light freighter just went for seven thousand more than we have, and a personal yacht went for three thousand more."

"Interesting." He rumbled, *"That is good cause for optimism. Were those totals off our total credits, or did that include my padding for fuel and supplies?"*

I huffed, marching down the street. "Of course I included your fuel and food estimates. I'm not so desperate to leave that I'd forget we need those to make it anywhere."

A low chuckle sounded in my ear. *"There are days when I wonder."*

Another huff served as my only response to the comment, leaving my words free to carry us further along. "I think we'll have a real chance next month."

"Assuming that any such vessels are among those being sold."

"Assuming that." I allowed, "But there's been at least two every month we've been here. Thirty more days and I really do think we'll finally be leaving."

"Something that we all eagerly look forward to." He said in reply. *"I must prepare to retrieve Johanna for escort to our temporary home. I shall inform her of the good news."*

I glanced at my wrist again, checking the time. She'd be just getting off from the restaurant, just as Irkan had just finished his day shift as a guard for the very same hotel we'd once stayed in.

Sadly that meant I was due to begin my own job sooner than I'd have liked. "All right. I'm heading to work, I'll see you both when I get back to the station."

He chirped an affirmative, which was about the only words of his native language I'd been able to decipher, and then cut the channel.

Three months.

Three months on Kagarraht, with one or two more to go. Thirty to sixty days.

After that we'd have another month of travel, give or take a week, and then we would arrive on Lushrivers. A world where we would be safe, be able to relax, and not have to do things like count every credit we spent on food, drink, or clothes. Where we wouldn't have to sleep on cheap cots in an apartment that was bare walls and floors.

It might even be a world where I didn't have to look at every person on the street, checking to see what kind of weapon they had. Evaluate how likely they were to come after me. What the odds were that they were an agent of either the Faithful or the local slaving guilds.

Whether or not they were one of ul Gothin's crew stalking me.

To say that I was looking forward to leaving would be a massive understatement. That wasn't to say that I wanted to spend another three to five months on Lushrivers... I really, really didn't. I wanted to go home, to the Empire, to Rerth, and Holde, and Jet. To call Huvu and catch up, to call Fyth and hear her voice again.

I wanted to go to Altair and just lose myself for a month or three.

The Empire may not have been perfect, I knew that better than anyone, but even the worst Imperial colony seemed a paradise compared to a planet like Kagarraht.

A mixed group of Naulians and Humans seemed ready to prove that. I'd noticed them at an intersection, loudly bickering about which bar they should go to next. Despite the fact that I was on the other side of the street, one of Humans spotted me striding past, smacking one of the others on the arm and pointing my way.

My brief hope that they'd assume I was a fellow pirate from my annoyed stalk was dashed upon the rocks when one of the Naulian men laughed. Within a breath the entire group had set off, turning to try and keep pace with me on their side of the road.

Pursing my lips, I lengthened my strides without looking like I was in a hurry or nervous. A little bit of subterfuge I'd gotten a lot of practice at these past few months.

It was a trick that I had figured out on my own during my time with packs who didn't want me, and one I'd perfected here.

A trick I'd learned from Rerth had been how to quickly map out a city in my head; to not rely on maps loaded on my wrist-comp. To walk and drive the streets, to recognize buildings, to feel which areas were safe, and which weren't.

I knew exactly where I was, and the best place to find shelter against the storm. At the next intersection I turned right, just in time as the men finally began to cross the street, one of them calling out something in a Human language that made the others laugh.

I didn't look back. Instead I looked to the people ahead of me, to the other side of the street. Watched the way their heads moved when they realized a pursuit was in the offering. That gave me a good idea at how far behind me the men were, telling me they hadn't started running me down. Not yet at least.

Keeping my strides long for the next block, I ignored a more understandable call in Caranat for me to 'start running, we want to see that ass shake!'.

The sudden attention from a driver cruising past warned me that they'd begun to lose interest in a slow chase just as I neared the next corner.

Fortunately for me my destination was right there, and a glance through the windows told me that I was in luck today.

Stepping through the bar's open door, I slipped past the harried looking Naulian woman acting as the hostess. Two long strides brought me to the very first table that was packed with pirates already throwing back drinks.

Not letting myself hesitate, I went straight for the woman at the head of the table, planting my hands on both of her broad shoulders from behind.

Yerra ul Gothin started to go for her gun at once; only the cackling laughs of her personal crew, and the way I started to dig my fingers into her muscles had her abruptly stop the motion.

"My apologies, Captain." I said, hearing the men entering the bar right behind me. "I was overdue to pay my respects."

The Thondian woman slowly relaxed, sinking back into her chair with a deep chuckle. "You are greatly overdue, Lori. Continue, and I may forgive your alien failings."

I dipped my head to the left in a clumsy imitation of a Thondian show of deference, but the approving whistles and grunts from her officers told me I'd done the right thing. Even if she couldn't see me, their reaction had her relaxing further.

The way the floor creaked and bent under my feet warned me that someone was behind me. I started to tense in preparation for being grabbed, only for whoever it was to curse just loudly enough for me to hear them. A few breaths later I felt them move away, the grumbling of several men fading as they departed.

"Who were they?" Gothin asked, still not turning.

"Drunks looking for someone to play with, I think." I replied, making sure not to let up on my massage.

Her drink rose to her lips, making me adjust my fingers as she took a drink. "And you fled from them?"

"Seven of them, one of me, and they were all armed." I said in my defense. "I didn't like the odds."

There was a deep huff, her heavy mug returning to the table. "Then you should be better prepared, little savanna."

I bit my tongue. Gothin liked me, in her own way, but she didn't need to know that there'd been several arguments about that in my pack. We all may have agreed that we needed more guns and protection if we could get them, that wasn't the issue.

The issue was how to do so. Irkan was in favor of simply buying them legitimately, and accepting that we'd need another few weeks worth of living on Kagarraht to make up that expense. Johanna was in favor of simply stealing them from whoever we could.

I'd been delaying. Spending money on things as expensive as shield-belts, or full armor, was something I really didn't want to do. At the same time, stealing it carried the implied risk that we'd be caught or implicated. That could make our stay here even more uncomfortable.

Right now using Gothin as our guardian was not ideal, but she was a powerful asset to have. She was a middling player, locally, from what I could tell, with a small fleet of corvettes that she used to raid on behalf of whichever of the larger pirate groups was paying better at the time.

"It's on our list of things to get, when and if we can." I said.

A finger tapped the side of her mug. "My crew are given proper protection."

I let out a sigh, "We're-"

"You'd be well paid." She spoke over me, "You know I value your insights, even if I do not believe your tale. A Mikiran pilot would be welcome, and I would even tolerate your Ark Fleet whore if she proves she truly knows her way around a ship."

My fingers pinched down on her skin, voice heating up. "Don't call Johanna that."

Gothin let out a deep huff, not even seeming to notice the pinch. "One year of service and I would take you to Alum."

"No, Gothin." I snapped, in the same tone. "It's not happening, so drop it."

There was one of those high-pitched, almost seething whistles from her lips. Before I could try to dodge, one of her hands snapped up, seizing my wrist.

"Ashahn's blood!" I hissed when she tightened down, shoes dragging when she effortlessly hauled me around her seat, her grip too strong to even think about resisting.

I swallowed as she pulled me into her lap, leaning in, forcing me to duck my head to the left if I didn't want her face pressing against mine.

"Watch. Your. Tone." Her growl was perfectly audible, her crew silent. Watching. "I tolerate your Human insolence because you gave me excellent service when you analyzed that data last month. It allowed me to plan our last raid in most profitable way."

"I-"

Her other hand shot up, wrapping around my throat. That grip tightened as well, betraying just how easy it would be for her to cut off my air. My own reflexes had me starting to inch my free hand toward my pistol... a motion that made her squeeze my wrist and neck a bit harder.

I shut up and stopped moving.

Gothin took a long breath, baring her exceedingly sharp canines when she resumed speaking. "My fondness for your mind does not give you leave to speak to me in that tone. Do you understand?"

My chin jerked in the smallest nod.

"Good." She said, though her words were still a growl. "Corrak? Get all of the information from our last run onto a tablet. Lori is going to go over it for us in repayment for us saving her, and in repayment for her lack of respect."

Her second in command grinned, already rifling through the bag hanging from his chair to find what he needed.

At the same time Gothin finally eased up, letting me get air into my lungs.

"I..." I cleared my throat, coughing once. "Have to get to work. I'm not saying I won't do it!"

She'd started to tense, but the quick addition merely had her tap a finger against the side of my neck in a silent warning.

"Give me a few days." I asked. "And I'll tell you what I think of whatever you send me, just like last time."

"...good." The finger trailed up, over my jaw, making me shudder a little in discomfort. "You remain clever, but weak, Ashe'lori. You are lucky I do not simply take your wrist-comp, and drain the funds you so desperately hide away."

I swallowed again, pushing my way out of her lap. She didn't stop me, her expression unreadable as I stood up.

The reminder that she knew what our plan was made my hands clench. I hadn't told her, I wasn't a fool, but she'd learned it anyway. Learned it because the heavy-set Thondian man at the far end of the table could hack nearly any system on Kagarraht, and she'd had him stalking us in the local Net the moment I'd drawn her attention.

She knew we were hardly spending any money. Knew I went to the monthly auctions for stolen ships.

Gothin was more than intelligent enough to place the sail on the horizon from there... and more than ruthless enough to start exploiting that knowledge for her own gain as much as we let her.

But there were lines.

One more clearing of my throat got rid of the uncomfortable sensation there, and let me speak clearly. "You could try, but you know I would die before I let you do that."

The pirate captain curled her dark lips in what could only technically be called a smile. "Yes. That is your final step, and that is why I push you to it every time we speak."

"Because you know I'll give in so long as it doesn't stop us from leaving when we can." I muttered, unable to stop myself from glaring a little. "Because you know that we need someone to protect us once every few tides. Without you around, we'd have been enslaved or killed weeks ago."

"Yes." She repeated, a bit more smugly that time. "That is the way of things in these Reaches. The Paragons favored me, the day we met. I intend to honor them by exploiting you for all you're worth for as long as I can. Be glad

I am not doing worse."

The truly sad thing was that I... was. Glad for her restraint, and glad for her protection.

I didn't like her. Didn't like the way she seemed fond of hauling me around, touching my skin and fur. How she insisted I prove myself by going over the traffic analysis of potential targets for her raids, making me complicit in her piracy.

But I'd been telling the truth about what her protection had meant to us. Without her I'd have been chipped by the Slaver's Guild in our second week. Killed by the Lort Gang in week five. Johanna would have been taken that same week. Irkan would have been slain with sorcery by Crescent deserters last month.

I'd have probably been raped today.

Rerth had once told me that an Intelligence Agent didn't have the luxury of liking the people she worked with. That we'd have to make deals with people we hated in order to get what we needed.

"Thank you." I forced the words out, stepping around her to take the tablet from Corrak. "I'll ping you when I've gone over this."

Gothin tilted her head to the right, smirking, and saying nothing else when I left, hoping I could make it to the shuttle depot on time to start my evening shift.

XVII

Hands shook me awake far too early in the morning, my own trying to bat them away before I realized it was Johanna leaning over me.

"Hey." She leaned back a little to avoid my initial flailing, "Come on, Ashe. I need your help. We've got a problem."

I didn't need more than her last word to wake up fully. I was sitting up, grabbing for the pistol next to my cot before she finished standing. "Who? Pirates? Faithful?"

Johanna shook her head, "Neither. It's Irkan."

Blinking, I stopped halfway through getting up as well, "Irkan? Was he attacked?"

"No. He..." My friend hesitated, then said more quietly. "...a ship came in with news. King Yulaz is dead. He got killed by mercenaries during his invasion of Terminus."

More blinking. "The Scarlet Tears' elder King? The one we were going to try and convince about the Faithful? *That* King?"

Her nod was solemn. "Yeah."

"...Ashahn's blood." I groaned, fingers gently putting my gun back onto the floor. That way I had both of them free to bury my face into, rubbing furiously. "Iriahn's.... ugh. What about the other King? He said there's two of them."

"I don't know." Johanna replied, "He just told me that the King was dead, and then he stormed off to the bar down the street."

That didn't really surprise me. Irkan hadn't told me nearly as much about himself as Johanna had, and I knew next to nothing about King Yulaz. What I did know was that Irkan had been absolutely confident that said King would both hear us out and believe us, and that he'd never spoken of the man with anything but the utmost respect.

If I'd heard that the Torlah had been killed...

...I'd have gone straight to a bar as well, even though it couldn't have been more than an hour past dawn.

Exhaling into my palms, I let my hands fall into my lap. "All right. Let's get dressed and go get him before he gets too drunk."

Johanna nodded, gently helping me get to my feet. A check of the time confirmed that I'd been asleep for a mere three hours. That was my excuse when it took me a second try to get my pants on, my companion not hesitating to snicker when we both realized I was halfway through putting them on backwards.

I got them on properly, and made sure to get my shirt on the right way on my first try. After that both of us grabbed our pistols; hers going onto her belt, mine in the shoulder holster. Armed as best we could be, we headed out into the early morning light.

"How was work?" Johanna asked as we hit the apartment's exterior stairs, making our way down from the third floor we lived on.

"Only had to reroute around one gun fight in the streets." I shook my head, really wishing I had a cup of tea in my hands. "So not too bad. No one tried to steal the bus either."

There was a quiet noise of approval. "Finally using the right word for a bus."

I elbowed her gently as we turned down another flight of the stairs, "Shuttle *is* the right word for one if we were in the Empire. And yes, I know we're not in the Empire right now, you don't have to say it."

She rolled her eyes at me. "I put up with the constant references to water and sailing and rivers, don't I?"

"You do." I allowed. "Not that I know any other references to put into my language."

"You would if we spoke Deutsch more often." She grumbled. "I don't care that Irkan can't understand it. Every other day, my language."

I sighed at the familiar argument, changing my words to those of her native tongue. "All right, but not every other day. When it's just us two, we'll speak it."

Her chin rose, but she was clearly pleased as she similarly changed languages. "Good. I'm going to hold you to that."

"Ja, ja." My arms rose above my head, tired muscles stretching out. "Did you sleep all right?"

"I did, until you pulled on my hair to try and stop me from getting up."

I blinked. "I did?"

She brought her thick mane around, over her shoulder. Hands stroking it almost protectively. "It's your new thing. Usually you miss, but today you got a pretty good hold on it. I have no idea how you didn't wake up when I pried it out of your fingers."

A bit of heat came to my face. I cleared my throat as we reached the street level, "Sorry. I didn't know I was doing that."

"I won't say it's fine, because it's kind of annoying." She paused, then added. "And painful. Next time I'm going to grab yours to wake you up."

I was fine with that, mostly because she wasn't threatening to stop sleeping next to me. I knew she still didn't really understand my need to have someone in bed with me every night. She'd heard my stories, of growing up with sixteen kids all piled together in a single bed. Of living with Half-Sword packs with eight of us sharing a single space.

But hearing the stories and putting up with my avid dislike for sleeping alone were two different things. She was tolerating my need for it, something I was more than thankful for, but there remained plenty of things about it that seemed to annoy her.

"All right. I'd probably deserve it." I said.

Johanna hummed, the pair of us walking west. "Having a dream?"

"Yes." I admitted, "A nice one, for once. Playing Strike-Wave with my childhood pack."

"And you thought my head was a ball to block?"

A bit more heat, "Um, maybe? Sorry, like I said. You know I'd be less likely to grab it if you let me cut it like you do mine."

She huffed, but there was a bit of a smile on her face. "Ashe. Your hair is a *mess*. Constantly. I have no idea why you love it so much, or why you make me trim it to keep it like that."

We promptly fell into our familiar argument about our fur, and why my medium length but ragged locks were far more attractive than her overly long mane. That banter went on for the full block to the nearest bar, trailing off to nothing only when we marched inside.

The Mikiran woman lurking on the other side of the doors sharpened her attention on seeing us.

"Savanna females." She growled. "They know this place has no drinks for them. What do they want?"

"Mikiran hostess." I replied, using the only description she'd ever given us. "Where's Irkan?"

Her long head turned left with a grunt. "At the bar and already drowning himself. Deal with him."

Taking that as permission, the two of us walked past her. In contrast to the kinds of bars I was used to, ones that catered explicitly to Mikira were far more brightly lit. They also lacked on booths, instead featuring only tables with the bowl shaped seats their species favored, seats that were absent at the bar itself.

Anyone drinking there had to stay standing, something that didn't seem to bother the squat aliens at all.

Oh. And it was doing a brisk business despite the incredibly early hour. Several dozen men and women were speaking in their chirping language over drinks, sharp teeth on display as they tore apart heavy breakfasts.

We got plenty of stares on the way across. So much time with Irkan had left me better able to read their body language and limited expressions. They weren't upset at our presence, nor looking down on us. Instead there seemed to be a general bafflement at what we were doing there.

I found our packmate at a corner of the bar, head tilted to one side so that he could pour half a pitcher's worth of amber liquid into his mouth.

And there was already an empty pitcher in front of him, which didn't bode well.

"Irkan." Johanna called his name before we got too close, giving him fair warning that we were present. "Mein Gott, you haven't been here twenty minutes yet!"

His only response was to tip the pitcher back a bit more, clearly aiming to simply chug the entire thing down. And since neither of us could get to him in time, or fight him for the beer even if we had, that was exactly what he did.

The empty plastic slammed down on the bar when we arrived, moving to stand on either side of him. Irkan growled low in his throat, glancing at each of us in turn.

"Ashe'lori." He rumbled. "Johanna. What are you doing here?"

"Taking you back to our apartment." I said. "None of us are supposed to drink alone, remember?"

"You do." Irkan countered.

"Only when cornered by pirates." I crossed my arms, "And never more than a single beer. You've already had ten times that."

He turned to fully face me, letting me see the extent of his annoyance. "Yes. I have. And I intend to have far more."

Johanna carefully grabbed one of the protruding sections of his shell, using the leverage to shake him. Well, she flexed her arm in a clear attempt to do that, but he only twitched.

"We get it." She said, "But can you get black out drunk in our apartment instead of public?"

He groaned and growled, but wasn't drunk enough to really argue with us. Not yet anyway. If we'd gotten here five or ten minutes from now, that might have been different.

As it was he still insisted on bringing plenty of it home with us. The bartender chuckled the entire time he filled up two travel pitchers. Handing them over to Irkan, I slid credits across the bar in exchange, and then Johanna and I did our best to get Irkan back.

Our companion tolerated us leading him outside, but he refused to talk with us. Instead he ripped off the top of one of the pitchers, working his way through the beer in the short time it took us to make it back to our building.

By the time we had our door opened, he was working on getting the other one open as well.

Not for the first time I wished we had actual furniture in the apartment. Instead of being able to sit at a table, where we might have a chance to steal the pitcher if he set it aside, we ended up sitting in a circle on the floor.

"So..." I gave him a chance to speak up, only continuing when he said nothing. "...did you ever meet the King?"

"No."

The flatness of his response didn't bode well, but I couldn't think of anything else to do besides sail onward. "Just respected him?"

One of his eyes locked onto mine. "Ashe'lori is not going to leave this sailor in peace until he speaks, is she?"

"I spent more than a year in a traumatized pack." I said quietly. "One where every person there was together because they'd been through something that rattled them. Every one of them said that talking about it helps clear your mental sea."

He showed me his sharp teeth. "And you desire to know more about my Kingdom. Information I have rarely spoken of."

That drew a genuine scowl to my face, and a wince to Johanna's.

"Irkan!" I snapped. "When has it been like that between us? Yes, I was being trained to be an Imperial Agent. *Yes*, I like knowing things. This isn't about that. This is me trying to help someone who I call a packmate."

Irkan started to growl only for Johanna to cut him off, her tones firm. "That was too far, Irkan. I don't call us family like Ashe does, but we've spent... God, more than a year now helping each other survive. Almost two years. If she was really after your people's secrets she'd have been working a lot harder at it before now."

A low growl, his clawed hands tightened around his booze... then his eyes lowered to glare at the ground instead of us.

"Perhaps." He replied. "My accusation was made... incorrectly."

I crossed my arms, not really forgiving him. "It was. I can go away and you can vent to Johanna if you really think I'm just spying on you."

Irkan's broad chest swelled, pushing out as he inhaled, then fell with the exhalation. His shake of his head seemed exhausted, defeated. "No. The sailor named Irkan apologizes to Ashe'lori. She is correct. We have shed blood together, and slain foes together. It is not like that between us."

A *look* from Johanna had me take a deep breath of my own, letting it out with my words. "Apology accepted."

She nodded in approval, looking between us. "Now that we're all calm again, how about you tell us what the war news actually is?"

He closed his eyes, deliberately setting the pitcher down before he could pick it up again. Only once it was settled did he begin speaking.

"The Kings launched an all out assault on the faltering Riush. Diversionary strikes attacked what colonies remained loyal to them, while our great fleet commenced an attack on Terminus itself." He explained. "The battle there was vicious. The Eldest Riush was slain early in the battle, but a packmate rallied what remained of their forces. They held long enough for the Crescent's Golden Armada and the Xenthan-Imperial Navy to arrive."

I nodded, "So they lost?"

To my surprise he moved his head in the negative. "No. King Yulaz was slain by the same mercenaries who slew one of the Princes early in the war. With his death, and the arrival of the Trahcon warlords, King Zaen asked for an armistice. It was accepted, and negotiations began."

He paused, visibly focused on his breathing once again, then said. "The surviving Riush, their last loyal retainers, and the mercenaries were allowed to leave Terminus. In exchange the system was surrendered to the Kingdoms."

I couldn't stop from making an impressed noise. "So the Mikiran people control their home system again?"

"They do." For a brief moment his almost sullen grief vanished; he straightened, voice deepening with pride. "Our homeworld may be a dead and blighted wasteland, but the Final Fortress of Remembrance is *ours* again."

Johanna looked impressed as well. "I can't imagine if the Ark Fleet took over a fortress above Terra, or Xentha. There must be celebrations all over the place."

Irkan preened for a brief moment, then he seemed to crash back down into the depths. "...there would be, if not for the loss of our great King."

She nodded sympathetically, "He was that loved?"

"Loved is not a term our people would use." He shook himself, quills wagging. "But... I suppose it is the one that aliens might. Our people had begun to fail. To descend into nothing. The great legacy of our blood, our stories, our names... it was collapsing before he rose."

"Really?" I cocked my head to one side, "I thought the Scarlet Tears were doing pretty well."

A stubby arm waved, "We appeared strong, yes, but internally we were weak. True, we raided. We mauled Cathia... but there was no follow up. We crushed their Fourth Republic, yet our Kings did *nothing* when the Kolkris forged their Crescent among its ruins. When those weak cities became a vengeful arsenal, filled with rage at what we had done. Our Kings ignored the rise of Empress Ravt, discounted her ambition. They did nothing but squabble, wage wars of words and blood between Mikira and Naule within our own borders."

I nodded slowly, getting it. "Your docks were rotting while the Elders boasted about how fancy their yachts were."

Irkan blinked slowly, then let out a deep chuckle. "Yes. An apt metaphor. When Yulaz challenged his father, when he inspired Zaen to challenge his cousin... he refused to let us fall. To become divided. He gave us pride in being the children of two fallen empires, filled our hearts with a determination to not let our Kingdom of the Scarlet Tears fall as our homeworlds did."

He fell silent for a moment, then went on. "More than that, his words were not idle boasting. He personally strode forward, crushing those pirates his father had allowed to fester in our stars. He rebuilt a fleet allowed to falter. Dismissed five hundred Generals in favor of those who knew how to truly lead warriors. He prepared us for the struggle he knew was coming."

"...sounds like he won, though." I pointed out. "I mean, he may have died, but he lead your people to victory."

"He did." Irkan allowed, eyes lowering, "But the war is not over. We hold Terminus, destroyed the Riush, and made peace with Empress Ravt... but the pirates who I spoke with claim that the war continues. The Crescent has refused peace. Cathia will not yield so long as the Kolkris live. It shall be a war of decades, of centuries."

Johanna nodded solemnly. "A war you need your best leader for."

"Yes."

I nearly asked about who would rule now. What the odds were that they would listen to us about the Faithful... but sanity splashed cold water on the thought. This wasn't the time.

"What was he like?" I asked instead. "I mean, he sounds determined and a good leader, but do you know what he was really like?"

Irkan smiled, picked up his final pitcher of ale, and regaled us with stories of his fallen leader until well after noon.

XVIII

Tossing my coat onto the back of the cafe's chair, I collapsed into the seat with as theatrical a groan as I could manage. Not seeing any point in being subtle about it, I put in the extra effort to slump over so that I could plant my forehead onto the table's surface.

"Kill me." I groaned into the wood. "I don't care about going home anymore. Just end it."

Irkan's deep laugh preceded the sound of a glass being pushed across the table. "Ashe'lori must live to deal with pirates. All know that I have no taste for it, and Johanna would long be slain."

Another groan came as I forced myself up enough to look at him. "If I never have to deal with pirates again, I will consider it a life well lived."

"That is the second such time you have made that statement." He nudged the glass of water a bit closer to my hand before sinking back in his own seat. "The repetition was not required. Not when your opinions are well known."

"Just making sure you remember." I replied.

He chuckled again, watching as I took the drink and sipped at it. He waited until I settled it down once more before saying, "What did Ul Gothin do this day?"

"Enough that I wish this was alcohol instead of water." I muttered, already picking it back up to take another sip.

His amusement faded, expression and posture turning serious. "Did she do something untoward?"

A slight shake of my head came as I lowered the glass again, a sigh coming after. "Not in the way you're thinking. No violence, no groping, or anything like that. She's just... ugh. Her usual self. No sense of personal space, likes to loom over me, fluff my fur, imply threats, that kind of thing."

"Threats?" He asked quietly.

"That she's going to find a way to make us work for her one way or another." My right shoulder rolled back and forth. "Nothing she hasn't said before, and nothing she can follow up on since her ships departed this morning."

He grunted. "I would state that to be a good thing, but we are now lacking a powerful warrior to protect us."

"It's both good and bad." I agreed. "But right now I'm more thankful she's gone than worried we'll get attacked and enslaved. For now. That might change depending on how things go over the next few weeks, or if she's gone long enough that the slaving guilds start asking about us again."

"Agreed." Irkan rumbled, taking up his own water. "We must be alert for such things, though I doubt that we shall be considered targets now."

I tilted my head a little, "Because of the war situation, you mean?"

There was a low sound in his throat. "Yes. Before, many worlds of the Riush were raided only by the daring. Those that feared they would recover, and punish those who had taken advantage of their distraction. Now that their state has collapsed, there are many easy targets in this coreward part of the Reaches."

Meaning the various slaving guilds were far busier going after worlds where they could seize people in bulk rather than trying to pick off a trio of marooned people in their local river. Especially when coming after us might make an enemy out of one of the more successful pirates operating from the planet.

Although... that was probably overstating it. Gothin would be annoyed, but I didn't think she'd be all that vengeful if we were taken while she was gone. The local guilds would know that. Still... they couldn't know it *for sure*. Especially with as touchy as Gothin liked to get with me, they might think that I was trading my body instead of reviews of trade lanes for her protection.

They might not think that Gothin liked me so much to come after me if I was taken, but they couldn't *know* that.

"Not worth the risk, maybe." I muttered, shaking my head around another sip of water. "A potential feud with a local pirate, for what? A whole two Humans and a Mikira?"

"Your kind is more valuable than mine as slaves." He noted. "You remain somewhat rare and exotic in this region, despite how many seem to find careers in piracy or as mercenaries."

"So we might be worth it?" I asked.

A clawed hand waved dismissively. "In peaceful times, I would be more concerned as I said. Unless we do something truly foolish, the slaving guilds are not my concern."

"Just the pirates and Faithful."

"Yes." Irkan agreed. "That the latter have not found us yet should be a balm. Yet each week that goes by leaves me more concerned."

My hum was cut off by a waiter approaching with two enormous glasses of tea. A quick glance at Irkan had him nodding, taking the one offered to him.

"I ordered for us." He confirmed, already pulling money out of his belt pouch and handing it over.

"Thanks." I said, taking my own glass from the waiter. "And thank you as well."

The waiter gave me a toothy grin, holding up the currency that Irkan had just given him. "A good tip just did."

Then he was ambling away, leaving us to our drinks. Mine was pleasantly sweet, and hopefully not poisoned. We both sipped at them in silence for a few minutes before I set the glass down near my water.

"I'm getting worried about the Faithful too." I admitted quietly. "Three months is two months longer than I thought it would take for them to find us. I suppose that's proof that whatever transmitters are inside of us don't link up to the DataNet. That none of them are here."

Irkan nodded once. "Yes. This sailor knows that Kagarraht is not a hub world. That it is unlikely they would randomly discover us, but after Aonu and Cashihto... he remains concerned."

Concerned enough to revert back to not referring to himself in the first person.

"Me too." I bit my lip, then lowered my voice further. "I think I'm going to side with Johanna."

He blinked. "In what regard?"

I took a deep breath, let it out. "I picked this cafe for a reason. Look across the street."

My companion did, and his eyes narrowed at once on seeing the Gunsmith's store just across the way. The display windows showcasing the full armor sets that they also sold.

"Ah. We are not going to simply purchase them then."

A clear statement rather than a question. "No, I don't think we are. I priced it out. To pay for full armor for all three of us, plus a pair of nullification grenades each, we'd set ourselves back two months."

The noise in his throat was displeased, leaving me to explain. "Irkan, armor's *expensive*. Especially good armor that would actually hold up long term in a firefight. Almost everything on sale here is... driftwood garbage."

"That, this sailor can believe." He grumbled, angling his head to drink more of his tea. "What of the armor we have already?"

I rolled a shoulder. "Either was just steal one less suit, or we get a properly matching set and sell it to boost our funds a little."

"Perhaps... but does Ashe'lori truly believe that illicit activity is our only option?" He asked.

Tapping the glass with tea in it, I hesitated for a long second before I let myself say it out loud. "Yes."

It was his turn to take a moment to breathe, to consider me.

"I see." He said finally. "What convinced Ashe'lori of this?"

"Gothin and Johanna." I said, then went on to properly explain. "I'm not saying that Gothin is going to come after us, I don't think she will. That being said, I don't know if I can say the same about her crew. Some of them... the way they look at me, at Gothin..."

Irkan nodded very slightly. "They watch her for weakness. Are curious if you may be a weapon to cut her with."

I tipped my own head, agreeing with him. "That's a problem. There's also what happened to Johanna at work yesterday. She'd have been a lot safer if she'd had a shield belt, or any kind of protection under her clothing. The Faithful armor she's got is too bulky for that."

He looked discomfited at the reminder that the restaurant she'd been working in had been shot up, and half a dozen people killed in a brawl between two minor gangs. A brawl that had rather decisively ended with a group of pirates simply killing both sides to protest the fact that their lunch had been interrupted.

None of the staff had been killed, but it had still left Johanna more than a little rattled.

She'd been even more rattled to realize she had to go back to work today. That a little thing like a dozen prospective customers being gunned down in the booths didn't amount to closing for even a day.

I didn't blame her for her reaction. It was one thing to expect to have to run for our lives from maniacs like the Faithful, to be paranoid that slavers or pirates might try and abduct us. But to be nearly killed as collateral damage while working in a diner? Shot by a random gangster drunk before noon?

It seemed so... depressingly pathetic. The kind of thing we really shouldn't have had to worry about.

The kind of thing that civilized people shouldn't have had to worry about.

Taking another deep breath, I followed it up with a long sip of my tea.

"It is convincing." Irkan said while I drank. "Though I question the wisdom of plotting such an action across the street, and in plain view. This sailor admits he is not an agent like Ashe'lori, but it still strikes him as foolish."

Swallowing, I set my glass down and explained, "This isn't our target.

I already checked it, and the security is way too good for me to deal with. Rerth or Jet probably could, but I don't have the hacking skills to circumvent what they've got set up."

"Then where?" He asked.

"Got a few options." I ripple-tapped my fingers on the table, nails clicking as each one came down then up again. "But we're going to need a few supplies first. Should be cheap from the convenience store next to us."

Irkan blinked slowly, then huffed. "And you required additional hands."

"Yup." I smiled shamelessly, "Finish our tea and go shopping?"

The huff became a laughing nod, both of us quickly downing the last of our drinks before rising.

We walked in a companionable silence. Leaving the cafe, we turned right, strolling into the broad lot already filling up with both ground and air-cars as people shopped. Picking our way through without getting run over or landed on, I grabbed us a pair of heavy bags once we got into the store proper.

Ignoring the food and alcohol aisles that were closest to the door, I led Irkan toward the quieter back half of the place.

"And... here we go." I grabbed three heavy cans that proclaimed them to be dark green. "Bag?"

He opened his, watching as I dropped them inside. "Paint?"

"From what I can tell, all of the good stores have protection. Pirates, gangs, or even the slaving guilds. That means whatever we steal has to not *look* stolen as soon as possible."

"Ah." He nodded. "Perhaps we make it look aged?"

I pointed at him with one hand, already turning back to the numerous color options available. "Good thought. More paint first, then let's find some kind of sanding or grinding equipment that's not that expensive."

Adding black, red, rust, and another two shades of green to our haul, we meandered up and down the aisles looking for anything I could think of.

I talked to him as I did, appreciating the feedback since I'd never *actually* done something like this before. I'd just been the support, the person dragged along.

"We'll need an escape vehicle of some kind." I said, checking over heavy grind stones meant for blades. They might work to make our armor look battered, but I didn't want to damage the protection. "There's every chance that I'll miss an alarm. We have to be in and out as quickly as possible."

"Stolen as well?" He asked.

"We're not buying one." I noted, glancing at him. "Does stealing a car upset you?"

"No." Irkan replied at once. "If we are able to do so, that is merely proof that the owner was insufficiently paranoid."

I couldn't stop a little snort. "You sound like Jet. Except he'd have just called them morons."

His mouth parted in a lazy smile, "We are upon a lawless world. Those who live here should know better."

That was definitely true. I certainly knew better. Or, well, I would know better if I actually had a car I wanted to keep.

"Can you steal one?" He asked.

"I think so." I said. "Might take me a few tries, but there's a lot of articles on the local net about it. I'm pretty confident I can make it work."

"If she is sure. What will the remaining plan be?"

"Johanna will be our driver" I went on, finally picking out something we could attack the armor with. "She'll stay in whatever car we find, and make sure no one takes it. I'll be doing the actual breaking and entering."

Irkan tilted his head as we got moving again, "And what shall my role be?"

My elbow lightly tapped his thick arm. "Muscle. You think I can carry three entire sets of armor? Probably more, since we're going to have to make it look like a general burglary if we can?"

"Not without tripping over it." He quipped.

"You make me sound clumsy." I protested, "I meant that I'm not strong enough."

"You are also not strong enough." He replied with an easy grin. "But you are quite the clumsy, tall savanna. Johanna told me of your struggles clothing yourself."

"That was one time!"

"Was it?" He asked.

My face warmed slightly. "...it may have been more than once, but that's not the point. You're going to come with me, wait for me to get in and disable the security, then help me get the equipment out."

He hummed, still smiling, but thankfully he stayed focus on the project.

"And how will you do that?" He asked.

"Still working on that part." I admitted, feet slowing as we entered an aisle full of cloth. "Today is just us getting the bare minimum. I'll probably have a longer shopping list once I pick the actual store that I think we'd have a chance to burgle."

Irkan's own amusement faded. His eyes watched as I started inspecting the various rolls and reams, trying to find one that would be good enough for what I needed.

"Ashe'lori is only partially trained, by her own admission. Does she truly believe she can do this?"

My fingers paused around a long strip of black cloth that was far too thin.

I was only partially trained. I hadn't even been with Intelligence for a full year before the Faithful had taken me. All I had was abbreviated training, what I'd picked up during our actual missions, and my various misadventures as an Imperial Conscript.

Could I successfully burgle a store that sold guns and armor? A store that would have to have functional security systems, given what kind of planet we were on? A store that would have plenty of armed men and women on call, ready to come and kill us for the temerity of stealing from them?

Could I?

I didn't know.

What I thought I knew was that if I didn't... if I didn't, I didn't like our chances the next time the Faithful caught us. I was positive that it was a *when* it happened, not an *if*. Maybe not here, but once we got to Lushrivers...

...if the Faithful had people on Aonu, then they'd have people there as well. If only to observe what was going on in one of the major powers in this region.

Maybe Irkan's people would be able to protect us.

Or maybe not.

"I can." I said with more confidence than I truly felt. "Because we have to be able to protect ourselves."

My friend's voice turned low, almost hungry. "Another difficult challenge."

"Yeah."

"Good. It is by such challenges that we define our names." He clapped me gently on the shoulder. Gently by his standards; I still rocked on my feet from the impact. "I look forward to seeing how we accomplish this one."

"Me too." I whispered before shaking my head once, raising my voice. "I need dark cloth. Very thick, something that we can use to make sure no one can see my face."

"Of course. Perhaps that one?"

I turned, saw the one he was pointing to, and headed off to check it.

XIX

I walked down the street as casually as I could, both hands warm in my jacket's pockets. Apparently winter wasn't quite done with the city just yet; our few weeks of steady warmth had vanished against a brutally cold wind.

That wasn't ideal for me, since it had fewer people walking on the streets.

"Never enough foot traffic when you need it." I muttered, pulling my shoulders in a bit as a particularly bad gust roared down the street. "Ashahn's ass it's cold."

The Naulian man striding past me grunted, "No shit, short-fur."

I had a sudden urge to give him a rude gesture. A sure sign that I'd spent too much time out here. Well, one sign. My deteriorating language was another one. I'd have to get that under control before I got back to the Empire or I'd stand out more than usual.

Exhaling a stream of vapor, I kept walking, glancing at the building across the street.

Red-Strong Arms and Armor was housed in a three story building, which towered over the two smaller businesses on either side. As far as I could tell the upper levels served as the owner's home, while only the ground floor served as their place of business.

Johanna, as the only one of us who wouldn't be approaching directly, had been the one to actually go in and check their inventory. The Naulian owners had tried to sell her exactly what we needed, but at a price I wouldn't have wanted to pay even if our budget hadn't been constrained.

With a bit of coaching, she'd been prepared and come back with a sketched outline of the interior, complete with what security cameras she'd been able to see inside. Most importantly, she'd picked out the interior door that had to lead either upstairs, or to the storage space with the actual arms and armor.

So I had something to work with on the inside.

On the outside, I was constantly updating my own sketched map.

The front and side doors were both heavy security models, and the glass windows were obviously armor-grade. The doors used both security consoles as well as a physical key slot. Watching endless videos on the local net, and buying a lockpicking kit, made me think I might be able to get around that second part.

I mean, maybe. If I had a lot of time and no one around to watch me fumble through it. Sadly the security consoles that I couldn't hack were an insurmountable obstacle.

"Two cameras watching each door even if I suddenly learned that skill." I rolled my neck, taking a final look before turning my head forward once again. The better to not be obvious about the fact that I was casing the building.

This was my tenth time either walking or driving past, each time wearing different clothing, most times with a hood or hat in place to obscure my features.

I didn't want to take any chances with this. Not any more chances than I already was.

So far it seemed to be paying off. Each time I'd gone past I'd picked out more details, or confirmed suspicions. Today's was confirmation on the cameras; two per door, one on the other two sides, and another one on a pole watching the roof.

But there wasn't one watching the patio on the second level, on the north side.

That patio door didn't look as well secured as the others. It probably still had an alarm, and a lock, but it might be a way I could get into the second floor. From there I could get down to the ground floor, get what we need, and then simply open a door for Irkan.

...of course he'd still be seen on the cameras. That would be a problem.

Blowing out another misting breath, I slowed my pace when I drew closer to a shuttle stop.

I'd hardly come to a stop when one of the heavy vehicles came around the corner, the driver slowing up at the sight of someone waiting. Old brakes groaned as it came to a halt, the door opening to let me see the Trahcon man sitting at the controls.

"Lori." His tarah rose a little in surprise. "What are you doing out here?"

"Hey Voln. Checking out a restaurant." I replied with a partial truth, climbing in to the shuttle's warmth. "Menu looked good, but their local Net's page lied about their prices."

Fer'voln snorted, "Of course they did. How far you going?"

"All the way to the main station. I'll walk home from there."

He gave me a vague wave, tapping the button to shut the doors. While he got the heavy vehicle into motion again, I walked past the mostly empty seats to a booth near the back.

Collapsing into it, I loosened my jacket before fishing my ear-piece out of a pocket. Getting it into place, I picked out Irkan's connection on my wrist-comp.

Normally talking in the open about this kind of thing would go against every bit of advice that Rerth, Holde, or Jet could have given me. It went against even my common sense of how to plot a crime.

But considering that the two Thondian men a few rows ahead of me were loudly discussing how badly they wanted to assassinate their Tarath, whatever that was, I didn't think me offering a few vague words would really increase our odds of getting caught.

Especially since I'd already checked all of the shuttles for listening devices, found four, and gotten a tidy bonus from the shuttle company for my efforts. I did similar checks at the start of each of my shifts, and I hadn't been finding anything, so I was reasonably sure no one would be recording me.

Still, I'd speak quietly. Just in case.

The connection chimed just a few times before he answered.

"Ashe'lori."

"All done and on my way back." I reported. "I think I've got two possible entrances for us."

"That is good. Do we have a time table?"

I shook my head even if he couldn't see the gesture. "Not really. Well, maybe. I've noticed what might be a pattern, but I want to do a few more checks to be sure."

"Of course." He rumbled, *"If we are to do this, it would not do to be impatient, or to have ill timing."*

"Definitely not. I think we can do it, I just need a bit more time to do research and prep." I bit my lip for a moment, considering, then said, "If I'm right, then when the pirate fleets are due back from their raids next week will be our chance."

Irkan made a noise of understanding. *"A good thing we have all requested that day off already."*

A good thing indeed. Most locals *wanted* to work that day; men and women flush with stolen goods and money tended to be free with both their money and their affections. At least to start with. The heavy drinking as the night went on tended to make those days some of the more dangerous around here, even by this world's poor standards.

Local citizens seemed inured to it, but we weren't.

"Yeah. Let's assume that'll be our day. If it doesn't work out, if they stay in instead of going out to party, we'll regroup and try again."

"Understood. Do we have everything that we shall need?"

"In theory, yes." And I really didn't want to spend even more money, even if the cost of supplies was a drop in the ocean. It hardly rated against how much we had saved up, or how much we would need. "I'll go over our supplies again as I finish up the plan."

I got the impression he was nodding, even if I couldn't see him either. *"Good. Is there anything else to discuss before your arrival?"*

"For us, no. Ask Johanna to call me?" I asked.

He grunted. *"I shall once she is finished bathing."*

"Thanks." I said. "I'll be back in a half hour or so."

"Very well. Until then, Ashe'lori."

Cutting the line, I got settled as comfortably as I could. Considering that I was sitting on extremely thin pads over top of metal, that wasn't all that much. The most I managed was to get my long legs stretched out under the seat ahead of me.

Left with little else to do, I watched the battered city flow past to either side. Half-listened to the increasingly graphic ways that the men ahead of me wanted to kill their apparent liege lord.

Ah. Apparently he was sleeping with the man on the right's bond. No, wait. He was sleeping with *both* men's bonds, and boasting about it to their faces.

"Aliens." I murmured in Deutsch, on the off chance they paused their ranting long enough to hear me. "Honestly. It's just sex."

They evidently didn't agree.

Rolling my eyes as the ranting got even louder, I caught the eye of a Trahcon woman doing the same thing. We both shared a smirk before she got off at the next stop, the two loud men getting off right after her.

That left me as the only one aboard, apart from Voln in the driver's seat.

With nothing else to do besides wait for either Johanna to call, or Voln to get us back to the primary station, I brought my wrist-comp back up. For a moment I considered sailing about the local Net, or else staring at my ideas regarding the burglary. Maybe trying to pick up a few skills with computers.

I was pretty sure I'd look at everything I really wanted to on the first, and I'd been doing little besides the second for the last week. As for learning hacking quickly, I'd found several helpful guides... except for the part where they assumed levels of proficiency I simply didn't have.

Picking a physical lock when you had tools designed to do just that wasn't all that hard a skill to learn. Overriding an electronic lock with minimal training in coding and electronics was something else.

So instead of depressing myself with my lack of knowledge in that field, I brought a note file up to start working on my next letter to Rerth. Something to send her once we were in a system where I had free DataNet access.

I already had more than a few of them ready to go. Two of them detailed everything that had happened on Last Stop, or as much as the three of us could remember. Another covered our trip and visit to Cashihto, while the fourth went over our very brief visit to Aonu.

This newest one went over our time on Kagarraht... and a disturbingly large portion of its contents was me trying to justify aiding a pirate in her raids.

And now justifying staging a burglary to secure proper equipment, though I was far less worried about that. Rerth had led us in doing just that on Nuevo Genova after all. We'd had to in order to survive, just like I was pretty sure we had to do the same to survive long term out here.

She'd still had to fill out plenty of paperwork to explain just why she'd done it, and she'd made me edit it during our trip to Trinity.

I was pretty sure I was missing a few of the lines, but it was the best I could do without the actual form.

Settling in to review and edit what I'd already written, I got through most of it over the next five stops or so. Which made it just typical when a very loud Trahcon pack boarded at the sixth stop, breaking my concentration.

Normally I wouldn't have had any problems refocusing, but the loud curse from one them warned me that I had a problem.

"Iriahn's fucking dick. Another short-fur? Their kind are showing up everywhere." A woman growled, glaring at me as she dropped into a seat near the front.

My eyes had already snapped up before she finished speaking, flicking across to count how many of them there were.

Five. Three women, two men. Plain clothes, not armor. No visible shield belts. Only one of the women had a gun openly on a hip holster. All five had their tarah raised in a clear threat display.

Ashahn's... blood.

Pursing my lips, I felt old instincts return. I casually let my eyes drop to my wrist-comp again, as if I'd only just looked up to notice who'd gotten on. My mind already sailing on, determining what the next stop would be, and how long it would take to get there.

Was this the first time I'd really had to deal with supremacists since the Faithful?

There'd been the one manager on Aonu, I supposed, but that hadn't been all that severe as such things went.

This felt like it could be.

My heart began to pick up speed, beating more quickly as the growls and complaints regarding my species continued.

A woman growling. "This planet was miserable enough, but it's only gotten worse since that pirate band with the stupid name showed up."

"The Black Flag Band." A man supplied. "Short-furs, every last one of them."

"Greedy ones." Spat another woman. "Arrogant and pretentious, like all their kind. Did you see the ones at the store last night? Demanding to be let to the front of the line, as if they were one of the Big Four."

"I bet that one is one of theirs." The first woman spoke again, clearly referring to me. "Did you see the way it looked at us when we got on board? Nahk. Go tell it to get off at the next stop before it gives us a disease."

"Gladly."

My eyes closed for the briefest moment, opening as the sounds of footsteps drew closer. I felt my fingers trembling, breathing quickening along with my heart. Familiar. It was all too familiar. Except...

...except I wasn't afraid. I had been, nearly every other time this had happened.

I should have been. There were five of them, one of me. I had a gun, they all had sorcery.

But their words... against the cutting fury of the Faithful, of the Burned Hand, their words hadn't been hurtful. Hadn't made me want to shrink. They'd just been...

...*annoying,* really.

I was on edge, perfectly understandably so given the danger, but I wasn't actually afraid like I should have been.

"Hey, short fur." The man had reached my booth, putting his hands on hips while he growled. "You-"

"Need to get off at the next stop." I interrupted him, surprising myself nearly as much as him, I thought. Turning my head, I met his blue eyes with my brown ones. "I heard you."

He blinked rapidly, tarah quivering. "What did you just say to me?"

I blinked once. "That I heard you, and that I'm getting off at the next stop. Did you need anything else?"

The man actually gaped a little, his tarah lowering in confusion. My refusal to either cower or fight had apparently thrown in him into a mental whirlpool he was struggling to get out of.

While he flailed for words, I glanced around him, spotting the next stop coming up. I rose to my feet, my feminine height causing me to loom slightly. That finally got him to react, voice lowering to a growl.

"We could kill you, short-fur."

"Yes." I replied simply.

"You'd best..." He trailed off, blinking. "What?"

"You could kill me." I told him. "There's five of you, all with sorcery, and all I have is a pistol. What's your point?"

"That... you need to be more polite!"

It was a struggle not to giggle, or laugh. After so many supremacists had come at me, insulted me, attacked me, tried to murder me.... this was honestly more pathetic than it was threatening.

"Of course, sir." I said with as straight a face as I could manage. "Would you mind stepping back so I can get off the shuttle, as ordered?"

I don't think I could have confused him more if I'd been trying.

"I... yes. Good. Get off, then." He stumbled for something more decisive to say, finally settling on. "And don't let us catch you on these shuttles again."

"I drive one." I muttered to his back as he turned away, retreating to the safety of his pack from the strange Human he'd just ran into.

Said packmates clearly hadn't heard what we'd been discussing, but my standing up had them all glowering. His waving for them to calm down, and my legs carrying me to the rear door, seemed to settle things.

It might not have lasted if I hadn't tapped the exit request button, and Voln casually pulled the shuttle over so that I could get off at the next stop.

Johanna finally called just as my feet struck the sidewalk, strides lengthening as I worked out the fastest way to the apartment from where I was.

"Hey." I said once I'd accepted the call. "I just did something and I can't decide if it was stupid or wonderful."

"*Mein gott. What?*"

I swallowed, "Uh. I ran into a pack of supremacists on the bus, and I talked around the man who came to confront me. I think I left him more confused than anything else."

"*Uh...*" She audibly swallowed, "*You did?*"

"Yeah."

"*...details?*" She asked.

I gave them as I began the long walk home... and found myself constantly looking over my shoulder for the Strike I was sure was going to hit me.

The pack stayed on the shuttle... and the attack never came.

XX

The raucous celebrations were well underway by the time we made our final approach.

My hands came up, tightening the crude black bandanna I'd sewn together. It covered most of my face, while a winter cap covered up my fur and everything else. A long sleeved shirt, dark pants, gloves, and a heavy backpack completed the outfit.

It was exactly as subtle as a hurricane, but it didn't need to be clandestine. It just had to make it as difficult as possible for anyone to identify me.

Approaching from the service street behind the line of businesses, I stopped at the first ladder I found. Clambering up the back of a store, I took a moment to catch my breath and collect myself.

The long strip of the building lay before me. The roof was mostly some kind of cheap gravel, with stone tile paths connecting various appliances. Just beyond the edge was a small gap, and then the store that I intended to burgle.

Nodding once, I settled my pack and got moving. Some instinctive part of me wanted to run, to get there faster. To be quick so that I wouldn't be spotted. Get this over and done with faster.

Reason told me that the few seconds I saved wouldn't be worth the exertion. Not when I was going to have to do a lot of physical labor in the very near future. Plus I was far enough away from the street that no one would be able to see me up here anyway, and the only building nearby with multiple floors was the one directly ahead.

I supposed someone on the larger shopping complex just to the west could have spotted me, but then what would they be doing up there at this time of night during a celebration?

Doing my best to keep my breathing steady and calm, I kept my chin up and alert as I approached the far end.

The gap between this building and the next was too far for me to easily reach.

The gap between it and the patio just above wasn't.

Not letting myself hesitate, I picked up the pace as I got closer, bringing me up to a short burst of effort. A leap at the last moment had my gloved hands slammed into the metal railing above, fingers frantically tightening.

Swallowing, feeling my legs swaying in the open air, I carefully began to swing myself a bit to the right. On my third swing I managed to contort myself to get a leg up, wedging that foot under the railing and the 'floor' of the patio.

My arms and abs still burned with the effort, but I managed to haul myself up. A second bit of movement got me up and over the short railing, grimacing when I nearly landed on a pair of empty bottles. More were piled up in a corner, apparently overflowing from a small bin.

"Classy." I muttered, experimentally trying the patio door. It was locked, which didn't surprise even if it disappointed. A closer look revealed a number pad set into the handle, which made me abort my thoughts about picking the lock.

Backup plan it was.

Flexing my fingers a few times let me make sure my gloves were still secured. A quick roll of my shoulders later, and I moved left, towards the back of the building. The patio may have ended well before the corner, but there remained a decorative ledge that seemed to mark where the second floor was.

Getting back up and over the railing, I tested my weight on that tiny ledge one foot at a time.

It held, but it was a real struggle to keep my balance with how little of my foot actually fit. Doing my best to will my heart to slow down, I carefully stretched myself out until one hand could grasp the edge of the nearest window. Using that to help stay upright, I eased my other foot out as well.

Then I shuffled along slowly and carefully, using my grip on the window more than my feet to actually stay secured. I didn't try to open it as I went past. Any half-decent alarm would have gone off, and signaled the owners to stop partying and come home.

So instead I kept going, using the corner of the building once I was past the window, edging my way around it.

There, overlooking the service alley, was another window.

One that was opened nearly every evening... and one that was open tonight. Just a crack, enough to let fresh air in, but *open* all the same.

"Now." I muttered, staring into what looked like a darkened bedroom. "To find out if there's a second lock, an alarm, or anyone home."

Reaching down, I slid my fingers in between the metal holding the glass in place and the stone of the building. A final nervous nod, and I gently pulled up.

It slid for a few inches... then caught.

I tensed on reflex, freezing in place. When no alarm sounded, I whispered a quiet prayer to Khash, and gave it a second pull in the hopes it was just stuck rather than running into a second lock...

...and for once, my prayers were answered. It came up. In fits and starts, and a few less than a subtle yanks, but soon enough I had enough of an opening to fit through.

I emerged into a dark office, an expensive looking chair sitting behind an equally nice desk. The contrast between them and the beer bottles stacked to one side was enough to have me shake my head again.

A quick look around let me see a security panel on the nearby wall. Meaning if I'd had any skills with computers, I could have simply turned it all off right from here. Let Johanna and Irkan walk in, nice and easy.

Taking a few steps closer let me check the two small displays, a relieved breath coming out when I read the glowing letters; 'Armed and Ready', and 'No Active Alert'.

Making yet another mental reminder to force Jet to teach me everything he knew, I moved around the chair and desk to approach the door. It opened without a sound, revealing a pitch-black hallway.

I hesitated there, then gambled by bringing my wrist-comp online. The blue glow revealed walls covered in the kind of cheap artwork you could buy from anywhere. More doors were on the left, but the right had an obvious stairwell.

A quick tap got the call started. "I'm in."

"*Good.*" Johanna said at once. "*You have no idea how stressed out I am right now.*"

"Pretty sure I do." I murmured, "I've done your job before. Are you in position?"

"*Yeah, I'll pull up as soon as you give the signal. Irkan?*"

His deeper voice replied at once. "*I have just entered the alley behind. I am ready.*"

"Good. Starting my sweep."

Walking towards the stairs as quietly as I could, I glanced down them to see a heavy security door at the bottom. The same one, I was sure, that Johanna had seen during her walk through of the store proper.

Considering the size of the building, and the size of the sketch that she'd given me...

...there was a chance that the storage for the actual goods was up here rather than down there.

Reversing direction, I paused before the first closed door, drew my gun from under my shirt, and made sure that the safety was off. Only then did I start checking each of them one by one.

A bathroom. Surprisingly clean.

A bedroom that was anything but.

A dining space with a small kitchen, more empty bottles.

A stairwell heading up to the third floor.

Another rather disgusting bedroom.

Biting my lip, I eyed the stairs up before dismissing them. I couldn't imagine that they'd keep their goods up there. Walking up two flights of stairs every time you had to retrieve something for a customer? It would have been incredibly aggravating to deal with.

"Nothing on the second floor." I reported, still keeping my voice down. "Heading to the first floor."

Johanna hummed, *"Okay. I don't see anyone on the street, and I don't see the owner's car either."*

"No one in back." Irkan completed the report. *"You remain secure."*

For now, . Exhaling, I once again made for that first set of stairs, though that time I actually went down them.

A very cautious push on this side saw it swing open easily, and without any screaming alarms or blinking lights. That part was good.

The part where there was a camera right above it on the other side wasn't.

I'd come prepared for that, though. Crouching down in the stairwell, I swung my backpack off and opened it up. My fingers quickly retrieved the heavy canister I needed for this part, my eyes double-checking the instructions in the light of my wrist-comp.

Shaking it several times, I carefully leaned out, keeping my head well below what I hoped the camera's view would be.

Then I sprayed it down with black paint.

I was certain that a real security system, the kind you'd find in the Empire, or used by the Faithful, would have started shrieking around then. Would have alerted the owner that a camera had been blinded.

But when I took another gamble, racing back upstairs to the office, I let out a sigh of pure relief on seeing the system still showing that no alerts had been triggered.

Far more confident, I slipped back downstairs, approaching the camera covering the service counter from the side. Spraying it down as well, I followed it up with the one watching the front door.

"Prep work done." I hummed, fighting against the strange urge to relax as I tossed the paint back into my bag. "Interior cameras are blind. Searching for our gear."

My packmates made happy noises, and repeated their reports that no one seemed to be coming to interrupt.

A short search revealed that Johanna had missed a small alcove behind the service counter. Stepping in revealed another stairwell heading down, and following it down revealed neatly organized stacks of arms and armor.

More bad luck there; the owners were very paranoid about the guns. They were all secured in their factory crates, themselves showing as locked, while the crates themselves were locked instead of metal cages. Worse, the lock itself clearly had an alarm rigged up to it, so there wasn't much of a chance I'd be able to pick us up some new weapons.

"Dammit." I growled on seeing a box of Nullifcation grenades just out of reach. "Bolt cutters. Should have had bolt cutters."

"*It's locked up?*" Johanna asked.

"The guns are." I replied.

"*Let's hope the armor isn't.*"

I couldn't help but dip my head in agreement, resuming my careful circle of the basement. My steps brought me to a veritable wall of ammunition being kept in an enormous collection of shelves.

As soon as I was sure that there wasn't a camera down there, I wasted no time in grabbing as many boxes of Imperial-Standard and Imperial-Two rounds as I could fit into the backpack. It was intolerably heavy when I pulled it back on, but that was a small price to pay.

Doing my best to ignore the way the straps were digging into my shoulders, I kept up my search until I found the stacks of armor. Like the ammunition it wasn't as secured as the weapons themselves, though I was pretty sure that was more a matter of practicality.

Someone breaking in and racing downstairs could grab a gun, attach a quick-charger, and be dangerous to the shop's owners very quickly.

Someone racing down here and trying pull armor on would still be trying to get even one piece linked up by the time someone came down to put them in their place.

The moment that I confirmed that they had a respectable variety of equipment, I said as much. "We've got what we need. Thondian, Trahcon, Mikira, and Human."

Not that we needed the first two, but stealing things for just a Mikira and two Humans would be a little too obvious.

"I'm going to drop the ammunition down to you, then start hauling all of this up to the front door." I reported. "We'll go with our second exit plan."

"*Confirmed.*" Irkan rumbled, "*I shall be ready.*"

What followed was an utterly miserable hour's worth of work; first running back up to the second floor, then carefully tossing the bag of ammunition down to Irkan. He caught it with a grunt, then lumbered off to link up with Johanna.

That left me to head back down to the basement to start the long effort of hauling crates nearly as tall as me up the stairs and over to the front door. The first was difficult enough, and left me panting a bit from the effort.

The second, third, and fourth were increasingly miserable. By the time I got the fifth one stacked up I was soaked with sweat and panting as if I'd just played two full games of Strike-Wave as a Sail-Runner.

The sixth was pure misery, and left me sitting on top of it, shaking from the effort.

"Approach." I rasped. "Soon as... soon as no cars are in sight."

"*Got it.*" Johanna replied.

"And make sure your faces are covered." I added.

"*Ja ja, we're ready.*"

It didn't take them long. Four minutes, tops, and Johanna was again in my ear telling me that they were about to stop outside. Not wasting another breath, I slammed my shoulder into the front door and threw it open.

The long silent alarm finally began to sound; a steady klaxon that had me grimacing even as the stolen truck squealed to a stop just outside. Irkan, his colorful shell covered in a badly stitched cloak, his quills spray painted black, leaped out of the back before Johanna had the truck at a full stop.

My arms were burning, but I'd more energy from somewhere. It didn't last beyond helping him get the first two in, but I managed that much before I just had to climb into the back. He quickly heaved in the remaining four, relying on me to use my legs to shove them into a neater arrangement, and then he was clambering back in as well.

"Go!"

Johanna was accelerating in a heartbeat, pulling us away from the scene of the crime.

We made it a full block before a car went screaming past the other direction, screeching to a halt in front of the store. Figures tumbled out, waving guns as they rushed inside, somehow not noticing us casually driving in the other direction.

"Must think we're still inside." I called to Irkan, very glad when we turned down a side-street, leaving them well in our wake. "Must have thought we were just regular traffic!"

"Indeed!" He shouted back. "Well done, Ashe'lori!"

I couldn't stop the pleased warmth from rising in my chest. Yes, it had been an illegal burglary. Yes, it had been exhausting, bad for my nerves, and left me soaked with sweat.

But it had still been... kind of fun. Especially since we weren't being chased at the moment.

I kept my ridiculous hat and bandanna in place until we were more than a mile away, finally taking them off once I was sure I was right about the lack of pursuit. The cold wind felt delicious as it ran over my fur, across my skin, and I found myself slumping against the truck's cabin.

"Hey." Johanna asked over comms, *"Are you sure we need to go through the rest of the night's plan?"*

I let my head fall back against the glass and metal. "Yeah. Let's not ruin this at the last moment. Straight to the communal parking, so we can take that other car we broke into."

Irkan grunted, easily keeping his balance near the back despite Johanna's somewhat unstable driving. "Assuming it is not stolen by another."

"Assuming that." I agreed.

If it was, we'd move our stolen goods into it, and then head home. We'd drop off Johanna and our equipment, Irkan and I would change, and then we'd head clear across the city to sell the excess to a shop that claimed to buy anything, no questions asked.

We'd sell them both the car and the extra armor if we could, and then take the shuttles back home.

I bit my lip, closing my eyes.

That money might be enough to give us room to work with in the next auction. Might let us get out of here in just a few weeks time. So close. We were so close.

We just had to finish tonight's project as cleanly as we'd begun it... and then pray no one caught us.

XXI

"Raised by one thousand by the savanna. Does Clan Howra match?" The Thondian Elder called, direction the question to a Naulian man whose own dark fur was streaked with white.

"Match and raise two thousand!" Came the booming reply, complete with a glare in my direction.

I met it, planting my hands on the chair ahead of me. The new armor looked hard used even with the green paint we'd splashed on, but I was hoping it gave me a more martial look.

So far it wasn't intimidating my remaining bidding rival for the old Thondian-made yacht being auctioned off.

"Does the savanna match and raise?" The Elder bellowed.

"She does!" I called without breaking eye contact. "Raise by three thousand!"

The leader of Clan Howra bared his teeth at me, one of his subordinates leaning to hiss something in his ear. The old man shoved him away with two of his arms, the other pair both raising to point at me.

"Match and raise by ten thousand!" He spat.

I clenched my jaw to keep from grimacing. That was right below our final line. "Match and raise by one thousand."

That same subordinate stormed back in, all four arms waving frantically. His voice wasn't quiet that time, "Father! It's a worn out old yacht that won't last the year!"

"We will refurbish it, and sell it for twice the price." The Elder barked. "Match and raise by five thousand!"

Ashahn's bloody....

Blowing out a frustrated breath, I turned to the man running the auction and bowed, tipping my head to the left like I'd seen others do. "Yield."

He bowed as well, though his head was angled in the other direction. "The Xanixik-35 Yacht has been sold to Clan Howra. Pick it up in Lot Seventeen by nightfall or it will be resold at the next scheduled auction. That concludes this month's sales. The next event will be in thirty days."

Dammit. That time I couldn't stop from making a fist, armor creaking as I lightly struck the chair in front me. A little gesture of frustration that made the old man who'd outbid me smirk some more.

Glowering at him for a heartbeat, I forced myself to turn away and withdraw.

My attitude was not improved when I ran into ul Gothin near the door, the enormous Thondian woman chuckling at my approach. Knowing better than to simply try and ignore her, especially when she beckoned for me to follow, I turned away from the exit to fall into step with her.

"So close." She offered, casually walking toward a side door. "Yet you remain stranded. Another few thousand and his pathetic Clan could not have matched your bid."

I took a deep breath, letting it out with my words. "Thirty days. We'll make enough this month that we'll get one for sure at the next auction."

"Assuming anyone brings in a ship in your price range." Gothin countered. "That is not a guarantee."

"There's been one every month so far, usually two or three." I replied. "So I think the odds are in our favor that there will be something available. Or are you going to outbid me to try and force us to work for you?"

That got me an amused little noise, "You are not worth *that* much money, little savanna."

Good. Her showing up and stealing any ship we tried to bid for had been a very real worry.

"Thank you." I said. "I don't mean to be impolite, but was there something you wanted in specific? Besides making sure that everyone in there thinks I'm one of your employees, I mean."

For the briefest moment I thought I saw surprise on her alien features. She collected herself quickly, smirking in her usual way.

"Such a quick mind." She said, sounding approving. "Be thankful for my presence. I do not doubt that Clan Howra would love to eliminate you after today's events."

That time I couldn't stop the grimace. "Ashahn's blood. Are they going to think that I drove up the bid just to cost them money?"

She waved a hand. "If you were independent, a random short-fur? Of course that is what they would believe. But as they instead believe you to be my personal analyst, as most do, they will simply believe I hoped to use the yacht as a decoy in some scheme."

A huff came out, shoulders drooping a little. "What data am I going over for you in exchange for your protection this time?"

Gothin casually reached down to a pocket, pulling out a detachable drive. She offered it, and I dutifully slipped it into one of the pouches on my belt.

"The Yera-Pollru Corporation's usual trade routes and sightings. I want to know how they are most likely to react to to the kind of chaos currently unfolding in the Reaches."

I nodded. "How soon do you need it?"

"My last cruise was most profitable. You have your final month here to do your best work." She said. "You may even utilize myself or my crew to protect you as needed for that time."

My throat worked as I swallowed, "Uh, I'm grateful, but may I ask why?"

Ivory teeth showed in her smile. "Your prediction regarding the last route was perfect, Ashe'lori. We took five full heavy haulers fleeing from a battle near Terminus. Their cargo is being sold, the crew and ships ransomed to their corporation for a fortune."

Oh. So... I'd done good then. Helped a pirate hit exactly the kind of target she'd wanted to.

A tiny wave of professional pride crested in my chest, then was mercilessly crushed on the shores of shame.

I'd been much, much happier not knowing just how she was using my information. My analysis and predictions. Perhaps I was a hypocrite, I'd burgled a store not two weeks ago, and stolen two cars in the process. Even *sold* one of those cars for profit.

But that was... small. Necessary to my return home, to my personal safety, the safety of those I called packmates.

I supposed I could make the same argument for helping Gothin. She was helping us, protecting us, in her own way. Making small time gangs and the other pirate bands ignore the people sitting on enough, or nearly enough, wealth to buy a small starship.

But it still just felt... *wrong* to help her, in a way that stealing body armor hadn't.

"I'm a mess." The tired groan came just as we reached a side exit, stepping out into the afternoon sunlight. "Ashahn's grace but I'm a mess."

"You are a savanna." Gothin replied, almost philosophically. "All of your kind are a mess. It is to be expected."

Considering most of the other Humans I'd met in my life had assuredly been more than a little storm-wracked mentally, I supposed I didn't have much room to argue with her.

So instead I simply patted the belt pouch with its drive. "I'll have it ready for you before we leave."

She nodded sharply, then simply swerved away when we reached the main street. The lack of farewells was apparently another Thondian thing, one that was thankfully easier to get used to than the endless posturing and power plays.

Not watching her go off, I instead walked down the street leading away from the starport. The first cafe catered only to the ranking members of the Big Four pirate gangs on Kagarraht. Thankfully the one just beyond it was more open, and that was the one I walked into.

Irkan and Johanna had claimed a table near the door, both in their new armor as I was, and I wasted no time in walking right over to them.

"No celebrating." I sighed at having to dash Johanna's hopeful expression, "Clan Howra drove it a few thousand above our limit."

She slumped at once, groaning. "God dammit. Thirty more days?"

I nodded tiredly, sitting down. "Thirty more days. The good news is that no one else stuck with the bidding anywhere even close to our limit. So long as there actually is a ship in our size and cost range next month, I think we're nearly guaranteed to be able to get it."

Johanna grumbled something, picking up her glass of tea and drinking. That left Irkan to shake his head at her behavior, comfortably leaning back in his seat.

"That remains within our expected time frame." He said, not sounding bothered. "An annoyance, to be sure, but we are in better condition now than we ever have been."

"True." I said. "On that, more good and bad news. Gothin's back, and is making sure everyone thinks she's our backer when it comes to bidding for a ship. She says it's the only thing stopping someone else from thinking we're running the prices up."

"Or," Johanna mumbled, "Just killing us for our money."

I flicked a hand her way, "Or that. Point is that she's back, and apparently the information I gave her was so good that she's open to us using her for cover whenever we need to. So long as I go over some more information for her, and have it ready by the time we leave next month."

The woman tilted her head, then shrugged by rolling a shoulder. "I guess it could be worse."

"It could be. You just gave me a Trahcon shrug, by the way." Isaid.

"I did not!"

"You did." Irkan and I said, though his slower way of speaking stopped both waves from hitting the sand together.

Not that it stopped Johanna from pouting, or us from chuckling.

Our waiter, a rather plain looking Hunter approached around then. I quickly glanced over the menu while Johanna and Irkan ordered, picking out a fish plate that sounded all right, along with the local dark ale I'd become fond of during our stay.

He retreated after a compliment of my scars, and I offered him a token appreciation of his long tarah that had him smiling.

With nothing to do but wait for our food, and not celebrate like we'd been hoping, I slouched forward a bit and turned to Irkan.

"So... you promised to talk to us about what we can expect when we get to Lushrivers." I said.

"I did." He eyed me, "When we have a ship. We do not have a ship."

I pointed a tired finger at him, "You know everything there is to know about me, and pretty much everything there is to know about Johanna. It's your turn to tell us something besides the fact that you were a sailor."

A clawed finger of his own rose, "The savannas are aware of how I was captured, and what became of my companions."

Johanna snorted, "Which we could have mostly guessed, Irkan. Come on. You've never said anything about your family, or clan, or house, or whatever you have."

He glowered at us, but the slight smile betrayed that he was more amused than upset. "Ashe'lori has infected Johanna with her lust for knowledge."

She groaned, "Do you have to say it like that? You make it sound like she gave me a sexual disease or something. Stop stalling already, and tell us who we'll be staying with once we make it to your home!"

There was a deep sigh, but he nodded once, taking a few moments to collect his throughts.

"Assuming we are not all kept in secure quarters by the armed forces?" He asked, cupping his water in both hands. "In such a case, I would presume with what you would call my House, though there is no word in

Caranat that truly describes it."

"Blood-kin?" I suggested.

"Some who dwell there are what you would call that, yes. Others are not." He shrugged slightly. "They are of my House, and I would shed my blood for them, as they would for me. Or you, if you are welcomed into our home."

"How many are there?" I asked, genuinely curious.

He scratched at his quills, thinking. "Hmm. When I departed, there were forty-three of us of age. Several were considering joining by.... you would say bonds."

"Marriage." Johanna supplied the loan-word.

"Yes, that." He nodded. "And several others may have become blooded adults in my time away. I cannot recall all of the children's true ages."

It was her turn to tilt her head, "You don't have any?"

Irkan... actually slumped a little, shaking his head. "No, to my shame."

She winced sympathetically, "No one interested, or too busy being an officer on your ship?"

A quiet hum. "Few are interested in a Mikiran sailor, young Johanna. It is not a profession that inspires others to attraction. The only woman who did found more comfort in the attentions of a man with higher rank that I. None showed interest since."

"I..." I hesitated, then admitted, "Have no idea how Mikira determine handsomeness, so I can't tell you that you're attractive. But you do have a proper Name now, right? That has to mean something, even for a sailor."

That earned me an almost startled look, and then a lazy smile. "I am considered average by those close to me, Ashe'lori. Although your other words have merit. A proper Name is one that may see options open to me that were once closed."

He went on a bit from there, describing his blood-pack. Evidently he was the eldest of five children, and his career in space had made him something of a disappointment to his family. His three younger brothers were all infantrymen in the Scarlet Tears army, while his sister served as a mechanic for an armored force.

An incredible pride entered his voice when he spoke of them, openly boasting of how well they'd done in their training. How they'd proven themselves in skirmishes with pirates and raiders in the run up to the war, how sure he was that they'd covered themselves in glory during the campaigns.

"Perhaps," He said as our food arrived, "They have even earned Names of their own. Few Houses have more than a handful. Our father and mother would be deeply honored to see so many of their children declared for the whole Kingdom to know."

Irkan paused, reaching for a small packet of spices. Tearing it open, he sprinkled it over the burnt meat on his plate. "Speaking of my Name, I shall require your aid to confirm it."

I nodded, already attacking my fish with a fork and knife, getting the meat off the bones. "Tell everyone what happened you mean, so that they agree you truly earned it."

"Yes. And I shall do the same for you." He said. "We are not a people who favor wasting time, so it shall likely be done when we are questioned on the Faithful."

Johanna hummed, slurping down some of the noodles she'd ordered. "But there's a chance it'll be separate, so we should be ready to have to tell the story twice."

"Good thing we wrote it down." I noted. "We can just read it to them."

"Less chance of us screwing it up." She agreed, already twisting more noodles around her fork. "Think we'll see any of your siblings while we're there?"

Irkan tossed his head back, swallowing the bit of meat he'd just torn off. He cleared his throat, lowering his gaze to ours once again.

"It is unlikely." He admitted. "Unless they were wounded or are on leave. Our father and mother shall be there, perhaps with other, lesser members of the House. None shall bother you, as I said. Your greater foe shall be the world itself."

I blinked, fork pausing halfway to my lips. "Why? Weather? Air?"

A hand reached down, slapping one of his trunk-like legs. "Gravity."

"Oh." Swallowing once, I ate my bite, finding the fish pleasantly flaky and well seasoned. Getting it down, I asked, "How far off Imperial standard?"

"A full half." He sounded amused when he went on, "The savannas shall find their strength returning most quickly!"

Johanna groaned even as I perked up a little, which made us both glance at once another.

"What? Oh God. I forget." She sighed, "You really want to get that muscled, don't you?"

"The fact that you don't is weird." I told her seriously. "Just like the fact that you think my fur is ugly like this."

"It is." She said, her voice flat.

"It is somewhat stringy, and bland in color." Irkan made me gasp when he offered his opinion, "Perhaps some brightness would aid Ashe'lori in attracting pleasurable attention. Green and blue, perhaps."

I eyed the very same colors on his quills and shell. "So I'd match you?"

"They are handsome colors." He replied with a grin. "Are they not?"

I considered him, humming. Tried to picture myself with streaks of green and blue in my fur. "...maybe."

"Oh no. No, no, *nein, nein, nein!*" Johanna smacked the table hard enough to make her plate rattle and me jump. "You're already a walking fashion disaster, I'm *not* letting you make it even worse!"

"But it might look good!" I protested

"It would be an abomination!"

Irkan's roaring laughter made half the restaurant look our way... but he kept at it, just as the two of us kept bickering about nonsense.

The three of us acting like the packmates we'd become.

Interlude
Rerth'riah

The conference room cleared of my packmates and subordinates alike, eventually leaving me alone to make my report.

A few taps of the controls dimmed the lights and locked the door, with a final command bringing the DataNet connection online. While it began the long sequence or relaying a signal all the way from Alum to Trinity, I got my rank badge loosened and ready to insert into the system.

The holographic display above the conference table flashed as the connection was made, a male voice echoing from the speakers even if no video came through yet.

"Confirm."

I slid the badge into the scanner, "Operative Rerth'riah, requesting a direct report. Code Twenty-Nine. Thirty-One. Forty-Five."

"..Confirmed." He said a few long breaths later. *"Will route inquiry to the Void Lord."*

"Confirmed." I replied, leaning back in my seat.

The Void Lord's subordinate, or maybe her packmate, didn't say anything else. He simply put the channel on standby, a text display popping up above the table telling me to wait.

It took the Void Lord a full quarter of an hour to accept the request, giving me plenty of time to finish putting my notes together. To collect myself, and prepare to recite what we had learned in three months on Alum. What we'd experienced in three months on Alum.

I rose to my feet when the screen flashed, revealing the Void Lord seated behind her desk on her flagship.

"Void Lord." I said, saluting.

"Operative Riah." She gave me a dismissive wave, sending me back

to my seat. *"You finally have your first report from Alum?"*

I bowed my head, "Yes, sir. I apologize for the delay, the situation here is more complicated than I anticipated."

One of her long, masculine tarah flexed. *"You mean that the Kolkris are causing problems."*

I didn't see any reason not to readily admit that. "They are both causing problems and genuinely assisting, sir."

"I'm sure." She drawled, casually leaning back in her own seat. *"Begin with the Embassy and Intelligence assets."*

Taking a deep breath, I nodded once, then began detailing our initial investigations. "We have cleared the principle Embassy staff and their packmates. They are all now secured aboard the *Granite Warhammer.* Sadly that is the extent of the good news. My packmate and our data analysts have confirmed that the Embassy's computer systems are completely corrupted."

Her eyes narrowed, a hand motioning for me to continue.

"We brought in Crescent teams to verify that, and they confirmed the same." I said, glancing at my notes before going on, "All Embassy communications were being routed to another system, and all saved records were being copied out as well. The Crescent team managed to track some of it to a data center in one of the world's southern arcologies. They raided it and took three prisoners."

"Interrogation results?" Delarah demanded.

"Two knew nothing, local workers who didn't know who they worked for." I paused, then said. "The third bit off her own tongue before the Crescent could stop her, and then immolated herself."

The Void Lord swore under her breath. *"What about Intelligence?"*

"Missing." I said.

"All of them?" She demanded.

"Yes sir." My hands clenched for a moment, then I forced them to relax. "Of the five Operatives listed, none were to be found in their last listed addresses. Records from commercial traffic found one using a known alias to depart Alum more than a year ago. We do not know if the others are dead or traitors. Of the sixty-two Agents assigned to the Far Reaches, we or the Crescent have confirmed deaths for thirty-eight of them. Five are still alive, but are being held in secure quarters on Cathia. The remaining twenty one have vanished."

I went in to a bit more detail there. Some of the killed Agents had been survived by their packs, who had similarly been picked up by the Crescent and were being held in a military compound on Cathia. Right now the Kolkris weren't about to let us interrogate them, or let them come home to the Empire, but they were alive.

And I had convinced Kolkris'irkah to give us records of the Crescent's questioning sessions. What we'd watched had generally born out a familiar pattern; ambushes in isolated areas, or attempts to drug food and drink. Exactly the kinds of attacks we'd seen from the Faithful in the past.

"*We need those citizens home, and as witnesses.*" Delarah said when I finished.

"Kolkris'irkah won't give them up. She knows they're leverage." I shook my head ."Not without concessions, ."

"*I will provide you a list of viable options within the week. What else do you have? What of your packmate?*"

I took a calming breath, willing my mental seas to remain smooth. "We have no word from her. Assuming the letter was genuine, she should have arrived at Lushrivers nearly three months ago."

Delarah tapped a finger on her desk. "*You desire to send someone there?*"

Of course I did. Ashe could have been there, could be imprisoned by the Scarlet Tears. They could be stopping her from sending word home, while they determined what she was doing there, what she knew.

"I do." I admitted, "But the war between the Crescent and the Scarlet Tears continues. There is no safe route there, not unless we dispatch someone as a Compact Observer."

The Void Lord didn't need me to tell her the problems with that idea.

Not when there were already several dozen such Observers in this region, and the other Compact nations would have to approve a new one. Nor could we fake one; the Compact itself was very clear on the consequences for such an action.

"We will be patient." I told her, out of a lack of any other viable options.

Her nod was sympathetic. "*I know what it means to have a packmate missing, Operative. If you do have any word or lead, contact me at once, and I will approve your pursuit.*"

"Thank you, sir. Regarding the Intelligence operation here, that is about the state of things. All known safe houses and training facilities have been stripped bare or else sold off to unaffiliated groups." I went on. "All but two data centers were similarly shut down. My people are going through those as we speak, but all of the information they've found on those servers precedes Director Tasir's posting."

Delarah's tarah flicked outwards in irritation. "*Delve deeply into them regardless. Perhaps there is something that was missed.*"

"I have already given my packmate orders to do so." I said. Jet would either handle it personally, or more likely, would simply assign some of the people we'd brought with us to work on that.

"*Good.*" She replied, looking pleased for the first time since the report had begun. That didn't last, given how unpleasant the information I'd given her was. "*So in summary, our worst fears are confirmed. The entire Far Reach branch of Intelligence is either dead or betrayed the Empire on behalf of these Faithful.*"

I could only nod, "That is our impression, yes sir. There is some good news."

She blinked once, then waved an arm permissively, "*Do share, Operative.*"

I took a deep breath, then let it out. "Before she vanished, Director Tasir had apparently given up on a response from the Empire. She began working directly with the Crescent, sharing information with them and coordinating activity against a person called the Matriarch."

A hand rose, and I shut up to let her speak. *"Who is this?"*

"Unknown at this time." I said. "A high-level asset of the Faithful at a minimum, likely another of the Burned."

A nod. *"Continue."*

I did. "She was involved in several strange events on Alum some years ago. Though they did not catch her, Tasir and the Crescent were able to kill numerous people the Kolkris and I now agree were members of the Faithful. They were preparing for further operations when Tasir and her remaining senior agents all vanished."

Taking a moment to glance at my notes, I nodded once and sailed on. "At the moment, the Crescent doesn't have much more information than that. However, members of a mercenary corporation did have direct contact with the Matriarch. Kolkris'irkah strongly implied that they knew far more than they have admitted about the Faithful."

"Where are they?"

"Recently returned to Alum." A glance at the time on the display. "By now an aircar will be waiting to take me to begin questioning them. Supposedly they also encountered another Faithful kill team during the war, operating on an Ark Fleet colony of all places."

"Interesting. I approve of your initiative." She tipped her head in a sign of that approval. *"Send everything you learn within the week, even if it turns out to be nothing. I trust everything we have discussed up until this point is documented?"*

"Yes sir. Of course."

"Good." Delarah repeated. *"Dispatch it at once by the secure channels. All of the Void Lords are sharing the information we are discovering, and forwarding it to the Torlah."*

My reports would be read by the Torlah? For a brief moment it felt like my hearts went out of rhythm, and it was all I could do to swallow.

"I will make sure they contain all relevant details." I promised. "Dispatch will go out at the end of the week with my interrogation of the mercenaries."

Delarah's cool stare told me that it had better be, or her prior approval wouldn't last. "*I trust that it will be. Your reports by then, and then you will join a broad channel conference the week after with the other Operatives I have assigned to the Near Reach investigations. The scope of the problem is becoming clear, and you must be informed.*"

"Yes sir, I'll be there." I said.

"*Trinity Out.*"

"Alum out." I waited for her to cut the channel first, leaving me to close my eyes, focusing on nothing but my breathing for several long moments.

Then I shut down the equipment, rose, and strode to the door.

Holde was waiting for me on the other side, casually leaning against the wall. One look at my tarah told him my mood, and he wasted no time in leaning in to give me a soft kiss.

I returned it more gently than I normally would have, breaking away slowly to tell him. "Our reports are going to be read by the Torlah. At least the summaries."

His eyes widened in shock, tarah rising along with them. "That's... oh. *Oh.* When?"

"A week."

"I'll get Jet's half cleaned up as soon as possible." He promised, knowing exactly what I feared. "What about the rest?"

I could only shrug. "We're still in her favor, and still have permission to go get Ashe as soon as we have a definitive lead. That's about the only good news. All reports are being circulated among the Eight Void Lords, plus the Torlah, and I'm supposed to attend a full DataNet conference of the Operatives in two weeks."

His long tarah fell as quickly as they'd gone up. My bond had no problems seeing through the shallow water, knowing exactly what that level of information sharing meant.

This was being treated as an extreme crisis. Something so large, so severe, that it couldn't be limited. That secrecy was being traded for speed and clarity.

It was not at all how Intelligence operated. Had, operated, I supposed.

"Our ways failed." I murmured, shaking my head. "Let us see if the Void Fleet's methods can save us."

"I'll pray to the Aspects." Holde replied, clearly meaning every word. "Do you want me with today?"

"I did, but we don't have much time to get things ready. Go, start getting the reports consolidated and summaries crafted. I'll handle the mercenaries with... is Ithi free today?"

When he nodded, I did as well. "Go. I'll be back tonight. And tell Jet he's not writing reports for just us anymore!"

Snorting, he waved as we separated, jogging off to inform our packmate of events. I headed the opposite direction, sending a quick message to Huvu'ithi, telling her to meet me at the aircar. Her reply came fairly quickly, and I only ended up beating her to the roof by a few minutes.

Thankfully she was in full armor, though her only weapon was a pistol on her hip. I briefly considered sending her back for heavier arms, then forced myself to remember that I was in a Void Fleet now.

Impatience was now a virtue I would need to cultivate.

I waited for her to climb in to the passenger seat, activating the self-driving function and entering the address.

"The River District?" She read, frowning as she pulled her restraints over the bulky armor. "Oh, those mercenaries. Shouldn't we bring a Half-Sword along?"

"We will if they are impolite today." I replied, resting my hands on the controls as the car lifted off on its own accord.

The steady acceleration pushed me back into my seat; the warm forest shielding the embassy quickly giving way to the outskirts of Alum's capital city. The glistening spires of the central districts were highlighted by the polar ocean beyond them, and the grand urban sprawl that covered the coastline.

"You look tense." Ithi noted a few minutes into the flight.

Pursing my lips, I... found myself admitting what had happened. "The Torlah herself is involved. Our reports are going all the way up to her, according to Delarah."

She blinked several times, then her burned tarah tried to droop. "Uh. I've read Jet's reports. They're-"

"I know." I interrupted her, fighting the childish urge to drum my fingers on something. "Believe me, I know. I also need to have these mercenaries interrogated and full reports drawn up on this Matriarch by the end of the week, and then I need to be prepared to brief the Near Reach Operatives the week after."

"Ah." The burly soldier nodded slightly. "The fast life of a Voider."

I grunted. "Yes."

She tilted her head, hummed again, then quietly sang. "We sail on calm seas, we sail in storms. We sail beyond the maps. We laugh and sing, roar and shout. We have no food, have no orders. Water ran out ten weeks past, so we drink nothing but the rum."

Rolling my eyes, I still heard myself murmuring in time with her. "We sail to the void between the stars. We sail to slay the beasts that dwell there. Come and sail with us if you dare."

Ithi chuckled, shifting her bulk around to try and get comfortable. "I still remember the first time I heard that damned song. Fifth Void Fleet bastards kept adding new lines, drew it out for an hour until my unit snapped and went after them."

"How did you do?" I asked.

"They pummeled us." She replied cheerfully. "They're impatient and half-mad, but they're damned good in a fight."

I smiled faintly. "Let us hope they are as good at uncovering secret terrorist cells."

"Yeah. And that she actually does let us sail out to pick up Ashe, once she makes it to the Tears' worlds."

I had to give Huvu'ithi that. No matter how much time had passed, no matter how likely it was that the message from Ashe had been a fake... she had never once lost confidence. Never once believed that her old packmate was long dead, or a tortured prisoner.

I didn't want to doubt. Did not allow myself to.

But it... seemed easier for her, than it was for me. Perhaps I simply knew too much. Was too old, too paranoid, too guilt-ridden over how many times I had ruined the poor Huntress's life.

True, Ashe had managed to nearly end her own career more than once. Rather spectacularly at that. But she'd have never had those opportunities if it hadn't been for me. For my mistakes.

"I..." Inhaling sharply when my voice faltered, I tried again. "I have never said this to you, but I said it to Ashe once. I am... I am sorry that-"

"Don't." Her hand shot out, grabbing my wrist. Ithi's eyes closed, her nose flaring as she took her own deep breath. "Don't, Riah. Tell me when she's back. Not before."

I could only nod, the air falling still.

It stayed silent in the vehicle until it began to circle around our destination; a mammoth complex built right up near the river that gave the River District its name. The place looked like a demented cross between a castle and an apartment complex, though I could see several painters hard at work covering bare walls in elegant designs.

One of the towers was already decorated in the theme of a storm, and it was at the base of that section that we landed in a small spot in the yard.

I'd give the mercenaries something else; they weren't slow.

By the time I'd shut the motor off and exited the vehicle, three of them in full combat armor were within ten yards. All Thondians, wearing full helms with their heavy plate, and all carrying some model of rifle I didn't recognize. They weren't pointing them at us just yet, but they were clearly alert.

Their armor was a dark navy with metallic trim, and the only logo that of an executioner's sword pointed down on their left shoulders.

The leader took a half-step forward, the other two spreading out to stop Ithi or I from hitting all three with a single spell.

"Imperials." A deep, masculine voice emerged from his helmet. He sounded more curious than surprised, which made me think that the Crescent had told the mercs more than they should have. "What are you doing here?"

"To have questions answered." I replied, automatically filling my voice with the tones of an officer who expected obedience. "I need to speak with whomever in your organization knows about a woman called the Matriarch, or about a terrorist group known as the Faithful."

His stiff body language gave me nothing to work with, neither did his tone. "Wait."

I crossed my arms, Ithi moving slightly on my right. Staying partially in cover behind the car, ready to cover me if she had to.

The Thondian shifted just enough over the next few minutes to make me believe he was talking to someone on a private line. I waited patiently until he finished, and his speakers activated once again.

"The Matriarch is known to the Reyja." He said. "However, those who know the most are on vacation, and refuse to be disturbed. Return in two months."

My fingers and tarah twitched, my power swirling into the air for a brief moment before I forced it back under control.

"That is unacceptable to the Empire." I said sharply. "The Faithful have slain and abducted Imperial citizens. We need answers."

"That," He replied, own voice flat, "Is not a problem of our House. The Reyja will see you in two months, if they desire to."

I felt Ithi's own anger rise, her crippled sorcery making power shift in fits and starts.

Forcing my own emotions to remain even, I said, "The Empire is coordinating with the Crescent in this matter. Kolkris'irkah told me to contact

Trenah'kolkris, who apparently resides here."

"The Reyja will *not-*"

I cut him off. "Tell Kolkris that Ashul'tasir is dead. Her blood-sibling assured me that would get her attention."

His low growl was magnified by his helmet's speakers, but to my vague surprise he muted it a moment later. The conversation that followed was more animated by Thondian standards; his balance shifted several times, head moving right, then left, then ducking.

Then he spoke again, voice sullen. "Rejya Kolkris informs you that Reyja Kean is not available. He is outside of the city on a hunt with his bond. You will be free to stay within the estate until his return, and she will provide what details she can regarding the Matriarch... provided that you do the same."

"Very well." I said with absolutely no sincerity. I'd already had to give far more to the Crescent than I'd desired, and I was not about to share critical Imperial intelligence with mere mercenaries. "We agree."

Something in his low whistle told me that he knew I didn't mean it, but he turned all the same, waving us toward the wooden doors just behind him.

"Welcome, Imperial." He said. "To the House of the Silver Blade."

XXII
Ashe'lori

I was leaning against the outside of the Rocky Shoal Restaurant & Tavern when Johanna finished her shift. She didn't walk out so much as she *stalked* out, lips pressed into a thin line while her hands were clenched into fists.

The food and drink stains covering her white uniform more or less explained her mood.

"That bad?" I asked.

"Worse." She muttered, the two of us falling in step with one another. "I'm drinking your ale as soon as we get home."

"Might want to shower first. I think you have beer in your fur." I said.

Johanna immediately reached behind her, pulling her long mane over her shoulder to check it. Muttered swearing began when she found the strands stuck together, disgust replacing anger on her face.

Smiling faintly, I patted her shoulder as we walked home. "Another drunken bar fight?"

"Two." Her voice was a growl. "And one Naulian woman who was annoyed at getting hit on by a man, so she threw her plate at him, *missed*, and hit me instead."

"That explains the stains on your pants." I said, trying to sound as even keeled as possible. Which was a bit of a struggle considering her pout and the amount of colors on her normally pristine uniform.

She gave me her best glower. "You can stop sounding like you want to laugh anytime now."

I quickly looked away before I could *actually* laugh at her. "Sorry!"

"No you're not."

"I'm sorry you had a bad day." I said as earnestly as I could.

There was a quiet huff, but that seemed to mollify her. for the moment. "Was yours as bad as mine?"

I shook my head. "Not really. I mean, I probably have more tea than blood in my veins right now, and the morning shift was a lot busier than my usual evenings. Just four hours of work wasn't all that bad though. No fights or shootings or anything."

"No really annoying riders?" Johanna asked.

"Nope, sorry." I said. "It was a pretty boring morning. Not that I'd be eager to do it again. Not even for the bonus pay that they gave me for covering the half-shift on short notice."

She grumbled a bit, clearly displeased that I hadn't suffered as much as she had. "It's always just one of us. Why can't we all be miserable together?"

I could only shrug, "I think the Aspects are making us miserable enough by trapping us here."

"I'd say that I don't believe in your Aspects, but I'm starting to." Johanna pursed her lips, kicking at a rock on the sidewalk. "Maybe that's just because everyone swears by their body parts around here."

"I'd offer to teach you, but I really only know the basics." I admitted.

She glanced at me, the pair of us turning on to our street. "You mean you only know a few dozen of them, instead of the few hundred that there are?"

"Pretty much." I said. "I mean, I know the important Aspects, and about Aysh, and that's really all you *need* to understand. You're supposed to talk to the priests if there's some part of your life that you need to pray about, and they tell you which Aspects to consult."

"You make it sound like they actually answer. Don't tell me you've heard that one you're always saying is ruining your life."

I shook my head. "The Aspects don't talk to people. Not like you say that the Human God is supposed to. It's all wrapped up in their, well, *aspects*.

If Ashahn is looking out for you, you might get a key inspiration at the right moment. If she's not, you might find an unusually powerful storm ruining your life."

My packmate huffed, "Sounds too easy to me. How do you know what's from one of your gods, and what's just you, or nature, or random chance?"

A shrug, "Faith, I guess. All I know is that I think that Aysh is real, and so are its Aspects. Plus, well, the Faithful apparently hate them. Even if they were as evil and warped as the Naule's old Sun Gods, I'd consider praying to them just for that."

Johanna went silent for a few long strides before saying, "It's sad, but I honestly can't argue with you."

Chuckling, I patted her shoulder again, drawing a small smile out of her as we arrived back at our apartment building. A few more minutes of walking up stairs brought us to our door, where a physical key along with a security code unlocked it for us.

Not waiting for even a breath, Johanna swept right into the bathroom, pausing just long enough to grab a robe to throw on when she was done. I, far more sedately, headed into our small kitchen and started pulling out snacks and drinks.

Knowing that it took her a long time to wash her fur even on a good day, I cracked open my bottle before hopping up onto the counter. Sitting as comfortably as I could manage, I brought my messaging application up, composing one to Irkan.

Johanna is home, we're both alive. She had another miserable day.

I was lowering my arm when his icon shifted color. A moment later he was typing a reply, leaving me to read.

Was anyone slain?

Snorting, I typed back, *No.*

Then it could not have been that miserable of a day. My own is merely dull.

Still getting off on time? I asked.

Yes. Shall the noble females be present to escort me?

I smiled, quickly sliding my finger over the mesh on my arm. *I suppose we can be, if we're not busy with anything else.*

Ashe'lori is not nearly so funny as she believes herself to be.

That drew another snort out of me, and a quick reply. *You laughed. Admit it.*

I admit nothing. I shall see you in an hour.

See you then.

Closing that application, I kicked my feet a few times, then sipped more of the ale. Not really feeling like checking what passed for news on the local Net, I let my eyes drift closed instead.

The only real sound in the place was that of the shower. Steady at times, others more random, chaotic as Johanna moved about. I steadied my breathing, focusing on that noise. Blocked out everything else. Indulged in the calm of meditation for a while.

I hadn't been meditating as much as I had on Last Stop. I probably should have, but despite our complaints, this world was hardly as bad as that one had been. I also wasn't suffering from the after-effects of what had been done to us on the barge.

Here, it had been easier to lose myself in the banal routines of my simple job. Spending every moment of my free time creating a mental map of this city, so that we would never be helpless. Doing research for Gothin to keep her happy.

Working with my packmates to keep our spirits up as best we could on this dismal world.

Taking a deep breath, I pushed it out, not letting myself drown in that thought. I had more than enough worries, that was true, but things weren't *that* bad. For once.

We had enough money. We had armor, and so far no one seemed to be sailing about looking for us. We still had our old weapons, and now we had plenty of ammunition for them. Gothin may have been... difficult, but in her we had some form of protection from the local gangs. From other pirate bands.

Soon enough we'd be leaving, and be on Lushrivers.

Soon enough we'd truly be going home.

My concentration finally broke when the water cut off. The last drops reaching my ears just before I heard Johanna begin furiously toweling herself off. That noise lasted for several minutes before she came out, wearing the black, silken robe she'd kept from our old yacht.

I had to hum appreciatively as she approached the kitchen. "You look better with wet fur like that."

She scoffed, "You mean with my hair a complete mess. And *no,* I'm still not letting you cut it ragged like yours."

"Your loss." Turning, I grabbed the bottle I'd gotten out for her. A twist of my fingers got the top off, and I held it out just as she arrived to take it.

"Thanks."

"You're welcome." I replied, picking my own up. We tapped them once, then drank together.

She joined me in sitting on the counter, though she took the spot opposite next to the sink. For a while neither of us spoke, we simply sipped our dark ales and enjoyed each other's company.

I was about to ask what she wanted to do tonight when she spoke first, her voice almost hesitant. "Ashe. You really think we're leaving here soon, right?"

"...yes?" I asked, "Johanna, we're leaving. We're going to be fine."

A hand waved, moving her bottle back and forth. "No, I'm not having that kind of crisis. I believe you. I just..."

I frowned a little, kicking my legs. "Just what?"

Her following sigh was almost explosive. "I know we agreed to drop it, but *please* Ashe. I want you to come with me to the Ark Fleet."

"Johanna." I made her name into a groan, "Not again."

"I don't mean forever. I mean, not at first. Wait, that's not right..." Johanna clenched her jaw for a moment, exhaled, then said more calmly. "I mean that I want you to come with so that I have more than just *me* to explain what happened."

I eyed her, then carefully set my ale aside so that I could plant my hands on my knees. "And I might have believed you if you hadn't stammered around it."

There was a long groan. "Yes, I want you to stay there with me. You... God above, Ashe. You saved my life more times than I can count. You helped keep me sane in that tiny cell on that barge. I... I know I haven't been the most useful. Before and after we had the yacht."

"You've been plenty useful." I countered.

Her head shook a little. "As an extra pair of eyes, sure, but... ugh. Ashe, I'm nineteen... or am I twenty now? I don't even know. My point is that I'm not stupid. I... I know *ships*. How to live on them, maintain them, fix them. I don't know... all of this."

I brought my arms up, crossing them. "And that was pretty important to us surviving at all once we got off Last Stop. Also, just being an extra pair of eyes has kind of been one of the things keeping us alive. Imagine how long it would have taken Irkan and I to raise the money by ourselves?"

"I guess, but..."

"No buts." I insisted. "There's no way that Irkan and I could have really managed this on our own. You were really the one keeping the yacht running, Irkan just flew it. And you'll be the one that's going to make sure our new ship is going to keep working once we buy it."

"I..."

"You're important to me, to us." I continued. "I wouldn't call you my packmate if you weren't."

Johanna sipped ale to buy herself time, cheeks actually turning a little pink... and then her eyes abruptly narrowed. "...and you're trying to distract me."

Dammit! I'd been so close.

"I am not." I said, even if the words were a complete lie.

"You are!"

I bit my lip, then let the words out. "All right, yeah. I am."

It was her turn to set her ale aside, the better to cross her arms and glare at me. "Just come with me to the Ark Fleet. Help me explain about the Faithful. See how Humans live for yourself."

"Johanna..." I drew the groan out even longer that time. "...really? I'm a citizen of the Empire. A *loyal* citizen. I don't want to trade my life there for one on a ship filled with people who hate my culture."

"It...." She struggled for a moment, then slumped, looking away. "...all right. I can't say that it wouldn't be hard. I just want you to see my home, I guess."

"And I want you to see what Altair is like. Show you the sights, take you drinking." I said.

Her lips turned down, eyes not returning to mine. "Would it be that bad, just to come with?"

I took a deep breath, then let it out. "Honestly, probably not. I could handle it. And I would like to meet your Onkel, your blood-siblings someday, just like I want you to introduce you to my packmates, new and old. I wouldn't turn down an order to go visit you, to back up your report to whatever your government is."

"Probably the United Captains since it'll be a security thing. I think."

My arms uncrossed, one hand waving. "Them. I wouldn't say no, Johanna. I'd even ask for the duty if it's an option. But..."

"It's not your home." She said quietly.

"It's not." I agreed, voice lowering as well. "Just like Altair's not yours."

Johanna chewed on her bottom lip for a moment, then asked, "What do you think is going to happen to Irkan, once we get back?"

I hummed, thinking about it for a moment. "He'll probably go back to being an officer in their navy, if he can. Maybe he'll even get a ship of his own if having a full Name really is that important to his people."

"Maybe."

Her tones made her concern clear. "Worried about him?"

"I'm worried about both of you." She said, even more quietly, still refusing to look at me. "I mean. I'm afraid for me, but I know that when I go home I'm... no one. Odds are pretty good I can spend the rest of my life in peace and quiet in my flotilla. Find someone to raise a family with, never be in danger again. But you and Irkan...."

I started to reply only to hesitate, giving her a chance to go on.

"You're both soldiers. I know, I know. Agent and Sailor, or whatever, but... he's going to jump right into a war he thinks is the greatest thing that's happened in his lifetime, and you're going to go tearing off after the Faithful." A sharp shake of her head broke her words apart, fingers clenching around her arms. "You're my friends. I don't want... I don't want to go home, then find out that you're both dead a few months later."

"Johanna-"

"Or have you messaging me every week, then suddenly stop." She went on, "Then have some Imperial I don't know call me to say that the Faithful took you *again*."

Those words made the waters in my soul churn a bit, if only because they were worries I'd been doing my best to suppress.

As much as I didn't want to think about it, or admit it, her fears weren't exactly misplaced. Once I was home I'd be debriefed, maybe given a few weeks or months to acclimate to being back, and then it would be time to return to work at Rerth's side.

Time to resume hunting the very same people who'd proven that they could capture me.

I'd escaped once, yes. Technically twice, if I counted Oshflara. I'd survived their attacks on Trinity. But if that trend continued... sooner or later, I would lose Khash's blessings.

Sooner or later I would run into them, by my choice or theirs. And my odds of survival in either situation weren't exactly good based on my past history.

"You'd be safer on the Ark Fleet." Johanna said, still quiet.

"I would be." I agreed, just as softly. "But... I can't, Johanna. The Empire's not perfect. I know it's not. But it's still... it's *home*. I have to go back."

Her head shook once. Twice. A hand grabbed her bottle of ale, bringing it to her lips so that she could down half of it as quickly as possible. I took a more measured sip, refusing to judge her for the reaction.

In moments like these it was easier to remember how young she was. How completely untrained she was for what we were going through.

I might not have been that much older than her, physically, but I'd been a conscript, a soldier, while she'd still been treated as a child. Spent time with people who had truly lost packmates and friends to violence. Had suffered through violence myself.

Until her time on the barge, Johanna's life had been quiet. Peaceful. Not ideal, certainly not, but nothing that would have prepared her for all of this.

"I can't promise you that I'll be fine." I said. "Because I don't know that I will be, once I get back. But I *will* message you every week once I make it home. If something happens to me... I'll make sure someone goes there to tell you in person. Not just some soulless message."

She sniffed once, nodded... and then resumed downing her ale.

That time I joined her, the two of us working our way through the bottles. What few snacks I'd gotten out were eaten in a comforting silence, the

239

pair of us moving so that we were sitting side by side instead of apart. She tried to go for a second ale when we finished, only for me to firmly insist on water.

Our playful argument about that helped relax us until it was time to go and guide Irkan home.

XXIII

Four days before the next auction, the Star-Runners and the Nurukin Gang both returned from their raids. They descended on Kagarraht in a swarm of drunken revelry. Freighters hauled down thousands of tons worth of inanimate loot, along with far too many new slaves for my peace of mind.

I breathed as shallowly as I could inside my helmet, walking with my packmates through the crowded starport. Doing everything I could to tune out the boasting of the pirates heading out to spend their 'earnings' on the town.

"It never gets easier." I muttered, knowing my microphone would transmit my words to the others' helmets. "Listening to them brag about what they've done."

Johanna shifted a little closer to me, making room for a group of boisterous Naule already downing ale. "It really doesn't. You hear them laughing about the slaves they took?"

"Yeah."

"Disgusting." She muttered.

Irkan merely let out a deep hum, saying nothing. Not that he was a fan of slavery, he seemed to view it as a general waste, but it didn't bother him like it bothered us. Nor was he bothered by the fact that we were surrounded by people who'd spent the last month finding ships and worlds to attack.

Mostly because the raids were still targeting the former colonies of his people's enemies, I thought. I was pretty sure that he'd react very differently if we ran into a group who boasted about hitting a Scarlet Tears world.

Thankfully things quieted down when we took the next right, striding down a long sky bridge that connected the main building to a waiting area. It was mostly empty apart from a small cafe, whose Thondian owners were beaming over the fact that their shelves had been picked clean.

Leaving them to finish closing and counting their earnings, I led the others over to one of the broad windows overlooking the grounds.

"Three!" I couldn't stop myself from sounding giddy, the prior discomfort fading away at once. "Look at them!"

Irkan chuckled as he came up on my right, head tilting a little. "They would not quicken my blood in any other circumstance, Ashe'lori. Even a glance shows them to be decrepit."

I waved impatiently at him, "I don't care how they *look*, I just care if they can get us to Lushrivers."

Johanna nodded sharply, "Definitely. A yacht and two small freighters?"

"Yes." Irkan said, "I believe that freighter on the right would be more ideal. The Yollim model."

I frowned inside my helmet. "Not the yacht?"

"The yacht shall be more expensive." He replied. "And it looks to be in the worst shape of the three. I cannot imagine that the interior is any better. The freighter on the right is a model I recognize. It is more courier ship than cargo hauler, meant for long distance travel in places like the Lost's Kingdom."

"Ideal for us." Johanna said, nodding once. "Enough storage for the food and water we'd need to make Lushrivers in a single trip."

"Precisely." Irkan turned, contemplating the ship on the left. "That vessel... a Ukkat light hauler. Short range, not ideal, but it could be made to work. I would prioritize it or the Yollim at the auction."

"Got it." I replied. "I'll bid on either the Yollim or the Ukkat, whichever they put up first. If the yacht is cheap, should I try for it anyway?"

He hummed, bringing a hand up before appearing to remember that he couldn't scratch at his chin. "If it is well below our threshold, then I do not see the harm. Any ship is better than no ship."

Johanna apparently agreed. "Definitely. Even if we have to fix it up a little, or clean it, so long as we have a functioning ship that can get us somewhere else... that's all I really care about right now."

I shrugged before making the pack's voice unanimous. "I'll try and win the Yollim if I can, but if not, any of the three should work out for us. Just don't buy the yacht right up against our limit."

With that decision made, we lingered for a little while to watch the pirates who'd been left behind to secure the ships they'd stolen. None of them seemed to be attaching bombs or anything, or hauling out anything vital to the ship's functioning. Mostly they seemed to be going through the standard routines; refueling them, pumping water in, that kind of thing.

Of course we'd still need to go over all of the systems as best we could when the time came. According to Irkan, sabotaging a ship's engines right before you sold it wasn't uncommon out here. If you combined that with a tracking beacon, you had an easy way to both recovering the ship you'd just sold, as well as pick up a few slaves who weren't bright enough to check for traps in their new vessel.

So we might *have* a new ship in four days, once the auction completed, but it'd probably be several more before we were actually ready to leave. Maybe longer, depending on what we found inside.

Still... I couldn't help but vibrate in excitement, wrapping an arm around Johanna and resting my other hand on Irkan's shoulder. My normal pessimism had drained away, replaced with the utmost confidence that this was finally it.

There was no way we'd lose on all three bids. Not after how the last few had gone. We'd win one of them for certain. A week longer, two at the absolute worst, and we'd finally be leaving this planet.

"We're going home!" I said, smiling down at the three battered ships. "Soon, we'll be on Lushrivers."

Johanna giggled, leaning into me. "We really be, won't we? Oh, we should celebrate tonight! Order some good food instead of that cheap stuff."

"Definitely." I said firmly. "Our budget can handle a good dinner. Irkan, any preferences?"

"Perhaps that first restaurant we discovered?" He proposed, "They had a fine balance of cost and quality."

"Johanna?"

"Sounds good to me." She said. "Let's go!"

We set off again, chatting happily about what we'd do once we got to Irkan's home.

"I will return to the Navy, of course." He rumbled as we casually walked back toward the entrance, taking our time to let more of the pirates pass through ahead of us. "Once we have told our tale to those of importance. I am sure that the pair of you will be allowed to live comfortably in our home until it is time to depart."

I stretched my arms out with a pleased little groan, "No more cover jobs sounds wonderful to me. You think we'll be given full DataNet access?"

His armored shoulders moved in a shrug, "I do not see why not. Neither your Empire nor Johanna's Fleet are currently enemies of my people. I would expect you to be able to arrange your passage home easily enough, and to send any messages you desire."

"How long you think?" Johanna asked. "I mean, how long will we be there?"

"Not long, I expect. A month, perhaps two? Much shall depend on how Rerth's Agent wishes to arrange her to return to her Empire."

I hummed. "I mean, heading home by way of Alum is really my only option, isn't it?"

"The only option with any degree of speed, yes." He agreed. "Which is a problem, as Alum is claimed by the Crescent of Cathia. To arrange for such a passage will be difficult with the war ongoing."

Oh. Right.

He went on, waving an arm toward Johanna. "It will likely be easier for you both to simply be moved by a Compact Observer, but how long it would be before one would consent to be used as a courier? I do not know."

Considering that they had the rather enormous job of making sure that the war out here stayed relatively 'clean'? I doubted any of them would really want to waste time picking up a pair of young women.

Then again...

"Maybe." I said. "I mean, there's a chance that any of them from the Empire would do it. If Imperial Intelligence creates enough noise about our problems with the Faithful, and how they're operating in the Empire. It might be a big enough crisis."

Johanna hummed, the sound making it easy to imagine her biting her lip inside her helmet.

"Maybe." She echoed. "But that's just the fast way home, right? Like you said, our people aren't at war with yours. We just need to arrange for safe passage through the war zone."

Irkan nodded. "Yes. That may take time, however. Several additional months at worst."

"I can live with that." She said.

"Me too." I agreed.

A few quiet months, safe and secure on Lushrivers, sounded wonderful. Doubly so if I really did get to arrange a live call to Rerth, or even if I was merely allowed to start exchanging routine messages with her.

She needed the full reports I'd been putting together, and I needed to know how my pack had been doing in my absence. Had to reassure Pack Tun that what had happened on Trinity had not been their fault. Had to check in with Huvu, with Fyth.

The former was going to yell at me for getting myself captured, but she'd be thrilled that I was still alive.

The latter.... I hoped the latter had forgiven me, and would be equally happy that I wasn't dead.

Our conversation trailed off as we neared the exit, and the press of men and women still streaming out. Fortunately most had already left, and so it wasn't the longest wait before we reached the doors.

Less fortunately the courtyard outside remained packed, and extremely loud. Part of that was simply a few hundred people all conversing, part of that was the constant stream of aircars coming and going. Another wave of shuttles coming down from orbit, bringing the crews of those ships too big to land, added their engines to the din.

Very glad for the helmet protecting my ears, I followed Irkan when he plunged into the chaos, cutting north. We followed the edge of the building, trying to avoid the worst of the crowds, making for the street exit on that side. While that one was busy as well, it wasn't nearly as overcrowded as the eastern one, leaving us able to get out into the city proper in just a few minutes.

"Eat there or take it home?" I asked.

"Home." Johanna said, a single heartbeat before Irkan said, "There."

The two of them exchanged a clear look, making me snicker before siding with my fellow Human. "I think I'd rather be home so we can get this armor off."

"And," Johanna added, "So we can drink without being paranoid about it."

Irkan let out one of his deep chuckles. "The female savannas make a convincing argument."

My reply, about how he seemed so easily convinced, was swallowed up by the thunderous roar of a ship's engines. Grimacing, I glanced up to see a massive barge slowly passing over the city. It was clearly headed to the eastern landing grounds that were reserved for the big ships, but it was low enough that it seemed to be disrupting some of the aerial traffic.

"Fools." Irkan groused. "They will be fined most heavily for coming over the city."

I shrugged. "I think they'll live with a fine. If they'd done that tomorrow morning, with thousands of hungover pirates laying around..."

A dark laugh. "True enough. Our poor companion shall bear the brunt of such attitudes, as always."

That was certainly true. Irkan and I had to deal with the occasional drunk, as did Johanna, but her morning shifts in the restaurant often left her dealing with extremely grumpy murderers still suffering the effects of what they'd done the night before.

"We'll get you something nice for dinner tomorrow as well." I said, turning to find Johanna still watching the barge even as it moved farther into the distance. "Johanna?"

Her head tilted, apparently not listening. until I reached out and grabbed her shoulder. "Johanna! You all right?"

"I... don't know." She said, her voice... odd. "I just... felt weird. It was... I don't know. Weird. Something about that ship is weird."

I blinked slowly, feet coming to a stop as hers did. Irkan needed an extra moment, but came to a halt as well, turning between us and the ship now turning to make its final landing approach.

"Weird?" I asked, trying not to sound baffled. "What about it is weird?"

Her weight shifted, arms coming up as though she wanted to throw them up, then simply fell limp. "I don't know! It was just... I couldn't stop looking at it."

Irkan crossed his own arms, "There is nothing special about it that this sailor can tell. A fairly standard cargo hauler, of Imperial manufacture."

It was as if he'd reached into my chest and grabbed my heart with his clawed hands.

"Imperial...?" I rasped, getting a hand up to tap the side of my helmet. It took me a pair of attempts, but I managed to get the zoom working enough to get a closer look. "Oh no. Ashahn's ass. No. Not an Imperial barge."

Johanna's hand found my arm, and from the way it shook I could tell she was squeezing down on the armor plate as tightly as she could manage. "No. Not now. It can't be them showing up *now.*"

"I..." I inhaled sharply, then let it out. "...I don't know. But it's the same model as the one we were trapped on, and if you felt weird about it then I'm definitely concerned. We have to check it out."

Irkan's own voice had turned serious just as quickly as mine. "Find the hunters before they can find us."

"Yes. We see if it's the Faithful, and if it is..." I shook my head. "Four days until the auction. We'd just have to make it that long. That or we put our emergency plan into action."

Johanna nodded, "Join Ul Gothin, you mean? Can we trust her?"

"No." I said. "But if our options are her, or the Faithful? That's not an option."

"Can't argue." She whispered. "How do we do this?"

I licked my lips, considering our options. Felt a pang in my belly that told me that food still had to be a priority. You couldn't focus on an operation on an empty stomach; you were all too likely to miss something if you were distracted.

"We get dinner."

Irkan turned away from the barge just as it vanished behind the skyline, "Is Ashe'lori certain?"

"Yeah. We'll have some time." I said, finding myself surprisingly confident in that. "They can't be here for us, or they wouldn't be that obvious. If it is the Faithful, they might just be here to buy slaves to take to Last Stop, or to use as target practice, or whatever unholy project they're working on now."

He nodded slowly, leaving me to fix the display on my helmet, letting out a deep breath. "We get food, take it home, and we pick up our weapons. As soon as we're done eating, let's head east and see just who came out of that barge. If they're not Trahcon, we can come back, laugh about being paranoid, and get a little drunk."

"And if they are?" He asked.

"If they are..." I swallowed, "If they are, then we'll have to decide if we're going to fight or flee."

XXIV

Even when we'd arrived at the barge to find a group of Trahcon conversing at the base of the crew ramp, I'd held out some hope that they weren't among the Faithful.

We'd stayed well back, stopping us from listening in, until two of them had broken off from the others. Not really hesitating, I made the call to follow them into the city to see just what they were up to. The others hadn't argued, though they'd been less certain of leaving me to be the one to follow them directly.

I hadn't really seen the choice. I may have been an amateur spy, but I'd gotten a *little* training in following people around a city. Irkan and Johanna hadn't. More than that, one person following someone was harder to pick out than three.

The two of them split off as we left the landing field, moving to keep pace down a side street rather than walking with me directly.

In truth I probably hadn't needed to send them away like that.

I didn't think the people I was following noticed me in the slightest. Not when they were too busy sneering at everyone around them.

"Pretty sure they're Faithul." I said across our comms, casually keeping pace about a half-block behind them. "They're doing everything they can to not come within a few yards of any alien on the street, and there's a lot of aliens on this street."

Johanna's frustrated groan sounded from my speakers, but it was Irkan who spoke. *"Where does Ashe'lori believe they are headed?"*

Consulting my mental map of the city, there was only one place I could think of in this direction. "Slave markets."

"Looking for more beasts to torture." His voice dropped to a growl. *"This sailor believes we should not allow them to return to their ship alive."*

In any other circumstance, I don't think I'd have even considered that as an option.

But for the Faithful?

For the Faithful, I found myself seriously thinking about it.

"If we can." I said finally. "There should be a shuttle station just across the street from the markets. Head there like you're waiting for a ride back."

"*Understood.*" He rumbled.

"*Ashe.*" Johanna spoke up, "*Are you going to be all right on your own?*"

I had no idea, but I couldn't admit that. "Yeah, I'll be fine. Just be ready in case they realize I'm following them. Or that I have a transmitter in me somewhere."

"*We will. And I'll start screaming if they realize that we have them too.*"

Smiling even though I knew she was deadly serious, I kept my focus on the two Trahcon just ahead of me. An intersection with groundcars flowing past had stopped them, along with a dozen other people. Faithful being Faithful, they'd halted well back of the mixed Thondians and Mikira waiting to cross.

Forcing my nerves deep under the surface, a hand casually resting on the gun on my hip helping steady the waves, I approached close enough to hear them speaking to one another.

"...given this assignment." The male of the pair was complaining, hands tugging his heavy vest more tightly around his chest. "We should be preparing for the second operation."

The woman on his left snorted, her arms crossing. "We would be if you had kept your mouth shut. You know how sensitive the Ascended is to her packmate's failures."

"Her outright disaster, you mean."

She shrugged, "Her fate is in the Gods' hands, now. And you should be glad of this duty. It will hardly be difficult, and we can cover ourselves in glory with the others later when the real operation begins."

He seemed to grumble for a moment, then said just loudly enough for me to hear. "It might be easy, but my skin is crawling to be surrounded by so many beasts."

And there it was.

"It won't be long." She replied, tarah flexing as the signals finally changed, letting the foot traffic begin moving. "Soon they'll be caged, as they should be. Come, we can..."

I let the distance between us grow a bit, trying to look like just another pirate strolling along in their wake. It wasn't as hard as it could have been; plenty of people around us were in full armor like I was. Few were Human, true, but I supposed I could have passed for an extremely short Thondian.

...that was actually not a bad idea. It would certainly help me avoid attention. Of course I'd need to learn their language. And how to hold myself as stiffly as they did. And learn that silent communication in how they positioned themselves.

All right. It probably wasn't possible, not without more training, but I *could* pass for a tall Trahcon woman in the right armor. I'd just need a helmet in that proper style. True, it wouldn't work to deceive other Trahcon, they'd pick up on my lack of sorcery quickly, but it could definitely work on other aliens.

"Should have thought of that before, Ashe." I muttered to myself.

Nothing to do about it now, except keep it as an idea for the future.

The slow pace of the man and woman ahead of me, mostly caused by their prejudiced refusal to get near anyone else, made it a fairly long walk to the city's largest slave market. I had to stop several times to avoid getting too close, or drawing their attention behind them. Mostly that meant window shopping, though at another intersection I managed to get into a debate with a Naulian over whether or not the Scarlet Tears or the Crescent was going to win the ongoing war.

"Of course we shall be victorious." Irkan huffed, having listened to

my side of the argument. *"That is hardly in doubt."*

Smiling to myself, I finally picked up the pace around then, watching as the Faithful vanished through the market's grand entrance.

The building itself was enormous, one of the larger ones in the entire city, and it was one of the busiest as well. Not because many people were actually buying other people, as far as I could tell. Instead most of the traffic seemed to be following the signs for numerous slave brothels, which made my stomach churn unpleasantly.

Doing my best to not think about what was going on in those areas, and similarly ignoring the massive advertisements for various slave-dealers on the walls, I followed the Faithful up a broad stairwell to the second level.

They sailed a straight course for one of the nearby shops. It was lit up with pink and blue lights, playing over miserable looking Naulians sitting in glass cages for anyone to inspect as they walked past.

I gave them a minute's head start, pretending to be checking out a sign for Trahcon men being sold; 'With implanted nullifiers!' according to the ad.

"Disgusting." I heard myself growl before I raised my voice, "Irkan, Johanna? I think you should come inside."

"Are we attacking them within the market?" Irkan asked.

I bit my lip, considering it before saying. "I think so. If we do it after they pay, but before they take the slaves..."

"The sellers shall not complain." He replied, understanding. *"And those slaves shall not be sent to the barge."*

"We can only hope." I said. "Head straight upstairs once you're in, first store on the right."

"Understood."

Trusting that they'd be on their way soon, I turned away from the disgusting advertisements, and strode into a shop whose contents were sure to improve my mood.

Inside I found the Faithful at a counter, in deep discussion with a tan-furred Naulian woman. Her expression, and the way all four of her arms were haughtily crossed, betrayed that their attitudes were already making their bargaining more difficult than it needed to be.

Another employee approached me before I could do more than glance around; finding the interior emptier than I would have expected, apart from the trapped souls in their glass cages all around the edges.

"Welcome." He greeted me in Caranat, giving me a toothy grin as he ambled over. "What kind of product are you looking for?"

Forcing myself to sound calm, I replied, "Right now I'm merely comparing my options. If I may have a few minutes to look?"

"Of course, of course." He waved his right arms permissively. "If you have any questions or preferences, please let me know and I will be happy to help."

It was incredibly disconcerting how polite and helpful he was, considering the nature of his 'product'. I could have been in a store for clothes, with a helpful man trying to help me find the best fitting shirt, instead of in a slaver's den looking over *people*.

I strolled slowly along, pretending to look over the miserable looking prisoners. None of them seemed to have any defiance left; none of them so much as glanced at me, keeping their sunken eyes on the ground instead.

That made it easier, in a way. To just... look past them. Not really see them.

To focus on my hearing, to listen to the argument at the counter.

"...offering you a more than a fair amount." The Trahcon man said, his voice rising in irritation.

"And I would be happy to make such a deal, but I *cannot* sell you our entire stock!" The Naulian woman snapped back. "A fifth of what we have is already promised to the 15ᵗʰ Flotilla! I will sell you the rest at that rate."

The Faithful scowled, tarah rising in an obvious threat display. "That is not enough for what we need."

"It is what I have! And you won't find anyone else here with those numbers, or willing to sell in bulk at that cost." Came the counter. "Not unless you want to bargain with a dozen other groups. Take the one hundred I have, and you can make up the numbers with *one* of the other sellers."

"We do not have time-" The woman beside him gave him a sharp elbow, making him hiss. "-what?"

"We don't have time to argue either." She countered. She was apparently the better actor between them; she sounded far more understanding and patient than her companion. "Take her deal, we'll find a second to make up the numbers. If they complain about us going over budget, they'll just have to understand."

The man tensed up further, but finally jerked his head in a sharp nod. "Fine. We'll take what you have."

"Excellent." Not that the seller sounded any happier. "Fill out the requisite delivery forms, and your payment information."

I came to a slow stop next to a red-furred slave, pretending to inspect her. That lasted until the male employee came back over, his expression far more apologetic.

"I am sorry, but it seems all of our product is spoken for now."

"I heard." I replied, "A shame."

He followed where my gaze seemed to be, nodding in apparent understanding. "Oh yes. The red hair is always very popular. I'm sure we'll have more product in soon. I can create an alert for you, if you wish?"

"No, thank you. I know the raiding schedule." I said, trying to sound just as polite. "I'll come by after the next return."

"Of course, of course." He smiled, not seemingly bothered. "If we get more reds, I will see about keeping one back for you. A small upcharge only."

I glanced right, to where the Faithful woman was entering information into the tablet she'd been given. The moment she handed it back I forced ice onto my nerves, and raised my voice.

"Thank you again, that would be most appreciated. A shame the river-sharks took them all."

The woman gave me a sharp glance, clearly irritated, but the man gave me something more. He turned sharply, tarah rising along with his voice.

"Then you should have been faster, short-fur." He spat. "Go buy a used up pleasure whore if you're that desperate."

His slur made my spine straighten up all on its own, my hand falling to the grip of my gun. "Do *not* call me that."

"I will call you what I like, *short-fur.*" He sneered. "Go. Scurry back to the mud your kind crawled out of."

I didn't have to feign the growl, adding an angry step forward. He mimicked me at once, traces of ozone coming through my helmet's cheap filters. Looking considerably more alarmed, the employee at my side quickly darted between us, all of his arms extended out to keep us apart.

"Now, now." He tried to chuckle, "Please don't fight with so much product around. How about the savanna stop holding her gun, and the river-shark withdraw his sorcery?"

The Faithful's reaction was everything I could have hoped for.

"Do not speak down to me!" He spat, right tarah flexing. The invisible spell rammed into the poor Naulian slaver hard enough to lift him from his feet, slamming him into the counter. He fell with a pained cry, the woman behind that counter snarling as she brought a hand down on something.

An a single alarm yowled... and both of the Faithful shrieked, hands rising to clutch at their tarah. Shouts from outside betrayed that their were more Trahcon who'd just been caught at the edges of the effect.

"That's an emplaced nullifer." She shouted, "You're paying double for that, gray!"

For a single heartbeat I feared that the Faithful would back down with their greatest weapon taken away, with their only defense removed. They recovered slowly from the pain only they could feel, from the deafening notes stopping them from calling on their sorcery.

And then my fears were proven unfounded, because both of them completely lost their minds.

"You *dare!?*" The woman shrieked, throwing herself over the counter, trying to strangle the much smaller alien. Both of them tumbled back in a flurry of confused limbs.

I didn't have time for that, because the man was coming right at me, fists raised.

At least he was, until I drew my pistol and shot him when he was just a few feet away.

His expression widened in shock when the round punched through his chest, his charge turning into a stagger. I think he tried to find the strength to keep going, until my second shot took him in one of his hearts.

Then he dropped in a heap on the floor, dark red blood pooling around him.

People were shouting outside, and the women were shouting behind the counter. I hesitated for a single moment, then ran forward, leaping over crumpled employee still trying to recover his wits. Landing next to the counter, I leaned over it to see the Faithful on top of the Naulian woman, slamming her head against the floor with each flex of her arms.

I didn't hesitate that time; I snapped my free hand down and grabbed her by her left tarah. Hard.

The woman yowled, her back arching as I pulled her up. She thrashed, losing her old on her victim, and managing to fight her way of my grip.

That was fine, because she'd straightened up to do it, and now I didn't have to worry about hurting the woman under her when I pulled the trigger again.

Said Naulian woman shoved the corpse off of her in a furious motion, "Fucking grays!"

Grimacing at the slur, and feeling my body beginning to shake, I held a hand out for her. "You all right?"

She snapped her attention to me, then to my hand as if baffled. Then she shook herself, and raised a hand up to take mine.

I pulled her up gently, then quickly caught her when she nearly tipped back over.

"I'm.... " She blinked several times, then slumped against the counter. "Oh. Not fine. Ugh... Jak? Jak? Are you all right?"

The man groaned as well, two hands fumbling to get a hold of the counter.

He was helped by a sprinting Johanna, my packmate sliding to a stop beside him, She got him upright as Irkan lumbered in behind her, his rifle held in both hands just in case.

They'd hardly entered before a trio of Thondians in extremely heavy armor came storming in, all three clutching shotguns.

"Report!" The lead man bellowed. "What was this?"

The woman I'd helped managed, barely, to wave an arm at them. "It's... settled. Damned grays lost their heads. Just an argument over who got to buy product."

There was a deep grunt, the weapons lowering. "And these three?"

"Helped." She blinked a few times, then asked. "I'll pay the fee for your medic. Think... things aren't right."

"Concussion." I turned to the Thondians, bowing my head to the left as I would to Gothin. "She got her head slammed on the floor several times."

Another grunt, though he gave me a similar bow to his right. "We'll dispatch the medic and a clean-up team. You've got that long to take anything you want from the bodies. And turn that nullifier off!"

I blinked, then nodded. "Thank you."

He was already turning away, striding outside. Shouting that it had been handled, and for business to resume.

Behind me I heard the two Naule fumble around for a moment before deactivating their security system, leaving my packmates and I to check the bodies of the two people I'd just killed.

I'd killed them. Both of them.

I'd killed two Faithful.

It was... I felt almost *giddy*. The terror of facing them again was gone, banished to the depths. Sure, I'd gotten very lucky in that they'd reacted even worse than I'd expected to a very mild insult. That this slaver's store had a nullification system ready just in case sorcerers tried to cause problems inside.

But I'd still done it. I'd beaten the people who'd haunted my nightmares for *years*, and I had done it easily.

"I can't stop shaking." I whispered, kneeling beside the man's corpse, pulling his wrist-comp off. "I thought this was going to be a real battle. That we'd be wounded, really struggle."

Irkan huffed inside his helmet. "Ashe'lori was lucky, and the Faithful were arrogant. I believe that we may continue to rely upon the latter if we work with speed."

I blinked, turning to him. "What do you mean?"

"This sailor has an idea. An aggressive one." He nodded to the two battered Naule, "We shall need them, and Ul Gothin's support, but it may give Ashe'lori the knowledge she so craves."

Another blink, then I felt my eyes widen. "You want to *attack* them? Attack the barge?"

"Yes." He said simply.

I swallowed, shifted my weight, glanced to where Johanna had just removed the dead woman's wrist-comp as well.

"...what are you thinking?" I asked.

He told me.

XXV

The slavers were all too happy to help us, once we made it clear all we really needed was their cargo haulers. The fact that the Faithful's payment had gone through probably helped as well, ensuring that they didn't blame me for throwing a stone into the water.

I'd really wanted to try and free a few of the slaves who'd technically been 'bought', but Irkan had been firmly against it. We didn't have the time or resources to actually do anything for them. All we would manage was to give them temporary freedom, false hope, and then a rapid return to enslavement.

And besides. Whatever fate awaited them would be kinder than the fate of those who might now be trapped on the Faithful's barge.

I still wasn't happy, but I'd struggled to come up with a counter-argument. Especially in the short amount of time we had to get everything together.

According to the slavers, deliveries like these were usually conducted inside of three hours. That was the length of the window we had to convince Gothin to help, and then arrange for her and as many of her pirates as she could get together to come and join us.

Most of that time was actually spent getting the critical asset we would need in the back of one of the slavers' massive delivery vehicles.

Once it was ready, we all piled in, forming up a convoy four trucks long, headed for the landing grounds.

Gothin herself was in the lead truck with me, sitting on my right as I drove. Like me she was in full armor, though hers was painted black and looked well cared for. She leaned forward as we drew near to the barge in question, an approving noise coming low in her throat.

"Well now. You were not lying, that really is an Imperial barge." She said. "Exactly the kind of vessel I could use to act as a supply ship to extend my raids, to hold stores and spoils."

"I am glad you approve." I replied, nervously tightening my grip on the controls. "We don't know how many living enemies will be on board, but there will be several dozen combat automations. They'll be the real danger, so you should focus on them first."

A hand dropped to her belt, patting the grenades there. "We can handle mere machines, along with sharks without their sorcery. This is an operation we have done many times, little savanna."

I swallowed, realizing I'd just stated the blatantly obvious to her. "Right, sorry."

To my surprise she actually chuckled, "Your first battle?"

"Not my first battle, but I'm not.... used to being on the offense." I admitted. "Most of the fights I've been in have kind of just swept over me."

"As shall this one, once it begins." Her stiff frame seemed to loosen, arms and legs shifting in preparation as we drew closer to the barge. "I see a welcoming party emerging to greet us."

There was indeed; two of the Faithful had emerged, wearing light armor but without helmets. Standing at the base of the crew ramp, they were waving for us to pull left, to where the massive side doors were slowly opening. I could see automations waiting patiently to receive their 'cargo', to haul them to the tiny cells.

"How close?" I asked, finding my usual shaking coming back. Memories of walking down ramps just like those into a swamp after months of terror and darkness coming back at the worst moment.

"Close. Pull right, just beyond them, back up towards the first ramp." Gothin ordered, her hands slowly shifting her long shotgun into her lap. "Follow their instructions."

I did, gently striking the brakes, making sure to keep control of the massive vehicle in the dirt I was driving on. Focusing on the controls helped me stay calm... mostly.

Turning left, I slowed to a stop, then put it into reverse, backing up toward the ramp as one of the Faithful moved so I could see him in the rear cameras. He waved me closer with rolls of his hand, beckoning me on until he was satisfied.

I stopped, locking the brakes but leaving the motor running at his gesture to halt.

"Wait." Gothin ordered patiently, watching as the remaining three trucks all rumbled placidly past; experienced pirates driving them into position.

I watched nervously as the Faithful behind began to come around, strolling up toward my door. "He's coming."

"I know. Lower your window when he knocks." She ordered. "Hallan? Activate on my signal."

"Ready!" Another Thondian woman replied from just behind us. *"At your word, Tarath!"*

The Faithful rapped hard on my door, stepping up onto the footrest just outside. A single sharp rap on the door had me lower the window as instructed, the man's tarah lifting in annoyance.

"Open the back up, let's get this over with." He ordered rather rudely.

"Now." Gothin said simply.

He had enough time to blink. "What-"

She leaned around me, shotgun sliding across my chest. The Faithful had just begun to gape when she pulled the trigger, and blew most of his head into bloody fragments.

A second later I heard a Trahcon woman shriek in startled pain as the heavy nullifier spun up behind us, powered by the truck's motor. It wouldn't last long before it drained the system, ten, maybe fifteen minutes, but the pirates had assured us that would be more than enough.

Wild shouting came from every direction as pirates surged out of the slavers' trucks, men and women already tearing into the waiting automations before the machines could react.

Gothin was out with them in a blur of motion, leaving me to shove my door open, staggering over the incredibly nauseating sight of the man she'd just killed.

The other Faithful who'd been outside hadn't lasted any longer; she was already down, Gothin's people storming up the ramps before anyone inside could try to retract them.

I ran after her, spotting Irkan and Johanna at the tail end of the pirates who'd been riding in the back of our truck.

The three of us stuck close to Gothin when she ran up the crew ramp, following directly in her wake, following the sounds of gunfire and screaming. They'd been a bit muted outside of the ship's hull, but that changed once we were within; the cacophony deafening in the confined interior.

Another of the Faithful was laying dead just inside, making me jump over her corpse, and a pair of shot up automations lay just beyond them.

"Primary cargo holds cleared." A man reported across comms. *"They're a third the size they should be, someone really overhauled this tub."*

"Sweep aft." Gothin barked, following the party making for the bridge. "Lori says there will be prison cells and more automations to mind them. I want a full inventory of what we've got aboard!"

"As you order, Tarath."

Licking my lips to wet them, I was about to ask how much resistance there had been from the machines when the gunfire just ahead of us picked up. The steady, professional shooting abruptly transforming into the constant roar of panicked, desperate fire.

And a high-pitched yowl that occasionally haunted my dreams cut through it.

"Ashahn's blood!" I swore, "It's one of-"

The cybernetically tortured Kelthi surged into view around a corner before I could finish the warning. It was moving on all fours, blonde fur matted with blood, metals claws and fangs coated with the liquid. There was no pause, no hesitation; it bounded right for Gothin, taking her startled shot across barriers before they collided.

Irkan surged past me, lowering his head as the thing wrenched the pirate's shotgun from her fingers with terrible ease.

He slammed into it just before it could lunge for her throat, ramming it off of her with his sheer mass. The thing shrieked as they went down, its lanky body pinned beneath him. It flailed desperately, until Johanna and I both rushed forward to help him.

She shot from too far away; sending a round skipping off of intact shields.

I simply shoved my gun against its forehead, then pulled the trigger three times.

The tortured soul went limp, the glow its artificial eyes fading out. Leaning back, I still shot it two more times, just to be sure. I wasn't about to take any chances. Not after what I'd gone through in those tunnels.

Behind us I heard Gothin recover, looking back to see her kick her weapon back into her hands. Her voice low, pensive.

"You really were telling the truth." She muttered, "By the Paragons... everyone on full alert! We've got some kind of cybernetic crap! You three, come on!"

Pausing just long enough to help Irkan up, we followed her around the corner to find the lead team a mess of blood. Most of them were still alive, though bleeding badly, and clearly in extreme amounts of pain.

"They get off on hurting people." I said, answering the unspoken question. "Killing you ends their fun."

Gothin grunted, "You, Ark Fleet .Can you bind a wound?"

Johanna jerked her head, "Yes."

"Help them, you too, Mikira!" She stepped over her men, storming forward with real anger in her shoulders. "Lori! With me!"

The Kelthi had apparently ambushed the pirates as soon as they'd opened the way to the bridge, because its open door was just beyond them. Within it was a woman in the silver robes of a Priestess of Iriahn, her hands practically flying over various systems.

Gothin shot her in the side without a word, sending her stumbling. She caught herself on the small captain's chair, slumping against it.

"Ah..." Green eyes snapped up to us, teeth baring in a snarl. "You dare!? You beasts *dare* to cut us off from our birthright!? To harm those of the True Faith?"

"Obviously." Gothin drawled. "Any final words?"

"We will purge this disgusting world of all your filthy-"

Gothin shot her again, and the ranting cut off. "Bridge secure. All teams report."

"Engines secure." Hallan reported. *"Only automations down here, and they didn't have proper arms. Just tried to beat us to death."*

A man I didn't know spoke up in a Cathian accent, *"Cabins secure. Three more crazies. They huddled around a grenade when we came in, blew themselves apart."*

I winced, listening as Corrack gave his own. *"Still securing the slave deck. There's several levels, and a lot of them back here, Tarath. All Naule, paired up in padded cells. Think this tub is half full."*

"Explains why they were at the slave markets." I offered.

Gothin nodded in agreement. "Move the prisoners to the main hold, we'll see if any of them will be useful to us. Everyone else, sweep the ship for sabotage or hold outs. The sooner we're sure it's ours, the sooner we can celebrate another clean prize."

A chorus of replies came back, all of them sounding pleased. I nearly asked what she would do with the Naule who'd been aboard, swallowed my words, and instead started poking at the bridge's consoles.

"She wipe them?" Gothin asked, moving to loom behind me.

"I think so..." I sighed as the navigation system came up, cheerfully thanking me for installing the base software. "Yeah. Full reset it looks like. Dammit. I was really hoping we'd get something from the systems."

Her hand struck my back hard enough to make me stagger, "Cheer up, little savanna. Your enemies are dead, I have a new support ship, and you'll still get any other data we find."

I ducked my head a little, straightening up. "Thank you."

"The ship *is* your thanks." She reminded me. "Come. If there is anything left for you, it will be in their personal quarters, or on their corpses."

The Faithful's apparent leader didn't have much on her. Just a wrist-comp that she'd similarly reset when she had realized that the end was coming for her. More revealing were the numerous burns under her robes, covering nearly half of her chest. I took a picture of those with my wrist-comp, then followed Gothin back out into the bloody hallway.

It turned out that the Kelthi had only killed one of her people; a Naulian man who'd gotten his throat opened up. The others had merely been covered in painful lacerations that had them snarling and cursing, but most were already upright now that they'd been bandaged.

Leaving them to organize themselves, Gothin led my packmates and I up a ladder to the floor above us, where more pirates were already straightening out what was left of the corpses.

Their leader, a slim little Trahcon man, shrugged helplessly when we arrived in a dining space.. and when Johanna made a retching sound at the mess waiting for us. "Blew themselves up, like I said. Crazy."

I swallowed, trying not to look at what was left of the three Trahcon. I couldn't even tell if they'd been male or female, there was so little left of them. "Uh... yeah. We can... check the cabins, then you all can have whatever we don't need."

He glanced at Gothin, and at her nod motioned for his people to let us move past to start checking out the crew's quarters.

Irkan struck up a conversation with the pirate as we reached the first of them, Johanna and I rifling through drawers while the pair of them conversed.

"I am most impressed with your crew, Ul Gothin." He said. "Most professional."

She whistled, but her tones were pleased. "Don't tell me you expected us to act like those fools you see in film? Rushing about, firing our weapons wildly, screaming and cursing all the while?"

He chuckled, "Of course not. Such fools do not survive to become as successfully lethal as your crew."

"Now there is a proper compliment. I insist you continue."

Rolling my eyes a little, I tuned out their discussion in favor of digging through silken robes in drawers. My search revealed nothing besides clothing, but Johanna made a noise of triumph behind me. Turning around, I grinned as she held up a small, leather-bound journal.

"It's got writing in it." She reported, skipping through a few pages. "Coded, though. At least I think it's code."

Code was fine. We could deal with that later, "Keep it. Anything else?"

"Drawer full of credits in four different currencies." Johanna replied, pulling out the drawer in question. I leaned over a bit, spotting physical Imperial coins in neat stacks beside three others. One I vaguely recognized as Ascendancy chits, but the other two escaped me. "Bonus pay for our pirate friends."

Gothin made another approving noise. Between the fact that we openly left the money for her, and Irkan's compliments, we apparently graduated to trusted enough to finish our sweep without her supervision. She moved off with her people to inspect the rest of the barge, leaving us to finish checking over the cabins.

Crew quarters numbers two and three didn't have anything that the first one hadn't; lots of clothes, some snacks, and some booze. Neither had paper journals as the first, though the third had a wrist-comp hidden underneath a pillow on the bed.

The fourth and final cabin was more ornate than the others; it had artwork squeezed onto the walls, the bed's covers were all rich silks, and there was a small bathroom directly attached.

"Strange." I murmured, frowning at it all from the doorway.

"Why?" Johanna asked, looking over my shoulder. "Looks like a Captain's quarters, or something."

I shook my head, "Yeah, I guess, but... I don't know. The art is too bright. Look at it, a sunrise on that wall, a quiet farm on the the other."

She hummed. "I mean, it's not the usual dour storms and stuff that I see in Trahcon stores and restaurants. That a big deal?"

"On it's own, no. It just doesn't fit the Faithful to me."

Stepping inside, the two of us went through our usual search pattern while Irkan kept watch outside. Clothes were again dumped on the floor, each drawer checked for hidden spaces. Aside from the obvious quality there wasn't much difference in here.

Not until I got to the drawer closest to the bed on my side, and pulled it open to find another of the leather-bound journals.

Pulling it out, I let it fall open to where a feather was being used to mark a page. A glance at the words revealed them to be a mix of random letters, but my attention quickly locked in on the bookmark.

"A Vekki feather." I frowned, holding it up. It was dark, so dark it seemed to absorb the lights themselves. Turning it over a few times, I glanced at the tip, not surprised to find it sharpened and ink-stained.

"Used as a pen." I said.

Irkan took a single step inside, looking at what I was holding. "Are you certain it is Vekki? Not merely avian?"

"Pretty sure." I bit my lip, putting the feather back into the journal. "If it is, I don't think they gave up a feather willingly."

"This sailor agrees." He said. "Johanna?"

The other woman shook her head, holding up a small bag that she'd apparently found. "A few more journals, all blank. More of those feathers too. Plus a strange little disc thing."

"Disk thing?" I asked.

She shrugged, reaching in to pull it out.

It was indeed a disk. There were no symbols on it, no words. Just a rainbow of colors spreading out in a fan shape from the bottom center. Johanna turned it over, revealing the same thing on the other side.

"Dunno what it's made of." She said, "Doesn't feel like stone, or metal."

Irkan shrugged, "Bone, perhaps?"

Johanna promptly chucked the thing back into the bag, rubbing her hands together. "Ugh. Really?"

"Considering the Faithful?" He asked, evidently rhetorically as he went on. "It would not surprise me."

"Me either. Johanna? Catch." When she got her hands up, I tossed her the journal I'd found. She made it vanish into the bag as well, hefting it over a shoulder.

With nothing else to check on this level, we headed past the disgusting scene in the hall, then back down the ladder. One of the pirates was waiting for us, and promptly guided us outside once again. There, near the base of the ramp, Gothin was giving a variety of orders, more of her people arriving in more conventional vehicles to assist in taking over the barge for their own uses while most of the others began casually forming up for their rides back to her main vessels.

Not wanting to interrupt, I held back a little, trying to loosen the tension in my shoulders. My fingers clenched, then relaxed, then my arms crossed so that I could wrap my hands around my biceps.

Today had gone well. Extremely well.

Maybe even *too* well.

I should have been thrilled, ecstatic, almost giddy. I should have felt like I had in that slaving den. We'd taken out an entire Half-Sword's worth of the Faithful, hopefully without the rest of their kind even knowing what had happened here. We'd bought ourselves the time we needed to get out, and from how openly happy she was, I'd turned Gothin from a minor asset into a real ally.

But something still felt...

I found myself turning back to look at the barge behind us. Found myself staring at its rounded sides, blunt stern. At the shadow beneath its bulk, the harsh lines of its landing gear.

It looked...

"Johanna?" I asked quietly. "Is it just me, or does the ship just look... *wrong* to you?"

My packmate turned, her own fingers drumming a quick beat on the straps of her bag. "I don't know about wrong, but that weird feeling is definitely back. Like... something's staring at me."

Irkan huffed, shaking his head. "I feel no such thing. It is a dull ship. Nothing more."

No. No it wasn't. I couldn't say *why* it wasn't, but some part of my soul was telling me to sail as far away from that barge as was possible. And not to wait around either. It was just... off. Something about it was off. Turning a dull, boring barge into an ache between my eyes.

I bit my lip, inhaled through my nose, then let it out. "It's a ship I want to get away from. Let's get out of here and not look back."

They didn't argue, and Gothin arranged for her second in command to drive us home.

XXVI

Irkan tolerated our sullen silence until we got back to the apartment, got our armor off, and took turns showering. Only then, when we were sitting on the floor of our dining space, eating warmed leftovers did he finally confront us about it.

"Today was a grand triumph." He huffed, glowering at each of us in turn. "We abused the arrogance of those who once harmed us to strike them down with ease. Yet instead of reveling, my savanna companions act as though today was a mournful defeat."

Johanna met his stare with one of her own. "It was too easy."

He waved a dismissive arm. "The Faithful are prideful fools who rely on their powers to the exclusion of all else. To them we are mere animals, to consider that we might attack their ship was beyond them."

I found myself shaking my head, agreeing with Johanna. "They are arrogant, yeah, and too reliant on sorcery to defend themselves, but that was still too simple."

A deep huff, and a snapping bite of his burnt loaf, came before his next words.

"Gothin handled her people professionally." He countered. "They were swift and vicious, as skilled pirates must be. We had surprise and numbers against an unprepared enemy. Such things lead to swift victories in battle, in war."

Idly spinning some noodles onto my fork, I fed them into my mouth, chewing as I thought more on it.

It was hard to argue with him about that part. The Faithful *hadn't* been ready for what was coming. They'd expected four trucks full of restrained or drugged slaves, little more than cargo, and had gotten something close to sixty battle-hardened pirates instead.

Automations programmed to deal with nothing more than helpless prisoners hadn't been equipped for that. None of the Faithful themselves had been armed. As he'd said, the idea that they'd be attacked had probably never occurred to them, and even if it had, they would relied on their sorcery as usual.

Of course, with the numbers against them, even if we hadn't had a nullifier... no. Even without the nullifier in place, I didn't think the small pack who'd been aboard would have been able to resist that much force. They'd have just killed a few more of Gothin's people before they died.

Irkan was right. They'd had no chance from the moment they'd entered this particular harbor.

But then why did I still feel so worried?

"You're not wrong." I said once I'd finished chewing. "The logic of why it was easy tracks. I'd bet that the Faithful have stopped here for slaves before, and never had any issues. If we combine that with their usual attitude towards aliens and it's easy to see why they wouldn't have been ready for what we hit them with."

Johanna knew me well enough to ask, "But you still think it was too easy?"

"Maybe not too easy, exactly." My shoulders rolled, "But... something still feels wrong to me. That barge. It just... *looked* wrong."

Another huff from Irkan, his quills rippling with his shaking head. "It was a standard Imperial barge. There was nothing unusual about it, beyond its owners and cargo."

Johanna upgraded her look to a full on glare. "And we're telling you that there was. I don't know what it was, but I'm telling you that there was something *wrong* with that ship. Something that made me want to get as far away from it as I could."

"...like the ship itself was watching me." I said.

Irkan narrowed his eyes, opening his mouth. Then he shut it, visibly worked to calm himself down, and then asked in a measured tone, "Describe it more clearly, if you can. I would understand."

We exchanged a glance, then Johanna motioned for me to stay quiet so that she could try to work through her thoughts. I nodded, eating more noodles, trying to do the same to my mental currents as she began speaking.

"It was... like being around Marzin again. Exactly like that." She nodded very slowly, picking up confidence. "Like I was near a predator that I knew could kill me at any time. No matter how cheerful he was, how innocent he acted, I *knew* he could step on me, or crush me in his hands, or eat me in a single bite."

She worked at her lip, exhaled through her nose, then ran a hand through her hair. "I know it doesn't make any sense. It was just a ship. But I felt like there was an enormous predator right there in front of me, just waiting for its time to kill me. That there wouldn't be anything I could do about it when it decided to act. Ashe?"

Coughing against the spicy noodles I'd just eaten, I took a quick swig of ale to calm down my tongue. Once I'd swallowed, I considered my own words for a few breaths before nodding once.

"It was something like that." I agreed. "It was like how I used to feel when there were supremacists around. When I could feel them staring at me, ready to hit me with a spell as soon as my back was turned. I kept expecting the barge to explode, or its engines to light off until we'd driven a few blocks away."

Irkan considered our words, his features settled into his equivalent of a deep frown.

"Predators." He said, almost musingly. "You both felt as though predators were prepared to attack you."

"Yes." I said at once, Johanna humming an agreement around her own food. "And you didn't feel anything?"

"Nothing of the sort. Merely the exhilaration of battle, of victory. The ship was merely a ship, as I have said."

Johanna glanced at him, throat working as she swallowed. "You finally believe us then?"

It was his turn to shrug. "Neither of my companions favors lies. I believe that you were disconcerted by the vessel, if nothing else. However, I do believe that barge is now Gothin's to deal with."

The other woman blew out a short breath. "Heh. True. Still, you think we should warn her? More than we already did, I mean?"

I grimaced. "Tell her that we have a bad feeling about her ship? I can't imagine her taking it seriously."

"What if something happens, and we didn't warn her though?" She pressed. "I know we've got just four days until the auction, but we might need longer to fix up our purchase. Gothin could make our lives really difficult if she finds... I don't know. Another of the Burned Hand in a hidden compartment or something."

My expression tightened further, but once again I couldn't argue with the logic.

With my packmates watching, I brought up my wrist-comp and began to type out a short message to the pirate. Warning her that Johanna and I had gotten discomfited by the barge as we'd left, that there was something profoundly uncomfortable about it, and asking her to be careful.

Sending the short message off, I comforted myself in doing that much. Johanna looked similarly relieved, Irkan satisfied with the course of action, and so we settled in to finish our meals.

Naturally Gothin called me two minutes later.

I'd hardly tapped the accept key before her deep growl came from the tiny speakers. *"Define your bad feeling."*

Exhaling, I repeated what I'd described to Irkan, then did the same for how Johanna had felt.

"Are your people feeling it too?" I asked.

"At first it was just the three savannas I have among my crew."

I swallowed when she didn't go on, "And now?"

"Now every Thondian among is as well, including myself." Her words dropped to an angry hiss. *"It is akin to a rival staring me down from across the bar, feeling the point in my back where he wishes to drive his knife. The Trahcon in my crew complain of a noise at the edge of their hearing. They suspect some kind device meant to mimic sorcery."*

That was possible, I supposed. Cybernetics meant to replicate a Trahcon or Vekki's natural sorcery did exist, even if they were expensive and rare. Not that cost would really be an issue; the luxuries we'd seen them indulging in, the Faithful were anything but poor. Such a device would explain the noise her subordinate Trahcon were hearing.

Not really the rest of it though. Sorcery was inaudible to those who hadn't evolved to feel it, or who didn't have those same cybernetics to give them some kind of sensation when it was used around them.

It certainly didn't cause anything like what we, and Gothin, had felt.

"Have you found any secret compartments or anything?" I asked.

"No, but I am bringing in my own automations to start scanning for just such things, and pulling the majority of my people back." Another pause, then more hard words. *"You will return at once to assist and observe. I will dispatch a ground-car."*

That wasn't what I'd wanted to hear, but... dammit. I didn't think we could say no either.

"All right." I said, "We'll be ready in a few minutes."

"Good."

She cut the channel before anyone could say anything else, leaving Irkan heaving out a heavy sigh and Johanna groaning.

"We have to." I told them firmly. "We need every bit of information we have on the Faithful for when we get home. Plus, maybe this will let us figure out just how they did... whatever it was they did to us on the ships that brought us to Last Stop."

Johanna didn't look happy, shaking her head slightly. "I was fine *not* knowing, Ashe."

"I-"

"-have to know." She interrupted, tiredly pushing herself to her feet. "That's just how you are. Come on, let's get our armor on."

Getting up as well, I returned to verbal salvo even while my hands gathered up the remains of our second dinner. "Knowledge is what banishes fear, Johanna. Knowing what's going on helps. Always has."

"Which of your Aspects is that?" She asked.

"Zurep, but the saying itself comes from Iatanai. That's the second big religion in the Empire." I explained.

Irkan picked up his own plate, following along as we made to throw out what was left.

"A strange faith." He said, "One that worships no deities, but instead devotes the soul to the gathering of information. I have often thought it strange that Ashe'lori is not a follower of such a way."

I could only shrug, tossing out the disposable bowl I'd been eating from. "I like a lot of what it teaches, but... I like the Aspects more."

He split off after that, heading to his room, while Johanna and I made for the one that we shared together. Our armor was still exactly where we'd left it less than an hour ago; in a giant pile on the ground.

Working together, it didn't take us long to pull the under-layer on over our clothing, then start fastening the heavier plates over top of it. We helped one another with the bolts that locked it all into place, and then making sure our fur didn't get caught when we pulled our helmets on.

I picked up my pistol, making sure the safety was set, while Johanna took up one of the remaining carbines. I grabbed one as well, getting it slung over my shoulder. Doing a final check of each other's gear probably wasn't necessary, but it was a bit of comforting routine that made me feel something like a soldier again.

Then we were in Irkan's room, helping him check over his own gear. A far more complicated process thanks to the way it had to connect to his shell, and how he had to connect his two-piece helmet around his long head.

Once we were finished it was a quick walk to the window, and I glanced outside to confirm that Gothin's driver wasn't here yet.

"Helmet check?" I asked. "No pirates outside yet."

Johanna tapped the side of her helmet, "Check?"

"Check." Irkan rumbled after doing the same. "Let us hope this does not take into the late evening. Our shifts begin early tomorrow."

A hum from Johanna. "We could always just quit. We've got the money we need, and I'm sick of serving drinks to rude *schweine*."

"If the savanna wishes, she may." He replied. "The sailor finds the antics of drunken pirates amusing, at times. Brawling with those foolish enough to dispute the bar's peace is engaging as well."

I snorted, leaning against the wall, still looking outside, waiting for a car to come to a stop beside our building. "You should have just joined a sparring league if you were that desperate to get into a fight now and then."

Our Mikiran packmate let out one of his deep laughs. "I did consider it. Sadly those best suited to my moderate talents charge for participation, with the money returned only for victories. As much as I desire the occasional challenge, I had no desire to set back our retreat from this world."

"Thank you." I said, and I meant it. "Are there leagues like that on Lushrivers?"

"But of course. My people indulge in many games of skill and strength." A pause, then another chortle. "The sailor must be cruel to Ashe'lori; she will find no Strike-Wave played there."

I groaned theatrically enough that Johanna laughed.

"I guess I'll just have to keep watching re-runs of Cathia and Alum's leagues." I let out a heavy sigh. "Maybe I'll try the Xenthan ones.... car's coming up."

Johanna shifted to the door, but didn't move to open it just yet. "How are we making sure?"

"I'll call Gothin." I said, already bringing my wrist comp up to do just that.

I'd just gotten my arm level with my chest when something slammed into it, driving my fist against my sternum, sending me staggering. Low-shield alarms shrieked in my ears, and I had no time to even react before a second bullet punched through the window, slamming into my shoulder.

The armor plate there simply shattered, wrenching me to one side, and assuredly saved my life as I fell out of view.

"Down!" Irkan boomed, throwing himself down at the about the same time as I collapsed to the floor, gasping against the pain in my shoulder and elbow.

Johanna did the same a second later, half-landing on top of me.

She was just in time to avoid the heavy burst of automatic fire that cut through the glass, the cheap walls, and even the door. Both of us curled up on instinct, my eyes wide as I watched the tracer fire whip past just overhead.

My helmet's display made things worse a few moments later, lighting up with a planet-wide broadcast.

ALERT. ALERT. SYSTEM UNDER ATTACK. ALERT. ALERT.

I had enough presence of mind to gape before the gunfire suddenly cut off...

...and the shrieking of the city's alarms began to fill the stunned silence.

XXVII

The pause brought on by the howling alarms lasted all of a few seconds before gunfire erupted once again, but it was the few seconds I needed to splash cold water over my soul.

Shaking my head, I managed to get my carbine loose from its strap, getting the safety off with my thumb. "We have to go!"

"Which exit?" Irkan's shout boomed out of my helmet's speakers, hurting my ears far more than the gunfire had.

"Our room!" I called back, "Johanna! Come on!"

To her credit she recovered pretty quickly, rolling off of my legs and crawling rapidly along the floor. I followed right behind, Irkan doing the same ahead of us as our unseen attackers kept sending rounds through the window and walls.

In between the bursts I thought I heard more people screaming furiously outside, and intermittent gunfire starting up around us.

By the time we made it to the bedroom there wasn't any doubt that our neighbors were protesting the attack on our building by replying with their own gunfire. That distracted our attackers enough to make them ease up on their shots into our apartment, letting us get upright and scramble to grab our emergency bags.

Each one had extra clothes, ammunition, food, water, and some of the wrist-comps we'd taken from the Faithul's bodies and their yacht. Johanna and I split the journals we'd found between us, quickly shoving them into our packs before hauling them over our shoulders.

Irkan was already slamming the window out of its cheaply built frame, sending a fire-ladder spitting out automatically..

He took a single look, highlighting himself as a target, and only when no one started shooting on this side did he swing out to scramble down. At my shout, Johanna followed him, leaving me to try and cover them with my short rifle until they hit the ground.

Then I got the weapon back over a shoulder, swung myself through the open hole in the wall, and went down the two-story ladder as quickly as I could without losing my grip.

Down below I could see that the streets were clearing rapidly. Men and women of every species were rushing out of bars and restaurants, practically stampeding one another in their rush to get back to the port. Some piratical instinct telling them not to get caught on the ground, I supposed.

A muted explosion nearby me had me flinch, then pick up the pace.

"Now what?" Johanna shouted as I got near the ground, "Isn't our emergency plan to run to Gothin?"

"It is!" I shouted back, my boots hitting the stone. "Head east, behind the building!"

We set off at a fast jog that became a sprint when someone began shooting at us from somewhere in the far distance. I risked a single glance over my shoulder, but couldn't even spot the flash of the weapon. They could have been in the crowd or on a building, I didn't know.

"Ahead of me!" Irkan boomed, shoving me out in front, "Your shields!"

Right. They hadn't recovered yet. I ducked as best I could, letting him take one or two shots to his intact protection until we were out of sight around the corner of the building. Only then did I start hammering on my wrist-comp, frantically trying to get Gothin back onto a channel as we slid to a stop, trying to gather our breath, collect ourselves.

The pirate didn't answer. She was probably trying to get her own people back to their light ships sitting helpless near the port. Get her crew back from the bars, brothels, and gambling dens they'd been partying in. Protecting us wouldn't be anywhere on her list of priorities right now.

We had to get away. Had to get off world, and she was our only real hope at boarding any kind of ship.

"Plan?" Irkan asked, hands finally getting his rifle settled in his hands rather than slung over one shoulder.

"Get off world." I said, hoping I sounded firm as I got my own weapon back into my hands. "With how much of a mess the streets are, we won't make it on foot. My work station is at Twenty-Fifth and Balk Street. We go there, steal a shuttle, and use that to circle around the worst of downtown."

Both of them nodded, not arguing with the plan, crude as it was.

Taking a deep breath, and hoping I hadn't just doomed us, I led us down the alley, then back out onto a side street.

It was far quieter than the main road, consisting mostly of small apartment buildings like ours. The locals were boarding themselves up as quickly as they could, bracing themselves for the storm that the alarms and gunfire heralded.

A few watched us run past from their windows, only for their faces to vanish as armored shutters came down to protect them.

That was a smart move on their part, because we didn't make it anywhere close to my shuttle station.

We didn't even make it to the first turn before two Trachon in light armor, gray with no other markings, came sprinting around the corner. Irkan was quicker than they or me; the moment they began to slow down, bringing weapons up, he snapped his own into line and opened fire.

The nearest recoiled as the shots played over his shields, flinching back. Their partner hesitated for a split second, saw Johaanna and I getting our guns pointed, then shoved the other back around the corner.

I still shot, just like Johanna did, but I didn't think our wild rounds hit anything beside the bakery behind them.

Irkan snarled at their flight, slowing for a moment, then abruptly swerved right. "This way!"

Startled, we both skidded to a stop, then scrambled to race after him. Rushing between the apartment buildings, I'd have lost track of where we even where if not for the compass on my helmet's display. Irkan led us east-northeast as quickly as his short strides would allow, then abruptly cut north to bring us out onto a different street.

It was a main run, packed with people rushing in every direction, and we had to link arms like children to avoid being separated.

"Hoping they won't shoot in this!?" I had to shout, even with our helmets, to be heard over the din around us.

"Yes!" He bellowed in reply. "West!?"

"Yeah!"

I think he grunted before plunging into the worst of the movement, dragging Johanna and I along behind him. We got cursed at by an entire pack's worth of Naule, but a group of Thondians were quick to take advantage by following along in our wake. They stayed there until we finished cutting across the street, ducking into an alley, the tall trio moving with the crowd.

The alley was disgusting, filled with garbage and things I'd rather not see, much less walk through, but no one shot at us as we used it to get to the back of the local shops.

"Ashe?" Johanna asked, her heavy breathing audible over our comms. "Do you think we missed some of the Faithful?"

I shook my head, our sprint slowing back down to a jog as we cut across an empty parking lot. "Yeah. They probably sent a few others out on other duties, and they came back to find their ship captured. They must have figured out that they couldn't attack Gothin's people, so they either followed us, or one of them turned a scanner on."

"And found us." She said.

"And found us." I agreed.

Irkan shook himself, head sweeping left to right as he kept a wary watch. I gave myself another mental splash of ice water, and started doing the same.

"And the attack?" He asked his own question. "It would have been wiser to seek to capture us. Determine what we knew."

I could only shrug, "Don't know on that one. Maybe they saw Gothin's driver coming, decided to kill us before we could leave. Maybe our transmitters have a way of just telling them which of their facilities we escaped from."

Johanna made an unhappy sound in her throat, "Probably tells them everything about us."

They probably did.

Since admitting that out loud wouldn't make any of us feel better, I tried to keep us focused on our task. "We seemed to have lost them for now. We keep sailing west, we get to the station, and we catch up to Gothin before she can leave."

"Right. Uh," She seemed to shake herself, "What's between us and there?"

I nodded ahead of us as we neared the narrow street, "This line of businesses, then residential spaces. Mixed homes and apartments, I think. Nearest shuttle stop is outside of a Thondian temple just two blocks that way, right on Twenty-Fifth."

Irkan nodded as well, then began to pick up his lumbering pace once more. "Then that shall be our landmark. We reach it, and follow that street to our destination."

For the third time we accelerated up into a sprint, or as much of a sprint as Irkan could manage. It was a slow run by our standards. Still, it seemed to be enough to keep us ahead of the people trying to murder us.

This section of the city had already emptied out. It made things almost eerie with how much noise was still coming from the main throughway just out of sight. The shrieking of the city's alarm system starting up again a few minutes later didn't help either.

More gunfire had us all flinch until we realized it was too distant; not directed at us. It came and went over the next few minutes, never really picking up, but never really going away either.

I had no idea what it meant. People defending their homes? Rivals seeing an opportunity to kill one another? Frustrated pirates trying to shoot their way through traffic?

It could have been any or all of those things.

It didn't really matter, because we'd just begun to approach the shuttle stop when we got further confirmation that we really were chipped; a ground-car came screaming around a turn well behind us, accelerating rapidly.

A single glance let me see a the fanned helmet of a Trahcon leaning out of the passenger seat before they started shooting at us.

"Run!" I yelped, "Temple!"

It was the only real bit of cover nearby; massive stone walls with a narrow entryway. I couldn't actually see inside, and could only hope that the stone was thick enough to be bullet-proof.

We ran for safety as rounds began to smack into the walls, the ground, and our shields.

The passenger kept up their carefully aimed fire until the car's brakes screamed, the driver swinging around to give their gunner a better angle.

Johanna and I barely got around the corner before they cut loose at full automatic.

Irkan didn't.

His shields held for the few steps it took for him to reach the entrance, then failed to let the rounds begin hitting the shell protecting his back. The natural protection turned a few of the bullets away... but a few cracked through it, drawing a scream of pain.

"Irkan!" Johanna's shriek was followed by a second, "Ashe!"

I jerked my head around to realize that Thondian in red robes had just picked her up off of her feet, and that a second was already grabbing me as well.

"Ashahn's-let go!"

A hand snapped down, deflecting my carbine before I could shove it against his chest, the man actually laughing as his other hand grabbed my chest piece and...

...and he picked me up with one hand, as if I was a little Meshicon.

"Such rude guests!" He boomed, casually turning to shove me against a wall. "And more come!"

Irkan tried to come for us, but his charge became a stagger. He fell to one knee, slumping against the wall, clearly gasping for breath.

"Irkan!" I'd just begun to struggle again when I saw more priests casually lurking on the other side of the entrance, clearly ready for what came next.

The first of the Trahcon in gray armor didn't have a chance. They stormed in, a shotgun in hand, smoothly bringing it around to aim at Irkan's helpless body before they realized we weren't alone.

A Thondian priest in green robes grabbed them from behind just as Johanna had been, heaving them around like a doll. The Trahcon, a woman from the tenor of their yelp, slammed into the next priest in line, who promptly wrestled the gun out of her hands with no particular effort.

Her sorcery hurled him away in return, slamming him into the stone wall with a grunt, but the first priest made a dagger appear against her throat before she could try to recover.

The second of the Trahcon came bolting in, then skidded to a halt.

I stared, gaping, as their helmet swung around... and then they very carefully dropped the pistol they'd been holding, both arms spreading wide in the universal motion of surrender.

It was only then that I realized that priests weren't the only ones in here.

Not by a long shot.

Looking over the shoulder of the man still pinning me to the wall, I could see a deep depression in the ground. In the center of it was a veritable forest of enormous columns, each one covered in writing. Surrounding them were benches arranged in tiers, and each on of those benches was completely occupied.

What had to be more than two hundred Thondians, their skin ranging from the black of space to the tan of fine sand, had all risen at the commotion.

And nearly every single one of them had a gun of some kind pointed in our direction.

"Oh." I gasped against the pain in my chest and shoulders. "Oh. Um..."

The man holding me showed me his teeth, but there was nothing particularly friendly in his smile. "You interrupted the morning sermon. Although I suppose that the alarms had already done so, so that cannot be held against you."

"...hurts." I managed. "Down?"

"Ah, I suppose." He eased me down to my feet, but didn't let go of either my chest or the hand holding my carbine. "Release the weapon, savanna, and we will tend to your Mikiran friend."

I swallowed nervously, glancing at the two Trahcon who already being marched to a small building that had been hidden by the enormous walls.

Irkan fell to his other knee, and I stopped trying to analyze what was happening.

I let go of the gun, the priest pulling it away.

"Wise." He turned at the waist, voice rising to a deep call "Doctor Wotiv! If you would honor us, we have a patient for you!"

One of the worshipers began making their way forward at once, tapping two others to follow them. I jerked my gaze away from them as my personal captor leaned in, regarding me with his dark eyes.

"As for you. You will give us answers. If they are reasonable, we may allow you to leave. If they are not, well." A stiff shoulder rolled. "I am sure that you can guess, savanna."

I could only nod before Johanna and I were marched off in the same direction as our attackers.

XXVIII

The building proved to be some kind of barracks. Johanna and I, plus the two Faithful, were forced onto cots and our helmets were taken away along with all of our weapons. Both of the Trahcon got Nullification collars put on, which made both of them clearly, if silently, furious.

They didn't openly complain though. Neither did we when all four of us got our wrists tied together with actual rope of all things.

I did my best to split my attention between what was being done to us, and to the men laboring to carry Irkan in on a cot. Biting my lip, I watched as my packmate was moved into a separate room, the supposed doctor vanishing inside with them.

That left us with just the four priests who'd disarmed us as our apparent guards, one of them growling at the Faithful when one of them tried to ask a question.

"Silence." He snapped. "Until the Highborn-Priest arrives."

The woman in question gave him a respectable glower, but kept her jaw clenched. After apparently realizing that her stare was only amusing the priests, she turned her green eyes on me instead.

I met her glare with one of my own, similarly staying quiet. The only sound came the muffled conversation from the room with Irkan, and the quiet creaking of a cot when Johanna shifted herself so she was a bit closer to me. Her movement had both of the Faithful snap their attention to the priests, only to look disappointed when the men didn't say anything.

That tense quiet reigned for nearly a quarter of an hour, and then a truly massive Thondian man walked in.

He had to be close to nine feet tall, and had to duck through the doorway even though it was sized for his species. Red robes with golden trim were parted just enough to reveal that he extremely well muscled, and wore a heavy stone medallion on a necklace.

His dark eyes slid over Johanna and I, then over the Faithful, taking us in.

Whatever he saw must not have impressed him much. He growled something in his own language that saw the other four priests all bow very low to their left, then withdraw out the same door he'd just used.

Once they were gone, he retrieved a heavy chair, settling himself into it.

"I presume," He said, a voice exactly as deep as I would have expected, "That everyone present speaks Caranat, or has a translator running."

"We do." I replied.

The shorter of the Faithful, the green-eyed one who'd been glowering at me, said the same in a Homeworld drawl. "We do, priest."

"Good." Thick arms crossed his chest, his body otherwise remaining perfectly still. "The savanna females shall speak first, as they were the ones clearly fleeing to our sacred temple. You will tell me why you disrupted our sermon, and which band protects you on this world."

Swallowing, I did my best to remain calm and explain. "We only sought a place to make a stand against the enemy coming after us, and thought your walls would do. If we'd known services were ongoing, we'd have tried to circle around instead. Um, as for your second question, we're protected by Yerra ul Gothin."

He blinked slowly, "A pirate whose name and ambitions are known to me. You are of her crew?"

Some foolish, desperate part of me wanted to lie and say yes. The more rational part of my brain told me to stay calm, and tell as close to the truth as possible.

And maybe imply a bit. Thondians seemed to like implying things.

"Temporary contractors." I said. "We analyze data for her, once in a while. Sometimes we meet for drinks, and she likes it when I massage her shoulders."

The senior priest, maybe the eldest priest, seemed amused by the answer.

"I see." He rumbled. "You may now be silent. River-shark females. Explain your tale."

The same Faithful spoke up the moment the last syllable left his lips.

"The short-furs lie." She spat. "They're a pair of slaves who escaped from us when we set down to refuel here, so is that turtle we nearly put down. All three of them have transmitter chips, I can give you the frequency to confirm the tracking signals."

"I may." The priest said. "Which group do you claim?"

"We have an arrangement with the 15th Flotilla." She offered.

His placid expression morphed into a scowl. "The 15th Flotilla loathes river-sharks. If you are to lie, make it believable."

Her tarah rose, the nullification bar around her neck humming dangerously. "I do not lie! We despise each other, but they accept our currency in exchange for fuel and supplies. It was their landing field that our ship rested on."

I couldn't stop myself from interjecting, "Past tense, because Ul Gothin seized it a few hours ago. You can confirm that with her."

"For which she will die!" The Faithful snarled, whirling on me once again. "Our ships have entered the system, and they will not depart until all of our property has been returned, and our fallen avenged!"

Johanna scoffed, speaking up, "Like you actually give a-"

"Silence!" The priest's shout made the pair of us flinch, but neither of the Faithful so much as twitched a tarah.

That seemed to impress the man more than their initial words had, just as our reaction seemed to cost us whatever favor my own first answers had. He said nothing for several minutes, simply glaring at us all instead. It was probably a power display; forcing us to wait for him to remind us that we were his prisoners or something.

Gothin did it all the time, though without the prisoner bit.

"Savannas." He finally resumed. "You shall speak the truth. Are you their property?"

Johanna spoke before I could. "No. Others of their organization abducted us, but then they dumped us on a penal colony and never talked to us again. At least until we shot our way off world."

He blinked slowly. "If you were in their power, it could be said that you were their slaves."

"A *slave*," She countered, rather testily, "Is someone forced to do some kind of labor for someone else on pain of death. They dumped us in a swamp and never interacted with us again."

A low chuckle came from his throat. "A prisoner, then, but not a slave."

I briefly considered adding that we were from the Empire, but Gothin's initial reaction to my story had me hold my tongue. He probably wouldn't believe me, and would think I was either trying to intimidate him into releasing us, or else trying to imply that Rerth might pay for our safety.

His reaction to Gothin's name made me think relying on her was our best river to stay in right now.

"Gothin can vouch for our story." I said, "If you let us contact her, or if you do so yourself."

Dark eyes flicked back to me. "I am considering it. And you, river-sharks? Do you offer the same guarantee should I contact the flotilla?"

"Yes." The talkative one of the two replied at once. "And if you would scan these pathetic creatures, you would find their slave chips."

The priest regarded them, then planted both hands on his knees and pushed himself upright. When he spoke again his voice lost any trace of softness it may have once contained.

"You think me a fool, *gray*." He growled the slur. "The savannas and their wounded companion are in full battle armor, well armed, yet you imply that they broke away from you only after your arrival? Did your vessels simply happen to have such equipment already sized for them?"

"They-"

He spat something in his own language, cutting her off, then went on in Caranat once more. "And the 15th Flotilla would never work with a gray, not even to take their money. It is a point of pride for them that they are extremists against your kind, to such a degree that not even the Scarlet Tears can tolerate them."

The Trahcon went silent, their glares solidly on him.

"That is not to say I am pleased with the savannas for bringing their battle here." He flicked his gaze our way, "But their words have the ring of truth, and are easily confirmed. You shall all wait here until I may contact the mid-caste pirate whom they claim as their protector."

I licked my lips, asking, "When she confirms our story?"

"You may depart as soon as your companion recovers, and payment is offered for the impact markers in our walls." The priest replied.

"And the Faithful?" I pressed

He seemed to sneer at the moniker, but understood who I was referring to. "They claim to know the 15th Flotilla. They shall be given to them to do as they wish with."

Relief crested over me at once. Gothin would definitely demand some kind of payment for this, but she'd definitely support us. Even better, the Faithful would be taken care of by someone else, buying us time to figure out what was going on in the city.

That relief broke when one of the Faithful slid to her own feet, standing as tall as she could, tarah uplifted.

"The ships in orbit are no lie, priest." Her own voice lowered to her best growl as well. It might have been intimidating if not for the sheer size of the priest staring down at her, or the timber of his voice compared to hers. "You would do well to give these pathetic creatures to us, and forget what happened today."

"You threaten, when you are powerless?" The priest bared his teeth at her. "Bold, but useless, little female."

It was useless. He wasn't going to change his mind, and her entire display was kind of pathetic...

...but it was distracting.

I don't know if it was my thoughts or a tiny bit of motion that made me snap my head around to the other Faithful, to realize that the standing one had moved to be between the priest and her companion.

A companion who'd somehow gotten her hands free, drawn a small knife, and was cutting the nullifier's band from around her neck.

"She's loose!" I yelped, scrambling to get up, bound hands grabbing Johanna's to pull her up as well.

The priest was a beat slow. That may have been my fault; my sudden movement drew his attention to us, had him stepping our way, and only when the still helpless Faithful stepped aside did he realize that the woman behind her was now free to utilize her sorcery.

She didn't throw a Strike at him.

She threw River-Fire.

Ozone filled the air in the heartbeat before a stream of blue-black fire roared out from a point near her chest, washing over the enormous man just as he tried to surge forward. He screamed in pain and fury, keeping up his charge through the fire, trying to get close enough to break her neck before she could kill him.

The other Faithful kicked out a leg, getting close enough to the fire to scorch her armor, tripping him up.

He went down, thrashing as the sorcerous flamethrower played over him.

I couldn't run away. Irkan was helpless in the building. I didn't know where the other priests had taken my guns, and my hands were bound.

But the ropes holding them together didn't stop me from using them to grab someone.

Letting go of Johanna, who was staring in horror at the clearly dying priest, I leaped over her cot, barely caught my balance, then rushed at the sorcerer.

She'd been too invested in making sure the priest suffered, and only saw me coming at the last moment. Letting her spell dissipate, she whirled, tarah flexing as though trying to call up more power, but I collided with her before she could focus it.

Our armor's crash was inaudible over the agonized bellows from the dying man on the floor. She was free to grab at me with her hands, but I was taller and stronger, able to drive her back through my sheer mass.

Her back slammed into the wall, and I got both hands around her left tarah.

I squeezed as hard as I could, and it was her turn to scream in agony. She thrashed, slamming her palms into my armored chest, frantically trying to shove me away. Instinctive Strikes lashed out as well, my armor's shields flashing at the impacts.

I held on until the other Faithful hit me in a tackle of her own, driving me into the cot the two of them had been sitting on. We went down in a tangle of flailing legs and arms, her hands going for my throat, my own grabbing hers and trying to shove them away.

She went for a headbutt, missed when I jerked my head to one side, leaving her bounce her head off the pillow instead. I tried to get my legs between us, to shove her off, only for her to slam her hip into my thigh, pinning my left leg under her weight.

Johanna's bound hands snapped down over her head, drawing the rope between them against her throat. The Faithful's green eyes widened in panic in the instant before my packmate hauled back, viciously choking her by pressing against the nullification collar.

A single rasping cry escaped her lips, "Go!"

I managed to turn enough to the see the other Faithful, still clutching at the tarah I'd grabbed, scoop up her helmet from where the priest's had left it near the door.

Then she was sprinting outside, more men bellowing in surprise... and then pain.

I tried to get up, to run her down, but the woman on top of me refused to let herself get pulled away. She kept her weight on my leg, and slipped her hands under mine, grabbing my own throat, stopping me from trying to tell Johanna that we needed her alive if we could.

I choked, trying to flail, only to feel her forehead slam into mine.

Pain and darkness came and went as the three of us struggled and thrashed on the cot. I managed rasping breaths once in a while, Johanna didn't let her manage the same.

Her grip loosened, growing weak.

I saw her eyes roll back, Johanna pulling even harder.

By the time the priests made it in, half of them bruised, the other half clearly burned, we'd thrown the Faithful's corpse onto the ground. Johanna was vomiting into a bucket, either from what she'd just done, or from the smell of the dying priest on the ground.

That horrible smell of burned flesh set off my own stomach, and I found myself expelling my own dinner into a garbage pale rather than answering the priests' furious questions.

The obvious use of sorcery to attack their leader was probably the only thing that stopped them from murdering us then and there. Or maybe it was their own own wounds left them too battered to do more than shove us back onto cots, and to pull their dying leader into a side-room, bellowing for the doctor to attend to him.

We sat in miserable silence, both of us trying to spit out the taste in our mouths, until we were interrogated for a second time.

I told them the same story we'd told their leader, told them what had happened to him. They listened, left, and eventually returned to say that a security camera had caught the fight and confirmed that we weren't responsible.

They told us that Irkan would live.

That we would stay until Gothin came to collect us, after which we were never to return.

XXIX

Gothin's people put us in the back of an aerial truck, flying low and dangerously fast to the field where her ships were kept. I had the briefest glimpse of several corvettes nearly the size of the Faithful's barge before we landed beside one, quickly being shoved up a ramp.

A drugged and unconscious Irkan was carried to the ship's medical spaces.

"Ark Fleet." One of our escort gave Johanna a rough shove in that direction, "You stay with the wounded. The Tarath only wants the other one."

She gave me a somewhat nervous look, which I did my best not to return.

"It'll be fine." I said with a confidence I didn't really feel. "Tell Irkan what happened when he wakes up."

"...all right." She allowed herself to be pushed along. Not that she could have really stopped the Thondian men and women around us, but she didn't make them abuse their strength.

Neither did I, letting the two on either side of me guide me down a different corridor.

A short walk brought me to an armored door along with a Naulian guard leaning casually next to the controls.

"Guns." He ordered, two hands held out.

I turned my carbine over, then my pistol, and stood still as he ran a short scanner over me. Once he was sure I didn't have any extra weapons hidden away, he tapped out a passcode to open up the bridge.

Then it was my turn to get shoved roughly forward, stumbling into the ship's dark command center.

Our host was standing in front of a holographic tank, her second in command seated nearby. Strangely there wasn't anyone else on the bridge. All of the other seats were empty, the stations clearly sitting on standby.

I'd hardly recovered my balance before the door slammed shut behind me, leaving me to awkwardly straighten up as best I could.

"Um, thank you for-"

Gothin interrupted me. "The barge is gone."

My teeth clicked as my mouth closed. I swallowed, then recovered enough to ask, "What?"

"It lifted off shortly after our discussion." She said, voice flat. "We barely cleared everyone who was on the ground near it before the primary engines activated. There were still fifteen of my people aboard, trying to determine if we missed someone, or if it was under remote guidance. All Naule or Mikira, they were the only ones who could be stand to be near it."

I carefully walked forward, taking a spot near the display without really looking at it. "Did they find out?"

Corrak provided the answer. "The last transmission we got from them was nothing but screams."

"Oh." It was the only word I was able to manage. One I repeated a stunned moment later. "Oh."

"Nothing since then." He went on, nodding to the holographic image. "The barge made orbit where a frigate fell in to escort it out. That was when more ships jumped in, including a blockader. It charging up its field is what caused the city's alarms to activate."

Swallowing, I finally looked at what they'd been reviewing.

A tiny version of Kagarraht hung in the center of the display, surrounded by smaller icons. I couldn't read any of it, it was all in their runic language, but after a few seconds I thought I understood it from the positions and the colors being used.

Local ships were in close orbit, staying above the capital city, blocking any approach from the interloping fleet. A few were flickering, maybe shooting at the two ships moving away from the colony, or maybe the system was just updating.

Either way I could pick out the barge and its escort, heading to link up with nearly two dozen ships lurking around the nearest and smallest of Kagarraht's moons. A bit farther out were the icons of the pirate ships too large to properly land, parked around the larger moon.

There was a lot more of them than there were Faithful vessels, but they'd be operating with minimal crews right now. Not really in any shape to engage in battle.

"What kinds of ships?" I asked, nodding to the group.

"Imperial ones." Gothin replied, her voice flat. "A blockader escorted by a full division of cruisers, or void-ships, or whatever they call them. A second cruiser division is in battle formation there, and they have five escort groups in system as well."

That... was a lot of ships. A lot more ships than I would have ever thought a group like the Faithful could possibly own.

Gothin apparently agreed. "I thought you claimed these people were mere terrorists."

"They are." I swallowed, "I mean, they're rich terrorists, but this is... this isn't right. The Empire isn't backing them. It can't be."

"Then explain." She growled.

I flailed for a moment, words tumbling out. "I don't know! Maybe they were raiding the reserve flotillas? Or faking scrapping of obsolete ships? Either way they have to be old! The Empire wouldn't just misplace an entire battle-group of modern ships!"

The pirate stared me down, then seemed to exhale. "Perhaps I am losing my mind, but I believe that you didn't know they had this level of force available."

My momentary relief was drowned when Corrack spoke again. "That may be, Tarath, but the invaders have made their demands clear. If we return their property, they'll withdraw."

"And," Gothin countered, "Do you or any of the officers actually believe that they would?"

"No." He said bluntly. "But the other bands will be trying to figure out just who it is that these attackers are referring to. We're taking a gamble sheltering the three of them."

Gothin's dark gaze slid until her eyes were on mine. "Her Empire will make it worth our while."

I swallowed, ducking my head. "The Empire really wants any information they can get on the Faithful. I'm sure they'll pay you very well for returning us, and more for records of those ships."

I had no idea if they actually would, but it was the only thing I could say in the moment. I'd definitely do my best to convince Rerth to give the pirate some form of pay if she got us home.

Corrack let out a deep grunt, bowing his head to his leader. "We're still with you, Tarath, but be careful. If the Big Four realize we were the ones who hit that barge, that might change a few minds."

"Then we'd best ensure they don't realize it." She replied sharply. "Keep everyone from the raid on their ships, and pay out a bonus to the entire flotilla from our reserve."

He nodded, rising to his feet. "I'll double the guards outside as well."

"Good. Go."

A final bow had him leave without another word, the door opening and shutting behind him. Leaving me alone with the pirate leader. Who was staring at the display without acknowledging me.

That lasted until I took a step toward the vacant chair, her attention snapping back to me sharply enough that I froze.

"Your Empire. Will it pay me?" She demanded.

"I... don't know." I had to admit it. "I *think* so. The Faithful were causing a lot of problems even before they abducted me, but I don't think anyone really thought they had warships. We didn't even think they had places like Last Stop."

"The world you claim you were taken to?" When I nodded, she let out a soft whistle between her teeth. The words that followed were ones I didn't understand, but the tone was that of someone cursing rather viciously.

Swallowing, I hesitated, then asked. "Please. If you want to turn us over to them..."

"Begging for freedom?" She asked harshly.

A tiny shake of my head. "Please just... just shoot us instead."

Gothin stiffened in obvious surprise.

"I mean that." I whispered. "We would all rather die than be taken by them. You have no idea what they do to people. What they'd do to us after we got away from them."

Her chest shifted as she took a deep breath, exhaling it through her teeth once again. "Let me guess. It would resemble that tortured thing that we killed on the ship."

"Only if we were really lucky." I said.

"I see." She crossed her arms, then let out a deep huff. "Stop looking at me like a broken slave, little savanna. I have no intention of turning you over. Not to a group like this. They would not honor any deal, and would mark us all for death simply for interacting with you."

"If you were lucky." I repeated, a little more bleakly. "Um. Do you have a plan then? Can we leave?"

A broad shoulder rolled. "It will depend on what the Big Four decide. They are already in conference with one another. If we are fortunate they will order everyone into space to drive these interlopers off."

"And if we're not?" I asked.

Another shrug. "Blockaders require enormous amounts of fuel to power their fields. It should be possible to simply wait them out."

It was my turn to take a deep breath, forcing my mental seas to smooth out. I had to stay calm. Had to think.

I'd learned a lot about pirates over the few months here, from talking with Irkan and with Gothin. One of the first bits of knowledge had been that pirates were not big on taking unnecessary risks. They were in their profession for wealth, not to die.

"They're going to try and hold out." I guessed.

"Likely." Gothin agreed. "Ships will likely be allowed to depart in limited runs on opposite runs, using the world for shelter as long as possible. To force these Faithful to choose between keeping their field up, to come closer to the planet, or else risking their prey escaping."

I bit my lip, nodding once as I thought I got it. "So they'll try and make the Faithful commit to attacking, or else give up and leave due to lack of fuel. Has this happened before?"

A nod. "A Scarlet Tears force attacked during the war, when the Big Four were still loyal to the Riush. What I just outlined was their exact plan. The Tears lacked enough numbers to risk a direct assault, and backed down after a week of posturing and skirmishes."

So the pirates would feel very confident in being able to make the Faithful do the same.

The question would be if the Faithful would be as willing to give up. On their own, I didn't think they would be. The Faithful were arrogant above anything else, and their pride had been hit several ways. We'd escaped them, killed some of them, and freed a host of their prisoners.

They wouldn't want to back down.

But this wasn't a clandestine raid, or a handful of their agents ambushing someone in a back alley. This was a full battle group openly blockading a world. Yes, that world was a pirate colony in the Far Reaches, but it was still a very public action.

The longer they stayed, the more people would become aware of them.

I felt myself frowning, turning to stare at the display again.

"Why?"

The word had been a whisper, but Gothin heard it clearly. "Why what, little savanna?"

"Why attack?" I asked, trying to puzzle it out. "Everything they've done up until now has been... not quiet, exactly, but they tried to be clandestine. This system has an active FTL buoy. It's out of character."

Gothin cocked her head slightly to the left, though she quickly returned it to a neutral position. "Do you know something so dangerous to them?"

I shook my head. "Just what we saw on Last Stop, but we already sent messages home with that information. Ashahn's blood, I've told you most of it. They'd have to know that the information would be out by now, and I don't think they had any idea just who we were until their barge.... the barge."

"The barge." Her voice dropped once again. "Whatever we missed aboard that killed my people."

"Something important enough they'd send in an entire fleet to get it out." I blew out a breath, bringing a hand up to run it through my fur. "Dammit. I really wish I knew what it was, or why they had so many ships to escort one barge. Or why they risked sending it here at all."

A deep hum from the larger woman came along with a wave at the display. "They wouldn't. No one sane would. That single barge must be one of many, a convoy lurking somewhere in deep space nearby."

I chewed on my lip, agreeing with her. "One barge not full of prisoners, so they stopped at a world with a large slave market to fix that."

"Likely."

"Do you think you could check the starport's records?" I asked. "For signs of other barges like that?"

"Are you paying?" She asked in return.

"If I can. Otherwise it would be something my packmates and Imperial Intelligence would want to know."

She tipped her head slightly. "Then I will consider investigating. For now, I believe that is enough. Return to your companions. Expect to be summoned tomorrow to tell me everything you know of these Faithful."

I nodded, "I'm guessing we're your guests?"

"Prisoners." She corrected without shame. "I do not bother with the pretense. Attempt to leave this ship and I will oblige your desire to be shot rather than be returned to the Faithful."

Even by Gothin's standards, that was a tad more blunt than I'd expected.

"Understood." I said quietly. "Thank you."

"I have never been thanked for holding someone hostage before." She sounded almost amused, one hand waving for me to go. "Begone, Ashe'lori."

I gave her a hesitant bow, and retreated to the door. It opened on my approach, revealing the same pair who'd escorted me here to begin with, and they wasted no time in pushing me away from their leader.

Not resisting, I followed their directions to where my companions were being held.

XXX

The eight days I spent as a prisoner on Gothin's flagship were, in all honesty, some of the most restful I'd had on Kagarraht. It wasn't that I appreciated being surrounded by pirates, or being confined to the small ship's corridors.

It was the fact that I finally didn't have a fake job to go to. I didn't have to be paranoid about how much a tall glass of tea cost at a restaurant. There wasn't any looking over my shoulders, checking to see if the men we'd stolen armor from were about to find us.

Instead I got to help tend to Irkan, lounge around a small cabin with Johanna, and help Gothin go over what little information we were getting about the situation in orbit.

Gothin and I's predictions regarding everyone's behavior had more or less played out exactly as we'd expected, which made me prouder than it should have.

The pirates had refused the Faithful's orders to turn over the people who'd attacked their barge, primarily because none of them were certain who had actually done it. Gothin certainly wasn't volunteering her name, and the hackers she had on staff had cleaned out what little evidence there'd been. Said specialists had also found the signals from the transmitters in our bodies, and jammed them a full day before the Faithful had ordered anyone emitting those signals be turned over.

While there was every chance that the Faithful who'd escaped would be able to give her compatriots our names, or Gothin's name, so far it didn't seem like she'd been able to. That or she'd been too focused on preparing her assault of the priest to listen to what I'd said.

End result? With the Faithful offering no real details that could be verified, the Big Four were apparently convinced this was kind of shake-down by Imperial renegades, and weren't cooperating in the slightest.

Just as Gothin had predicted, they'd begun sending out small groups of ships on trajectories that took them well away from the Faithful's ships. The Faithful had moved in response, sending our their own light forces to skirmish with the pirates, force them back, but no real damage had been done on either side.

It was all a calculated waste of the Faithful's time, fuel, and supplies.

A waste that seemed to be paying off from the increasingly furious transmissions coming from that Blockader, demanding cooperation under a wide variety of threats that were mostly serving as fodder for laughter in bars.

That finally changed on day nine.

I sighed, taking the single seat in our cabin after yet another meeting with Gothin. It wasn't a Trahcon-type room, meaning we all had our own beds set into the walls rather than sharing a single broad one. My packmates definitely appreciated the difference, even if I didn't.

Irkan was laying on his stomach, rough patches covering the cracks in his shell, while Johanna was stretched out on her own cot. Both perked up at my entry, waiting for my daily report.

I gave them the bad news. "The Faithful have started raids on the surface. They brought in three of those barges, and came in under their cruiser's guns. Landed near a village on one of the other continents and destroyed it."

Johanna bit her lip, asking, "Did they violate the Compact?"

"No. They weren't that stupid." I said, very much wishing that they *had* been that stupid. Even pirates would have known what that meant, and called in everyone they could. "Killed anyone who resisted, then marched the survivors and any civilians they could catch into the barges before lifting off again."

Irkan stirred as best he could, groaning a little before speaking. "What was the local reaction?"

"The band operating out of that village was a minor... I don't know. Subsidiary? Vassal? They worked for the Nurukin Gang. They wanted to lift off to engage, but none of the others did." I said.

"Foolish." He muttered. "Now the Faithful know they can remain in close orbit, and they could engage any ships attempting to lift off."

I nodded, "That's what Gothin said, and it looks like that's what they're doing. The blockader and the other cruiser squadron are moving in from the moon, and they're pulling in their escort forces too. The pirate ships still in orbit are moving onto opposite orbits."

There was a quiet groan from Johanna. "God dammit. That close, they can shut off the blockader. Only turn it on when ships try to lift off and run for it."

"Agreed." Irkan exhaled, closing his eyes. While he wasn't in danger of dying anymore, the priests and pirates had done a surprisingly good job of patching him up, he still tired extremely easily. "It will greatly prolong their ability to linger. The longer they do, the more strife shall occur between the local groups."

I could only agree. "Yeah. Gothin is hoping they attack the surface again, but make another of the Big Four angry. If two of them want to fight, there's a chance the others will go along with it. There's more than enough ships here to drive them off."

A tiny shake of his head. "Only with heavy losses. The most powerful vessels are those in the second moon's orbit, and they are too lightly manned to be effective. No shuttles will reach them with crew either."

"...that's a problem." I admitted. "But it's about where we're at right now."

Johanna rubbed tiredly at her temples. "Waiting for the Faithful or the pirates to get tired of how things are, and actually do something?"

"Yeah." I said.

She let her head fall back onto her pillow, theatrically throwing an arm over her eyes. "Better happen soon, or Gothin's going to start charging us rent."

"Don't say it out loud or she just might." I muttered.

"Ja, ja." Her arm lowered enough to cover a yawn, "How long does she think it will take though?"

"She has no idea, but the pirates can't afford to just sit around forever. Two more weeks, maybe three?" My shoulders rolled. "That's her best guess before the smaller bands stop listening and try to leave the system anyway."

"And us?" She asked.

I took a deep breath, then let it out. "If there's a mass-breakout, Gothin says she's going to lift off, and that we're going with her to Terminus. If the Scarlet Tears will pay for us, she'll leave us in their care, and hopefully they'll take us to Lushrivers."

"Possible." Irkan rumbled quietly. "What is her plan if my people do not believe I live, or that we are worth the coin?"

"Gothin will take us to Alum. There's an Imperial Embassy there, and sometimes Ark Fleet traders come through." I said. "She'll give both the same offer, along with the Crescent. If none of them accept, then she'll drop the two of you off there and keep me."

Johanna abruptly sat up, "What!?"

I winced at the volume, holding my hands up. "I'll have to pay off her.... investment in us by working for her, but I convinced her to let you two try and get home from Alum. Try and contact Imperial Intelligence for me, and arrange for my pack to pay for my freedom."

"She'd *enslave* you!?" She demanded, swinging herself around to a seated position.

"....more or less." I said quietly. "But you'd be on a pretty safe planet, with a good chance of getting home. Plus there's an embassy, like I said. I'll give you my identification number, and Rerth's contact information. She'll believe you, and come and pick me up."

"I don't care about us, we're not leaving you as some Thondian pirate's *slave*!"

My own voice rose again, "We don't have a choice, Johanna! She gave me her plans, and told me to deal with it! If it comes down to that, I'll be all right! I won't be *happy,* but I know you and Irkan will get in contact with the Empire. You'll get me free."

Her jaw clenched along with her fists. "I'm not leaving you behind like that."

Irkan let out another tired groan. "Would the savannas calm themselves?"

"You," She whirled on him, fur flying with the speed of it. "Don't get an opinion! You think slavery is completely fine!"

He twitched, blinking rapidly. Not that I blamed him; I was a bit taken aback as well.

"Johanna-"

She didn't let me finish. "No! We're not letting you do that."

"That's just the worst case scenario." I tried to get her to calm down. "We'd need four different groups to all refuse to believe us about who we are to even get to that point. Plus, there's every chance that something will happen here to give us a chance for something else."

"But-"

That time it wasn't one of us interrupting one another.

Instead the pale lights snapped off, then came back on a deep blue at the same time as an alarm began to howl from speakers. All of us flinched in surprise, then looked up just as Corrack's voice replaced the obnoxious klaxon.

"We've got incoming toward the city! All crew prepare for ground and boarding action!"

Ground and boarding!?

I wasted a few breaths gaping, recovered myself, and lunged for the drawers holding my armor. "You heard him! Armor!"

Johanna had paled, but scrambled out of her bed to start grabbing her own. "We don't have our guns!"

"I'll get some!" I promised, "We have to protect Irkan!"

Said packmate was trying to heave himself up as well, "The sailor can protect himself."

"You can barely walk!" I countered, yanking my under-suit out, and somewhat frantically getting my shirt up and over my head. "Can you even get your armor on by yourself?"

"I can and shall." He growled, shuffling to where his own gear was stacked in a neat pile.

Shaking my head, I left my pants on, they were tight enough to fit under the first layer of protection. Practice combined with fear helped to get Johanna and I into our equipment in record time, though we were lacking both our helmets and weapons. Not really knowing how I'd get either of those back just yet, I raced over to help a far slower Irkan instead, Johanna doing the same.

It was probably a sign of how wounded he really was that he didn't try to shake us off. He just held his arms out, letting us get everything into place with minimal fuss.

We'd just finished when our door opened of its own accord, and I found a Naulian woman I vaguely recognized as one of Corrack's usual assistants. Like us she was in full armor, though hers looked honestly battered rather than our pretend-battered.

"Here." She growled, tossing a heavy bag onto the floor. "Everything we took from you. Boss wants both of the savannas up on the bridge, and the Mikira needs to get to medical. He's the new door guard for the doctors."

Yanking the bag open revealed our helmets, carbines, and our pistols.

Johanna grabbed her usual carbine, with Irkan and I grabbing one of each. As soon as the weapons were settled, and we had our headgear on, we headed out.

The Naulian led a shuffling Irkan toward the ship's small medical suite, while Johanna followed me towards the bridge. While I could hear plenty of movement all around, there weren't all that many people heading deeper into the ship, so we weren't obstructed on the way.

For once the armored doors were open, and every station was manned. Gothin stood at her usual place at the holographic display, snapping out what sounded like commands to her people.

Not wanting to interrupt, I moved in just enough so that she definitely noticed me, but stayed silent until she finished and waved us forward.

"A Crescent scout entered the outer solar system." She announced. "The Faithful seemed to be sending an intercept group when two more arrived at different vectors. Not sure what they're doing this far from the main sieges, but their presence caused the Faithful to lose their patience."

One look at the display told me what she meant by that.

"They're coming for us." I swallowed on seeing just how many icons were detaching from larger ships. The leading elements were already entering the atmosphere, escorted by those lighter warships that could safely come down to the surface. "Uh. Where are they headed?"

"Here." Gothin replied. "I believe they have decided to simply sack the city."

"Oh." I licked my lips, grateful that the headgear hid my reaction. "Are we lifting off?"

Her head shook. "No. Shields are up just in case, and our guns are ready to deal with anything that comes too close, but we're staying on the ground."

"Why?" Johanna asked.

"Several fools already attempted to lift off. A cruiser's secondary battery cut them apart." Gothin replied. "Unless we all lift off at the same time, anyone trying to be the first to leave is an obvious target. We stay and fight on the ground."

"Oh." She said. "Um, what do we do?"

"Stay put in this room until told otherwise." The pirate ordered. "Ashe'lori? What's Imperial doctrine for a landing like this? And don't tell me that they aren't actually Imperials, my information says that they follow your tactics when fighting like this."

I blinked. "Information from where?"

She gave me a flat look. "Doctrine. Now."

Confused, I told her what I knew. "Uh. If they're trying to envelope the city, we'd land as close as possible depending on the defenses. Wind Formations, that's the professional soldiers, would strike in first to try and take out anti-air and ground-to-space emplacements. Then the conscripts would roll in."

"You've seen that?"

"Only in Ah-Cycle drills." I said. "I was never in a real combat unit, but I've been in a war-game where we practiced that. Once."

Gothin didn't exactly look pleased. "Once. By the sacred Pillars... I suppose once is more experience with your Empire than the rest of us have. Assuming they identify us as the ones sheltering you, how would they approach?"

I bit my lip, feeling my mental seas churning as I thought on it.

"I only really know the doctrine for conscripts." I admitted. "Um, we'd use a lot of artillery to keep you pinned and distracted. Hit the intersections in the city to stop ground movement, then make a heavy push toward our main target. I don't think the Faithful will be patient enough to set up heavy guns though."

A deep grunt from the taller woman. "We are agreed on that. I expect diversionary attacks on every other landing field, force the other bands to focus on defending just themselves."

Johanna cleared her throat, "So make them do what every pirate group would want to do anyway."

"Precisely, Ark Fleet." A tight shake of her head. "Cause chaos and confusion, then I expect them to rely on the survivor who fled to guide their main attack directly to us."

My companion's helmet shifted to me, then back to her. "Are you going to give us up if that happens?"

"No."

I couldn't help but blink. Not at the response, but at the lack of hesitation. "Really?"

"I have a buyer for you." Gothin replied. "One that will pay well, and one that I feel certain will not betray me. Like you, they further assured me that the Faithful would not honor any deal struck, and that any who crossed them are marked for death or worse."

"Who?" I pressed, "Imperial Intelligence?"

"That is for me to know, and you to learn. Now be silent. The first waves approach."

Silently fuming, I felt Johanna gently put a hand on my shoulder, then not-so-gently give it a rough shake. A wordless plea for me to quiet down and stop risking Gothin's anger over my need to know everything I could about the Faithful.

Taking deep breaths, I let her turn me so that we were both watching the display as the first waves of the Faithful began to land on the outskirts...

...and a hopelessly chaotic battle began.

XXXI

The Faithful were badly outnumbered by the local pirates and gangs whom they were attacking. There were still far more of the terrorists than I had ever hoped there would be, but it was still a force of a few thousands attacking a city of millions.

If this had been an Imperial city the attackers would have been easily repulsed.

Sadly for us it was about the farthest thing from an Imperial outpost.

According to Gothin, the pirates in Kagarraht's largest city were divided into at least forty separate groups. Few of which could agree on anything besides keeping the city *mostly* peaceful so that they all had a market for their stolen goods.

Coordination in the face of the enemy collapsed as soon as the first wave struck our shores, with every group prioritizing the defense of its own ships and territory. The Big Four pulled all of their people back to protect the main starport, and refused to let anyone else approach.

That led to fighting between the pirates, when several smaller bands who had ships there tried to flee in the wake of the first attacks. When they approached the port they were shot at, told to pull back, and promptly tried to shoot their way in instead.

Gothin let us listen to the mess of signals, threats, calls for help, and declarations of hatred while she directed her people to continue digging in all around her small flotilla.

I'd been impressed by her people's professionalism when they'd stormed the barge, and I was equally impressed by the way they prepared for the inevitable battle.

Shuttles were positioned to create fortified positions, cars and carts turned over to make barricades, and sentries were sent to give us ample warning. Heavy guns were broken out of arms lockers, positioned to protect the ramps leading into each ship, whose own massive weapons were kept primed and ready to fire.

It was those weapons that fired first; driving off a Faithful assault shuttle that tried to make an approach near our landing field.

And for the first ten hours of the engagement, that was the extent of our involvement.

Gothin rotated her people to get meals, including us, and we checked in on Irkan to find him asleep in a medical bed. The ship's doctor, a bitter old Trahcon elder, had apparently insisted. He didn't want the only person assigned to guard him to be too tired to do the job, and didn't want us lingering around and being in the way either.

We'd gone back to the bridge, and been told to sit on fold-out chairs near one of the walls while the battle continued elsewhere.

Mostly we spent the time messing around on our wrist-comps. Finally loading translation software that one of Gothin's people promised wasn't full of viruses, then getting it running so that we could actually understand most of what was being said.

I didn't really believe it didn't have viruses, but the need to communicate finally overcame my desire for security.

The Faithful continued hit and run attacks on the south and west sides of the city through the morning and into the afternoon. Their light ships came in close a few times, exchanging missile volleys with their piratical counterparts to cover more assault shuttles coming down, and then would pull back.

The longer that the battle wore on, the worse the situation inside the city seemed to get. More gangs turned on one another, more pirates chose flight over resistance. Those few who tried to make for orbit didn't last long, while those who stayed close to the ground and simply flew to more remote locations fared better.

Gothin was openly discussing possible locations to move to with her officers when the Faithful progressed beyond mere raking operations. When their main assault finally began.

"Here they come." She cut off further conversation as the ship's display lit up, bright red markers appearing all over the map of the city. "Paragons damn that bitch those priests let escape!"

312

Swallowing, I rose from my seat to get a better look.

I nearly wished that I hadn't. That tide of red was progressing rapidly from the Faithful's main landings in the south-east of the city, cutting through the outer districts, heading for the north-eastern landing fields.

Right where we were sitting.

"Corrack, ground status!"

Her second in command replied at once, "Sending out the alert. We'll be ready, Tarath, but they won't die for nothing."

She grunted, glancing to her right. "Hak! Orbital report?"

The Trahcon woman there brought one hand up, apparently listening to something on the comm pieces covering the tips of her tarah. Then her broad face split into a wicked smile, "They've arrived! A Crescent battle force just slammed right into the blockader's field, they're deploying now!"

I sucked in a quick breath, speaking up, "Can they win?"

"They've got a battleship and three heavy cruiser squadrons, so I'd hope so!" Hak called back, no one chastising me for speaking up. "They're flaring their engines up and coming in hard!"

A wave of relief crested somewhere in my chest, my eyes moving to see Gothin looking rather smug.

"The Crescent are your buyers?" I demanded.

"Honestly, I did not expect them to come for you so directly, but we came to an arrangement." She replied. "They proved incredibly interested when I contact them, the week after you mentioned they might also be an enemy of these Faithful."

I vaguely remembered saying something like that during one of our talks at the bar, early in our relationship. I hadn't even considered that she might contact them directly. Especially not before we'd really come to any kind of accord.

In any other circumstance the fact that she'd been looking to *sell* me almost from the start of our interactions would have been incredibly concerning.

In that moment?

"I'm not complaining about the rescue." I assured her, smiling inside of my helmet. "What's the plan now?"

"Hold out until the Faithful shift to engage the enemy in orbit, then break for space ourselves." She replied, turning back to her officers. "I want every ship ready to do just that."

Corrack nodded, striding over to the same communications officer, both of them quickly working together to get those orders sent out. Johanna came up to stand beside me, her hand finding mine as we watched the Faithful fighting their way closer.

"The Crescent." She shook her head. "Irkan won't be happy about going to Cathia instead of Lushrivers."

"He'll be upset, but he'll be alive and free to *be* upset." I replied. "And I'm sure we can get him transferred home. I can't imagine the Crescent would really be that upset about releasing one Tears officer. One that missed pretty much the whole war as it is."

"Let's hope so." She replied, squeezing my hand for a long moment before we let go by mutual accord. "I-"

"Contact!" A booming shout cut her off, a Thondian at another station shouting. "They're moving their light ships in!"

"Evacuating?" Gothin demanded.

"Moving too fast! I think-fuck! Brace!"

I didn't even manage to get a hand out towards the display before the entire ship seemed to lift off the ground, then slam back down. Johanna bounced off of me, men and women all around swearing as several more impacts sent everyone stumbling or clutching at their consoles.

Somewhere around the fifth blow I managed to grab on to the display's ring, holding on tightly while Johanna got a hold of my armor to keep herself upright as well.

That gave me a good view as flashing icons appeared all over the primary starport.

As the Faithful brutally violated the Compact's edicts against orbital bombardment by flattening the entire facility, obliterating most of the surrounding city blocks in the process.

More markers were appearing all over the place, popping up too fast for me to even try to understand them. One I didn't need any help grasping were three Faithful corvettes that shot past just overhead, using the brutal distraction to sweep over the city without resistance.

"Contact! Air-drops!" Someone howled over the general comms.

"Engage!" Gothin bellowed, recovering faster than anyone else in the bridge. "Signal all ships, lift!"

We were too deep in the ship to hear its weaponry firing, or to hear the pirates outside engaging, but I could well imagine the cacophony of it. And besides, there was more than enough noise inside with everyone shouting at one another, systems being called off as the ship's power plant was brought up to full power.

"They're landing on the ships, we've got no angle Tarath!"

"Charges! They've got charges!"

"More coming in from the south! Cut down the aircars!"

"They're jumping clear!"

My heart clenched when the ship shuddered, and a woman to our left began swearing, then reported, "Engines two and three just went red!"

Gothin swore as well, then reached out and ripped her helmet off of her belt. A swift motion brought it over her features, air hissing as it locked into place. "Prepare to receive borders! Any ship capable of withdrawal is to do so! Everyone still on the ground, pull back to defend cabin to cabin. We hold until the Crescent make their own combat drop! Orbital status?"

"Faithful are moving off!" Hak called after a moment, "They're reforming into a battle formation, and they dropped the nullification field! I don't think they'll be in position for another bombardment!"

"Crescent?" She demanded.

"Uh.... there it is! An assault ship just jumped in, opposite side of the planet! Crescent Admiral says we just have to hold out for a little while, they're deploying forces to come straight for us!"

A dark but relieved cheer went up at that, even if the pirates kept their focus on the systems in front of them.

"Good." Gothin waved an arm at her, "Broadcast that to all of our people, make sure they know we're not holding for nothing!"

"Yes, Tarath!"

"You two," She went on, stabbing a finger at us, "With me to the main ramp!"

I felt my limbs begin to tremble as we dutifully followed her, the Naulian men who'd been standing guard outside of the bridge following us in turn. Everywhere more pirates were settling in to intersections and doorways, checking over weapons. Speaking in low, furious tones about how the pay had better be worth what was coming.

Was Gothin about to try and turn us over to the Faithful, despite everything?

I sent silent prayers to a dozen Aspects that she wouldn't. That they'd stand and fight, and that we'd be able to hold out until the Crescent came.

And even if they fought... this wasn't going to be like our prior battles with the Faithful. These apparently weren't the usual, sorcery-obsessed types we'd been able to overcome in the past.

These ones were perfectly content to use guns, wear armor, and generally accept that we lived in a modern age.

"I need to be visible." Gothin informed us as we marched through the ship. "They fight better if they know I'm directly watching them. You two will keep anyone from attacking me from behind. Enemy or friendly. Understood?"

"Johanna's not really a soldier." I tried, only for Gothin to shake her head at once.

"The Ark Fleet bitch will be one today, or she won't live to see tomorrow." Her hands pulled a short-barreled shotgun off her back, priming the weapon with practiced ease. "You hear that, Ark Fleet?"

Johanna's growl had a bit of a tremor to it, "I heard you, sand-elf."

The slur only made the pirate chuckle. "Your Paragons gave you spirit at least. Keep it when you're bleeding and burnt."

I threw a sharp elbow into Johanna's side before she could say anything hot in reply. It stopped her from speaking, but even with her face covered her furious glare was rather obvious.

Of course her dislike for the pirate leader faded when we reached the open hatch, and the long ramp heading down to the ground.

The city we'd lived in for the past four months was in flames.

Fires were making black smoke billow upwards from a dozen different locations. The occasional tracer rounds flew into the evening sky, shot by unknown parties against equally unknown targets. A missile abruptly screamed down from somewhere, only to detonate harmlessly in the air. Cut down by a laser maybe.

And to the west...

...to the west an enormous, roiling cloud of dust was still settling from the blasts that had torn apart the colony's premier harbor. That must have killed thousands, tens of thousands, in moments.

I had a dozen seconds to take all of that in before gunfire began roaring far closer, forcing me to pay attention as the leading edge of the Faithful's assault arrived.

Trahcon in full armor darted closer, using their sorcery to bring their cover with them; wrecked cars, pieces of crashed shuttles, and even random debris forming into shelters at their direction.

The pirates were doing their best to break up their formations, and here and there I thought they managed it, forcing the Faithful back. The problem, as far as I could tell, was that the ship's guns were silent, and I saw the reason when I jerked my gaze around in time to see the enemy already on top of a nearby corvette.

They scurried away from a heavy turret even as it rapidly spat out rounds, shooting down a pair of approaching aircars, then an explosion made me flinch.

Once the flash faded, I realized that they hadn't actually destroyed the turret, but they *had* jammed it in place, leaving it useless.

"Focus fire above!" Gothin must have seen the same thing, "Clear them off our ships!"

A chorus of affirmatives came over comms, but I was pretty sure her people had already been doing their best. The problem was the ships were just too big, too tall, for anyone on the ground to really manage it.

Johanna started to bring her rifle up, clearly aiming for the same group I'd spotted, when the other problem revealed itself.

Gunfire abruptly slammed into my head and shoulders, sending up sparks from my shields. Yelping, I threw myself backwards on panicked reflex, stumbling back into the ship just before a man in full armor landed right where I'd been.

Either Gothin had a rear-display in her helmet, or she'd simply realized what was happening, because she whirled around before he could try and cut her down from behind.

Slamming his rifle aside with one hand, she drove her shotgun against his helmet with the other before pulling the trigger. What was left of him hadn't finished falling when more gunfire roared in from overhead, hitting Johanna and Gothin in equal measure.

Johanna flinched back just as I had, scurrying back into the ship, Gothin following with more anger than fear in her audible swearing.

She'd just about reached the entryway when a grenade fell, bouncing off her shoulder. Watching it ricochet toward me, I felt my body move, a leg lashing out as if the canister was a Strike-Wave ball.

I sent the thing flying out into the open, the detonation coming a few panicked heartbeats later.

"Back!" Gothin snapped, already spinning around, "Cut them down when-"

A second grenade dropped, and it was too far away for any of us to try and throw it back. Instead of detonating in an explosion, it began vomiting greasy smoke and obnoxious flares. All three of us flinched, our helmet displays lighting up painfully against the Eclipse grenade.

We scrambled back, the fog chasing us down the hall.

Johanna was the quickest that time; she fired blindly into the cloud as she backpedaled, keeping enough self-control to use short bursts. I got my carbine up just in time to see the distinctive flash of shields being hit, and pulled my own trigger at the same time as Gothin.

The Faithful's charge turned into a stagger as their protection failed, their upraised sword faltering as all three of us shot as rapidly as we could, finding the weak points in their armor.

"Tarath!" Corrack's bellow came just as blind gunfire came at us instead, forcing us to duck back even farther to where the pair of Naulian men were holding the first intersection. A wave of my hand had Johanna fall back to catch her breath, leaving me to lean over the shorter man to keep watch. *"They've breached the cargo bay!"*

"Seal the lift!" She shouted back, "I want guns at every utility junction!"

"Confirmed!"

Gothin fired a round or two from her weapon, an action I copied when a wild burst snapped past me.

"Fleet status?" She called.

It took him a moment to reply, the aimless gunfire picking up from the other side, making both the Naulian pirates join us in trying to discourage anyone from coming this way.

"Most of the Faithful seem to be evacuating!" He reported, *"The only group that isn't are the ones here! Crescent assault shuttles are burning hard*

our way!"

As if they'd heard him, the Faithful upped their assault at that very moment.

Another of those damned Eclipse grenades came ricocheting down the corridor, spewing flares and smoke in equal measure.

I braced myself, expecting a charge, and thought I was ready.

Then a hulking figure with glowing red eyes came sprinting through the smoke, bellowing in rage when the first startled gunshots slammed into shields protecting its otherwise bare form.

He'd been Thondian, once. Before the Faithful had decided to turn him into something else.

I could see where metal had been roughly shoved into his flesh, covering him in armor and shields. Where his muscles had been bulked out beyond anything natural, where his legs had been replaced with metal that let him begin covering the distance between us far too quickly.

"By the sacred-"

Gothin didn't get to finish her oath before it was on us, and the roars of more came echoing down the hall.

XXXII

I lost track of everything except for the creatures whose rush seemed to be directly aimed at me.

My finger started yanking the trigger down as quickly as I could, my left hand doing its best to help the gun steady. I couldn't tell if my rounds were hitting; everyone else had opened up on the same target. His shields collapsed in a matter of seconds, the following shots striking armor and flesh in equal measure.

His charge turned into a stumble, and then he was simply trampled by those following behind, all of them roaring in unison.

I kept shooting, some desperate part of me wishing I had a heavy shotgun like the pirates were using.

Gothin's shotgun boomed nearly as quickly as my gun, both of the Naulian pirates blasting away with their own weapons, all of us desperately trying to scythe down the tortured souls before they could make it to close combat.

Three more dropped.

The fourth reached one of the pirates as he died, burying the smaller alien under his mass, leaving space for the fifth to leap over them, coming right at me.

My frantic shots couldn't breach his protection before a massive hand simply ripped the gun out of my fingers, the metal screaming as he simply crushed the barrel in the process. A leg lashed out in a blur when I tried to jump back, catching me in the stomach.

The blow drove the air from my lungs, and sent me crashing to the ground at Johanna's feet.

She'd missed what we'd been shooting at from her sheltered position, but she'd apparently heard enough to set her own weapon to automatic as well.

It flashed just above me, roaring in a continuous sound as she poured fire into the man with no restraint, her voice raised in a startled scream. He jerked, howled, made it a single step forward, then pitched sideways with a dozen wounds covering the floor in blood.

"What was-"

Johanna's words were cut off when another of the men burst around the corner, her startled gunfire not as accurate the second time. A desperate lunge of my arms let me grab his metallic legs before he could reach her, stumbling him just enough for her to dodge.

Then one of the Naule was around the corner, cutting the man down with a precise head shot.

Thanks were on my lips when Gothin scrambled back into the same corridor as us, a Faithful with a blade following in her wake. Blue-black fire wreathed the weapon, letting it effortlessly carve through her subordinate before the man could finish turning back around.

My stomach rolled at the way his headless body fell, legs and arms struggling to get me upright. Nearby Johanna shot for the third time. She wasn't any more accurate, but enough of the panicky shots hit the Faithful's barriers to draw their attention.

They hesitated, then ducked back around the corner before Gothin could join in.

"Back!" The pirate shouted, holding her shotgun with one hand and ripping something off her belt with the other. "Catch!"

I had to lunge to catch the weapon, realizing it was a shotgun identical to the one in her hands. Fighting to get my balance steady, I was still trying to find the safety when yet another of the cyber-Thondians came bolting around the corner, the Faithful right behind, using them as a living shield.

Both of the other women opened fire at once, blood spraying when the man's shields proved to be down. He began to fall, and some vague instinct warned me of their plan a heartbeat before it happened.

"Watch out!" I shouted, legs shoving me sideways against the wall just in time to avoid the corpse when sorcery hurled it forward.

Neither Johanna or Gothin had been as ready, but the pirate's reflexes were better. She managed to mostly avoid it, only a tumbling arm striking her, while Johanna took the full force of the impact.

Shaking fingers found the weapon's catch just as the Faithful came for me; that blazing sword dredging up old fears. I screamed as I pulled the trigger, the heavy round slamming into their chest. Their shields took the blow, but it was enough to make them stagger, their wild swing missing my arms by inches.

I shot them again, followed quickly by Gothin shooting them twice in rapid succession.

The sorcererous fire faded into nothing as their corpse fell, leaving my trembling hands able to pull the body off of my packmate.

"Thanks!" She gasped, taking my hand, letting me pull her up. "God. God. Not more of those things."

"I-"

Gothin gave me a hard shove, pushing me down the hall. "Not the time, short-furs! Move! Corrack! Report!"

There was so much echoing gunfire I'd barely been able to hear her, even over comms, and Corrack's voice was even more covered up by the noise.

"-*breached both sides!*" He shouted, "*Other ships are holding!*"

"All crew out of the bow hatch!" She bellowed in reply, "Tell the *Serpentine Cut* to cover our retreat to their ramp!"

"*At once!*"

Gothin led us in a rush down that corridor, slamming a hand on a console as we passed. The security door slammed shut bare seconds after Johanna and I got through it. Her lack of concern definitely inspired us to try and keep up, especially when she did it again at another door.

We ran into more pirates in the next corridor. One of them had dragged a heavy gun out, and was sending monstrous bursts down a long corridor filled with more of the tortured Thondians.

"Seal and withdraw!" Gothin's order had them abandon the gun entirely, picking up their small arms and scrambling after us.

The next security door sealed shut over the hunting-scream of one of the cybernetic-Kelthi, a single glance over my shoulder letting me see the thing pounce on a pirate who'd fallen behind.

I was grateful the slamming metal stopped me from seeing more than the first spray of blood.

A short sprint later had us bursting into the ship's forward hold, where I was incredibly relieved to spot Irkan among those who'd gathered there. I recognized most of the bridge crew as well, but there could only have been a dozen or so others.

"Tarath." Corrack slammed a fist onto a button, sealing the last doors behind our party. "They're using breaching charges to get through the barricades. They nearly took us on the bridge, we have minutes, at most."

"Little time to recover then." She replied, already striding forward. "Open the ramp. We move as a group, any wounded in the center. Straight line for the Serpent, their guns will cover us."

Everyone nodded, taking those few seconds to catch our breath.

My own was more labored than it should have been. As bad as it had been on Nueva Genova, or in the final run on Last Stop. Sweat was making my clothes and armored suit stick unpleasantly, and I couldn't figure out a way to properly hold the Thondian-sized shotgun in my hands.

On my right, Johanna was trembling as badly as I had to be, even if I couldn't tell how severely I was shaking anymore.

Irkan took a few steps over as we waited for Gothin to adjust the ramp's controls, his movements casual and steady in a way that ours weren't.

"Calm yourselves." He murmured in his deep voice. "This is but our next challenge to glory, my friends. We shall complete this task as we have completed each one before it."

Right. Right. This was just one last trial. The last one before we would truly be free to go home. All we had to do was make a run to the next ship in line, and hold out inside it. It wouldn't be long, couldn't be long, before the Crescent arrived.

Plus, most of the Faithful were fleeing. They'd have limited numbers here, and so many of them had to have already died. It would get easier. It had to get easier from here.

Gothin's hand hovered above the console, her head and chest turning to look over the surviving crew of her flagship. "Nullifier check! I have one!"

"One!" Corrack replied.

"One!" A Trahcon man called.

When no one else said anything, she nodded. "Jahr! Yours comes out ahead of us, then we go down. Corrack! First sorcerer you see, hit them. Mine is our reserve."

Both men nodded.

"Form up to run!"

We all slid a few steps closer, nearly everyone standing right on the ramp rather than at the base of it.

Gothin's hand came down. Whatever she'd done to the ramp's controls had it simply drop without anything to slow its descent. It slammed into the grassy soil, sending everyone stumbling, but the press of bodies and helping hands make sure that everyone stayed upright.

"Stay with Irkan!" I shouted to Johanna, keeping up with his shorter strides when he began his lumbering run. "Come on!"

We ran into the open to find that the battle hadn't abated outside. Gunfire was flashing everywhere, as was sorcery. The Faithful had created bunkers and barricades wherever they could. Combined with the pirate's own efforts, they'd turned the landing field into a maze of burning and broken wreckage.

Bodies were everywhere, but most of them were either Faithful or their cybernetic puppets. The pirates must have been successful in retreating into their ships, and if ours was the only one that had been breached, then we really did have a chance.

We just had to survive the winding jog, our little mass of people shooting at any bits of motion that we could see.

Gothin's personal crew cut down a group of wounded Faithful trying to pull back, then dealt with a trio of the cybernetic-Thondians when they tried to rush us.

The first shuttle screamed past not long after that second group was slain, its side doors open as it nearly crashed on top of the same ship we were trying to reach. Those Faithful who'd taken out its dorsal guns scrambled inside, its engines leaving a trail of black along the corvette's hull when it took off again.

"They're retreating!" A Naulian woman shouted. "They're leaving!"

It was the last thing she said before a *creature* bounded over the burning cart it had been hidden behind, seized her head in its long mouth, and simply ripped it off of her body.

A bellow of rage preceded one of the Thondians simply tackling the thing, ramming his gun into its belly, firing wildly the entire time.

He killed it, I think, but three more pounced on him within seconds...

...and tore him apart in a flurry of claws.

If my heart had been going fast before, it felt as though it was going to burst out of my throat when I got my first glimpse of the things.

Half-cybernetic, like most of the Faithful's help, they had long, skeletal heads with six gleaming eyes. Patches of fur were visible where metal hadn't covered it up, and each of their four legs ended in metallic claws. Long tails whipped back and forth as they devoured their prey.

And they were massive. As tall as Irkan at the shoulder, and they probably weighed as much as he.

Gothin had done well to keep her people disciplined, but seeing one of their number being eaten alive in front of them was too much.

They fired wildly, sprinting at everyone's best speeds toward the promised safety of the next ship, ignoring Gothin and Corrack shouting for them to stay together.

All their gunfire did was prove that these things had shields as well, and drew their attention away from their grisly meal and toward the panicked mob. Either following unheard orders, or simply acting on instinct to chase fleeing prey, the three bounded after the fleeing pirates, letting out shrieking howls as they did.

"Behind!" Irkan's shout was our only warning before another of the things came rushing at us from that direction. It was fast; impossibly fast, reaching him before any of us could get our guns aimed.

Our Mikiran packmate roared through his helm when it leaped on him, ducking his head, then throwing it back just in time to rake his horn against the thing's chest. Blue blood sprayed from the wound, drawing an horrible shriek, claws raking at his shell and armor.

They went down, thrashing. I shot it but only drew flaring energy from its shield, only for Corrack to come to our rescue.

The enormous man slammed into the thing, angling his body to drive an elbow and hip into it at the same time. The impact drove it off of Irkan, leaving Johanna and I, plus another pirate, free to shoot it until its shields failed.

It died in writhing, screaming pain, flailing enough that it collapsed back on top of Irkan's legs.

Legs now coated in both blue and brackish-brown blood.

"Irkan!" Johanna's frantic shove didn't move the thing pinning him down, and Corrack was too busy shooting at another to aid her. "Ashe, help-"

A feminine bellow cut her off, "Beasts!"

I whipped my head around to see Gothin and the rest of her bridge crew scrambling back toward us. All of them were shooting at an armored figure as it strode forward, their rounds turned aside by a Cloak of Ashahn.

The boiling, rolling storm of energy around the Faithful was everything it had been in my nightmares. Exactly as it had been when the Burned Hand had mocked us, tortured us, and been ready to kill us before Tasir had sacrificed herself.

"Pathetic!" The voice wasn't the Burned Hand's, I didn't think, but she had the same disgusted sneer. "Your very existence is an affront to me, but I shall be kind! Tell me the order in which you wish to die!"

Gothin raised her gun, then froze when more of the cybernetic creatures leaped into view to either side of us. Then another trio came prowling in, blood dripping from their jaws, forming a broad circle around us.

Trapping us.

"Oh God." Johanna's voice was flat. Dead. "God in heaven. Not like this."

I felt my tongue go over my lips... and my eyes go up as more shuttles lifted off, vanishing. As the deep roar of more became audible over the echoes of gunfire and screams.

The Faithful were leaving. Retreating. This one... this one was staying behind, to kill us. To finish us off while the others fled.

That meant the Crescent was nearly here. They had to be.

My gaze fell back to the Faithful. Hearing her mocking us, hearing Gothin trying to stall for time. Knowing it would just make her the first target because she'd spoken up.

We didn't have time. The Faithful would toy with us until the last moment, and then she'd kill us all before help could arrive.

Unless...

"Stay with Irkan." I said, "Stay here."

"Ashe, what are you doing!?'

What I had to do to keep my pack safe.

I strode forward, getting up to a jog just as Gothin's people retreated back from a long tendril of sorcererous flame, their leader flinching as well when it scorched her armor.

"You think to delay me?" The Faithful taunted. "You think yourself clever? Then you may die-"

My voice rose in a shout, finally my turn to cut one of them off. "Blessed is Ashahn, Wrath of Aysh!"

The faceless helmet snapped to me at once, her words twisting into a scream of fury. "You dare invoke false-gods!?"

Taking a final, deep breath, I turned my jog into a sprint, a hand shoving Gothin in the side as I ran past her, charging right at the Faithful.

"She is our inspiration, our dreams!" I continued the common prayer, bracing myself for what I knew was coming. "She is the storm that tests us!"

That horrible fire came at me when I was still a dozen paces away. It wasn't focused; it didn't burn me alive in an instant, but I still screamed as the heat washed over me. Saw my visor crack, felt my under-suit begin to melt.

Felt the familiar pain of burns.

My thumb jammed down on the grenade I'd pulled from Gothin's belt, the dial already turned down to zero.

The nullification bomb went off with a whine that somehow cut through everything in the moment before the Faithful let out a new scream of fury, the fire vanishing as if it had never existed.

She was less a yard away, reeling, and completely unprepared when I rammed into her, armor crashing as I bounced back a step, both of us struggling to keep our feet.

Her hand went for her sword.

My hands pushed my shotgun against her chest.

She froze. "You can't-"

I pulled the trigger.

Her broken body fell at the same time as one of the creatures hit me from the side, slamming me onto the ground. A forelimb pinned my gun to the ground, the other's claws raking at the scorched protection over my chest and arms.

I couldn't stop from screaming in pain, in fear as its fanged mouth descended. The open jaws came down on either side of my head, forcing me to stare down its throat, my exhausted thrashing not doing anything to make it get off.

And then... never closed its mouth.

It just stayed like that, pinning me down, torturing me until my screams turned to desperate sobs. My vague thoughts of sacrificing myself for my packmates, for my friends, vanishing in those horrible moments. Of wanting to live, wanting that more than anything else.

The thing kept me there until I realized it wasn't breathing anymore.

I was still choking, still crying, when it was finally shoved off of me, Gothin becoming visible as she slumped to her knees on my left.

"...stop sobbing, little savanna." She tried to order, but her voice was a beaten as I felt. "They're here."

Gasping a few times to get some breath in me, I managed to prop myself up on my elbows to see figures in dark armor swarming in. A few wore heavy coats, and seemed to be giving orders even as more shuttles came down to disgorge even more of them.

They were killing the creatures everywhere. Concentrating their fire to cut them down with a cold efficiency.

"Come on. Up. You need to help me explain this mess."

The pirate grabbed my burned arm, and I heard myself let out a whimper before the world went blessedly dark for a while.

XXXIII

I woke up to the numbing, floating feeling I recognized from strong painkillers, and the wonderful tugs of someone brushing my fur. Not wanting whoever it was to stop, I kept my eyes closed, and did my best to keep my breathing even.

"I know you're awake." Johanna said, "You can stop faking."

I tried to say something playful back, but found my throat so dry that all I managed was a rasping cough. A moment later I felt a straw pressed against my lips, with cold water following.

"Better?" She asked, pulling it away when I twitched a hand to tell her I was done.

Opening my eyes was easier than I expected it to be. The lights were dim enough to not really hurt them either, leaving me blinking a few times. I was laid out in a pretty standard medical bed, monitoring equipment I'd seen before all laid out on my left.

What was different was the size of the medical space; it was far larger than the Imperial units I'd been in before. Large enough to comfortably fit additional chairs, one of which was right up next to me, and where Johanna was sitting.

She looked tired, but otherwise all right.

"Yes, thanks." I said, feeling stronger already. "Where's Irkan?"

A hand waved to the far wall. "In the room next to you. He'll live, but he was cut up pretty bad on top of the gunshots. He woke up this morning for a bit. I think he was all right until he realized we're on a Crescent ship. That's... he's not happy about that."

So he had taken that badly then. At least he was alive. We all were.

"Are we safe?" I asked.

My former cellmate shook her head, a somewhat helpless expression on her face. "I don't know to be honest. The Crescent sailors made it pretty clear they don't like me, or you, or Irkan, but they've got orders to take us to Alum."

"Oh." Grimacing, I reached around for the bed controls. Johanna found them first, getting me into a vaguely seated position with a few taps of the buttons. "Are you all right?"

She gave me a somewhat flat look. "Three days ago I watched you charge a sorceress like a maniac, and the only two people I trust have been unconscious until today."

"...but are you all right?"

"Mostly. I still want to slap you, but the mercenaries escorting us have been letting me explore the ship." Her shoulder rose and fell in the Human way. "It's been keeping me distracted, just like you're trying to distract me right now."

"Was not." I said at once.

"Was too." She countered, something almost like a smile on her lips. "How do you feel?"

I thought about it, then said, "Drugged. How bad?"

In response she reached out, grabbing the blanket that had been covering me. A steady pull brought it down off my chest, my waist, then left it bunched up around my knees.

The better to let me see just how many patches were covering various parts of my body. My legs and arms were the worst, with strips of medical tape covering up pads in clear patterns that I recognized even before Johanna began speaking.

Her voice quieted a little. "You have sorcery level burns almost everywhere your armor plating wasn't covering you. That cybernetic hund clawed up your left arm and right leg too, but it was killed before it really dug in. One regenerator session patched it up."

"Could be worse." I murmured.

"Should have been." She countered. "What were you *thinking*? All we had to do was live for another minute or two!"

"I didn't think we had a minute or two." I said in reply. "I thought she'd set the creatures on us as soon as the Crescent arrived, or more of Gothin's people came out. I thought if I could take her down, maybe the things wouldn't be under control."

She closed her eyes, shaking her head. "You thought they'd all jump you, and ignore us."

"...maybe." I offered.

"This is a pack thing, isn't it?" She demanded.

"...maybe." I said again. "I wasn't going to let them kill either of you."

Johanna clenched her jaw, exhaling through her nose. "I... I don't even know what to say to you at this point. I'm.... I'm so happy we're alive, you're alive, and I'm... proud? Flattered? God above, I don't know. I want to slap you as hard as I can too."

"You probably could." I volunteered. "I'm floating enough I don't think I'd feel it."

That finally got her to laugh, a quick one that had her wipe her eyes on her sleeve. "Don't... don't get me started."

I smiled, letting my head sink into the pillow. "We really going to Alum?"

"Supposedly." A pause, then a hand reached out, grasping mine. "One of the mercenaries told me that your pack is there."

My heart skipped a beat, a desperate, yearning hope entering my voice. "They are?"

She nodded, "They wouldn't give me details, but they said Rerth'riah is there with a whole bunch of other stuck-up Imperials, their words, and they were being paid to get you back. That they started planning this since Gothin contacted them."

I tried to say something. I don't know what, if I'm being honest, but no words came out. Something between a laugh and a sob was all I managed, my eyes welling up with tears.

How many months had it been, since I'd been taken? Since we'd all been taken? No, it was too long to be counted in months. Years. It had been nearly two years since that day on Trinity. Since I'd last seen my packmates. Last seen the woman who I'd once blamed for ruining my life, and who had also stepped in to try and give me everything I'd wanted.

Two years.

Two years surviving on that barge, on Last Stop. Making our desperate escape, skipping from world to world in a stolen yacht. Surviving as best we could on a pirate colony, trying to make that final, short leap to safety. Finding a wall of rain waiting for us right before the end...

...and surviving to make it anyway.

"Don't start. Don't..." Johanna's groan turned into a sob of her own, hands rising to try and wipe away her tears.

I didn't bother, just let mine run down my cheeks until she got up, wrapping her arms around me gently.

We sobbed into each other's fur until we didn't have any tears left, until broken laughter replaced it. I managed to get my own arms up, hugging her as best my tired limbs could. She didn't even protest when I kissed her cheek before we broke apart, both of us smiling.

"We made it." I told her.

"We did." She kept smiling, tugging my blanket all the way up and over me again. Using it to dry my face, then leaning it to use it on her own. "I'm... I'm supposed to go get someone to talk to you. And get you food."

"Thank you."

Giving me a final pat of my fur, she slipped out of the room, leaving me to catch my breath.

I was just feeling as if the drugs would carry me back to sleep when she returned with a tray full of food, and a Trahcon woman in a dark uniform, a heavy coat stretching down near her ankles. She walked with the aid of a cane.

The walking stick, and her generally stiff motions, made me think of an Elder, but her face was that of a rather handsome Guide. The serpentine tattoos curling around one eye, then trailing suggestively down her neck, were particularly interesting to my fogged mind.

"Good to see you're awake." She said, her accent not quite local, not quite any of the Imperial flavors I could identify. "I'm told Human men usually don't like their women scarred, which is a shame because you've got an impressive collection now."

Johanna huffed as she brought the tray over, getting it into my lap. "She's grayborn."

The Trahcon blinked once, tarah quivering, then grinned. "Ah. Then I expect you're rather pleased."

I wasn't sure if I was pleased, but I didn't really mind either, and said so. After that, I asked a question of my own, "May I have your name?"

"Reyja Call'adda, of the Silver Blades." She gave me a Thondian style bow, thumping her cane once in front of her. "We're your escort, and we get to make sure you haven't been turned by the Matriarch's people."

Pausing in the effort of picking up my fork and knife, I blinked at the term. "The who?"

"Faithful, I think you call them." Adda said, "I'm going to ask you about your past, and your relationships, see if-"

"-if I react?" I finished for her. "I know that trick."

"Good, then you won't be upset when I call you a liar." She replied, "Eat up first, then we can get started."

I got through about half of the food before my arms refused to rise when I ordered them to, forcing Johanna to feed me the rest. Our guest seemed incredibly amused by that, calling her a good packmate, but otherwise appeared content to wait.

Then she went through the exact same thing that Ashul'tasir had once done to us on Last Stop. Asking about my past from the earliest I could remember, pressing me on every detail, and routinely calling me a liar, telling

335

me that my streak of bad luck was impossible.

The only real differences were that I kept a hold of my emotions, and she seemed to be checking information on her wrist-comp as we spoke.

"All right." She said once we'd gotten as far as my last stop on Trinity. "I think that's good enough. Not sure why we have to bother, I'm sure your Imperial friends are going to interrogate you for weeks after this."

"Months." I predicted.

A hand waved, turning her wrist-comp off so that her grip could return to her cane. "That's about all I had for you today. You have any questions for us?"

Feeling surprisingly awake for having eaten, I nodded at once. "Who are you, really? Why did Rerth send you?"

"Checking to see if she actually sent us?" She asked.

"Yes." I said, only belatedly realizing I shouldn't have been that blunt. I blamed the painkillers.

Fortunately the mercenary looked more amused than insulted. "Don't worry about being paranoid, huntress. That's the kind of survival instinct our people really respect. As for your question, we're people who've run into your enemies before. One of us in particular *would* have reacted if you questioned him about his past."

I sucked in a breath, "He was Processed?"

"If by 'processed', you mean someone wiped his memories and put something else in there? Yeah." Her genial expression faded into something uncomfortable. "And we ran into someone else we're sure went through the same thing, except he didn't come out anything close to sane. You'll get the whole story, but not today. Promise."

"I..." I wanted to know. I *needed* to know, but... I was safe now. We were all safe now. It could wait. For a little while. "...thank you. Um, did we save the wrist-comps we took? The journals?"

Adda nodded. "Our people are going through them for anything useful. You'll get to sit in on the final results in a couple of days, if you're up for it."

Johanna scoffed, "It's Ashe. She'd crawl there even if she was dying so long as you promised to give her information on something she's researching."

I tried to deny it, and felt heat rise to my cheeks when I realized that I really couldn't.

Our host chuckled, "I think that's enough for now. Doctors said you need rest, but that you should be upright pretty soon. We have to take a long route to avoid the main campaign theaters, so it'll be five weeks or so before we make Alum."

"Can we send messages?" I asked.

A shrug. "I know Cieran won't care if you do, but the Crescent Captain might. I'll ask and let you know tomorrow."

"Thank you."

"Welcome, little huntress." She gave us a final little wave, then walked slowly toward the door. "Rest up. You'll be back to your Empire with answers before the next tide."

My smile returned, tired body sinking into the wonderfully comfortable bed, knowing that we were truly going home, that we might finally have answers to so many questions.

Finally.

Epilogue

I limped down quiet corridors, carefully checking each corner to make sure that Johanna wasn't going to suddenly appear.

She'd been taking her role as my and Irkan's caregiver extremely seriously, and finding out that I'd gone exploring when I was supposed to be in bed would definitely make her angry.

Which was cute, but excessive.

My body may have been rather stiff, and sore, but I was more than capable of walking around. After more than a week of laying in a bed, I *needed* to be up and walking around or else I'd start shaking. I needed to see if the dichotomy between the mercenary soldiers and Crescent sailors was as Johanna had claimed.

So far, it seemed like she'd been perfectly accurate.

The few crew I'd passed had taken one look at me, then pretended like I didn't exist. Which was an upgrade over insults and glares, I supposed, if not all that much of one.

In contrast the mixed-species mercenaries seemed incredibly amused that I was up and about, and seemed almost conspiratorial when they promised to not tell Irkan or Johanna. One of the Thondians had even directed me to the nearest lounge, promising I could relax there.

With no real destination in mind, that seemed as good a harbor to sail for as any other.

I found it a few minutes later, the door opening automatically at my approach. Inside was...

"By Ashahn's bloody grace." I blinked rapidly, stepping inside and looking around.

I'd expected the kind of lounge I was used to on ship's. A few comfortable tables, maybe a cooler for drinks and snacks, and a couple of screens to watch things on.

Instead I found myself in an extremely cozy tavern. And I meant *tavern,* not a bar. Everything was plated in dark wood, the lighting was purposefully dim, and an entire wall of liquor was protected by a thin cage to hold the bottles in place.

Walking that way, I idly poked one of the stools at the half-bar near the alcohol, and found the cushion just pliant enough to comfort.

Another look around let me find the expected flat-screens worked into the walls, but there were also projectors in the small tables. I considered sitting down, seeing what there was to watch, but the wall of colorful bottles kept drawing my attention.

"Maybe just a look." I murmured, carefully walking around the bar to start poking at them. "And maybe a small drink."

I quickly found a section devoted to bottles from the Empire, and even found a whiskey I remembered liking on my third assignment. That was good. What wasn't was the cage holding the bottles in place was locked with a passcode.

"Dammit."

An amused, masculine voice had me jump slightly, banging my hip on the bar behind me. "The password is one-two-three-four-six."

I whirled around to find that two people had entered the room in perfect silence, dressed casually in dark clothing.

The speaker was Human, pale skinned and dark furred, and just a bit taller than me. His fur was nearly as long as Johanna's, tied loosely behind his neck, while the bit around his mouth was trimmed short apart from two long sections he'd braided below his chin.

He was lean, and looked fairly dangerous with the scars around his left eye, but not nearly as lean and dangerous as his companion.

The snowy-white Xenthan with her blood-red eyes watched me the same way I'd seen more than a few pirates do; trying to decide if I was worth the trouble of attacking or not. A stiff shake of her head, making her long mane rustle softly, hopefully meant I was safe for now.

"Um, thank you." I said after a startled moment, "Did you want something while I'm back here?"

The man looked amused, speaking again in a sharp Cathian accent. "I make my own drinks. Just grab whatever you like and find a seat."

Hesitating for another moment, I did as instructed. Grabbing the whiskey I'd been looking at, I found a small glass under the bar, then slipped around it to take one of the tall stools to sit on.

The Human walked around me, pulling out a bottle without looking as he went past, then grabbing a second. I glanced to my left to see the Xenthan woman sitting two stools away, resting her chin on one of her massive hands.

"You..." Up close I realized she was wearing a necklace of some kind. One with... one with bones, rank badges of various types, and what looked like a long metal claw.

A claw I recognized.

"...were you the one that killed the thing attacking me, on Kagarraht?" I asked.

"I did." She replied, her own accent a lilting, rolling thing.

"Thank you." I said.

She blinked her enormous eyes very slowly, her forked tongue running over dark lips. "I would have rather killed the sorceress that you recklessly charged. Or killed you. Either would have been a more impressive triumph than a mutilated animal."

I swallowed, "Oh. Um, thank you for not?"

The man let out an amused little breath, pulling out more glasses, along with more bottles. "Be gentle with the girl, Voya."

That red gaze went to him, "You do not care for me because I am *gentle*."

"True." He seemed to smile, starting to pour the liquid with easy motions. "But she's an ally at the moment, so ease up."

She huffed, looking away sharply enough to send her mane rustling again.

Glancing between them, I cleared my throat and tried to learn something, my bottle sitting idle next to my empty glass. "Ally for the moment?"

He tipped his head, switching which bottle he was pouring from. "Yes. Our past experiences with your Empire were... mixed, to put it politely. That being said, these... what did your report call them. Faithful?"

"Faithful." I confirmed.

A nod, and another bottle-swap, "These Faithful are a long-term problem we've been preparing to work on. I was hoping to finish our vacation first, but then your packmate showed up on Alum and that plan went straight to the deeps."

I blinked. "You met Rerth?"

"I did. She's a real commanding bitch, you know that?"

A startled giggle came out before I could stop it. "Yeah. Yeah she is. I still love her."

He gave me a brief grin, then nodded to my drink. "You going to pour that or what?"

I poured myself some, watching as he finished making the mixed drink he'd been working on. Within a minute or two he had a pair of glasses filled with a pale blue liquid, complete with a little foam on top. He passed one to his evident partner, keeping the other as he stayed upright across from us.

We sipped our drinks in silence, and I found the straight liquor just as pleasant as I remembered it being.

I waited until they'd set their glasses down before asking. "What do you know about the Faithful?"

"A lot and not much, same as you." He replied, resting one arm on the counter. "Enough to not be surprised at all by what was in your reports about what happened to you, what you saw, or what happened on Kagarraht."

"You read my reports?" I blinked, then blinked again, "How? Ashahn's blood, did you hack my wrist-comp?"

He surprised me with a Trahcon-style shrug, and then again by completely admitting it. "Of course we did. We're mercenaries. Our survival depends on knowing everything that's going on around us. And besides, us being here to talk to you is our way of paying you back for the information."

I sipped more whiskey to buy myself a few breaths to think. It was more than a little annoying that they'd gone through my things like that. I hadn't liked that even when it had been Rerth doing that, but... well, they were here to give me information in return.

It could have been worse.

"So..." I eyed him, frowned some more, then made a guess. "You're the one that Adda told us about. The one who was Processed."

A tip of his head. "Yes. My name is Cieran Kean. That's Voya en'Chi. We're long-term enemies of the Matriarch, or Faithful, or whoever they really are."

"Ashe'lori, but you knew that." I took a fortifying sip of my alcohol, then sailed on. "What did they really do to you?"

"It's a long story." He replied, "But I'll tell you about it, and about our other encounters with the Faithful, if you tell us what happened on Last Stop. Your own words, not a dry report."

I hesitated... and nodded.

"Okay. Tell me everything, and I'll do the same."

He nodded, sipped his drink, and then he told me his story.

Appendix A: Kahsandale

The largest faith in the Empire, and one that has inserted itself into the very language. Kahsandale is a hybrid pantheistic/monotheistic religion that holds there to be a single being that was either born with the universe or who was responsible for its creation. This was a very common feature of most pre-Unification religions, and was one of the few things most of the original priests agreed on.

As this penultimate being is far beyond any mortal's ability to contemplate it, or at least for them to do so and remain sane, it split itself into myriad aspects and lesser images in order to guide and shape the mortals within its new universe.

This allowed the majority to adequately explain to themselves, and the Trahcon people, why there were so many lesser deities and differing interpretations. People who followed different faiths were not 'wrong' so much as they were simply ignorant of the whole truth.

When they later expanded into interstellar travel, it also enabled them to include alien faiths into their own pantheon; simply believing that the 'God' or 'Gods' seen by other species to simply be more aspects of the original divine being; 'Aysh'.

As could be expected this does not usually go over well with other species. While some faiths do tolerate some degree of a merger, most actively reject Imperial theology. The exceptions tend to be those groups brought into the Empire, which will often find dedicated priests and collaborators working to merge the faiths as best as possible.

Aysh

The true divine being, either the creator or the first soul of this universe, Aysh is also the location to which all souls travel to after death, with the soul being a spiritual core representing a being's consciousness and will.

Depending on which particular branch of Kahsandale is being followed, its believed that these souls will either be judged by Aysh, by merely those souls within of their own kind, or by a variety of Aspects created

343

simply for that purpose.

Regardless, those that are deemed to have lived a worthy life are allowed to return, to rejoin Aysh in peace. Those deemed unworthy are subjected to what is known as 'the cycle'. Their souls are purged of their active memories, punished for their transgressions, then are forcibly re-incarnated into a newborn to try again.

Aspects

Exactly who or what the Aspects of Aysh are can vary, but at a minimum they are usually considered to be its representatives to the beings of its universe. While unimaginably powerful by merely mortal standards, they are 'contained' enough to speak to living beings without destroying them as Aysh would.

While there are hundreds of Aspects even before one includes the absorbed gods, angels, and demons from alien religions, those originally of Zulflaran origin follow a distinctive pattern; they are beings of Duality.

Each has a positive and a negative, as pre-Imperial Trahcon would view it, trait. This notion of balance seems to pervade through the faith, with destruction and creation being held up as the two inevitable truths that must always follow one another.

The Cult of Ashahn

The largest sect of Kahsandale is the so-called Cult of Ashahn. Not officially organized, it is more of a cultural phenomenon. Its origins can easily be traced to Airalon Invasion, where luck or fate saw more temples of Ashahn preserved through the era.

While forced to compromise, their over-representation saw lower level priests slowly expanding the number of traits given to Ashahn in comparison to the other Aspects. While a crack-down did eventually occur some decades later, the social inertia had already begun.

In the modern interpretation, Ashahn is the greatest Aspect of Aysh, the first to appear before the Trahcon. More than mere inspiration, she gathers the positive traits of Architecture, War, Justice, and both forms of Sorcery... to start with. While these are the most common, it is not unheard of for her to take the traits of other Aspects as well.

Her negative aspects remain more limited, focused on death and destruction by the storm. By leaving her unbalanced, with far good than bad in her nature, those early priests ensured a great deal of effort would be made praying for her favor .

A side effect of this cult's prevalence is that dedicated priests to other Aspects rarely do more than acknowledge Ashahn's existence. This can often lead to snide remarks and open arguments when high ranking priests meet to discuss doctrinal matters, and low-key prejudice against those who only worship at Ashahn's temples.

The Cult of Sorcery

A far more modern movement than the Cult of Ashahn, the Cult of Sorcery is heavily tied into Trahcon-supremacist movements. Found mostly on smaller colonies in both the Empire and Near Reaches, the Cult of Sorcery is made up of a dozen different smaller movements who agree on the basics.

While there are differences between them, all venerate Mahkahs and Velshen. They hold that, as the Trahcon are natural sorcerers, then those Aspects are the parents of their species. More extreme sects go farther; claiming that their natural talents are proof of Aysh's divine favor.

Priests who ascribe to these cults often build dual-temples to both Aspects, and advocate for the use of sorcery over technology. As nearly all aliens lack such talents, discrimination against them is littered through their preaching and lessons.

Other Sects

In mainline Kahsandale, the primary doctrinal argument revolves around the Aspects and their precise relationship with Aysh. While most citizens believe that the Aspects are just that; Aspects of Aysh, composed of like-minded souls in a kind of spiritual hive-mind, who all operate in accordance to the greater purpose of Aysh without having true free will of their own.

In contrast, a significant minority reject this. Instead they view the Aspects as independent beings. Still reated directly by Aysh, but existing as individual creatures who inhabit the immortal plane inside their own society.

Aysh is their distant parent, their silent ruler, but does not directly control them anymore than Aysh directly controls the living. These groups are far more likely to offer worship to the Aspects directly, and believe they are the ones who stand in judgment over those who will be, and who not be, allowed to merge with Aysh after death.

Beyond this are many smaller groups, several of which are more atheistic. The most predominant of these believe that Aysh and its Aspects are not 'gods' so much as they are immeasurably powerful beings from another dimension, most likely the same realm the Trahcon draw their sorcerers energy from. To them dying is simply the act of transferring ones soul from one reality to another, an endless cycle of transformation.

Appendix B: Historical Torlah

Mahro'tuni   Reigned: I0-0 to I0-72
Description: The last War Leader and first Torlah, it was Mahro'tuni who effectively created the Empire through sheer force of will in the wake of the Airalon invasion. Militaristic, abrasive, and harsh, she won loyalty by never ordering a task she herself was not willing to perform.
Fate: Retired, dying peacefully in her estate on Zulflara.

Tizu'amiar'kahdel   Reigned: I0-72 to I0-487
Description: Created the majority of precedents of the limits and extensions on the Torlah's power, and finished solidifying the governmental structure.
Fate: Died in office; old age.

Julro'rush'tohnay   Reigned: I0-487 to I1-85
Description: Oversaw the first calendar reset to a new age when contact with the Ovoolur led to renewed conflict with the Airalon. Personally commanding the first naval actions, he helped develop Imperial battle theory during the early stages of the war.
Fate: Killed in action against the Airalon.

Madel'nixte'honsha   Reigned: I1-85 to I1-254
Description: The only non-military Torlah, she is still considered the greatest of them all. In her time she created the Chashti'tahza, reformed the Delne'lir, oversaw final victory over the Airalon, and was instrumental in the transformation of the Compact.
Fate: Assassinated by the Union of Tribes to start the First Compact War

Ghai'jahth'delarah   Reigned: I1-254 to I2-301
Description: The first Chashti'tahza to ascend to the rank of Torlah. She commanded the Empire through the First Compact War, but had little interest in non-military affairs and primarily focused on reforming the armed services in the aftermath.
Fate: Retired, died peacefully in Torlah Mahro'tuni's estate on Zulflara.

Hirra'wohl   Reigned: I2-301 to I2-520

Description: Fought beside the other Compact nations in the Second War against the Airalon Remnants, establishing the Imperial Watch, and then the initial stages of the Wars of the Storms. He also greatly expanded the colonial growth programs despite the numerous wars during his reign. The last Torlah to not be a member of a Delne'lir.

Fate: Died in office; old age.

Wih'torsi'shar   Reigned: I2-520 to I2-781

Description: Considered the most unlucky of the Torlah. Not adept at politics, she was unable to unify the Imperial Government during the Wars of the Storms, leading to heavy losses and a lack of strategic direction. Her exhaustion left her unable to properly handle the reunion with Cathia, and saw her retire in the aftermath.

Fate: Retired, died peacefully in her estate on Abantia.

Flyo'cruth'tohnay   Reigned: I2-781 to I2-1011

Description: A cautious woman who sought to correct the problems encountered by her predecessor, while expanding the old colonial programs. Saw the discovery and addition of the Meshicon, and affirmed their unique status in the Imperial system.

Fate: Died in office; old age.

Vurrah'bon'rahku   Reigned: I2-1011 to I2-1497

Description: A logistical specialist uninterested in ruling, she left most of the day to day operations of the Torlah to her packmates. Her lack of a foreign affairs specialist was a leading cause for tensions that eventually turned into the Colonial Wars near the end of her reign.

Fate: Died in office; old age.

Rahk'reth'tun   Reigned: I2-1497 to I2-1658

Description: Firmly believing in Imperial expansion into the Near Reaches, he would be continually frustrated by his geopolitical rivals. Despite a successful Compact chastisement against the Kingdom of Sacred Blood, his failure to reconcile and reinforce the Third Cathian Republic led to a backlash and his early resignation.

Fate: Retired, died peacefully in Torlah Mahro'tuni's estate on Zulflara.

Sulu'yorah'delarah   Reigned: I2-1658 to I2-2055
Description: Eager to restore Imperial glory, she took up and refined her predecessor's plans for an invasion of the Near Reaches. Executing them to perfection, this resulted in the conquest of numerous Naulian colonies in addition to their homeworld. She then led an equally successful defense against the Concordat and Federation when they attempted to exploit the situation.
Fate: Died in office, old age.

Kradahr'iston'nirand   Reigned: I2-2055 to Current Day
Description: Began her reign dealing with the consequences of conquest, focusing on colonial development and the integration of the Naule. This problem was only worsened when Humanity was discovered, and rapidly conquered, by an enterprising Chashti'tahza. She is already having similar political problems to Torsi'shar, and is believed to be overworking herself to try and keep things under control.

www.ingramcontent.com/pod-product-compliance
Lightning Source LLC
Chambersburg PA
CBHW032138190626
46814CB00005BA/1744